ABOUT THE AUTHORS

THAT'S BUTT-HEAD. HE'S PRETTY COOL. HE HANGS OUT A LOT AND WATCHES TV. OR ELSE HE CRUISES FOR CHICKS. YOU KNOW, HE JUST KEEPS CHANGING THE CHANNELS AND WHEN A HOT CHICK COMES ON HE'LL CHECK OUT HER THINGIES. IT'S PRETTY COOL. HEY, CHECK THIS OUT. "THE PEN IS MIGHTIER THAN THE SWORD." WAIT. WAIT. "THE PENIS MIGHTIER THAN THE SWORD." THAT'S WHAT I'VE GOT, HEH HEH HEH M HEH. WRITING'S COOL!

UH, THIS IS BEAVIS. HE'S A POET, A STORY-TELLER, A WUSS, A FARTKNOCKER, A DILLWEED, A DOORSTOP AND A PAPERWEIGHT. HUH HUH, AND HE'S A DUMBASS. PLUS HE'S A REAL WUSS. HE'S NEVER GOTTEN ANY. HE LIVES AT HOME WITH NO WIFE AND NO KIDS. JUST HIS PET MONKEY, HUH HUH. BEAVIS HAS WON MANY AWARDS, INCLUDING MY FOOT KICKING HIS ASS AND MY FIST IN HIS FACE. EVEN THOUGH I LET HIM HANG OUT WITH ME, IT DOESN'T MEAN I'M INTERESTED IN DUDES, OR ANYTHING. MOSTLY I JUST KEEP HIM AROUND SO I'LL LOOK EVEN MORE STUDLY AROUND CHICKS. COMPARED TO HIM. BEAVIS, I MEAN.

MTV — MUSIC TELEVISION®

BEAVIS AND BUTT-HEAD
READING SUCKS

THE COLLECTED WORKS OF BEAVIS AND BUTT-HEAD

MIKE JUDGE

  BOOKS

NEW YORK   LONDON   TORONTO   SYDNEY

BOOKS

POCKET BOOKS, a division of Simon & Schuster, Inc.
1230 Avenue of the Americas, New York, NY 10020

Introduction copyright © 2005 by MTV Networks, a Viacom Company
Chicken Soup for the Butt copyright © 1998 by MTV Networks
The Butt-Files copyright © 1997 by MTV Networks
Huh Huh For Hollywood copyright © 1996 by MTV Networks, a division of Viacom International Inc.
Ensucklopedia copyright © 1994 by MTV Networks, a division of Viacom International Inc.

MTV Music Television and all related titles, logos, and
characters are trademarks of MTV Networks, a division of
Viacom International Inc.

ISBN-13: 978-1-4165-2436-6
ISBN-10:   1-4165-2436-3

This MTV Books/Pocket Books trade paperback edition November 2005

10 9 8 7 6 5 4 3 2 1

POCKET and colophon are registered trademarks of
Simon & Schuster, Inc.

Manufactured in the United States of America

For information regarding special discounts for bulk purchases, please contact
Simon & Schuster Special Sales at 1-800-456-6798 or business@simonandschuster.com.

These titles were previously published individually by MTV Books/Pocket Books

Pages 96, 98, 194, 290, constitute an extension of this copyright page.

Dear Friends of Reading,

As I write this interduction, the summer is coming to an end, the leaves are falling, and hundreds of kids across the land are being forced to leave their televisions and return to school and read books and stuff. It's like a national tragedy.

We all know that reading sucks, but why not take a moment to savior the good points of the book you are now holding in your hands. And how do I know you are holding this book in your hands right now? And not something else in your hands? Uh huh huh.

One good thing about this book is that they had to destroy thousands of trees and use a bunch of dangerous chemicals to make it. Huh huh. Cool. So please enjoy this collection of our finest work. All you have to do is sit there and turn the pages. It's a good way to make use of your butt. Uh huh huh. Because like they say on television, a butt is a terrible thing to waste.

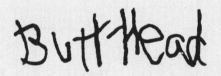

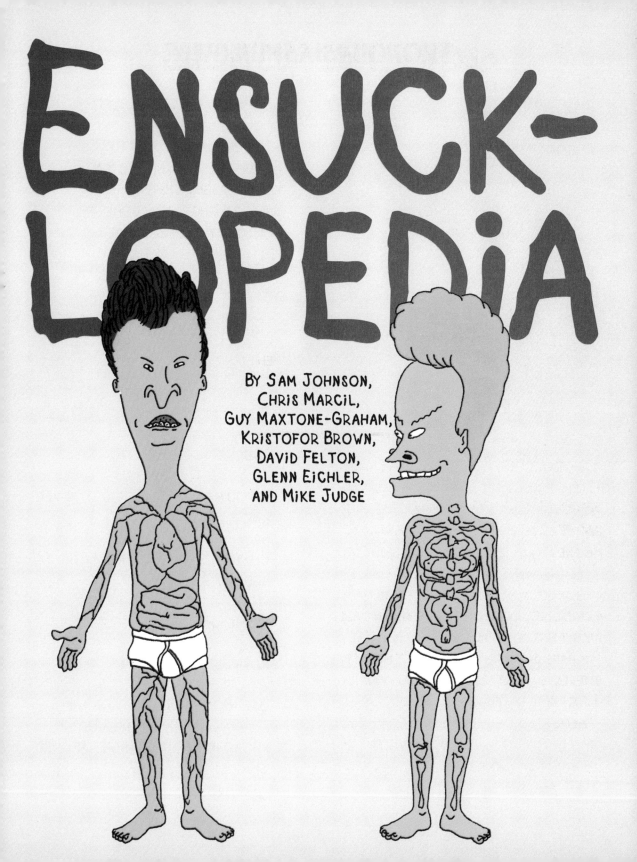

ENSUCK-LOPEDIA

BY SAM JOHNSON,
CHRIS MARCIL,
GUY MAXTONE-GRAHAM,
KRISTOFOR BROWN,
DAVID FELTON,
GLENN EICHLER,
AND MIKE JUDGE

PRONOUNSIASHUN GUIDE

ASS	"ASS"
ASSWIPE	"ASSWIPE"
UH, ANYTHING IN SPANISH	"HAMANA POR QUENO SALSA, PLEASE"
DILLWEED	"DILLHOLE"
BUTT	"BUT." THE SECOND T IS SILENT BUT DEADLY, HUH HUH
DRIVE THROUGH, PLEASE	"RIPERUEBLEEV"
69	LIKE IT'S SPELLED
THE F WORD	"FART"
THE S WORD	"SUCKS"
BOOB	IF YOU HAVE TO ASK, YOU'LL NEVER KNOW
VULVA	UH, THAT'S SOME SCIENCE WORD, I GUESS. ASK DARIA
WEINER	"PENIS," HEH HEH HEH
BEAVIS	RHYMES WITH "WEINER"
HOOTER	SEE "BOOB." SEE TWO OF THEM, IF YOU CAN. (BUT, SERIOUSLY, PRONUNCIATE IT "THINGIE" AROUND CHICKS)

Aa

CLASSIFIED ADS

PERSONALS

DO YOUR FRIENDS TEASE YOU...
...Because your thingies are so big? This, like, very sensitive (in more ways than one, huh huh) guy wants to heel your emoshunal wounds, or something. I'll take a hands-on approach to your problem, uh, problems. BOX 69.

YOU: BEAUTIFUL, STACKED MODEL
Me: Handsome sex machine named "Butt-Head." Come to Butt-Head! BOX 69.

OZZY OSBOURNE TYPE
Seeks Christina Apple Gate lookalike. Must know how to rock. And how to do it. Oh yeah, and if, like, you're the real Christina or that Baywatch chick and you're reading this, then you should definitely respond. I'll let you star in some, uh, home movies. Huh huh huh huh. BOX 69.

DO YOU LIKE HOLDING HANDS...
...Walking on the beach under the, huh huh, moon,

PERSONALS

quiet evenings by the fi-- TV, and candlelight dinners? Then don't call, cause we, like, don't have time for any of that crap. Only call if you're, like, interested in doing it and stuff. BOX 69.

SWM, 14
SKS (uh, that stands for "seeks," not "sucks") one SWF 4 SX (that stands for "sex." Heh heh heh). Um, XYZ, PDQ, LMNOP and PB4UGO2BED. BOX 69.

ARE YOU A HOT CHICK?
Two young studs seek hot chicks for, uh, you know, huh huh huh huh. Send a letter and a naked photo. That'd be cool! But don't worry that much about the letter, if your not that good at writing and stuff. Poster-sized would be fine. For the photo, we mean. BOX 69.

ARE YOU A DUDE?
Then quit reading this, fart-knocker! These classified ads are for chicks only. BOX 69.

PERSONALS

FREE LESSONS...
...In, like, how to do it. Only the seriously hot need respond, or something. BOX 69.

WANNA HAVE INTERCOURSE?
You know, like, SEXUAL intercourse? Heh heh heh heh heh! I wrote "sexual intercourse!" BOX 69.

BUSINESS OPPORTUNITIES

MAID WANTED
Must know how to polish wood. Huh huh huh huh. BOX 69.

PETS

ADOPT A MONKEY
Small, friendly, playful monkey, likes to "fetch bones." Heh heh m heh heh heh! Now seeking new owner. Current owner spanks him frequently. Answers to the name of "Little Beavis." BOX 69.

FOR SALE

SPERM
Huh huh huh huh huh. Heh heh heh heh m heh heh heh. Box 69

THE HUMAN BUTT, BY BUTT-HEAD

THE BUTT IS THE MOST IMPORTANT PART OF THE BODY. THAT'S HOW COME THE BUTT RULES. GOD GAVE US THE BUTT SO THAT WE COULD, LIKE, HAVE SOMETHING TO TALK ABOUT. THE FIRST BUTT WAS INVENTED LIKE, A LONG TIME AGO BY THE SAME GUY THAT INVENTED THE TOILET. THE BUTT HAS A CRACK IN IT, HUH HUH HUH HUH. GOD PUT A CRACK IN OUR BUTTS SO THAT WE MIGHT HAVE TWO BUTT CHEEKS INSTEAD OF ONE. SOME ANIMALS LIKE FISH DON'T HAVE BUTTS. THAT'S WHY THEY SUCK. OH YEAH, I ALMOST FORGOT, THERE'S ALSO YOUR BUTTHOLE. IT'S LIKE, IN THE MIDDLE. I COULD WRITE A WHOLE BOOK ABOUT THE BUTTHOLE.

HOW THE BUTT WORKS.

INSIDE YOUR BUTT THERE'S ALL THIS COMPLICATED STUFF THAT LIKE, MAKES TURDS HAPPEN. THERE'S ALL THESE TUBES AND STUFF. THEN THE TURDS COME OUT OF YOUR BUTT, HUH HUH. (SEE ALSO: TURDS)

MAKE YOUR OWN BUTT.

YOU CAN MAKE YOUR OWN BUTT AT HOME. YOU GET TWO THINGS THAT ARE LIKE, ROUND AND THEN YOU LIKE, PUT 'EM TOGETHER. HUH HUH HUH. IT LOOKS LIKE A BUTT. CLAY WORKS PRETTY GOOD. YOU CAN ALSO MAKE A FACE OUT OF YOUR BUTT BY DRAWING EYES ON ONE OF YOUR BUTTCHEEKS AND THEN LYING DOWN SIDEWAYS. OH YEAH, YOU HAVE TO PULL DOWN YOUR PANTS FIRST. YOU CAN MAKE A BUTT OUT OF YOUR FACE BY DRAWING A BIG CRACK DOWN THE MIDDLE, HUH HUH. THEN LIKE INSTEAD OF CHEEKS YOU HAVE BUTT CHEEKS. (SEE ALSO: TURDS, MAKING YOUR OWN; PLAYDOUGH, FUN WITH)

OTHER STUFF TO CALL YOUR BUTT.

THE BEST THING TO CALL YOUR BUTT IS YOUR BUTT, BUT SOME PEOPLE LIKE TO CALL IT OTHER STUFF LIKE "ASS" AND "REAR" AND STUFF. WHEN BEAVIS WAS LITTLE, EVERY WEEK AFTER HE TOOK A DUMP HIS MOM USED TO SAY, "AREN'T YOU GLAD TO GET THAT OUT OF YOUR SYSTEM?" SO SOMETIMES WE CALL YOUR BUTT YOUR "SYSTEM," HUH HUH. LIKE, "CHECK IT OUT. YOU CAN SEE HER SYSTEM, HUH HUH HUH."

THE NADS, BY BEAVIS

THE NADS ARE COOL. I LIKE TO TALK ABOUT NADS. NADS. NADS. NADS! INSIDE YOUR NADS THERE'S ALL THESE LIKE, MOLECULES AND STUFF THAT CAUSE ALL THESE COMPLICATED CHEMICALS TO MAKE YOUR WEINER GET BIG WHEN YOU SEE A CHICK. THAT'S HOW COME WHEN THEY CHOP OFF A HORSE'S NADS, IT TURNS INTO A WUSS. SOMETIMES I GET A BONER WHEN I WATCH BAYWATCH. CHEMICALS ARE COOL!

SHUT UP, BEAVIS! YOU'RE NOT TELLING IT RIGHT. THAT'S NOT HOW YOUR NADS WORK. THERE'S ALL THESE TUBES IN YOUR NADS CALLED THE SEMINEFEROUS TUBULES. THEY'RE REALLY IMPORTANT BECAUSE IF YOU DIDN'T HAVE 'EM YOU'D LIKE, NEVER GET MORNING WOOD OR ANYTHING. THEY HOOK UP YOUR WEINER TO YOUR NADS. THEY'RE ALSO HOOKED UP TO YOUR EYES. IF YOU'RE LIKE, WATCHING TV AND YOU SEE A CHICK IN A BIKINI, YOUR EYES TELL YOUR SEMINEFEROUS TUBULES IN YOUR NADS TO MAKE YOUR WEINER GET BIGGER. SOMETIMES THAT HAPPENS TO BEAVIS WHEN HE SEES A DUDE. HUH HUH HUH.

SHUT UP, BUNGHOLE.

THE MUCOUS MEMBRANES

THIS IS THE PART OF YOUR BRAIN THAT MAKES YOU REMEMBER MUCOUS. MUCOUS MEMBRANES ARE REALLY IMPORTANT CAUSE IF YOU DIDN'T HAVE 'EM YOU'D LIKE, FORGET TO PICK YOUR NOSE. THAT'S WHEN YOU GO, LIKE, INSANE IN THE MEMBRANE OR SOMETHING.

THE KERMODIAL BUTTNOIDS

THE GLANDS THAT MAKE YOUR BUTT STINK.

THE FERBICAL NAD CLOBULES

THEY'RE THESE THINGS IN YOUR NADS THAT MAKE IT HURT WHEN SOMONE KICKS YOU IN THE NADS. THEY ALSO MAKE YOUR NADS ITCH. SOMETIMES THEY CRAWL UP INTO YOUR BUTT AND MAKE YOUR BUTT ITCH. HAVING YOUR BUTT ITCH SUCKS, BUT I LIKE SCRATCHING MY BUTT WHEN IT ITCHES. IT'S THE DAMNDEST THING. (SEE ALSO: THE HUMAN BUTT)

THE VIRGINIA

UUUHH...HUH HUH HUH HUH. WE DON'T KNOW MUCH ABOUT THIS.

Bb BACON

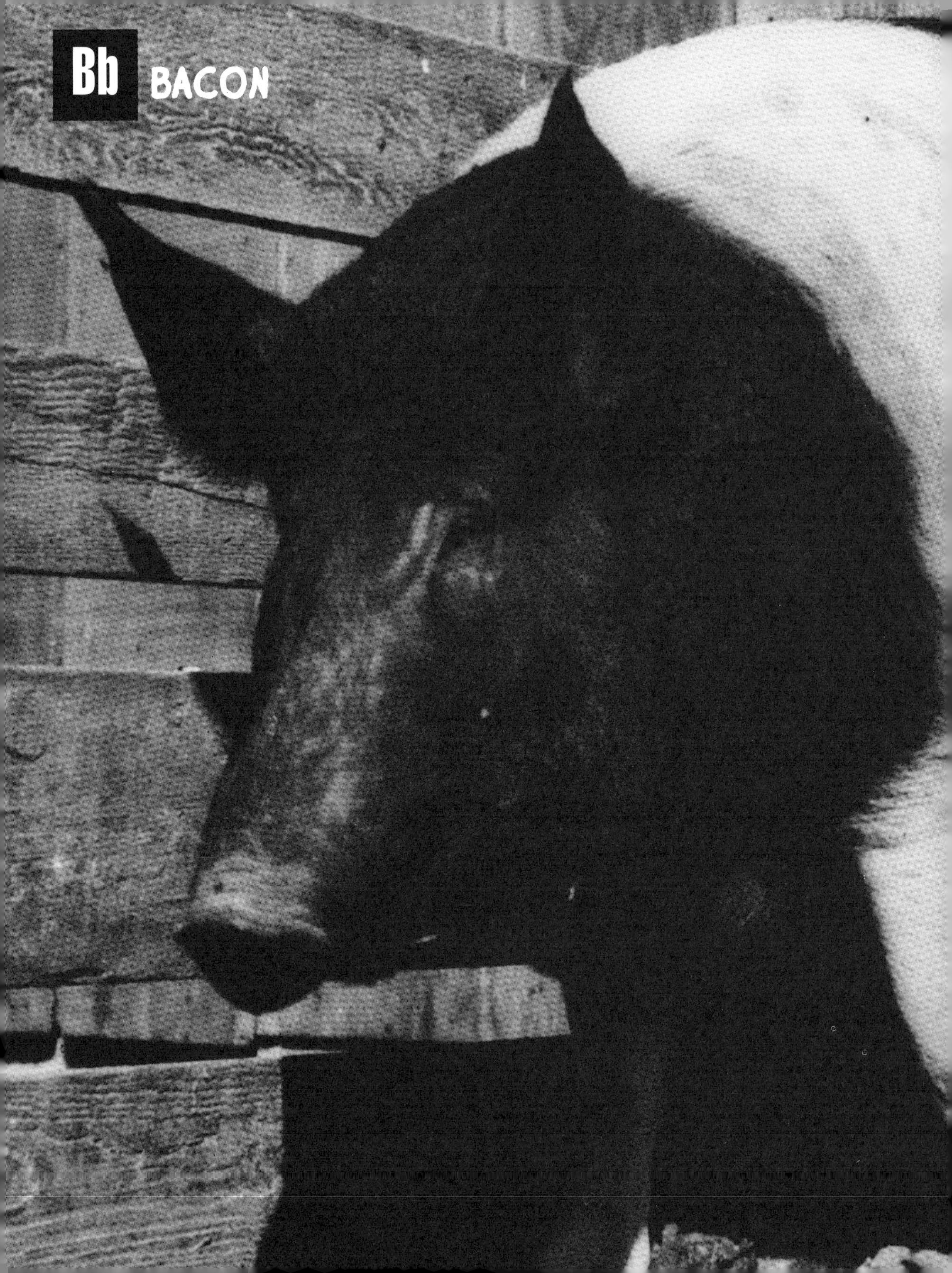

CC CREATION (THE STORY OF)

A LONG TIME AGO, LIKE DURING THOSE GIRAFFE PARK TIMES,

THERE WAS THIS DUDE, GOD, AND HE WAS, LIKE, REALLY BIG, AND LIKE, EVERYWHERE,

BUT NOBODY COULD SEE HIM, CAUSE HE WAS LIKE INDIVISIBLE OR SOMETHING.

SO HE COULD, LIKE, GO IN CHICKS' LOCKER ROOMS UNDETECTIVE, EXCEPT THERE

WERE NO CHICKS OR LOCKER ROOMS OR ANYTHING ELSE. THERE.

SO HE SAID, "THIS SUCKS." THEN HE SAID, "LET THERE BE STUFF."

AND LIKE THERE WAS THE EARTH AND STUFF.

AND GOD THOUGHT THE EARTH WAS PRETTY COOL,

BUT STILL NO NAKED CHICKS, SO HE MADE ONE. AND A NAKED DUDE, TOO.

AND THEY, LIKE, DID IT A BUNCH OF TIMES, AND THEY GAVE BIRTH TO ALL THE PEOPLE

IN THE WORLD (SCIENTISTS CALL THIS THE BIG BANG THEORY). BUT THEY

DIDN'T HAVE ENOUGH MONEY TO TAKE CARE OF THEM ALL, SO THEIR KIDS HAD

TO, LIKE, GO TO OTHER COUNTRIES TO FIND JOBS AND STUFF.

BUT BY THEN MONKEYS HAD LEARNED TO USE POWER TOOLS SO LIKE

THEY HAD TO COMPLETE WITH THEM FOR JOBS AND IT WAS HARD.

HUH HUH. HARD. SO THEY DID IT SOME MORE.

CC CHICKS

THERE'S THIS JOKE, HUH HUH, ABOUT WHAT THE PERFECT CHICK LOOKS LIKE. IT'S PROBLY PRETTY FUNNY. BUT LIKE, THIS PAGE IS MORE LIKE A SCIENTIFIC GUIDE AND STUFF THAN A JOKE. AND SO YOU CAN GET LIKE THE MOST EXACT IDEA OF WHAT A PERFECT CHICK IS, WE DECIDED TO DRAW IT INSTEAD OF PUTTING A PICTURE HERE AND STUFF. PLUS ALL OUR PICTURES OF PERFECT WOMEN ARE KINDA WRINKLED BY NOW.

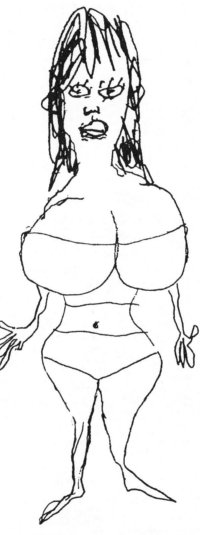

HEAD—LIKE, A PERFECT CHICK SHOULD HAVE LIKE A REALLY HOT FACE, BUT LIKE, DON'T WORRY ABOUT IT CAUSE THAT'S LIKE THE LEAST IMPORTANT PART OF ANY CHICK CAUSE LIKE YOU CAN ALWAYS WEAR A BAG ON YOUR HEAD, HUH HUH. BUT LIKE, IN THE HEAD AREA, IT'S BETTER IF A CHICK HAS A PERFECT FACE THAN LIKE, A PERFECT BRAIN? CAUSE THEN SHE STARTS THINKING STUFF AND SAYING JUNK LIKE, "QUIT LOOKING AT MY THINGIES." IF A CHICK STARTS TALKING A BUNCH A CRAP LIKE THAT, IT'S LIKE A SIGN SHE MIGHT NOT BE PERFECT.

THINGIES—A CHICK SHOULD HAVE REALLY BIG THINGIES, BUT NOT SO BIG THAT IT'S LIKE SICK OR SOMETHING. ACTUALLY THAT WOULD BE OK. BUT AT LEAST MAKE SURE THEY'RE ATTACHED TO A CHICK, AND NOT LIKE THE THINGIES THAT FAT DUDES HAVE AT THE BEACH. ONE TIME BEAVIS TRIED TO COP A FEEL OFF A FAT DUDE AT THE BEACH AND LIKE, THE DUDE KICKED THE CRAP OUT OF HIM. HUH HUH. HE WAS FAST FOR A FAT DUDE.

HIPS AND BUTT-AL AREA—LIKE, A CHICK SHOULD BE CURVY HERE. IF YOU ASK YOURSELF, UH, IS SHE CURVY ENOUGH? AND YOU CAN'T DECIDE THE ANSWER, THINK OF LIKE ONE A THOSE

GLASS THINGS WITH SAND IN IT THAT'S SPOSED TO KEEP TIME. I THINK IT'S CALLED A SAND WATCH OR SOMETHING. EXCEPT PUT EYES AND LIKE HAIR ON THE TOP, AND LIKE SKIN INSTEAD OF GLASS, AND LIKE BLOOD AND INTESTINES AND CRAP INSTEAD OF SAND. IF THE CHICK YOU'RE LOOKING AT KIND OF LOOKS LIKE THAT, AND SHE HASN'T LIKE CALLED THE COPS YET OR ANYTHING, THEN YOU CAN SAY, "NICE BUTT, HUH HUH" AND REALLY MEAN IT. CHICKS LIKE IT WHEN YOU SAY STUFF LIKE THAT AND YOU'RE NOT LYING. IT'S CALLED SINCERENESS.

LEGS—LEGS HAVE TO BE GOOD-SHAPED, AND LIKE, LONG. BUT IF THE CHICK IS SHORT, AND HER LEGS CAN'T BE LONG, THEN THAT'S OK TOO, AS LONG AS THEY'RE GOOD-SHAPED. ALSO, SHE SHOULD SHAVE THEM, BUT LIKE, WE'RE TALKING ABOUT WOMEN ANYWAY, AND NOT LIKE A COLLEGE CHICK WHO WALKS AROUND WITH LIKE HAIRY LEGS AND BOOKS AND STUFF.

SHOES—WE ALMOST FORGOT CLOTHES SO WE'RE GONNA TALK ABOUT IT HERE. BUT SINCE THIS IS LIKE THE PERFECT WOMAN, WE'RE GONNA FORGET THE CLOTHES AFTER ALL. HUH HUH HUH HUH.

SO LIKE, THAT'S THE PERFECT WOMAN. IF YOU'RE GOING LIKE, "WHOA, WHAT ABOUT OTHER STUFF, LIKE PERSONALITY OR SOMETHING," DON'T BE, CAUSE IN OUR SCIENTIFIC OPINION AS DUDES, A CHICK ONLY GETS A PERSONALITY IF SHE'S UH, UNPERFECT, JUST LIKE THE WAY A DUDE WHO CAN'T KICK PEOPLE'S ASSES WILL LIKE DO HOMEWORK AND STUFF. IT'S CALLED EVERLOTION OR SOMETHING.

Keep The Tip, Huh Huh

I never thought this letter was true until it happened to me, or something. One time I was at the arcade at the mall and there was this really hot chick playing the video game next to me. She was, like, really well built, with two thingies and stuff? Oh yeah, she had brown hair. Or maybe she was blonde, or a redhead, I forget. Maybe she was bald, huh huh huh. But she did have two thingies, I remember those pretty well.

Anyway, she dropped her quarter on the ground and as she bent down I could tell she was, like, trying to give me a good peek at her ample thingies. Quick as a flash, I stepped on her quarter and gave her a look that said, "Come to Butt-Head!"

She was getting pretty hot and bothered. Really, you know, wanting to get her quarter back. I was, like, thinking about taking the quarter and dropping it down my pants. Huh huh, that woulda been cool! Then, with this really sexy smile and thingies that were still pretty big, she said, "Move your foot, you moron, or my boyfriend will kick your ass."

I've never seen her since, but I'll always remember that special time we shared together and stuff. She wanted it.
—*Name and address withheld.*

She Wears A Bra

Eh, heh heh, there's this chick in my class? And I like to stare at her, and stuff. She must not mind, cause she'll just sit there when I'm staring at her, and pretend not to notice. She looks really hot! That's just, you know, judging from the back of her head. I bet the rest of her is pretty hot, too.

She must be pretty stacked, cause if you look really closely at the back of her shirt, you can tell she wears a bra. You can see all the wires and pulleys and stuff through her shirt.

Heh heh m heh. "Pulleys!" Um, "Pull these!" Heh heh heh. "Pull these, puh-lease!" That would be cool! —*Name and address withheld.*

School's Hard

Uh, there's this chick in our class. Beavis really wants her and stuff, even though she doesn't know he exists. And even if she knew he exists, she probably wouldn't like him, cause then she'd know what a wuss he is, huh huh huh!

Anyway, one day Beavis was, uh, looking at her a little too long? Then Van Driessen asked him to come up to the front of the class to write something on the blackboard. Huh huh huh huh huh, he had a stiffy!

So Beavis, like, wouldn't go up to the blackboard. And when Van Driessen asked him why not, he said, "Uh, because I have an erection."

Huh huh huh huh huh, what a dumbass! He probably could have gone up to the blackboard anyway, and people wouldn't have noticed, cause his weiner's pretty small. Everybody laughed at him, including the chick he'd been staring at. Beavis spent the rest of the day in the school psychoticist's office. I don't even think this chick is very hot.—*Name and address withheld.*

Mom Yes, Apple Pie No.

Uh, I had sex once? With Beavis's mom, huh huh huh.

Shut up, fartknocker.—*Name and address withheld.*

French Lessons

Eh, heh heh, I was, like, hanging out in my dorm room late Monday night when --

Beavis, you dumbass, you weren't in a dorm room. You were sitting on the couch watching "Baywatch."

No way. I was in, like, a dorm room studying for, like a big French exam or something, when all of a sudden I heard this knocking sound.

That was the sound of me hitting you on the head, dumbass.

No way! It was like this really stacked French chick. And she said she was there to help me study for my exam, by, like doing it with me. Heh heh heh.

Beavis, you've never even met any French chicks. Except for Madame Palm and her five daughters, huh huh huh. All that happened on Monday is you saw "Baywatch" and then you spanked your monkey.

Oh yeah.—*Name, address and weiner withheld.*

2

3   10

7

1. STAGE. This is the place where, like, it all happens or something. Like, the fat dude in Crowbar comes up to the front here, and squats down and starts groaning. That's when it's like, magic time or whatever.

2. SPEAKERS. This is what the music shoots out of. It's like, there's two kinds of music: loud and sucky. You never hear sucky music at concerts, unless you got ripped off, or it's, uh, jazz or something. Loud music shoots out into the air and right into your brain, huh huh. And like, everything shakes and stuff, even your brain. Your whole body's shaking and vibrating and whatever, and it's like that saying of how you can't even hear yourself think. But it's like, so what. Thinking's a pain in the ass anyway. Huh huh. Ass. Plus Beavis likes it cause he can't hear any of the other dudes who live in his head either.

3. SECURITY GUARDS. There's all these dudes here in front of the stage who like talk to each other with walkie-talkies and stuff. They're like, uh, striker unit 12, we got a situation in Baker sector, over. Huh huh. Get the hell back from the stage dammit or I'll split your head like a Halloween pumpkin. These dudes would be just normal asswipes except that they go to more concerts than anybody. So that makes them a little higher up than just normal asswipes.

4. BACKSTAGE. Member how I said it all happens on the stage? Uh, well, like some other stuff happens over here, backstage. They have food, and beers, unless it's one a those bands that had to bust themselves cause they got messed up on beers and stuff. They have slushies or something, I guess. And this is where Ozzy keeps all the animals and stuff that he's gonna bite the heads off of during the show. And like, this is where all the uh, huh huh, chicks leave their boyfriends before getting on the band bus so they can do it. Uh, you can't see the bus on this picture cause uh, I think the driver went over to the Hinky Dinky to pick up some coleslaw or something. For the chicks.

5. LIGHT BOARD. There's this big table thing at the back here and it's got all these knobs on it and crap, and like, a bunch a wires in it. It controls all the lectricity and stuff. And there's this big fat dude who sits there and like, doesn't even listen to the music hardly, he just messes with the knobs and tells people he's gonna come down and kick their ass if they don't quit leaning against the board. Huh huh. I think he's, uh, scared cause of the lectricity. But it's like Beavis took a whiz on some lectrical wires one time and it just like, turned his weiner black for a couple weeks.

6. MOSH PIT. This place rocks. It's like, people hitting you and pushing you and jumping on your neck and kicking your face and hitting your head with their knees and knocking you on the ground and stomping on your nads and falling on top of you and elbowing your chest and stuff. It's like a big, cool family.

7. TEE-SHIRT SELLERS. If I was smart, I'd like go down to the St. Vincent of Paul and buy all the old used tee shirts for about a penny and then like write Gwar on them and sell them at a Gwar concert for 50 bucks. Huh huh. It's a total ripoff and stuff. Good thing I'm not smart or I'd probly be ripping you off right now.

8. BEACH BALL. Before the concert, people are like, we have nervous energy or something, we need to be zapped by high-intensity sound. Or they're like, the opening act sucks. So they throw a beach ball around sometimes, or one a those frisbees or a glow stick. One time Beavis tried to get people to throw around this flat empty coffee can he picked up off the highway. I guess they were like, too excited cause, like, nobody threw it back after we chucked it real hard into the pit. It was still a pretty good idea. For Beavis.

9. DANCING CHICK. There's usually a chick right over here who like sways back and forth and spins around like she's listening to different music from what everybody else is. Listening to. And then you go over and go like, hey baby. And she keeps dancing and stuff and acting like you're not even there. And then you go, let's get it on, fox. And she keeps dancing. And then you're like, okay, forget you. There's other chicks in the sea.

10. STAIN. Usually there's a stain over here. And your feet stick on it. It could be like, somebody's drink, or like some puke or something. Or it could be blood or like a dead animal. In the end, you never find out what it is, and you stop thinking about it. But when you were thinking about it, it was cool.

BUTT-HEAD'S REPORT CARD

GRADE REPORT

HIGHLAND HIGH

(A=Excellent; B=Outstanding; C=Above Average; D=Good; F=Not Very Good*)

STUDENT NAME: *Butt-head*   GRADE: *N/A*

Language Arts   F   D   C-   F

Inner conflict, self-esteem problems prevent full self-expression – DVD

> UH, THIS WOULD BE COOL IF THEY TALKED ENGLISH OR SOMETHING.

Introduction to Business Arts   D-   F   D   B-

"Butt-O-Gram" marketing project a stroke of adequacy – MW

> I PUT THE BUTT IN PEOPLE'S BIRTHDAYS. BUSINESS IS COOL.

Science Arts   D   D   D-   D

HAS BEEN INTERESTING TEST SUBJECT; OTHERWISE A WASTE OF A ZYGOTE – SJK

> I CHECKED IF EVERYTHING WAS, YOU KNOW, "ANATOMICALLY CORRECT."

Math I   C-   D   D-   F

Must learn to stop laughing at the word "algebra" – DVD

> HUH HUH HUH HUH HUH.

Basic Hygiene   F   F   F   F

This student is a maggot – BB

> IF GOD WANTED ME TO WASH, HE WOULDA MADE ME SMELL LIKE A SHOWER, OR SOMETHING.

Beginning Spanish   D   D   D   F

Debe morir Butt-head – JST

> LO SUCKO MI POCHO HAMANA HAMANA TO YOU TOO, DILLWEED.

Physical Education   D   D   D   D

Figure of ridicule is all the figure he'll ever have – BB

> THIS WAS THE CLASS WHERE THEY KEPT ASKING THE TRICK QUESTIONS, I THINK.

Socio-Cultural Studies   C   C   C   C

Excellent attendance! – DVD

> VAN DRIESSEN SAID I MISUNDERSTOOD OTHER CULTURES JUST THE SAME AS MY OWN.

*As the result of a recent court ruling, the meaning of the "F" grade has been changed from the pejorative term "Fail" to the stern but less emotionally damaging "Not Very Good." Some parents may also want to implement their own "curve" to compensate for any regrettable but unavoidable Western European ethnocentrism which may have occured in class.

DREAMS and

DREAMS ARE COOL, CAUSE IT'S LIKE YOU'RE STILL WATCHING TV EVEN THOUGH YOU'RE SLEEPING. THE ONLY THING THAT SUCKS ABOUT THEM IS WAKING UP. SOMETIMES YOU HAVE TO GO BACK AND SLEEP ALL DAY, JUST TO FINISH A DREAM. BUT, LIKE, WHATEVER IT TAKES OR SOMETHING.

SOME DUDE ON TV SAID YOUR DREAMS ARE SPOSED TO MEAN SOMETHING. LIKE, IF YOU KILLED A BUNCH OF BUGS DURING THE DAY, THAT NIGHT YOU MIGHT DREAM ABOUT KILLING A BUNCH OF BUGS. SO WE, LIKE, DECIDED TO ANALEYES SOME OF OUR COOLEST DREAMS.

BUTT-HEAD'S DREAM: SO LIKE, I HAVE THIS ONE WHERE I GO OVER TO BEAVIS'S HOUSE, AND I JUST WALK IN, BUT I CAN'T FIND BEAVIS ANYWHERE. BUT THE BATHROOM DOOR'S OPEN AND I CAN SEE BEAVIS'S MOM, AND SHE'S EATING BANANAS IN THE BATHTUB. SO I'M STANDING THERE, CHECKING OUT HER WET THINGIES AND THINKING THIS IS COOL, WHEN SHE TURNS TO ME AND ASKS ME TO WASH HER BACK. BUT INSTEAD, I SAY I HAVE TO PEE. AND SHE SAYS 'THAT'S NICE.' AND THIS IS THE WEIRD PART... WHEN I WAKE UP AFTER THE DREAM, I HAVE A STIFFY, AND I REALLY HAVE TO PEE.

BEAVIS' ANAL-EYESEES: HMM... THAT'S WEIRD. I WONDER WHERE I WAS?

BEAVIS'S DREAM: OKAY, SO I HAVE THIS DREAM THAT I'M IN SCHOOL, EATING A PLATE OF BLOODY BRAINS AND LISTENING TO OZZY BACKWARDS, WHEN A VOICE TELLS ME TO GO DIG A GRAVE. SO I'M HANGING OUT IN THE CEMETERY, LAUGHING AT DEAD PEOPLE'S NAMES, WHEN I SEE ONE THAT SAYS 'WINGER'. ALL OF A SUDDEN THIS HAND COMES UP THROUGH THE DIRT. AND THIS PERSON STARTS CLIMBING OUT, AND IT'S ACKSHULLY WINGER, BACK FROM THE DEAD! ONLY HE'S GOT A CHAINSAW AND HE WANTS TO KILL ME! SO I'M RUNNING AND RUNNING, AND FINALLY, I GO, 'THIS IS STUPID. WHY AM I RUNNING FROM WINGER?' SO I TURN AROUND AND KICK HIM IN THE NADS, AND HE STARTS CRYING. AND I SAY, 'GO BACK TO THE GRAVE WHERE YOU BELONG, BUNGHOLE!' SO HE DOES.

BUTT-HEAD'S ANAL-EYESEES: WHOA! THAT'S PRETTY COOL. I GUESS WINGER'S A BIGGER WUSS THAN WE THOUGHT! HUH HUH HUH.

Nightmares

BEAVIS'S DREAM: SOMETIMES I HAVE THIS DREAM WHERE I GO DOWN INTO THE BASEMENT AND A GIANT SPIDER WITH A FLAMING SKULL HEAD CATCHES ME IN HIS WEB. AND JUST AS HE'S GONNA EAT ME, I WHIP OUT A NAIL GUN AND START SHOOTING HIM IN THE NADS. AND ALL THIS GREEN STUFF STARTS POURING OUT OF HIS GUTS, AND THEN ABOUT TWO THOUSAND BABY SPIDERS COME RUNNING OUT. BUT I DON'T HAVE ENOUGH NAILS TO KILL THEM ALL. BUT IT'S OKAY, CAUSE THE BABY SPIDERS START EATING THE BIG SPIDER AND IN BETWEEN BITES THEY LOOK AT ME AND SAY 'THANKS, BEAVIS.' SO I WATCH THEM FOR A WHILE AND THINK 'THIS IS COOL,' UNTIL I FALL ASLEEP IN THE WEB. AND THEN I USUALLY WAKE UP IN MY BED THE NEXT MORNING, AND THERE'S A BUNCH OF SNOT ON MY PILLOW AND STUFF.

BUTT-HEAD'S ANAL-EYESEES: HUH HUH HUH... YOU'RE A DUMBASS!

BUTT-HEAD'S DREAM: SO LIKE, SOMETIMES I DREAM THAT I'M ABOUT TO DO IT WITH A CHICK, BUT I CAN HEAR BEAVIS IN THE OTHER ROOM, LAUGHING REALLY HARD... AND IT'S PISSING ME OFF, BECAUSE HE'S EITHER LAUGHING AT ME, OR ELSE I'M MISSING SOMETHING REALLY COOL ON TV. SO I TELL THE CHICK I'LL BE RIGHT BACK... AND WHEN I GET TO THE LIVING ROOM BEAVIS IS DEAD. BUT THERE'S A PRETTY COOL SHOW ON TV.

BEAVIS' ANAL-EYESEES: WHAT DO YOU MEAN I'M DEAD?! HOW DO YOU KNOW I WASN'T FAKING IT?
CAUSE YOU WERE DEAD.
NO I WASN'T.
YES YOU WERE.
DON'T MAKE ME KICK YOUR ASS, BUTT-HEAD!
YOU CAN'T KICK MY ASS. YOU'RE DEAD.

BEAVIS'S DREAM: OH YEAH? WELL SOMETIMES I HAVE A DREAM WHERE I KILL BUTT-HEAD, AND HE'S DEAD.

BUTT-HEAD'S ANAL-EYESEES: UHH... THIS MEANS BEAVIS IS A LIAR. HUH HUH. THE END.
NO WAY! WE'RE NOT DONE!
YES WE ARE. HUH HUH.
CUT IT OUT, BUTT-HEAD! I'VE GOT A LOT MORE DREAMS! I GOT DREAMS ABOUT SNAKES AND VAMPIRE BATS AND FOREIGNERS AND GWAR...
DEAD PEOPLE DON'T DREAM, DILLHOLE.
I'M NOT DEAD!!!
OH YEAH? WELL, I GUESS WE'LL JUST HAVE TO WAIT AND SEE IF YOU WAKE UP TOMORROW. HUH HUH. GOOD NIGHT, BEAVIS. I'M GOING TO BED. HUH HUH HUH.

Dd SELF-DEFENSE

UM, LIKE, GETTING YOUR ASS KICKED ALL THE TIME SUCKS, HEH HEH. IT'S LIKE, YOU GOTTA TEACH YOUR ASS TO KICK BACK. YOU GOTTA LEARN TO SELF-DEFEND YOURSELF. HEH HEH. THAT'S WHAT I'M GONNA TEACH YOU HOW TO DO. AND LIKE, YOU GOTTA DO EVERYTHING I SAY BECAUSE I'M NOT ALWAYS GONNA BE AROUND TO HAUL YOUR ASS INTO THE FIRE OR WHATEVER. HEH HEH.

THE BASIC STANCE

UM, FIRST, YOU GOTTA LEARN THE RIGHT WAY TO STAND. STAND LIKE THIS, WITH TWO FEET ON THE GROUND. THAT'S LIKE, THE BEST WAY TO STAND. IT'S EASY, AND UM, PRETTY COMFERBAL. PLUS, IF YOU HAVE TO LIKE FALL DOWN OR SOMETHING, YOU'RE ALREADY STANDING UP, SO YOU'RE IN THE PERFECT POSITION.

THE NAD KICK

LIKE THIS IS THE MOVE THAT LIKE, MY WHOLE SELF-DEFENSE PROGRAM IS BASED ON. IT'S JUST A QUICK KICK MOTION DIRECTLY TO THE NADS. HEH HEH HEH. REALLY FAST AND REALLY HARD. RIGHT IN THE NADS, HEH HEH HEH. JUST MAKE SURE YOU ALWAYS TRY TO GET INTO FIGHTS WITH PEOPLE WHO HAVE NADS.

PLAY DEAD

SOMETIMES, IF YOU, LIKE, IGNORE A PROBLEM, IT GOES AWAY. SO LIKE, IF YOU SUDDENLY PLAY DEAD WHILE SOMEBODY'S KICKING YOUR ASS, THEY'LL LIKE GO AWAY. SOMETIMES.

THE LOOGIE HOCK

UM , EVEN IF LIKE, YOUR ASS HAS BEEN KICKED ALREADY, YOU CAN SELF-DEFEND YOURSELF HOURS, EVEN UM, DAYS LATER. YOU JUST HOCK A LOOGIE INTO THE PERSON WHO KICKED YOUR ASS'S CUP. HEH HEH HEH. THERE'S ANOTHER MOVE THAT'S A LOT LIKE THIS MOVE, BUT DIFFERENT, KNOWN AS THE CUP A WHIZ, HEH HEH.

THE STOMP

IF YOU HAVE TO SELF-DEFEND YOURSELF AGAINST LIKE, BUGS AND STUFF, OR LIKE ONE OF THOSE FLOWERS THAT'S GOT POINTY THINGS ON IT, OR LIKE A GUY WHO'S ALREADY DOWN ON THE GROUND, YOU CAN DO THE STOMP. HEH HEH. IT REALLY HURTS, HEH HEH.

FRIENDSHIP

AFTER YOU'VE LIKE SELF-DEFENDED YOURSELF, TRY TO BE FRIENDS WITH THE PERSON. THAT WAY THEY WON'T WANT TO KICK YOUR ASS AGAIN AND YOU CAN LIKE, JUST GET ON WITH YOUR LIFE. PUT IT ALL BEHIND YOU. HEH HEH HEH HEH. GET ON. BEHIND.

A Typical Self-Defence Snario

"The Basic Stance"
BUTT-HEAD: "GIMME THAT FROG, ASSWIPE. NOW. HUH HUH."
BEAVIS: "NO WAY, BUNGHOLE."

"Playing Dead"
BUTT-HEAD: "YOU WUSS. I BARELY TOUCHED YOU. HUH HUH. MY FROG, NOW."

"The Nad Kick"
BUTT-HEAD: "AAAAAAAGH!"
BEAVIS: "M HEH HEH HEH HEH. ASSWIPE."

"The Stomp"
BEAVIS: "GIMME SOME A YOUR SLUSHY, YOU WUSS. HEH HEH HEH. WUSS."
BUTT-HEAD: "UH HUH HUH OW HUH OW."

"The Cup a Whiz"
BEAVIS: "HEH HEH HEH HEH M HEH HEH."
BUTT-HEAD: "UUGH. GET OVER HERE AND HELP ME, ASSWIPE."

"Friendship"
BUTT-HEAD: "BEAVIS, AS SOON AS MY NADS FEEL BETTER I'M GONNA BEAT THE CRAP OUT OF YOU."
BEAVIS: "HEH HEH HEH. DRINK THIS—YOU'LL FEEL LOTS BETTER. HEH HEH HEH."

DAHMER, JEFFREY – UH, I HEARD HE, LIKE, SOLD ARMS TO THE MILITARY, OR SOMETHING, HUH HUH HUH! SOME DUDE'S ARMS, I MEAN. OH YEAH, AND HE'S LIKE REALLY SMART, CAUSE HE'S GOT LOTSA BRAINS, HEH HEH. YOU KNOW, LIKE, OTHER PEOPLE'S BRAINS? HUH HUH, YEAH. AND THAT DUDE HAS MORE GUTS THAN ANYBODY ELSE, BUT HE COULDN'T OUTRUN THE COPS CAUSE HE'S GOT TWO LEFT FEET. AND THEY HAD TROUBLE TAKING HIS FINGERPRINTS CAUSE HE'S ALL THUMBS. AND THEN HIS LAWYER COST HIM, LIKE, A LEG AND AN ARM. PLUS A HEAD AND TWO NADS, HUH HUH. WAIT, I GOT ONE, BUTT-HEAD! NOW HE'S, LIKE, PISSED CAUSE THE CAFETERIA IN JAIL DOESN'T SERVE CHICKS' FINGERS, HEH HEH HEH. THAT'S PRETTY GROSS, BEAVIS. OH. OH YEAH.

DAMME, VAN – THIS GUY KICKS ASS. HE KNOWS KARATE STUFF, AND LIKE, HOW TO KILL PEOPLE, AND THE STUFF HE DOESN'T KNOW, LIKE ENGLISH, MAKES HIM EVEN COOLER. CAUSE WHEN MOVIE DUDES KNOW ENGLISH, THEY JUST SIT AROUND AND TALK AND CRY AND STUFF INSTEAD OF GETTING TO THE BUSINESS AT HAND, WHICH IS KICKING ASS. BUT AS LONG AS VAN DAMME STILL SPEAKS EUROPEAN, EVERYTHING SHOULD BE COOL.

DENADULATION – THIS CHICK CUT OFF THIS GUY'S THINGIE, AND THE GUY HAD TO SHOW UP AND BLAME HER, RIGHT ON TV. AND ALL THROUGH THE TRIAL THEY KEPT SAYING "PENIS." "WHEN DID YOU CUT OFF HIS PENIS?" "IS THAT WHERE THE PENIS WAS FOUND?" "IS THIS A PHOTOGRAPH OF YOUR PENIS?" NOW WHENEVER YOU SEE THAT GUY'S PICTURE ON TV, LIKE ON THE NEWS OR ON RENALDO, IT SAYS UNDERNEATH HIS PICTURE, "WIFE CUT OFF HIS PENIS." AND WHENEVER HE GOES INTO A RESTAURANT, PEOPLE SAY, "THERE'S THAT DORK WHOSE WIFE CUT OFF HIS DORK." AND WHEN PEOPLE ASK HIM FOR AN AUTOGRAPH, HE WRITES, "BEST OF LUCK TO BETSY. SIGNED, THE GUY WHOSE WIFE CUT OFF HIS PENIS." THEY SHOULD WRITE A BOOK ABOUT HIS LIFE AND CALL IT "WHERE'S WOODROW?" HUH HUH HUH HUH. THAT WOULD BE COOL.

DESERT NAM – THE FIRST WAR SO COOL THEY PUT THE WHOLE THING ON TV. THERE WAS, LIKE, THIS SODOMY INSANE DUDE TRYING TO MUSCLE IN ON OUR CHICK, KUWAIT? SO WE KICKED HIS ASS. IT WAS COOL, CAUSE EVERY TIME THE ARMY FIRED A SHOT THAT HIT, THEY'D MAKE A MUSIC VIDEO ABOUT IT AND SHOW IT ON CNN. PLUS THE REPORTER DUDE WAS LIKE A WEREWOLF. HE RULED.

DICK – A WUSSY DUDE'S NAME. IT'S SHORT FOR "RICHARD." AND BEAVIS.

DILLHOLE – (SEE BEAVIS. HUH HUH HUH HUH)

DILLWEED – (UM, LOOK AT BUTT-HEAD. HEH HEH M HEH HEH)

DOG – HOW COME SOME ASSWIPES HAVE A BIG UGLY DOG AT HOME THAT DOESN'T EVEN WEAR CLOTHES AND WALKS AROUND NAKED ALL DAY EXPOSING ITS WEINER AND LICKING ITS NADS. AND THEY FEED IT STEAKS AND CALL IT THEIR BEST FRIEND AND SAY "GOOD DOGGIE," WHENEVER IT TAKES A CRAP IN SOMEONE ELSE'S YARD. BUT IF THAT SAME DOG WAS ME OR BEAVIS, THEY'D SMACK US SILLY AND MAKE US SEE A COUNSELOR? NEXT TIME SOME BUTTMUNCH HAS A "TALK" WITH YOU, JUST SAY, "HEY, WHY DON'T YOU GET ROVER SOME PANTS AND MAYBE HE'LL STOP MAKING A POPSICLE OUT OF HIS OWN BUTT!"

DOLPHIN – THIS FISH WITH A HOLE IN ITS HEAD THAT LIKES TO EAT BALLOONS AND STUFF. THE DOLPHIN LIKES TO EAT BALLOONS AND STUFF, I MEAN. I DON'T KNOW WHAT THE HOLE LIKES TO EAT. SOMETIMES TUNAS GET CAUGHT IN THE NETS FISHING DUDES LEAVE OUT FOR DOLPHINS, WHICH REALLY SUCKS, CAUSE TUNA FISH TASTES PRETTY GROSS.

DOPPLER EFFECT – THE DOPPLER EFFECT WAS NAMED AFTER THIS DORK NAMED DOPPLER WHO WENT AROUND NAMING STUFF SO PEOPLE WOULD THINK HE WAS A SCIENTIST. SOMETIMES WHEN BEAVIS FARTS, IT MAKES A LITTLE BROWN STAIN IN HIS UNDERPANTS. I'M GOING TO NAME THAT THE BUTT-HEAD EFFECT, AND THEN I'LL, YOU KNOW, GET SOME.

DOUCHE – A FEMININE HIDING PRODUCT, OR SOMETHING.

DUMBASS – UH, YOU SHOULD BE ABLE TO DO THIS ONE, BEAVIS, HUH HUH HUH. UM, OKAY BUTT-HEAD. EH, HEH HEH, A DUMBASS IS DEFINED AS, UM, YOU KNOW, A DUMBASS? IT'S JUST, LIKE, SOMEONE WHOSE BUTT IS AS SMART AS HIS BRAIN, OR SOMETHING? YOU KNOW, LIKE A DUMBASS. THIS IS HARD.

DUDES AND CHICKS

THERE'S LIKE TWO DIFFERENT KINDS OF PEOPLE IN THE WORLD, DUDES AND CHICKS, EXCEPT FOR THIS ONE DUDE WE SAW AT THE STATE FAIR WHO'S LIKE A DUDE AND A CHICK, HUH HUH. ME AND BEAVIS ARE DUDES, SO LIKE, WE KNOW A LOT ABOUT LIKE WHAT DUDES THINK ABOUT AND STUFF. HUH HUH. MOSTLY, WE THINK ABOUT CHICKS, SO I GUESS THAT MAKES US EXPERTS ON THEM, TOO. HERE'S SOME A THE STUFF WE KNOW.

A DUDE'S BRAIN IS LIKE DESIGNED FOR COMPLICATED STUFF LIKE SCIENCE. LIKE, FOR COUNTING BEERS AND EXPERIMENTING ON BUGS OR WHATEVER.

A CHICK'S BRAIN IS BUILT TO THINK ABOUT SIMPLER STUFF, LIKE ME AND BEAVIS. HUH HUH. AT ALL TIMES.

THESE ROCK-SOLID MUSCULAR MAN ARMS ARE USED FOR KICKING THE ASSES OF DUDES WHO LOOK AT MY WOMAN.

CHICK ARMS ARE BUILT FOR HOLDING ME, AND LIKE, CARRYING STUFF TO ME. NACHOS AND CRAP.

CHICKS HAVE THESE THINGIES THAT STICK OUT. IT'S LIKE, THEY EVOLUTIONED AFTER CHICKS STARTED WEARING BRAS. IT WAS LIKE, I LIKE MY BRA, BUT IT'S ALL LOOSE AND STUFF. I KNOW, I'LL GROW SOME THINGIES! HUH HUH.

THIS IS A DUDE'S PACKAGE. HUH HUH HUH. IT'S LIKE WHERE HE GETS MOST OF HIS IDEAS FROM.

A DUDE NEEDS PERFECT LEGS LIKE THESE FOR RUNNING AFTER CHICKS AND STUFF. AND LIKE, KICKING OTHER DUDES IN THE NADS, LIKE BEAVIS, HUH HUH.

A CHICK'S LEGS ARE SPOSED TO WORK CLOSELY WITH HER ARMS TO HELP CARRY MY STUFF TO ME. IF THEY WON'T COOPERATE, THE CHICK SHAVES THEM AS PUNISHMENT.

How To Like Talk To A Chick

Sometimes it's hard talking to a chick. Heh heh heh heh heh heh. But, like with chicks? It's like, they say stuff, and like, you have to think of what to say back, and by then they're already getting in some dude's car instead of yours just because he, like, has a car. Here's like some tips on how to like get a chick's attention and then hold it. Heh heh heh. Hold it.

* First, unzip your pants a little bit. Like halfway. That's so, like, the chicks you're talking to will start to, uh, unconshusly think about them. Your pants.

* Like, every time you're about to say something, open your mouth really wide and lick your lips, heh heh. It's a chick turn-on.

* When you first meet a chick, say something that like, shows you like really care about them or whatever.

Something like, "I think I can see your nipple." Heh heh. That's called a ice breaker.

* Sometimes, like, a joke can break the ice too. Something like, "It looked so nice out today I'm not wearing pants." Heh heh. Or like, that one about the dude who goes like I can't hear you cause I got a banana in my rear. Heh heh heh.

* When the conversation dies down, change the subject. Go, "Uh, do you wanna go do it somewhere?" That way there's like, no awkward silences and stuff.

* After about a minute or something, when you've said all there is to say, that's when you make your move. You should try to talk to chicks near where there's a clock so you know when a minute's up. Heh heh. Up.

HOW TO GET A DUDE'S ATTENTION

Like, a lot of chicks ask me and Beavis for advice about dudes, huh huh. They all want to know how to get a dude's attention. Or at attention, huh huh. I always tell chicks the same three things:

* Take off your shirt, huh huh.
* Uh, please take off your shirt.
* Dammit, I said please. Get back here and like, take that thing off. Okay, just unbutton it a little. The top button. Huh huh. OK, bye now.

WHAT A DUDE SAYS AND WHAT HE REALLY MEANS

Um, heh heh. Like, hi. Heh heh. Um, let's like, let's go somewhere and um do it. Heh heh heh. Yeah. Nice thingies.

TV is cool. Like, they should make glasses that have like two TVs on the inside so you could like put on your glasses and you'd just be watching TV. Heh heh. You'd be on your bike watching TV. I wonder what my bike is doing right now. Somebody's probably like, riding it. Heh heh m heh heh. Riding it. Ride! Ride! Ride! My next bike is gonna be made of nachos. And like, then I can ride and eat and watch TV. Hey, where'd that chick go? She was here just, um, like, 20 minutes ago.

Ee EXCUSES THAT, LIKE, WORK

UM, EXCUSES ARE LIKE THESE THINGS YOU USE TO GET OUT OF STUFF, HEH HEH. IT'S LIKE MONEY, EXCEPT THEY DON'T BUY NACHOS, THEY JUST BUY TIME. AND LIKE, YOU CAN'T WAIT FOR STEWART BEFORE SCHOOL AND TAKE HIS. NOT EVERYBODY USES EXCUSES, BUT THAT'S CAUSE MOST PEOPLE AREN'T LIKE AS UNTELLIGENT AS US. HEH HEH. HERE'S SOME EXCUSES WE USE TO LIKE GET OUT OF STUFF.

* UM, A DOG ATE IT. HEH HEH. THEN HE PUKED IT BACK UP AND LIKE, ATE IT AGAIN. HEH HEH. THEN, WHEN HE PUKED IT UP AGAIN, HE JUST LIKE, ROLLED IN IT, HUH HUH. IT WAS MESSED UP.

* UH, HUH HUH. I COULDN'T GET TO WORK ON TIME CAUSE MY NADS HURT. HUH HUH.

* THIS FAT DUDE GEORGE BET US THAT LIKE WE WOULDN'T SPANK OUR MONKEYS AND THEN HIM AND HIS FRIENDS WERE LIKE BETTING TOO. UM, THIS DUDE JERRY AND ELAINE, WHO'S A CHICK, AND THIS OTHER DUDE NAMED CREAMER OR SOMETHING. AND SO LIKE WE WEREN'T DOING IT, HUH HUH. BUT LIKE, CREAMER DID IT AND THEN LIKE, HUH HUH, SO DID THE OTHERS, INCLUDING THE CHICK, WHO'S LIKE, NOT EVEN SPOSED TO HAVE A MONKEY, BUT SHE DID IT ANYWAY. HUH HUH. AND LIKE, THAT'S WHY WE COULDN'T DO THE HOMEWORK CAUSE WE WERE TOO BUSY NOT SPANKING OUR MONKEYS. BUT THEN DURING THE COMMERCIAL, WE DID. HUH HUH.

* UM, WE CAN'T LIKE PRECIPITATE IN THE CAN GOODS DRIVE CAUSE LIKE, WE'RE ALLERGENIC TO METAL, HEH HEH. UNLESS IT'S HEAVY.

* WE DIDN'T DO THE HOMEWORK CAUSE BEAVIS'S MOM HAD TO GO GET HER STOMACH PUMPED.

* UM, HEH HEH, WE DIDN'T DO THE ASSIGNMENT CAUSE WE WERE WATCHING EDUCATIONAL TV INSTEAD. YOU KNOW, LIKE A SHOW ABOUT THOSE THINGS, UM, DINOSSERS, HEH HEH. THEY WERE THOSE PURPLE THINGS WITH TEETH AND THEY LIKE, HUNG OUT WITH THE LITTLE CHILDREN AND SANG SONGS ABOUT NUMBERS AND CRAP. AND THEN THEY WENT SUXTINCT UNTIL A LITTLE LATER WHEN BIG BIRD CAME ON. THEY SAID ON THE SHOW YOU COULD GET A CLASS CREDIT FOR WATCHING.

* MY PEN RAN OUT OF INK. CAUSE LIKE I USED UP ALL THE INK WRITING, UH, TO THOSE POOR KIDS IN CENTRAL INDIANA.

* THESE DUDES JUMPED US AND LIKE MADE US GIVE THEM OUR HOMEWORK AND UM THEN THEY WENT TO THEIR SCHOOL AND LIKE, CLAIMED IT WAS THEIR HOMEWORK EVEN THOUGH IT WAS OURS. I HEARD THEY GOT A A ON IT. DON'T TRY TO FIND THEM CAUSE THEY LIVE IN ENGLAND OR LIKE BRITAIN OR SOMETHING.

* I HAVE THAT THING. UH, ATTENTION DEFI... UH, DEFI... HUH HUH HUH, DEFECATE. HUH HUH HUH HUH HUH.

* UH, WE'RE LATE FOR WORK CAUSE LIKE, WE WERE OUT FISHING WITH THE PRESIDENT OF BURGER WORLD. UH, HE SAID IT WAS OKAY SINCE HE'S THE PRESIDENT, AND ALSO THAT YOU HAVE TO LIKE CLEAN THE FRYER FOR US. HE SAID HE WAS PROBLY GONNA FIRE YOU UNLESS YOU LIKE GIVE US SOME MORE VACATIONS. HUH HUH.

Ff FOREINURZ

FRENCH DUDES

FRENCH DUDES LIKE TO SAY "OOH" A LOT. LIKE, "OOOH-LA-LA! VOOLEY VOO TAKE A LOOK AT THE POOH ON MY SHOE?" HEH HEH HEH.

FRENCH DUDES GET A LOT OF CHICKS, CAUSE THEY KNOW HOW TO FRENCH KISS, AND STUFF. PLUS THEY'VE GOT SOME, LIKE, MAGICAL WAY OF TICKLING. THIS WOULD BE OKAY IF THEY JUST GOT A LOT OF FRENCH CHICKS, BUT SOMETIMES THEY GET AMERICAN CHICKS TOO, WHICH SUCKS CAUSE THEN THERE'S LESS CHICKS FOR ME AND BEAVIS.

OH YEAH, AND FRENCH DUDES ALL THINK THAT SHARI LEWIS CHICK IS A GENIUS JUST CAUSE SHE, LIKE, TAUGHT A GOAT TO TALK.

CHINESE DUDES

YOU DON'T WANNA FIGHT CHINESE DUDES CAUSE THEY'RE ALL, LIKE, GOOD AT TAI-DYE AND STUFF, WHICH THEY LEARNED A LONG TIME AGO FROM THAT MARC POLIO DUDE.

PLUS THEY'VE HAD A LOT OF PRACTICE FIGHTING GODZILLA.

ANOTHER COOL THING ABOUT CHINESE DUDES IS THAT THEY CALL EVERYONE THEY MEET AN "AH-SO", HUH HUH HUH.

ENGLISH DUDES

ENGLISH DUDES ARE LIKE ENGLISH, BUT THE WEIRD THING IS, THEY DON'T TALK ENGLISH.

YEAH, HEH HEH. IT'S LIKE, WHEN THEY SAY "BUM" THEY'RE NOT TALKING ABOUT SOME DUDE BEGGING ON THE STREET, THEY'RE JUST TALKING ABOUT HIS BUTT.

HUH HUH. AND THEY SAY OTHER WEIRD STUFF LIKE, "IT'S TIME FOR TEA AND SPANK MY MONKEY."

YEAH, REALLY. ENGLISH DUDES ARE WAY TOO INTERESTED IN TEA.

MEXICAN DUDES

MEXICAN DUDES LOVE AMERICA ALMOST AS MUCH AS AMERICANS DO. LIKE, THEY NAMED THEIR WHOLE COUNTRY "SOUTH AMERICA" CAUSE THEY LOVE AMERICA SO MUCH. MAYBE THEY WERE HOPING WE'D RETURN THE FAVOR, AND THEN THE MOST ASS-KICKING COUNTRY IN THE WORLD WOULD BE CALLED "NORTH MEXICO." BUT INSTEAD WE JUST NAMED ONE STATE "NEW MEXICO." IT'S LIKE A CARNATION PRIZE OR SOMETHING.

THE ONLY WORDS THEY HAVE IN MEXICAN ARE, LIKE, FOODS: "NACHOS, TACOS, BURRITOS, TOSTADAS, CHIHUAHUAS AND CHIMICHANGAS."

YEAH BUT, UM, SOME OTHER MEXICAN FOOD ACKSHULLY HAS ENGLISH NAMES, LIKE RICE, BEANS, BURRITOS AND NACHOS.

WAIT. WAIT. UM, OH YEAH.

CANADIAN DUDES

JUST KEEP WALKING NORTH FOR ABOUT A MILLION MILES AND YOU'RE BOUND TO RUN INTO SOME CANADIAN DUDES. THEY'LL BE THE PEOPLE IN THE HOUSES MADE OUT OF ICE WHO SPEND ALL THEIR TIME HARPOONING WHALES. IT'S PROBLY A PRETTY COOL LIFE, BUT THE COLD WEATHER MUST REALLY, YOU KNOW, SHRIVEL YOUR THINGIE. LIKE YOU'D NOTICE WITH BEAVIS, HUH HUH.

SHUT UP, BUNGHOLE. CANADIAN DUDES HAVE, LIKE, A HUNDRED DIFFERENT WORDS FOR YELLOW SNOW.

DUTCH DUDES

NOT MUCH IS KNOWN ABOUT DUTCH DUDES, EXCEPT FOR THIS ONE KID WHO GOT HIS PICTURE ON ALL THE PAINT CANS AFTER HE PUT HIS FINGER IN A DYKE.

HEH HEH M HEH HEH. "CANS."

Ff THE FUTURE

IT'S IMPORTANT FOR A GOOD ENSUCKLOPEDIA TO HAVE STUFF ABOUT THE FUTURE. UH, BECAUSE KIDS IN THE FUTURE CAN STILL USE THIS BOOK TO CHEAT OFF OF. SO WE DID THAT THING. RESEARCH. LIKE WE WATCHED, THAT SHOW ABOUT THE, UM, DUDES IN THE SPACE SHIP AND THEY LIKE FLY TO DIFFERENT PLANETS OR WHATEVER AND THEY GET PHASERED ALL THE TIME. I THINK IT'S CALLED CHEERS. IT SUCKS. AND, UH, IN THE FUTURE, IT WILL STILL SUCK. HERE'S SOME OTHER STUFF.

PEOPLE'LL COME FROM MILES AROUND TO WATCH THESE LIKE HUMAN AIR HOCKEY GAMES. IT'LL BE COOL.

LIFESTYLE

PROBLY THE BIGGEST QUESTION FOR ANY WUSS WHO GIVES A CRAP ABOUT THE FUTURE IS LIKE, WILL THEY FIND A WAY TO MAKE TV NOT SUCK? AND THE ANSWER IS NO, TV WILL NOT NOT SUCK, AND SINCE TWO WRONGS LIKE NUTRISIZE EACH OTHER, THAT MEANS TV WILL STILL SUCK. BUT THERE WILL BE SOME COOL THINGS. LIKE YOU'LL GO, "THIS SUCKS, CHANGE IT," AND LIKE, THE TV WILL AUTOMATICALLY FIND YOU SOME CHICKS AND EXPLOSIONS.

ALSO FOOD WILL BE DIFFERENT. BUT LIKE, IF THEY WANTED SOME REAL PROGRESS WITH FOOD, THEY SHOULD MAKE NACHOS THAT COME ALREADY CHEWED, OR LIKE INVENT HOT DOGS THAT COME IN THE FLAVORS OF FRUITY WHIPS SO IT'S LIKE, WHOA, A WHOLE MEAL IN A ROLL, THIS MUST BE THE FUTURE.

THERE'LL BE A LOT OF TECHNOLOGY CRAP TOO. WHEN YOU CALL SOMEBODY UP ON THE PHONE, FOR INSTANT, THEY'LL BE ON THIS LITTLE TV ON YOUR PHONE, SO IN THE FUTURE, PEOPLE WILL TRY TO CALL WHEN PEOPLE ARE IN THE SHOWER, OR, HUH HUH, DOING IT.

LIKE, IF YOU SEE A TV WITH A SHARP POINT ON IT, IT'S PROBLY FROM THE FUTURE. IN THE FUTURE, TVS WILL BE EXTRA BIG LIKE THIS SO THEY CAN FIT MORE SHOWS INSIDE.

LIKE, IN THE FUTURE, YOU'LL BE ABLE TO CALL UP PEOPLE ON TV. YOU'LL GO UM, HELLO, BLOSSOM? YOUR SHOW SUCKS, HEH HEH HEH. THEN YOU CAN HANG UP AND LIKE, CALL THAT CHICK RHODA OR THAT ONE DUDE. HOGAN HERO.

TRAVEL

IN THE PAST, DUDES WENT SLOW. THEY RODE ON COWS OR SOMETHING, WHICH THEY HAD TO START BY SAYING, "GET UP." THEN THEY SAID, "THIS SUCKS. WE GOTTA GO FASTER! FASTER! FASTER!" THEN THAT DUDE CHEVY CHASE INVENTED THE CAR. BUT IT'S STILL NOT AS COOL AS IT COULD BE, CAUSE LIKE, A LOT OF CARS STILL DON'T PEEL OUT. BUT IN THE FUTURE, WHEN THEY'RE POWERED BY, LIKE, TECHNOLOGY OR SOMETHING, ALL CARS WILL FINALLY HAUL ASS. SO THERE'LL BE LIKE SKID MARKS AND GUYS RUNNING LIGHTS ALL OVER THE PLACE. THE FUTURE WILL BE COOL FOR ITS OUTSTANDING CRACKUPS.

THE FUTURE ALSO LIKE HAPPENS IN SPACE. THEY'LL HAVE THESE ROCKETS WITH THE POWER OF, LIKE, A THOUSAND M-80S, AND THEY GO TO OTHER PLANETS, LIKE, UH, MILKY WAY OR SNICKERS OR WHATEVER IT IS. AND WE'LL LIKE CIVILIZE IT WITH BURGER WORLDS AND HIGHWAYS AND STUFF. BUT, LIKE, NO SCHOOLS CAUSE WE DON'T WANT THOSE ILLEGAL ALIENS UP THERE LEARNING HOW TO KICK OUR ASS. THEN ME AND BEAVIS WILL MOVE TO ONE OF THOSE PLANETS TO LIKE COLONY IT AND NOT HAVE TO GO TO SCHOOL. HUH HUH HUH. WE'RE PRETTY SMART.

BUT THE COOLEST THING WILL BE THAT PEOPLE WILL HAVE THESE JETSON THINGS. THEY'RE LIKE BACKPACKS, ONLY THIS STUFF SHOOTS OUT THE BACK AND YOU CAN GO UP IN THE AIR, LIKE A BIRD, HUH HUH, AND DO STUFF LIKE BIRDS DO, LIKE PINCH LOAFS ON PEOPLE. IT'S PRETTY COOL, HUH HUH HUH. BUT LIKE, BY THEN THEY'LL HAVE LIKE A INVENTION OR SOMETHING THAT LIKE SHOOTS A LASER FROM YOUR HEAD TO A BIRD'S BUTT WHEN IT CRAPS ON YOU. HUH HUH. SO PINCHING LOAFS ON SOMEBODY'S HEAD WON'T BE AS COOL THEN AS IT IS NOW.

NOT EVERYTHING IN THE FUTURE WILL BE COOL. THERE'S STILL GONNA BE WUSSES LIKE THIS WITH BOOKS AND THINGS IN THEIR BACKPACKS. DUMBASS.

ECONOMICS

ONE OF THE BIG THINGS ABOUT ECOLOGICS IN THE FUTURE WILL BE ROBOTS. ROBOTS ARE THESE THINGS THAT'LL DO THE WORK HUMANS DON'T WANT TO DO, LIKE PICK UP AFTER YOU FOR THE HUNDREDTH TIME. THE COOL THING ABOUT ROBOTS IS, WE WON'T HAVE TO DEAL WITH A LOT OF BUTTMUNCH CUSTOMERS AT BURGER WORLD ANYMORE, CAUSE THEY'LL JUST LIKE SEND THEIR ROBOTS TO PICK UP THE FOOD FROM US. UH, WOULD YOU LIKE FRIES WITH THAT, YOU STUPID METAL FARTKNOCKER? HUH HUH HUH HUH.

JUST LIKE NOW, SOME JOBS WILL BE COOLER THAN OTHERS IN THE FUTURE. COOL JOBS WILL BE HOVERCRAFT REPAIRMAN, WORKING ON LIKE A VIDEO SEX PHONE, AND BEING OZZY. MOST OTHER JOBS WILL STILL SUCK.

CHICKS

CHICKS WILL BE DIFFERENT IN THE FUTURE. THEY'LL, LIKE, PUT OUT. CAUSE, UH, THEY'LL BE SMARTER, SO THEY'LL DIG US MORE. PLUS WE'LL BE LIKE OLDER, AND LEARNED WHATEVER IT IS OLD DUDES LEARN TO LIKE, MESMERIZE CHICKS. AND EVEN IF THIS PART OF THE FUTURE DOESN'T WORK OUT EXACTLY RIGHT, WE CAN PROBLY GET THOSE DUDES WHO MAKE ROBOTS TO MAKE US A ROBOT CHICK TO DO THE WORK HUMAN CHICKS WON'T DO. HUH HUH HUH HUH. THE FUTURE IS COOL.

POOR DUDES WILL HAVE AUTO-CHICKS LIKE THIS. AND IF YOU'RE LIKE RICH, YOU CAN GET ONE WITH A TV IN HER STOMACH.

THIS IS AN OLD PICTURE. LIKE, NOW WE KNOW IN THE REAL FUTURE, ROBOTS'LL BRING NACHOS.

Gg FEELING GOOD PAGE

WHEN YOU'RE SITTING AROUND, AND THINKING THAT LIFE SUCKS, YOU'RE PROBABLY RIGHT. BUT USUALLY THERE'S SOMETHING YOU CAN DO TO MAKE YOURSELF FEEL BETTER, HEH HEH. UNLESS YOU JUST DID IT, HEH HEH. THEN YOU CAN THINK ABOUT STUFF THAT MAKES YOU HAPPY. HERE'S LIKE A LIST.

TURDS. LIKE, WHAT IF THERE WERE NO TURDS? THERE'D BE LESS TOILETS. OR MAYBE NOT, BUT IT'S STILL LIKE A COOL SUBJECT. TURDS.

WHEN IT'S LIKE A NICE DAY OUT, LIKE ON A SATURDAY, AND YOU WAKE UP AND GO, HM, IT'S A NICE DAY, IT'S LIKE SUNNY AND STUFF. MAYBE THERE'LL BE SOMETHING GOOD ON TV.

ACCIDENTALLY RUNNING OVER SOMETHING ON YOUR BIKE. THEN BACKING UP AND RUNNING OVER IT ON PURPOSE.

IT'S GOOD TO BE IN AMERICA CAUSE LIKE, ALL THE SIGNS AND STUFF ARE IN A LANGUAGE YOU UNDERSTAND.

HOT CHICKS WHO HAVEN'T HAD THEIR BOYFRIENDS KICK YOUR ASS YET.

ONE TIME I WAS RUNNING BAREFOOT IN THIS VACANT LOT AND I CUT MY FOOT REALLY BAD. AND I WAS ALWAYS BUMMED ABOUT IT UNTIL ONE DAY I THOUGHT, WHOA, IF I'DA BEEN CRAWLING NAKED ON MY STOMACH IN THAT VACANT LOT, IT COULDA CUT MY WEINER.

LITTLE KIDS ARE KINDA COOL. WHEN THEY LET YOU HANG OUT WITH THEM.

LOOK REAL CLOSE AT A FLOWER. THINK ABOUT HOW LONG IT TOOK THE FLOWER TO GROW ALL ITS FLOWER CRAP. IT'S KIND OF INSTRESTING, SPECIALLY CAUSE IT ONLY TAKES LIKE A MINUTE TO RIP IT APART.

SOMEWHERE, OUT AT A NACHO FARM OR LIKE A CHEESE FACTORY, THERE'S LIKE A SNACK FOR ME THAT HASN'T EVEN BEEN MADE YET. THEY BETTER HURRY UP, CAUSE I'M GETTING LIKE HUNGRY.

IF YOU'RE PISSED CAUSE ALL YOU DO IS LIKE SIT AROUND AND WATCH TV ALL THE TIME, JUST GO LIKE, WELL, IT'S BETTER THAN SITTING AROUND AND NOT WATCHING ANYTHING.

NADS ARE PRETTY COOL.

HARD – (SEE BEAVIS)

HEAD, CHICKEN – WHAT A CHICKEN RUNS AROUND WITHOUT FOR A FEW MINUTES AFTER YOU'VE CUT IT OFF. ITS HEAD, I MEAN. ALSO, LIKE, IF YOU GET THE RIGHT TRAINING AND LIKE KNOW SOMEBODY, YOU CAN GET A JOB AT THE SIDESHOW BITING THEM OFF. SOME DUDES HAVE ALL THE LUCK.

HEAD HUNTERS – THESE DUDES THAT, LIKE, GO UP TO CHICKS AND ASK THEM FOR, YOU KNOW, SOME OTHER DUDE'S HEAD ON A PLATE. UM, NOT TO BE CONFUSED WITH DUDES THAT HAVE PLATES IN THEIR HEADS, HEH HEH HEH!

HERTZ, ROD – UH, JUST ASK BEAVIS. HUH HUH HUH HUH HUH.

HOLIDAY – A DAY OFF WHEN YOU DON'T HAFTA GO TO SCHOOL OR WORK OR DO ANYTHING THAT SUCKS, CAUSE IT'S A DAY OFF. SOME HOLIDAYS ARE COOLER THAN OTHERS. LIKE, FOR ONE DAY EVERY OCTOBER THERE'S A "JULY FOURTH" HOLIDAY CELEBRATING WHEN WE OFFISHULLY TOLD ENGLAND THAT WE WERE GOING TO KICK ITS ASS. THAT'S PRETTY COOL! BUT THEN THERE'S, LIKE, "PRESIDENTS' DAY" WHICH CELEBRATES TWO PRESIDENTS' BIRTHDAYS, BUT YOU ONLY GET ONE DAY OFF CAUSE THEY WERE, LIKE, TWINS. OR MAYBE THEY WEREN'T TWINS, BUT THEIR PARENTS JUST DECIDED TO CELEBRATE THEIR BIRTHDAYS ON THE SAME DAY TO SAVE MONEY ON PRESENTS AND STUFF. PRESIDENTS' DAY SUCKS!

HORMONE – HOW DO YOU MAKE A HORMONE? UH, WHAT DO I LOOK LIKE, THAT SNOOP DOGGY HAUSER DUDE?

INDIAN BURN – KINDA LIKE, WHEN YOU SPANK SOME DUDE'S ARM FOR HIM? IT GOT ITS NAME CAUSE THIS IS HOW INDIANS WOULD START CAMP-FIRES, BY RUBBING TWO DUDES' ARMS TOGETHER.

THEY DID THIS SO OFTEN THEY, LIKE, WOUNDED THEIR KNEES, OR SOMETHING.

INFORMATION SUPERHIGHWAY – UH, IT'S LIKE THIS, UH, SUPERHIGHWAY FULL OF, YOU KNOW, INFORMATION? LIKE IN THE ADS: "HAVE YOU EVER HAD A MEETING IN YOUR BARE BUTT? WELL, YOU WILL, AND THE COMPANY THAT'LL BRING IT TO YOU IS T&A, OR SOMETHING." HUH HUH HUH! NO WAY, BUTT-HEAD! THE INFORNICATION SUPERHIGHWAY IS, LIKE, WHERE DEATH TRUCK FIGURES OUT WHO TO KILL NEXT.

INSECT – EH HEH HEH, IF YOU REALLY WANNA KNOW WHAT AN INSECT IS, JUST SCRATCH YOUR BUTT OR YOUR NADS OR SOMETHING AND THEN CHECK UNDER YOUR NAILS. ANYTHING YOU SEE THAT'S STILL MOVING IS PROBLY AN INSECT.

INTELLIGENCE – THAT'S THIS THING IN YOUR HEAD THAT'S LIKE GAS IN A TANK. SOMEBODY PUT SUGAR IN BEAVIS'S, HUH HUH. SHUT UP, BUTTWIPE. SERIOUSLY, THOUGH, LIKE YOU CAN FILL UP AN EMPTY GAS TANK, BUT IF YOU'RE NATURALLY UNINTELLIGENT, THERE'S LIKE NO WAY YOU CAN GET GAS FOR YOUR HEAD, OR SOMETHING. THEY SAY SCHOOL HELPS, BUT THEY'RE JUST TRYING TO SEE IF YOU'RE DUMB ENOUGH TO FALL FOR IT.

INTERCOURSE, HAVE SEKSUAL – (SEE IT, DO)

IT, DO – UH, YOU KNOW, THAT'S LIKE WHEN YOU AND A CHICK, LIKE, HAVE SEKSUAL INTERCOURSE? OH YEAH, AND IT'S ALSO "A CONJOINING OF THE MALE AND FEMALE GENITALS FOR THE PURPOSES OF PROCREATION" OR SOMETHING. I'M NOT SURE WHAT THAT SECOND THING MEANS, BUT THAT'S WHAT IT SAID IN THIS BIG DICTIONARY IN THE LIBRARY AT SCHOOL. HUH HUH, I WROTE "BIG DICTIONARY!"

HEAVEN

When he judges your life, God doesn't look at cool stuff you did like kicking guy's asses and stuff. It's like you have to do different stuff for God to think you're cool. Like, you have to pass his initiation rituals, like church. And then you get to go to his clubhouse, which is like heaven. And this is what's in it.

Clouds – Heaven is like built of clouds. So like, when you see a lot of clouds in the sky, it means that somebody is like stealing construction materials from like a new development in heaven.

St. Peter – St. Peter has a big book that has everything you did in it. That's like a big deal in heaven, books and stuff. It's like, they should change that expresso to, "It's like I died and went to college, or something." Also, don't make fun of Peter's name, or he'll put lightning up your butt.

Angels – All the people who worshipped God on earth and like meant it get to be angels. That means they get to fly around and play old time guitars and stuff. But what sucks is that only God and Jesus and his like roadies get to have beards and stuff. It's like ZZ Top's family or something.

"No Chicks" Sign – It used to be in olden times that they wouldn't let chicks into heaven. Then they changed the rule in the 60s, but they still said, "Thou shalt not, like, do it." But probably people sneak off and do it anyway.

Pearly Gates – Heaven is famous for its pearly gates, which were, uh, built in 1914 at a cost of 20 thousand dollars. Huh huh. They're probably

ALSO LECTRIFIED, BUT NOBODY REALLY KNOWS. SOME SAY YES, SOME SAY NO.

GOD'S THRONE – GOD SITS ON THIS BIG THRONE AND LIKE TIMIDATES PEOPLE INTO BEING WUSSES. BUT HE DOESN'T SIT ON IT ALL THE TIME. IT'S LIKE WHEN SANTA'S IN THE MALL. SOMETIMES HE HAS TO GO AND LIKE SIT ON THE OTHER THRONE, HUH HUH. HE'S GOT A SIGN THAT GOES, "GOD WILL BE BACK AT 1:30."

LOST PLANES – SOMETIMES, WHEN PLANES DISAPPEAR OVER THE BERMUDA TRIANGLE, THEY WIND UP IN HEAVEN, AND THEY HAVE TO LIKE CIRCLE AROUND UNTIL ALL THE PASSENGERS DIE OF NATURAL CAUSES. THEN THEY GET TAKEN INTO HEAVEN OR WHATEVER, AND GOD USES THE PLANES FOR HIS AIR FORCE.

TVs – THEY HAVE LIKE BIG SCREEN TVs IN HEAVEN, AND YOU CAN WATCH LIKE ANYONE'S LIFE YOU WANT. IT'S LIKE, YOU CAN SAY, "STEWART'S LIFE SUCKS, CHANGE IT," AND YOU CAN WATCH PEOPLE LIKE DOING IT, HUH HUH. BUT THEN THEY BLOCK THE TVs FROM LIKE SHOWING THE GOOD PARTS.

PETTING ZOO – HEAVEN HAS LIKE A COOL PETTING ZOO. LIKE, ALL THE ANIMALS ARE LIKE REALLY FURRY AND SOFT AND YOU CAN LIKE FEED THEM SANDWICHES AND LIKE SMALLER ANIMALS AND STUFF AND THEY LIKE IT– UH, BEAVIS. SHUT UP.

WANTED POSTERS – EVERYBODY'S SUCH A WUSS IN HEAVEN THAT WHEN WE GET THERE, WE'LL PROBABLY BE ABLE TO KICK PEOPLE IN THE NADS AND RIP OFF CANDY AND STUFF FOR A COUPLE YEARS BEFORE THEY FINALLY PUT A REWARD ON US. THEN WE'LL GO HIDE OUT IN HELL FOR A WHILE, AND JUST GO UP TO HEAVEN WHEN WE NEED SOME CLOUDS OR SOMETHING.

PULL MY FINGER: HISTORICAL STUFF THROUGH THE AGES

THOR, THE NORTH GOD OF THUNDER

A LONG TIME AGO THERE WERE THESE, LIKE, NORTHMEN OR WHATEVER WHO WERE REALLY STUPID. WHENEVER THEY HEARD THUNDER, THEY DIDN'T KNOW IT WAS CAUSED BY WEATHER STUFF. THEY THOUGHT IT WAS CAUSED BY SOME BUTTMUNCH NAMED THOR WHO LIVED IN THE SKY. HUH HUH. DORKS. THEY THOUGHT WHENEVER SOMEONE PULLED HIS FINGER, HE WOULD FART LIGHTNING. SOMETIMES IN A REALLY BAD STORM, HE WOULD FART SO MUCH HE WOULD PRACTICALLY TEAR HIMSELF A NEW CORNHOLIO. THAT'S WHY HE WAS CALLED THOR. HE WOULD GO AROUND AND SAY, "I'M THOR." AND PEOPLE WOULD SAY, "YEAH, WELL MAYBE YOU SHOULD GET YOURSELF A NEW *BUNGHOLE!*"

THE RIDDLE OF THE SPHINCTER

IN ANCIENT EGYPT THERE WAS THIS THING CALLED THE SPHINCTER THAT HAD THE HEAD OF A MAN AND THE BODY OF LIKE A DOG. HE WAS REAL WISE AND ALSO HE COULD LICK HIS NADS WHENEVER HE WANTED. ALSO HE WAS LIKE 200 FEET TALL, AND HE HAD THIS RIDDLE THAT IF YOU GUESSED IT RIGHT YOU GOT TO DO IT WITH HIS DAUGHTER WHO HAD LIKE 50-FOOT BOOBS, BUT IF YOU GUESSED IT WRONG YOU GOT KILLED. SO, LIKE, EITHER WAY YOUR FRIENDS HAD SOMETHING TO WATCH.

ONE DAY SOME EGYPTIAN DUDE WHO HAD A STIFFY TO SEE THE BOOBS TRIED TO ANSWER THE RIDDLE. THE SPHINCTER SAID, "WHAT HAS FOUR LEGS IN THE MORNING, THREE LEGS AT NOON AND --" NO WAIT, UH -- "WHAT HAS THREE LEGS IN THE MORNING --"

UH, HUH HUH -- "THE ANSWER IS BEAVIS."

SHUT UP, DILLHOLE!

ANYWAY THE SPHINCTER ASKED HIM THIS REALLY HARD RIDDLE WHICH THE EGYPTIAN GUY DIDN'T KNOW, AND SO HE PLEADED WITH THE SPHINCTER, "OH MIGHTY SPHINCTER, PLEASE DON'T KILL ME, I DON'T NEED TO SEE THE BOOBS." SO THE SPHINCTER SAID, "PULL MY FINGER." AND WHEN THE GUY DID, THE SPHINCTER'S 20-FOOT NOSE FELL OFF AND CRUSHED HIM.

AND ALL THROUGHOUT EGYPT-LAND, PEOPLE THOUGHT THAT WAS COOL. AND THEY BOWED DOWN AND WORSHIPED THE SPHINCTER. AND THEY NAMED A PART OF THEIR BUTT AFTER HIM.

MOTOR LISA, BEFORE AND AFTER

LEONARDO DA FONZI WAS A FAMOUS FOREN GUY WHO TOLD CHICKS HE WAS A PAINTER SO THEY WOULD TAKE OFF THEIR CLOTHES AND GET NAKED. THEN HE'D GO TO THE BATHROOM, AND THE CHICKS WOULD SAY, "HEY LEONARDO, WHAT'RE YOU DOING IN THERE?" AND HE'D SAY, "I'M STRETCHING MY CANVAS," OR, "I'M PRACTICING MY STROKES," OR, "I'M SQUEEZ-ING PAINT FROM MY TUBE." HUH HUH.

DA FONZI HAD THE HOTS FOR THIS STUCK-UP BIKER CHICK NAMED MOTOR LISA WHO HAD REALLY BIG HOOTERS. BUT SHE WOULDN'T LET HIM SEE THEM, EVEN THOUGH HE BEGGED HER. HE SAID, "I AM AN *ARTEEST.* I WANT TO, LIKE, PAINT ZE NIPPLES OR SOMETHING. AND THEN WE CAN, YOU KNOW, DO EET." BUT MOTOR LISA GOT ALL HUFFY AND SAID, "I AM SAVING MY HOOTERS FOR THE MAN I MARRY," AND THAT KIND OF CRAP.

DA FONZI DECIDED TO LOOSEN HER UP. HE ASKED MOTOR LISA TO PULL HIS FINGER. THE SOUND OF HIS FART MADE HER SMILE. HE PAINTED HER SMILING. THEN HE PAINTED HER AS SHE GOT A WHIFF OF THE FRUITS OF HIS MIGHTY FARTULENCE.

THE DECLARATION OF INDEPENDENTS

How America told that sucky country Britin to shove it up their butthole.

∗ ∗ ∗ ∗ ∗ ∗ ∗

Like on the fourth of July, 1976, a bunch of old dudes wrote the Declaration of Independents and blew off a bunch of fireworks and bottle rockets.

It's kinda like, Britin is this little dingleberry of a country. So these dudes took this piece of paper and just wiped Britin, and told them to get off our butt.

Uhhh, four score (huh huh) and uh, a bunch of years ago, we the people, like, declare our independents or something. And the rockers red flare, the bombs bursting in air. Uhhh... like, most dudes are created equal (except Beavis) and have certain aliens rights. like, the right to bare chicks and the right to remain silent. Cause sometimes you gotta fight for your right to party. With liberty and justice for all. Amen. Uhhh... Thank you, Cleveland.

— John Hancock

PULL BEAVIS'S FINGER

GET A SMALL CARDBOARD BOX AND CUT A HOLE IN THE BOTTOM. THEN TAKE SOME, LIKE, STUFFING AND PUT IT IN THE BOX SO NOBODY CAN SEE THE HOLE. THEN GET SOME RED PAINT AND PAINT THE INSIDE OF THE BOX, SO IT LOOKS LIKE THERE'S BLOOD IN THERE. THEN CUT OFF ONE OF BEAVIS'S FINGERS AND PUT IT IN THE BOX.

NEXT TIME YOU'RE AT A SWIMMING POOL, JUST, LIKE, TAKE A LEAK IN IT. THE GOOD THING IS, YOU DON'T EVEN HAFTA TAKE YOUR BATHING SUIT OFF TO DO THIS.

Jj PRACTICUL JOKES

CALL UP, LIKE, A SPORTING GOODS STORE OR SOMETHING? AND ASK IF THEY HAVE LIKE, A CASE OF VOLLEY BALLS. HUH HUH HUH HUH. "BALLS!"

CALL SOMEONE UP AND ASK THEM IF PRINCE ALBERT IS STILL SITTING ON THE CAN.

BUILD YOUR OWN MONSTER, JUST LIKE THAT DR. FRANKENBERRY DUDE, AND THEN TURN IT LOOSE IN THE GIRLS' LOCKER ROOM. THEY'LL PROBABLY ALL COME RUNNING OUT WITH THEIR CLOTHES OFF.

CALL UP ONE OF THOSE PHONE SEX NUMBERS, HUH HUH, BUT MAKE IT A COLLECT CALL, SO YOU DON'T HAFTA PAY. THAT'D BE COOL!

M HEH HEH, HERE'S A REALLY FUNNY ONE: CALL A CHICK UP AND ASK HER IF SHE WANTS A DATE.

HUH HUH, YOU DUMBASS, BEAVIS. THAT'S NOT A PRACTICUL JOKE.

SHUT UP BUTT-HEAD. THEY ALWAYS LAUGH WHEN I DO IT.

NEXT TIME YOU'RE AT A CARNIVAL? GO IN THE HOUSE OF MIRRORS AND TAKE OUT YOUR WEINER.

BUY A WHOLE BUNCH OF BALLOONS. YOU KNOW, THE KIND THAT'S FILLED WITH HELIUM? AND TIE THEM ONTO YOUR SCHOOL. ONCE YOU GET ENOUGH BALLOONS, YOUR WHOLE SCHOOL WILL GO AWAY. I SAW TODD DO THAT ONCE. REALLY.

GO TO A NUDE BEACH.

CALL SOMEONE UP AND SAY YOU'RE FROM THE PHONE COMPANY, AND THAT YOU'RE GONNA, LIKE, TEST THEIR PHONE LINE. THEN DON'T TEST THEIR PHONE LINE.

DISGUISE YOURSELF AS ONE OF THOSE MONEY MACHINES THAT BANKS HAVE. WHEN SOME RICH DUDE COMES ALONG TO MAKE A DEPOSIT, YOU CAN JUST KEEP ALL HIS MONEY.

TELL SOME CHICK THAT YOU LOVE HER, SO SHE'LL DO IT WITH YOU. HUH HUH HUH. BUT DON'T FALL FOR THIS TRICK IF SOME CHICK SAYS SHE LOVES YOU.

Jj J IS FOR JOBS

THEY SAY THAT MONEY MAKES THE WORLD ROUND OR SOMETHING. BUT LIKE, YOU CAN'T SIT ON YOUR ASS AND EXPECT TO GET ENOUGH MONEY TO DO COOL STUFF LIKE HANG OUT. THAT'S WHERE, LIKE, JOBS COME IN.

THERE ARE LIKE TWO KINDS OF JOBS: ONE IS CALLED "JOBS," WHICH IS FOR JOBS THAT SUCK, AND THE OTHER KIND IS CALLED "CAREERS," WHICH ALSO SUCK, BUT FOR LONGER. HERE'S LIKE A FEW JOBS THAT PEOPLE DO, NOT INCLUDING GETTING US PISSED OFF, WHICH IS LIKE A JOB ALMOST EVERYONE HAS.

DOCTOR – THIS GUY OPERATES ON YOU AND GIVES YOU SHOTS AND STUFF. BUT IT'S NOT AS MUCH FUN AS IT SOUNDS, CAUSE LIKE YOU HAVE TO GO TO SCHOOL EXTRA FOR IT. ON THE OTHER HAND YOU ALSO GET TO SEE CHICKS NAKED, WHICH IS AS MUCH FUN AS IT SOUNDS, HUH HUH.

BUSINESSMAN – TO BE A BUSINESSMAN, YOU HAVE TO WEAR A TIE AND HARD SHOES AND SIT IN THESE THINGS. MEETINGS OR SOMETHING. IT'S LIKE CHURCH, EXCEPT IT LASTS ALL WEEK AND THE GUY IN CHARGE DOESN'T OFFER YOU NACHOS TO STAY FOR "CHOIR PRACTICE." BUT, LIKE, A LOT OF BUSINESS-MEN MUST WORK FOR THE CIA OR SOMETHING CAUSE NOBODY KNOWS WHAT WORK THEY REALLY DO. SOME PEOPLE SAY THEY DO NO WORK AT ALL, EXCEPT IT IS PRETTY HARD TO TIE A TIE.

FARMER – THESE GUYS GROW MILK AND TREES AND FOOD, AND THEY LIKE PLOW FIELDS, HUH HUH. THEN THEY LISTEN TO COUNTRY MUSIC AND WALK AROUND TELLING TRAVELING SALESMEN NOT TO DO IT WITH THEIR DAUGHTERS. IT'S PRETTY COOL, EXCEPT FOR THE COUNTRY MUSIC. AND PLUS, IT'S COOL TO HAVE LIKE A DAUGHTER, CAUSE IT MEANS YOU MUSTA DONE IT ONCE, EVEN IF IT WAS A LONG TIME AGO, HEH HEH HEH HEH. OR LIKE YOUR WIFE DID OR SOMETHING.

LUMBERJACK – HUH HUH. JACK. THEY CUT DOWN TREES AND YELL SOMETHING, IT SOUNDS LIKE "TEN-FOUR" OR SOMETHING. THEN THEY LIKE TAKE THE LOGS AND TURN THEM INTO PENCILS AND MATCHES AND STUFF. WORKING WITH LOGS IS PRETTY COOL. JUST ASK BEAVIS.

COLLEGE MUSICIAN – LIKE, THIS IS A COOL JOB, EXCEPT YOU GOTTA GO AROUND SAYING HOW EVERYTHING'S ALL MESSED UP AND STUFF, AND YOU'RE LIKE ALL PISSED OFF ABOUT IT. PLUS YOU HAVE TO PLAY SUCKY MUSIC, BUT IF YOU WENT TO COLLEGE, YOU PROBABLY GOT TAUGHT TO <u>LIKE</u> SUCKY MUSIC, SO IT'S NOT SO BAD. EXCEPT SUCKY MUSIC, UH, SUCKS, SO MAYBE IT IS. BAD. ANYWAY, ALL THE COOL MUSICIAN JOBS ARE GONNA BE TAKEN BY US, SO COLLEGE MUSICIAN IS ALL THAT'S GONNA BE OPEN.

SOLDIER – LIKE, WHEN YOU'RE IN THE ARMY, ALL THE CHICKS GO, "HEY, SAILOR!" AND YOU GET TO WEAR TATTOOS AND STAND AT ATTENTION, WHICH WE'RE LIKE ALREADY REALLY GOOD AT, HEH HEH. THE ARMY IS ALSO COOL CAUSE THEY CAN TEACH YOU HOW TO KILL A MAN WITH YOUR BARE HANDS, BUT IF YOU'RE LIKE A BAD STUDENT, THEY GIVE YOU A GUN.

COP – YOU GET TO BE ON TV AND SAY THINGS LIKE "WE BUSTED THE PERP," AND STUFF. AND, LIKE, YOU GET TO SAY, "YOU'LL HAVE A LOT OF TIME TO THINK ABOUT THAT WHERE YOU'RE GOING, PUNK." AND, LIKE, "ASSUME THE POSITION." HEH HEH. WHEN YOU SAY "ASSUME," YOU SAY A WORD THAT HAS "ASS" IN IT. IT DOESN'T GET MUCH COOLER THAN THAT.

GARBAGEMAN – LIKE, WHAT CAN YOU SAY ABOUT A JOB THAT LETS YOU RIDE ON A TRUCK AND THROW STUFF AROUND AT 5 IN THE MORNING AND GO THROUGH PEOPLE'S CRAP? UH, NOTHING. EXCEPT THAT IT'S PRETTY COOL. ALSO THIS IS A GOOD JOB TO HAVE IF YOU'RE GOING OUT WITH A CHICK, CAUSE YOU CAN GET HER PRESENTS AND STUFF FOR FREE.

CONSTRUCTION WORKER – THESE GUYS GET TATTOOS AND TAKE COFFEE BREAKS AND BUILD STUFF AND, HEH HEH, THEY LAY PIPE. AND IN A LOT OF JOBS, IF YOU'RE FAT IT SUCKS, BUT HERE A GUT IS LIKE A BADGE OF HONOR. IF YOU HAVE A TATTOO AND A GUT, YOU'RE LIKE A KING, OR SOMETHING. PLUS THEY ALSO KNOW HOW TO TALK TO CHICKS. LIKE, THEY DON'T TALK, THEY JUST WHISTLE. IT'S LIKE A LOVE SONG OR SOMETHING.

IMPORTANT THINGS

- IN THE DESERT, YOU CAN DO A LOT MORE STUFF WITHOUT GETTING CAUGHT BY THE COPS.
- IF YOU HAVE INSURANCE, YOU CAN CUT OFF YOUR ARM AND GET, LIKE, A MILLION DOLLARS.
- YOUR MOM MAY OWE YOU MONEY. SO YOU SHOULD GET A LAWYER. I, LIKE, SAW IT ON OPRAH.
- YOUR MOM MAY NOT BE YOUR MOM AFTER ALL.
- NEXT TIME YOU PICK UP A HANDFUL OF DIRT, JUST REMEMBER THAT IT MIGHT HAVE ONCE BEEN AN ANIMAL TURD.
- THE WATER IN THE TOILET MAKES YOUR TURDS LOOK BIGGER THAN THEY REALLY ARE.
- EATING MAKES YOU GO TO THE BATHROOM.
- YOU CAN STILL GET WOOD WHEN YOU'RE REALLY OLD.
- YOU DON'T GO BLIND FROM, YOU KNOW.

TO KNOW

- You can't run out of sperm from, you know.
- It's against the law to make a chick do it with you. That's why guys have to, you know, make friends with themselves.
- Jail dudes get to watch TV all day.
- Roosters wake people up in the morning. Roosters are sometimes called cocks. Huh huh. So don't be surprised if you get woken up by morning rooster. Huh huh huh.
- Sometimes bald dudes have hairy butts.
- Oprah says fat people can't help it.
- School counselors never tell you that instead of going to college, you can buy a car.
- A lot of chicks sleep naked. The really hot ones.

HEY BABY.

LI LITERATER

You know those things? They got like paper inside and you like use them for smashing bugs and stuff, unless there's nothing to smash and so you just like read em or whatever? Those things are called books. This is like a list of the best books ever wrote.

Moby Dick

Um, heh heh. What's big and white, heh heh. And there's like, lots of sailors on it, heh heh. Heh heh heh heh heh. Um, the book sucks, but like, the name of it makes up for all the sucky parts. I wouldn't um recommend it or whatever unless you're just looking for a book with a good name. Stewart says there's a dude with a wooden leg in it, but, like, big deal. I've got one of those myself. Heh heh. See it? Heh heh m heh heh.

Naked Biker Magazine,

August 1993-Uh, huh huh, this is a magazine that we got for free at the Swif Mart, huh huh huh. It's mostly about chicks who like to ride around on motorcycles naked. It like teaches you stuff. Like stuff about motorcycles and chicks and how they're like pretty much the same. Plus it's like easy to hold with one hand. Huh huh huh.

Where the Wild Thing Is

Huh huh huh. In my pants, huh huh.

Curry Greg or something

Um, this is this book and it's about this little monkey dude and he like lives with this other dude with a yellow hat, heh heh heh. Yeah, and like the monkey is um real curry or whatever, so he like gets in trouble and stuff, heh heh, cause he like messes with stuff. And then the yellow hat dude has to go save the monkey dude's ass. Heh heh. Hey Beavis. Does he ever spank the monkey? Huh huh huh huh huh. Heh heh heh heh. Shut up, Butt-head. He's not like that. It's a good book. It's like, instresting or something.

MATCHBOOK FROM THE CLASSY CAT LOUNGE

ONE TIME, VAN DRIESSEN MADE US WRITE A BOOK REPORT ABOUT ANY BOOK WE WANTED TO. AND, UM, LIKE, WE DID IT ON A BOOK OF MATCHES. HEH HEH HEH HEH. AND LIKE, HE HAD TO LET US DO IT, CAUSE HE SAID IT COULD BE ABOUT ANY BOOK WE WANTED. AND YOU KNOW WHAT? IT WAS A PRETTY GOOD BOOK. HEH HEH. VAN DRIESSEN STILL GAVE US A D, THOUGH. FARTKNOCKER.

DEATHSPAWN #396

THIS IS THE DEATHSPAWN ONE WHERE DEATHSPAWN KILLS THAT DUDE BY LIKE PUNCHING HIM IN THE HEAD AND PULLING OUT HIS BRAINS AND THEN SHOWING THEM TO THE DUDE BEFORE HE DIES. HUH HUH HUH. DEATHSPAWN RULES. IT'S LIKE, IF HE TOOK OUT BEAVIS'S BRAINS AND SHOWED THEM TO HIM, HE'D SEE LIKE CHICKS' THINGIES AND NACHOS AND SOME TOILETS AND LIKE A BUNCH OF CRAP LIKE THAT. HUH HUH.

SHUT UP, BUNGHOLE. HE WOULDN'T EVEN BE ABLE TO FIND YOUR BRAINS CAUSE THEY'RE LIKE IN YOUR BUTT, HEH HEH HEH.

BEAVIS, YOU'RE LIKE SICK OR SOMETHING. SERIOUSLY.

THE CATCHER IN THE RYE

THIS IS ABOUT THIS KID AND, UM, I THINK HIS NAME WAS CATCHER OR SOMETHING. HE, LIKE, SWEARS ALL THE TIME. THAT'S PRETTY COOL. PLUS HE CALLS PEOPLE PHONES, HEH HEH. LIKE, UM, THAT DUDE IS A BIG PHONE. AND HIS SISTER'S NAME IS PHONE TOO. HEH HEH. CATCHER'S LIKE STUPID AND MESSED UP, BUT HE'S COOL. HE'S KIND OF LIKE CURRY GREG, BUT NO HAT GUY.

LORD OF THE RINGS

WHEN YOU SMASH A BUG WITH THIS BOOK, HUH HUH, THAT BUG STAYS, UH, LIKE SMASHED. HUH HUH. THIS BOOK IS COOL.

INTRODUCTION TO BIOLOGY

HUH HUH HUH. YOU KNOW HOW, LIKE, WHEN A DOG GETS HIT BY A CAR AND THERE'S LIKE ALL THE GUTS ALL OVER THE PLACE? THIS BOOK TELLS YOU LIKE THE NAMES OF ALL THE GUTS AND STUFF. HUH HUH. PLUS IT'S GOT LIKE A DRAWING OF TWO CHICKENS DOING IT. HUH HUH.

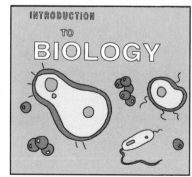

Mm UH, HUH HUH HUH HUH

ADJUSTING YOUR SET
BATTING PRACTICE
BEING YOUR OWN BEST FRIEND
CHANGING YOUR OIL
COOKING SOME SHEET MEAT
DISHONORABLE DISCHARGE
DOING SOME RAPID ONE-ARM PULL-UPS
EMPTYING THE PAYLOAD
FATHERING SOME PLEASURE
FIRING YOUR SQUIRT GUN
FIST-KEBABING
FREEING THE WILLIES
GETTING YOUR PALM RED
GOING BACK TO NATURE
GUNNING THE MOTOR
HITTING THE BATSMAN
HOMECOMING
HONING THE BONE
IRONING SOME WRINKLES
JUNIOR OLYMPIC POLE VAULTING
KNUCKLING YOUR KNOB
LAUNCHING THE HAND SHUTTLE
LECTRIFYING THE CATTLE PROD
LETTING SOME AIR OUT OF YOUR TIRE
MANNING THE COCKPIT
MASHING THE MONSTER
MEASURING FOR CONDOMS
MILKING YOUR BANANA
PEELING THE CARROT
PLAYING HAND HOCKEY

PLAYING THE PIPE ORGAN
PUD WRESTLING
PUNCHING YOUR WAY INTO HEAVEN
ROASTING YOUR WEINER
ROLLING YOUR JAM JOINT
ROUGHING UP THE SUSPECT
SELF-WHITTLING
SENDING OUT THE TROOPS
SHAKING THE THERMOMETER
SHIFTING GEARS
SHOOTING SOME SEEDS
SNAKE CHARMING
SOLOING
SPEAR FISHING
SPEED KNEADING
SPREADING THE MAYO
SQUEEZING OUT THE TOOTHPASTE
STAFF MEETING
TAKING A SHAKE BREAK
TAMING YOUR SNAKE
THREADING THE NEEDLE
THROTTLE THE BOTTLE
TOSSING THE JAVELIN
TUGGING YOUR TAPIOCA TUBE
TUNING THE ANTENNA
VIRTUAL SEX
VISITING MR. O.
WALKING THE LOG
WEDDING REHEARSAL
WHITEWATER WRISTING

History of

HEAVY METAL KICKS ASS. IT'S AN ART FARM OR SOMETHING. YOU SHOULD, LIKE, CRANK IT IN THE MORNING, CAUSE IT'S BETTER THAN THAT COFFEE CRAP, AND IT TAKES YOUR MIND OFF STUFF THAT SUCKS. PLUS IF YOU CRANK IT LOUD ENOUGH, YOUR NEIGHBORS WILL START TO GET INTO IT, TOO.

HEAVY METAL HAS BEEN COOL FOR, LIKE, CENTURIES. BESIDES ALICE COOPER AND KISS, ROB HALFORD USED TO DRIVE A MOTORCYCLE ONSTAGE AND IRON MAIDEN HAD A DEAD DUDE NAMED EDDIE CHASING THEM AROUND. THESE DAYS, GWAR WEARS THESE HUGE COSTUMES AND GETS IN THESE BIG FIGHTS AND THERE'S BLOOD EVERYWHERE. IT'S LIKE, A MESSAGE OR SOME THING.

BUT ASSWIPES DON'T RESPECT HEAVY METAL AND IT PISSES COOL PEOPLE OFF. UNTIL SOMEBODY, LIKE, FINALLY GAVE METALLICA AN AWARD JUST SO THEY WOULDN'T GET THEIR ASS KICKED. NOW THE WHOLE WORLD REALIZES OR SOMETHING... HEAVY METAL RULES!!!

SOME RADIO DUDE SAID HEAVY METAL OWES A DEBT TO DUDES LIKE HENDRIX AND LED ZEPLIN. BEAVIS SAYS IT'S ONLY, LIKE, FIVE DOLLARS.

ALICE COOPER WAS THE FIRST DUDE TO DO COOL STUFF ONSTAGE. HE USED TO PLAY WITH SNAKES AND CUT OFF HIS HEAD. (GOOD THING HE DIDN'T PLAY WITH HIS HEAD AND CUT OFF HIS SNAKE. HUH HUH!)

KISS WAS THE COOLEST, CAUSE NOBODY KNEW WHO THEY WERE, BUT, LIKE, EVERYBODY WANTED TO BE THEM. GENE SIMMONS EVEN SPIT BLOOD AND BREATHED, UH, STUFF. BEAVIS SPIT BLOOD AFTER I SMACKED HIM ONCE.

heavy metal

Ozzy bit the head off a bat just to show how cool he was. It worked. Beavis tried to do it but the bat bit him on the tongue and he got rabies again. What a dumbass!

AC/DC's singer sang "I'm on a Highway to Hell" and then he died. So he was, like, right. They got a new singer and I think he drives them around and stuff too.

If Slash could see anything, he could look for a cool band to join.

If you're in Metallica, you're, like, not supposed to smile, cause they lost a Granny Award to Jethro Tull, and that really pissed them off! So they made an album that kicked even more ass and then they won. But they're still pissed.

Mm MEDICUL ADVISE

CONDISHUN	CURE
DINGLEBERRIES	TRY WIPING NEXT TIME
PATIENT IS PARALIZED	UNTIE STEWART
DIZZINESS, VOMITING	TURN OFF THE BON JOVI VIDEO
BLADDER PAIN	TAKE A WHIZ
HAIRY PALMS, LOSS OF EYESITE	GET RID OF YOUR MAGAZINE COLLECTION, BEAVIS
SCALY FLAKES OF DEAD SKIN FOUND ON SHOULDERS	QUIT SCRATCHING YOUR BUTT BEFORE YOUR PICK YOUR EARS
FREQUENT FARTING	GET THE HELL AWAY FROM ME
PENIS TOO SMALL	HUH HUH HUH HUH. YOU WUSS!

LLEWELYN, DOUG –THIS IS THAT DUDE FROM PEOPLE'S COURT WHO LIKE GIVES OUT THE PRIZES TO THE CONTESTANTS OR SOMETHING. AND, LIKE, WHAT THEY DON'T TELL YOU IS THAT IF YOU GO ON THE SHOW AND LOSE, WAPNER TELLS DOUG TO KICK YOUR ASS BEFORE HE SENDS YOU TO PRISON. JUSTICE IS COOL.

LOSERS – HEH HEH. THESE ARE DUDES WHO LIKE, THEY CAN'T GET CHICKS SO THEY GO HANG OUT IN FRONT OF THE MAXI-MART ON A FRIDAY NIGHT AND STUFF. UM, WE HANG OUT THERE TOO, BUT IT'S DIFFERENT CAUSE WE'RE ONLY THERE CAUSE THERE'S NOTHING GOOD ON TV ON FRIDAY NIGHTS.

LOVE – LOVE IS LIKE THIS CHEMICAL IN YOUR HEAD THAT MAKES YOU WANT TO HANG OUT WITH A CHICK EVEN IF, LIKE, YOU'RE NOT GONNA DO IT WITH HER SOON. THERE'S PROBLY PILLS AND STUFF THEY HAVE NOW THAT YOU CAN TAKE TO STOP THAT.

LOUD – LOUD IS LIKE THE PERFECT VOLUME FOR MUSIC. LIKE, IF YOU HAVE TO ASK, "IS THIS LOUD ENOUGH?" AND WE CAN LIKE HEAR YOU ASK IT, THEN YOU SHOULD TURN IT UP SOME MORE.

LUST – (SEE LOVE)

MAN-EATING – "MAN-EATING" IS LIKE THE BLACK BELT FOR ANIMALS. IT'S LIKE, ONLY ANIMALS LIKE A SHARK OR A VULTURE OR SOMETHING KICK ENOUGH ASS TO BE CALLED MAN-EATING. AND LIKE ANDERSON'S POODLE, WHO'S LIKE REAL OLD AND JUST LIKE LAYS AROUND A LOT, SHE'S MAYBE A YELLOW BELT ANIMAL. IF SHE'S LUCKY.

MARBLES –THESE ARE THESE THINGS YOU PUT IN YOUR NOSE WHEN YOU'RE A LITTLE KID AND THEN YOU GO TO THE HOSPITAL. THIS IS THEIR ONLY PURPOSE.

MEAT – HERE'S THE KIND OF MEAT WE CAN SHOW YOU. THE <u>ONLY</u> KIND, BEAVIS.

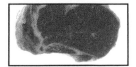

MICROWAVE –THIS IS A MACHINE THEY DEVELOPED DURING THE WAR TO LIKE FLY PLANES AND BLOW UP CITIES, AND NOW WE USE IT TO HEAT UP BURRITOS. SOMEBODY TOLD US THAT IF YOU STAND TOO CLOSE IT MAKES YOU SO YOU CAN'T HAVE BABIES, BUT THAT'S DUMB, CAUSE ONLY CHICKS HAVE BABIES.

MOMS – MOMS ARE COOL CAUSE THEY'RE ALWAYS LIKE GIVING YOU STUFF. FIRST, THEY GIVE YOU LIFE OR WHATEVER. THEN THEY GIVE YOU CLOTHES AND LIKE WALKING LESSONS OR SOMETHING. THEN, WHEN YOU'RE LIKE MATURE, THEY GIVE YOU TWENTY DOLLARS TO GET OUT OF THE HOUSE WHEN YOUR UNCLE COMES OVER. MOMS ARE COOL.

MONEY – IT USED TO BE THAT PEOPLE DIDN'T USE MONEY TO GET STUFF. LIKE, A GUY WHO WAS A NACHO FARMER, HE WOULDN'T SELL HIS NACHOS, HE'D JUST TRADE THEM FOR TVs OR SOMETHING. THEN, LIKE, HE'D TRADE A TV FOR CLOTHES. DUMBASS. BUT THEN PEOPLE GOT TIRED OF CARRYING TVs AROUND, SO THEY INVENTED MONEY, AND THE DUDES WHO INVENTED IT GOT TO HAVE THEIR PICTURES ON IT, WHICH WAS PRETTY COOL.

MUSTACHE – "MUSTACHE" IS LIKE FRENCH FOR "LIP BEARD." IT'S LIKE DIFFERENT FROM THE HAIR ON YOUR HEAD CAUSE YOU ONLY GET IT ONCE YOU GET YOUR TEST HORMONES. A LOT OF THE DUDES ON THAT COPS SHOW HAVE MUSTACHES. THEY MUST HAVE, LIKE, A LOT OF TEST HORMONES.

MUTANT – IF SOMETHING MESSES WITH A DUDE'S NATURAL STRUCTURE BEFORE HE'S BORN, HE BECOMES A MUTANT. THEN HE GOES FLYING AROUND KICKING ASS AND MEETING MUTANT CHICKS WHO WEAR COSTUMES THAT SHOW OFF THEIR THINGIES. ON THE OTHER HAND, IF A DUDE JUST GETS DROPPED ON HIS HEAD AS A BABY, HE BECOMES BEAVIS.

 **PETS**

PET	ADVANTAGES	DISADVANTAGES
DOG	* IF THERE'S ANOTHER DOG ON YOUR BLOCK, THEY'LL PROBABLY TRY AND DO IT, HUH HUH! * A DOG WILL SOMETIMES EAT ITS OWN VOMIT.	* WHEN IT WON'T EAT ITS OWN VOMIT, IT CAN BE REALLY HARD TO MAKE BEAVIS CLEAN UP THE COUCH.
CAT	* CAN BE TRAINED TO TAKE A DUMP IN A BOX. BEAVIS ENJOYED SHOWING THE STRAY CAT WE FOUND HOW TO DO IT.	* THE BOX GETS PRETTY GROSS AFTER A FEW WEEKS, UNLESS YOU ALSO HAVE ONE OF THOSE DUMBASS DOGS THAT LIKES TO SNACK OUT OF IT. UH, SHOULD THIS BE UNDER "DOG" OR SOMETHING? * NEUTERING A CAT CAN BE EXPENSIVE. AND YOU CAN ONLY HAVE IT DONE ONCE PER CAT.
GOLDFISH	* FLUSHABLE.	* IT TURNS OUT THEY DON'T REALLY HAVE ANY GOLD IN 'EM.
TURTLE	* THEY CAN'T GET AWAY SO EASY.	* WON'T EAT GOLDFISH.
BEAVIS	* YOU DON'T HAFTA PET HIM CAUSE, LIKE, HE PETS HIMSELF. HUH HUH. * IF YOU ALSO HAVE A DOG, YOU CAN FEED 'EM BOTH DOGFOOD.	* FLEAS. * MORE LIKELY TO FETCH A TURD THAN A STICK.
TAPEWORM	* YOU DON'T HAFTA BOTHER GOING ANYWHERE TO BUY IT OR FIND IT OR ANYTHING. A DOCTOR JUST ASKS FOR A TURD SAMPLE AND THEN TELLS YOU THAT YOU'VE GOT A PET TAPEWORM. * WHEN YOU HAVE ONE YOU CAN EAT A TON MORE NACHOS AND CANDY AND STUFF BEFORE YOU'RE FULL.	* THE DUMBASSES IN YOUR GYM CLASS WILL LAUGH AT YOU IF YOUR PET TAPE-WORM FALLS OUT WHEN YOU'RE DOING SQUAT THRUSTS. * ONCE IT FALLS OUT IT'S NOT COMING BACK. WITHOUT HELP, HUH HUH.
STEWART	* NONE. MAYBE PAY-PER-VIEW.	* WON'T RUN AWAY THE WAY SOME OTHER PETS DO.

Pp

THE PRESIDENTS OF THE U. S.

GEORGE DOLLAR	GEORGE ADAMS	GEORGE JEFFERSON
HE'S BALD. HUH HUH	SOME OTHER DUDE	STEVEN TYLER
CHRISTOPHER COLUMBUS	LINCOLN JEFFERSON	JFR
ELVIS, DUMBASS	MARTIN LUTHERING	THE OATMEAL GUY

 THAT FELIX GUY	 RINGO SOMETHING
 GEORGE ADAMS JEFFERSON	 THE GUY FROM THE 20

 LIKE, A DOBERMAN WOULDA BEEN GOOD	 THAT FORIN DUDE
 RONALD RAYMOND	 DANIEL DAVE LEWIS

 PRESIDENT SOMEBODY	 UH, HE GOT BUSTED OR SOMETHING
 RONALD RAYMOND	 MONT RUSHMORE

 NORMAN STORM	 RONALD RAYMOND
 THE GUY WITH THE COOL NAME	 THE GUY FROM SCHOOL. McVICKER

P
Polite

H
Helpful

O
Opportunistic

N
Natural-sounding

E
Enterprisers

Opportunity Doesn't Knock —It Rings!!!

CAREER ROCK '94— IT'S FOR YOU!

Why are you here at Career Rock '94? Because your guidance counselors know <u>you're</u> ready for the fast track: the tough jobs in fields like food service, sanitation, and corrections. But why listen to their "authority-figure noise"…when you can start <u>making</u> the noise in a career with Jackpot Telemarketing, Inc.!

Before we get started, be warned. **If you hate making quick money while sitting in your favorite easy chair, STOP reading right now!** Try and earn your pay working in some dead-end job instead. (<u>If</u> you can!) Be careful, though—you might blow all of your hard-earned cash on some "get-rich-quick" scheme. Meanwhile, your friends who have a telemarketing career will be piling up the cash while *never* leaving their homes!

What's the difference? *Most get-rich-quick schemes* **say** *they're "sure things," but they really* **aren't**. *A telemarketing career* **is**. *Here's why:*

- **No risk.** Other salespeople have to buy shirts, ties, even hard shoes. You don't. You can be making money without even getting dressed!

At Jackpot Telemarketing, the only thing we want you to spend is time!

• **Big rewards.** We don't keep our employees tied down to a flat salary. They earn <u>unlimited</u> commissions! Just as long as you keep selling, you keep earning! Soon, you'll learn the money-making secret of the big corporations—volume. And you'll be putting it to work for you!

The phone is ringing—with opportunity. You can answer it, and say "Hello" to a fulfilling telemarketing career. Or you can hang up, and spend the rest of your life searching for fun and excitement. The phone is ringing—but it won't be ringing forever.

Beavis + Butt-head: Please implement soonest!

Burycut

Beavis, check it out he wrote "Plow"

PUT YOURSELF ON OUR PHONE!

We don't want you to leap into your exciting telemarketing career sight unseen. So here's a realistic sample of what to expect once you sign up with Jackpot Telemarketing:

Customer: Hello?
You: Hello, is [customer's name] at home?
Customer: Yes, this is [customer's name].
You: Hi, my name is [your name] from Jackpot Telemarketing. May I take some of your time to discuss an exciting financial opportunity?
Customer: Well, to be honest, I'm a little suspicious of telemarketers.
You: I understand. But when you hear about this exciting financial opportunity, you may feel quite differently.
Customer: Could you send something in the mail, please?
You: I could, [customer name], but by the time you received it, it would be too late to take advantage of this exciting financial opportunity.
Customer: You've convinced me. Tell me more.
[Later]
Customer: Thank you! Before, I didn't like telemarketing very much. But you've changed my mind. Please call me again if you have anything to offer.
You: I will. Thank you very much.

Note: Phrases such as "big money," "quick money," "easy money," and the like are not specific promises. Jackpot Telemarketing assumes no responsibility for telephone company charges you may incur. No representation is made by Jackpot Telemarketing concerning the efficacy or legality of products we may offer you to telemarket. Full liability, civil and otherwise, is assumed by the employee. Jackpot Telemarketing is no longer affiliated with Score Telemarketing, Pot O' Gold Telemarketing, Stretch Limo Telemarketing, or Lord's Way Cosmetics. As a matter of policy, Jackpot Telemarketing does not respond to customer or employee complaints.

Pp PUBLIC SERVANTS ANNOUNCEMENTS

LIKE, WHEN YOU'RE AS COOL AS WE ARE, PEOPLE WANT YOU TO MAKE THESE PUBLIC SERVANTS ANNOUNCEMENTS, SO LIKE LITTLE KIDS WON'T DO COOL STUFF OR SOMETHING. EXCEPT THEY HAVEN'T ASKED US YET, CAUSE THEY MUST BE SAVING US FOR SOMETHING IMPORTANT. SO, LIKE, JUST IN CASE, DO ALL THE STUFF WE SAY, AND LIKE DON'T DO ALL THE STUFF WE SAY DON'T. DO.

* LIKE, DO OTHERS THE WAY YOU WOULD WANT THEM TO DO YOU. HUH HUH HUH HUH.

* IF YOU'RE REALLY PISSED OFF AT SOMEBODY, COUNT TO TEN AFTER KICKING THEIR ASS.

* DON'T PET A STRANGE DOG UNLESS IT LOOKS LIKE IT MIGHT BITE YOU. THEN LIKE PET IT AND TRY TO MAKE FRIENDS WITH IT AND LIKE, GIVE IT A HUG.

* DON'T GET A FAKE ID. THEY NEVER WORK.

* IN CASE OF EMERGENCY, BREAK SOMETHING.

* ALWAYS KEEP A SPARE SET OF BATTERIES AROUND TO THROW AT BEAVIS.

* STAY IN SCHOOL, ESPECIALLY ON LIKE TACO DAY.

* DON'T LISTEN TO WINGER.

* MAKE SURE YOU PLAY YOUR STEREO LOUD TO DROWN OUT ANYONE WHO'S GONNA GIVE YOU CRAP ABOUT IT.

* IF YOU CAN'T SAY SOMETHING NICE ABOUT SOMEBODY, CALL THEM AN ASSWIPE.

* RESPECT YOURSELF.

* OH YEAH—MAKE SURE YOU WASH YOUR HANDS AFTER YOU RESPECT YOURSELF.

* UH, WHY DO YOU THINK THEY CALL BEAVIS DOPE, HUH HUH.

* SHUT UP, ASSWIPE. HEH HEH.

* DON'T EAT AT BURGER WORLD. WITH YOUR EYES OPEN, ANYWAY.

* DURING A TORNADO, DON'T GO ON THE ROOF WITHOUT A CAMERA.

* UH, HUH HUH HUH. DON'T DO IT WITH A CHICK UNLESS YOU'RE IN A CONDOMINIUM. HUH HUH HUH.

* UM, HEH HEH, DRIVE THROUGH, PLEASE.

Pp FUN WITH PLAYDOUGH

PLAYDOUGH IS COOL. YOU CAN PULL IT, AND POUND IT, AND ROLL IT BETWEEN YOUR HANDS. HUH HUH. SOMETIMES BEAVIS PLAYS POCKET PLAYDOUGH.

SHUT UP, BUTTMUNCH!

THE DIFFERENCE BETWEEN PLAYDOUGH AND, LIKE, YOUR MONKEY IS THAT WHEN YOU PLAY WITH IT IN CLASS, IT'S CALLED ART. HERE IS SOME OF MY AND BEAVIS'S BEST WORK WITH PLAYDOUGH. SOME OF IT WE EVEN GOT A GRADE ON.

BUZZCUTT'S TURD LOG

A THING WE SAW ONCE IN DARIA'S PURSE

BEAVIS'S NADS

OFFICIAL PRESIDENTIAL LOAF

SIAMESE TURDS

WORLD'S LONGEST BOOGER

TURD LOG MADE BY A GIRL

THINGIES

MR. TURD

MORNING WOOD

VOMIT

THE HUMAN BUTT
(SEE ALSO: ANATOMY SECTION)

Rr APPLIANCE REPAIR

MOST PEOPLE DON'T KNOW HOW A TV WORKS. THAT'S WHY YOU GOTTA GO TO TECHKNOCKER COLLEGE. BUT EVEN THOUGH WE'RE NOT TECHKNOCKERS, WE'VE SEEN ENOUGH TV TO PRETTY MUCH KNOW HOW IT WORKS, AND WHAT YOU DO WHEN IT SCREWS UP.

STEP 1 SMACKING AND POUNDING

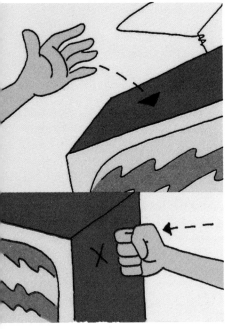

TV PICTURES COME IN THROUGH THE WIRE AND HOOK UP WITH A LITTLE WIRE-SIZED TV INSIDE YOUR TV. THEN THE LITTLE PICTURE GETS BLOWN UP TO THE BIG PICTURE YOU SEE ON YOUR SCREEN. SO LIKE, A PICTURE OF AN EXPLOSION, IT GETS BLOWN UP TWICE, HUH HUH. THAT'S PRETTY COOL.

BUT ANYWAY, WHEN YOUR TV PICTURE IS MESSED UP, IT'S PROBLY BECAUSE ONE A THE KNOBS ON THE LITTLE TV IS MESSED UP. BUT DON'T OPEN THE TV TO TRY AND FIX IT CAUSE YOU'LL GET LECTRICUTED, AND THEN, EVEN AFTER THAT, IT'S TOO COMPLICATED. JUST SMACK IT. SMACK IT NOT SO HARD AT FIRST, THEN WORK YOUR WAY UP TO WHERE IT GETS FIXED.

YOU CAN WARM UP ON BEAVIS IF YOU WANT TO. HUH HUH HUH HUH.

AFTER A WHILE, IF YOU SMACKED IT RIGHT, AND YOUR TV'S NOT TOO MESSED UP, YOU'LL FIGURE OUT JUST WHERE IT'S GOTTA BE HIT TO FIX IT. IT'S LIKE ITS H-SPOT OR SOMETHING, HUH HUH. THAT'S WHEN YOU MOVE TO POUNDING IT WHEN IT'S BROKEN. MAKE A FIST, LIKE YOU'RE GONNA KICK SOMEONE'S ASS, BUT ONLY USE THE SIDE OF IT. IF LIKE YOU'VE BROKEN YOUR HAND TRYING TO FIX SOMETHING ELSE, USE A HAMMER.

STEP 2 KICKING

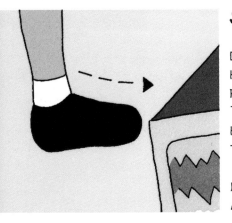

SMACKING AND POUNDING IS UM THE METHOD RECOMMENDED BY DOCTORS OR WHATEVER, BUT SOMETIMES A TV WON'T LISTEN TO REASON, HEH HEH. THAT'S WHEN YOU GOTTA CALL IN THE BIG GUNS, EXCEPT THEY'RE FEET, NOT GUNS. KICK THE TV HARD, RIGHT IN THE NADS. AND, LIKE, IF YOUR TV DOESN'T HAVE NADS, THEN PRETEND IT DOES. KICK IT REALLY HARD. NO, HARDER THAN THAT, YOU WUSS. NAIL IT! NAIL IT! IF YOU'RE DOING IT RIGHT, THE TV SHOULD FALL OFF THE BOX OR WHATEVER YOU HAVE IT ON.

MOST OF THE TIME, KICKING DOESN'T WORK, BUT IT'S CAUSE NOTHING WOULDA FIXED THE TV ANYWAY, AND LIKE AT LEAST YOU TAUGHT IT A LESSON, HEH HEH.

OTHER APPLIANCES

MOST OTHER APPLIANCES, LIKE A REFRIGERATOR, OR, UH, A BOOK, AREN'T LIKE AS COMPLICATED AS TVS. SO THERE'S LIKE NO USE TRYING TO SMACK THEM, CAUSE IT WON'T HAVE ANY EFFECT. KICKING MIGHT WORK, IF YOU HAVE LIKE GOOD BOOTS, BUT OUR PROFESSIONAL ADVICE IS TO JUST THROW WHATEVER IT IS OUT AND GO BACK TO WATCHING TV.

PERMANENT RECORD

UM, THIS WAS IN OUR PERMANENT RECORD, HEH HEH.
GUESS IT'S NOT REALLY PERMANENT.

LYNDON BAINES JOHNSON ELEMENTARY SCHOOL

To All Our New, Substitute, and Student Teachers:

I know there are a lot of questions you have about the procedures and customs here at L.B.J. Elementary. But I'm going to skip over all of those questions in the interest of going directly to your two biggest concerns.

Beavis and Butt-head are not to be trusted out of your sight. They are not to be trusted in your sight. You must never allow them to get behind you. Do not let them approach you at the same time. Do not "pull their fingers," even if Beavis cries. If they do come to your desk, together or separately, make them stay three to four feet away from it. If possible, stand up and keep your chair between you and them. At all times, be aware of the shortest exit path. Do not give them scissors. Do not give them rulers. They should not have glue, pens, erasers, paper or pencils. Ask them to remove their shoelaces when they enter your class. If possible, invite them to sleep through class. Avoid encouraging them to speak. Avoid speaking to them. If you must speak to them, do not be understanding, concerned, or "nice." Discourage others in your class from befriending or in any way helping them. Keep them apart from the others. If you can, put them in a box. Tell them it is a new learning tool from space. Keep the box sealed and instruct them not to laugh or speak as oxygen is limited. Tell the others it is really a box for very sick people and that they should not get close as they, too, may get sick. Pile several desks around the box. Leave the classroom with the others. Do not look back. Lead the others to the gym and hold class there. Barricade the doors.

Teaching is a rewarding, though demanding, profession. In the past few years, too many talented young teachers have decided that the demands outweigh the rewards. I hope, however, that by following these few simple guidelines, the trend can be reversed.

Sincerely,
Ms. Anne Camfey
Second Grade Teacher
L.B.J. Elementary School

Rr

RADIO

Free -Take One

KJWM (Highland's
Classic Hit Machine)
Program Guide

	Monday	Tuesday	Wednesday
	6-10AM Ian and Larry in the Morning. I Hate Mondays. Larry crank calls the bosses of KJWM listeners. Plus a tape of Dan O'Keefe at his weekly alcoholics support group	**6-10AM** Ian and Larry in the Morning. I Hate Tuesdays. Larry crank calls the spouses and children of bosses of KJWM listeners	**6-10AM** Ian and Larry in the Morning. Hump Day! Ian and Larry crank call the clients and customers of the businesses KJWM listeners work for. Plus a tape of Dan O'Keefe soliciting a prostitute
	10AM-2PM Bobby Cool. Lunchbreak: "Where are they now?" Today: Jimi Hendrix	**10AM-2PM** Bobby Cool. Lunchbreak: "KJWM RockVault" Today: Thirty minutes of "Freebird"	**10AM-2PM** Bobby Cool. Lunchbreak: "KJWM Komedy Klub" Today: Louie Anderson on being different
	2-6PM Dan O'Keefe's Afternoon Soundoff. Live Call-In. Today: Is the media killing America?	**2-6PM** Dan O'Keefe's Afternoon Soundoff. Live Call-In. Today: Morning Radio—enemy of Democracy?	**2-6PM** Dan O'Keefe's Afternoon Soundoff. Live Call-In. Today: Is management ignoring the fact that people here want to ruin me?
	6-10PM The Rock'n'Roll Whore! KJWM's Sheila Delmuzzo plays bands she knows "intimately." Tonight: Sam and Dave	**6-10PM** The Rock'n'Roll Whore! KJWM's Sheila Delmuzzo plays bands she knows "intimately." Tonight: Three Dog Night	**6-10PM** The Rock'n'Roll Whore! KJWM's Sheila Delmuzzo plays bands she knows "intimately." Tonight: The Dave Clark 5
	10PM-12AM Sextalk with Dr. Joy. Being your own best friend. Concerns, questions, getting started	**10PM-12AM** Sextalk with Dr. Joy. How could it be wrong when it feels so right? Knowing where and when to be your own best friend	**10PM-12AM** Sextalk with Dr. Joy. Ten signs that say you need to give being your own best friend a break
	12-6AM Bob Atherton's Nightowls. As an unpaid intern, Bob has been instructed not to speak on the air. Please report him if he fails to comply	**12-6AM** Bob Atherton's Nightowls. If you are unhappy with the selections Bob plays, report him immediately to Hit Machine management and he will be dealt with	**12-6AM** Bob Atherton's Nightowls. Bob thinks that because he is a radio major he knows more about radio than anybody here. But he doesn't. Report him

"Greetings, people of Highland. Don't forget to enter the Classic Hit Machine's Royal Pain in the Ass Contest. Just send your name, address and number on a postcard addressed to me, Rocko, the Classic Hit Machine Robot, and if you're entry is chosen, we'll broadcast Ian and Larry in the Morning from your home.

Thursday	Friday	Saturday	Sunday
6-10AM Ian and Larry in the Morning. Take this Job and Shove It. Ian crank calls the same bosses Larry crank called on Monday	6-10AM Ian and Larry in the Morning. T.G.I.F. Larry and Ian crank call the families, co-workers, bosses and clients of KJWM listeners. Plus a tape of Dan O'Keefe's humiliating testimony in divorce court	6-10AM Welcome to the Weekend. KJWM intern Bob Atherton with four hours of solid rock. You don't want to sleep through this! But don't beat yourself up if you do	6-10AM Rock, Roll, Redemption. Rev. Stiv Razor preaches a message of love through Christian rock
10AM-2PM Bobby Cool. Lunchbreak: "Request Line" Today: Anything by Emerson, Lake & Palmer	10AM-2PM Bobby Cool. Lunchbreak: "Block Party Friday" Today: Twelve in a row from Yes	10AM-2PM Revolution. Beatle-ographer Peter Delmarco. Today: "Norwegian Wood"—36 alternate takes	10AM-2PM Soaptown Bob Atherton spins the hits you love washing your car to! As an intern, Atherton is not allowed to speak on the air. Report him if he does
2-6PM Dan O'Keefe's Afternoon Soundoff. Live Call-In. Today: Ian and Larry—suspension or prison?	2-6PM Dan O'Keefe's Afternoon Soundoff. Live Call-In. Today: What to listen to when one KJWM dj is in prison and two others are dead	2-6PM KJWM Listener Poll's Top 3 Million Rock Songs Countdown. Today: numbers 2,345,695 through 2,345,634. Compiled by Bob Atherton	2-6PM Styx and Stones. A random selection of hits representing the spectrum of quality. Compiled by Bob Atherton
6-10PM The Rock'n'Roll Whore! KJWM's Sheila Delmuzzo plays bands she knows "intimately." Tonight: Take 6	6-10PM The Rock'n'Roll Whore! KJWM's Sheila Delmuzzo plays bands she knows "intimately." Tonight: The Moody Blues with the London Symphony Orchestra	6-10PM Listener Poll Top 3 Million Songs, continued. Songs 2,345,634 through 2,345,575	6-10PM Whatever! Grizzled Rock Veteran Vince Skulty plays obscure, unlistenable music, and rambles pointlessly for long intervals. Check it out!
10PM-12AM Sextalk with Dr. Joy. First aid for abrasions and blisters. Have I permanently ruined my best friend?	10PM-12AM Sextalk with Dr. Joy. What to do while your best friend is healing, a preview of tomorrow's KJWM Listener Poll Top 3 Million Rock Songs Countdown	10PM-12AM Listener Poll Top 3 Million Songs, continued. Songs 2,345,575 through 2,345,545	10PM-12AM Hello, Highland. Public forum hosted by Dr. Ron Quiring. Tonight: The General Trend Toward Rising Cancer Rates in the Tri-County Area and the implementation of the new Incinerator—Are They Related?
12-6AM Bob Atherton's Nightowls. Bob Atherton took out KJWM executive secretary Molly Carlson but he forgot his wallet and now he doesn't even say hi. He should be fired except he's just an intern	12-6AM Bob Atherton's Nightowls. And if Bob Atherton doesn't call me soon, he's gonna deal with my brothers, one of whom wrestled at 170 for Highland	12-6AM Bob Atherton's Nightowls. When a person gives herself up to you in a intimate way, and then you take 13 dollars for a cab out of her purse while she's still sleeping, you're not being respectful	12-6AM Bob Atherton's Nightowls. Do not have margueritas with Bob Atherton. His penis is bent and has a mole on it. Like a growth. Plus, it's very, very small. He is a dog

That's right, they'll come to your house, broadcast from your bedroom, and use your phone to crank call Buckingham Palace, home of the Queen of England! But hurry up and enter—this is our most exciting contest ever! Beep, spleep, biddy-biddy-bleep! This is Rocko, saying Rock On!"

QUIET – The opposite of "rock." I guess it's Latin for "suck" or something. It's like when you're sposed to shut up and let other people live in peace, or whatever, even if the other people's quiet is as loud to you as your noise would be to them, or vice versa. Either way, it sucks.

QUICK – (see Kwik)

QUIZ – This is a thing they do at school that sucks more than homework, but doesn't suck as much as a test. Van Driessen says it's just something to make sure we're listening in class. But it's like, if that's all you need to know, why don't you just ask us if we're listening. Like, it takes us a lot less time to say no than to fail a stupid quiz.

QUALITY – They put this big "Think Quality!" sign up at Burger World one time. But we didn't pay too much attention to it cause it said "think" and stuff, and then they took it down after all the newspaper articles. Maybe it was some kind of new burger they were planning, but they never explained to us what it meant, so it must have tasted bad or something.

RABIES – You can get rabies from a dog bite. But not every dog bite, cause I like expearminted on Beavis, and most of the time, when you're sposed to lie down and like foam at the mouth, he just ran around screaming. Then one time he thought he had it and he bit me. That's when I had to give him some shots from Dr. Knuckle Sandwich.

RATS – Rats are like the sharks of the animal kingdom. They just take what they want, and nobody gets in their way, specially cause what they want is garbage. It would be cool to have a rat as a dog, cause then you wouldn't have to buy it Rat Chow or whatever and plus the animal people wouldn't care if you like did science on it, heh heh heh.

REMOTE – Sometimes you see old TVs at like a yard sale with these knobs on them and you're like, "Whoa, no remote, what's the deal?" Back in those days, they say, you had to like get up and go over to the TV to change it. Like, it was almost less work to study than to watch TV. So the remote is like a great invention, since now you can change it from a show that sucks into one that also sucks, only not as much.

ROACH MOTEL – This one should be simple. It's just like a roach trap, right? It's like the prison for the bugs who don't get sentenced to death. But people get confused. Like one time Daria called our couch a big roach motel, even though there was a whole box of 'em the social worker had given us right where she could see it. And they weren't even unwrapped. Daria's not as smart as people think sometimes.

ROCK – Music rocks if it's cool and if, like, the louder you play it, the cooler it gets. If you thought it was cool and then you play it loud and it sucks, then it was probably college music or something. Or, if you think it's cool, and then you play it loud, and you think it sucks, and then you play it louder, and it sounds cool again, then something's wrong with your stereo or maybe the song just has a sucky part, like a lot of them do.

Ss SPORTS

SPORTS ARE STUPID, CAUSE THEY MAKE YOU EXERCISE, AND YOU CAN'T DO 'EM UNLESS YOU'VE GOT LIKE TEN OTHER GUYS AND A FOOTBALL STADIUM OR SOMETHING.

ME AND BEAVIS FIGURED OUT THAT THE MOST IMPORTANT THING IN SPORTS IS THAT YOU SCORE, HUH HUH. SO WE STARTED MAKING UP SPORTS THAT WERE COOLER AND FUNNER.

BREAKING STUFF -
YOU JUST TAKE STUFF AND YOU BREAK IT. AND YOU GET POINTS FOR EACH PIECE. LIKE IF IT BREAKS INTO FIVE PIECES, YOU GET, LIKE, I GUESS IT WOULD BE FIVE POINTS.

THROWING OUT THE GARBAGE -
YOU GET LIKE A LOT OF GARBAGE, AND YOU STAND ABOUT TWENTY FEET FROM THE TRASH CAN, AND YOU THROW GARBAGE AT IT. IF YOU GET IT IN, YOU GET TWO POINTS. IF YOU MISS, YOU GO WATCH TV.

FLY TENNIS -
OPEN ALL YOUR DOORS AND WINDOWS SO FLIES CAN GET IN THE HOUSE. THEN KILL THEM WITH A TENNIS RACKET. EACH FLY IS WORTH 15 POINTS.

WHO CAN STAY AWAKE THE LONGEST-
TRY TO STAY AWAKE AS LONG AS YOU CAN. YOU GET A POINT FOR

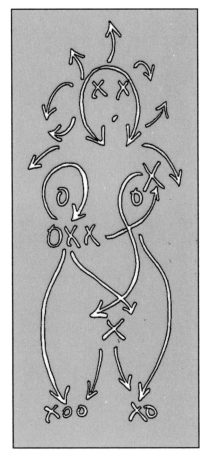

EVERY HOUR YOU STAY AWAKE. THE FIRST ONE TO FALL ASLEEP IS A WUSS.
(SEE ALSO: SLEEP DEPRIVASHUN)

SPITTING FOOD -
JUST LIKE PUT SOME FOOD IN YOUR MOUTH AND SPIT IT AT STUFF. IF YOU HIT IT, YOU GET A POINT.

LONG DISTANCE PEEING -
SEE HOW FAR YOU CAN STAND FROM THE TOILET AND STILL GET MOST OF YOUR PEE IN IT. OR AT LEAST SOME. PEE. AFTER YOU GET REALLY GOOD, TRY TAKING A LONG DISTANCE DUMP. ONE POINT FOR NUMBER ONE, TWO POINTS FOR NUMBER TWO.

THROWING STUFF -
YOU JUST PICK UP STUFF AND THROW IT AS HARD AS YOU CAN. WE HAVEN'T FIGURED OUT HOW YOU SCORE POINTS, BUT IT'S STILL PRETTY COOL.

SLAMMING THE DOOR -
I TAKE ONE DOOR AND BEAVIS TAKES ANOTHER DOOR. WE TAKE TURNS SLAMMING IT AS HARD AS WE CAN. WHOEVER SLAMS IT THE LOUDEST GETS A POINT. THE FIRST ONE TO A THOUSAND POINTS WINS.

FIGHTING -
LIKE, WHENEVER I GET BORED, I JUST SMACK BEAVIS IN THE FACE. AND I KEEP HITTING HIM UNTIL HE HITS ME BACK. THEN, WE'RE LIKE, IN A FIGHT. EVERY TIME I PUNCH BEAVIS, IT'S WORTH A POINT. EVERY TIME I KICK HIM IN THE NADS, IT'S WORTH TWO POINTS. THE ONLY PROBLEM IS THAT I ALWAYS KICK BEAVIS'S ASS, AND THEN HE DOESN'T WANT TO PLAY ANY MORE SPORTS. SO YOU SHOULD SAVE THIS FOR LIKE YOUR FINAL EVENT OR SOMETHING.

THIS SEWER PIPE IS COOL. BUT IT WOULD BE COOLER IF IT WAS REAL SMALL, SO THE STUFF CAN SHOOT OUT REALLY FAST. GOVERNMENT IS STUPID.

Ss SEWERS

SEWERS ARE COOL CAUSE THEY'RE A HIGHWAY FOR TURDS, HEH HEH. IT'S LIKE, WHEN YOU FLUSH, YOU'RE SAYING, BYE, LITTLE FELLA, HAVE A NICE TRIP, SO LONG. MOST PEOPLE, AFTER THEY SAY BYE OR WHATEVER, THEY DON'T EVEN THINK LIKE WHERE THE TURD'S GOING. NOT US. LIKE, WE'RE ALWAYS THINKING ABOUT THAT KIND OF STUFF, HEH HEH. WE'RE NATURALLY INQUISITOR.

* BEFORE SEWERS PEOPLE JUST PINCHED LOAFS IN THE WOODS OR SOMETHING, HEH HEH. (SEE ALSO: TOILET, ILLUSTRATED) AND THEN THEY SAID, IT'S TOO FAR TO WALK, I'LL JUST GO IN THE PIPE. AND THEN IN A LITTLE WHILE, SOMEBODY POURED WATER IN THE PIPE, PROBLY BY ACCIDENT, AND LIKE, PRIESTO, SEWER. A LOT OF INVENTIONS AND STUFF GET INVENTED BY ACCIDENT. LIKE THE LECTRIC GUITAR, THE FIRST GUY JUST FOLLOWED THE CORD FROM THE OUTLET, AND HE WAS LIKE, HM, I'LL BE DAMNED, IT'S A GUITAR.

* IT'S COOL TO MAKE VIDEOS IN SEWERS CAUSE THEY DRIP WATER, WHICH IS LIKE COOL IN A VIDEO. NO ONE KNOWS WHY IT'S COOL, OR WHO DECIDED IT, BUT IT IS. AND PLUS LIKE PEOPLE THINK SEWERS SUCK, WHICH IS COOL FOR BANDS THAT THINK LIFE SUCKS, BUT THEY LOOK COOL, SEWERS I MEAN, AND ALL BANDS TRY TO LOOK COOL, EVEN LIKE THE ONES THAT THINK LOOKING COOL SUCKS.

* A LONG TIME AGO, THIS LITTLE KID FLUSHED THIS FAMILY OF SEA MONKEYS DOWN THE TOILET. AND NOW THEY LIVE THERE AND LIKE EAT HUBCAPS AND STRAY DOGS AND STUFF, THOUGH MOST OF THE TIME THEY PROBLY LIVE OFF TURDS TOO, I GUESS.

* SEWERS USUALLY END IN A RIVER OR A LAKE OR A TREATMENT PLANT OR SOME OTHER PLACE. A TREATMENT PLANT IS THIS PLACE WHERE THEY LIKE TREATMENT THE TURDS SO THEY DON'T GROSS PEOPLE OUT. LIKE, IN OUR TOWN, THEY ADD THIS OILY STUFF THAT GIVES THE WATER THIS BURNED SMELL. IT'S COOL, AND YOU CAN GET OUT OF SCHOOL IF YOU TELL VAN DRIESSEN YOU DRANK SOME.

* THIS ONE TIME A RAT CRAWLED OUT OF A SEWER AND DIED RIGHT IN FRONT OF US. IT WAS COOL.

* ANOTHER TIME THE SEWER DUDES LEFT THEIR MANHOLE COVER OPEN SO WE CHECKED IT OUT. IT KICKED ASS. WE WERE GONNA CLIMB ALL THROUGH THE SEWER SYSTEM AND CHECK OUT EVERYBODY'S TOILET, BUT BUTT-HEAD FELL IN SOME CRAP AND HE SAID WE HAD TO GET OUT BEFORE WE SET OFF THE WARNING SYSTEM OR WHATEVER. SO WE DEFINITELY KNOW THAT LIKE SEWERS HAVE GOOD SECURITY.

22 May

10:00 p.m. Me and Beavis decide to try staying up all night. It's, like, a good skill to have, cause night is when most chicks do it. If you're gonna score you gotta know how to stay up late. And how to "stay up" late. Huh huh huh huh.

10:29 p.m. We each drank twelve sodas to be sure and stay awake all night. We figure it'll be hard to fall asleep if we hafta keep getting up to take a whiz.

10:47 p.m. M HEH HEH HEY HEH. THAT LINE ABOUT "STAY UP" LATE WAS PRETTY FUNNY. BUTT-HEAD JUST EXPLAINED IT TO ME.

11:04 p.m. Nighttime T.V. sucks. There's nothing on but a bunch of fartknocking shows about the news, or something.

11:38 B.M.

Huh huh, that's "p.m.", dumbass!

No WAY, BUTT-HEAD, it's B.M.! MAHH HEH. I took A DUMP AT 11:38. OH YEAH, I ALMOST FORGOT THE OTHER THING I DID...

11:39 P. HEH HEH HEH HEH.

12:00 AM. THE STROKE OF MIDNIGHT.

12:23 A.M. THE STROKE OF 12:23.

12:47 A.M. THE STROKE OF —————

Dammit Beavis, no-one wants to read about that!

OH YEAH, HEH HEH. SORRY ABOUT THAT. I GOT THIS DIARY CONFUSED WITH MY MONKEY-SPANKING DIARY.

2:30 a.m. Late night television sucks! Most stashuns have a sucky band playing the Notional Anthem, and now they're showing nothing but a bunch of static.

3:31 a.m. Watching the static on T.V. gets kind a boring after awhile.

3:39 A.M. WHOA! Heh Heh Heh. If you stair at the static on TV long enough, you start halloocinating, and then you can see a naked chick floating there. NAKED CHICKS RULE!

3:48 a.m. I've been trying to halloocinate from looking at the T.V. but I can't even get like dizzy. When Beavis thought he was halloocinating from watching the static, he musta been, like really halloocinating, or something.

3:53 a.m. I just remembered that Stewart said we could go over anytime and play with his new video game.

4:29 a.m. Stewart lied to us. We'll hafta kick his butt tomorrow. Or cane him. Huh huh huh huh. That would be cool.

4:45 A.M. EH HEH HEH. First offisttul sign of MORNING. I HAVE MORNING WOOD! HEH HEH M HEH.

5:18 a.m. Beavis ackshully got a smart idea. We could call up one of those 24-hour phone sex chicks now, when she'll probably be in bed and extra horny.

5:35 a.m. All she wanted to talk about was, like, "Do you have a credit card and what's the number on it?" We couldn't remember what we did with Anderson's credit card, so I hanged up. But then Beavis was really pissed off. Huh huh huh! He was getting a woodrow just talking about credit cards with the chick. Fartknocker!

5:36 A.M. DUMBASS!

5:37 a.m. Stut up Beavis, you turdwipe!

5:38 A.M. EH HEH HE HIM, DILLHOLE!

5:39 a.m. Don't make me kick your ass. Beavis.

5:40 A.M. BUTT-HOLE!

5:41 a.m. I kicked Beavis's ass, huh huh huh. I punched him so hard he fell asleep.

5:42 a.m. Early morning T.V. sucks.

Ss LIKE, UH, SONGS WE WROTE

(SOMETHING IN) MY PANTS

THERE'S SOMETHING IN MY PANTS
THERE'S SOMETHING IN MY PANTS
THERE'S SOMETHING IN MY PANTS
AND I THINK IT'S GROWING.

I DON'T KNOW WHAT MAKES IT GROW
THE WAY YOU LOOK, THE CLOTHES
    YOU WEAR
MY HAND IN MY POCKET, YOUR SMELL
    IN THE AIR
ALL I KNOW IS IT'S GOT TO BE FREE
GOTTA GET SOMETHING STRAIGHT
    BETWEEN YOU AND ME

CHORUS
THERE'S SOMETHING IN MY PANTS
THERE'S SOMETHING IN MY PANTS
THERE'S SOMETHING IN MY PANTS
AND I THINK IT'S GROWING.

(REPEAT CHORUS. REPEAT AGAIN.)
YEAH. IT IS.

IF I SAID I LOVE YOU

WOULD YOU TAKE OFF YOUR SHIRT IF
    I SAID THE WORDS?
WOULD YOU?
IF I SAID I LOVE YOU, WOULD YOU, LIKE,
    JUST TAKE OFF THE SHIRT?
WOULD YOU?

BECAUSE, BABY, IF THAT'S WHAT IT
    TAKES TO PROVE I WANT TO SEE YOU
    WITHOUT A SHIRT,
I'LL SAY IT.
I MEAN, IF LIKE, THE ONLY WAY I'LL SEE YOU
    WITHOUT YOUR SHIRT IS TO SAY
    I LOVE YOU,
I'LL SAY IT.

IF YOU TOOK OFF YOUR SHIRT BEFORE
    I EVEN SAID IT, THOUGH,
THAT WOULD BE COOL. SAVE ME
    SOME TROUBLE OR SOMETHING.
BUT REALLY, LIKE, IF THE ONLY WAY TO
    GET YOU OUT OF THE SHIRT IS TO SAY IT,
THAT'S COOL, TOO.

BECAUSE, BABY, THE IMPORTANT THING IS TO
    GET YOUR SHIRT OFF.
GET YOUR SHIRT OFF.
LIKE, THE IMPORTANT THING IS TO GET THAT
    DAMN THING OFF.
YEAH, GET IT OFF.

HAPPY TUNE

HUH HUH HUH
HUH HUH.

UH HUH HUH HUH.
HUH HUH HUH.

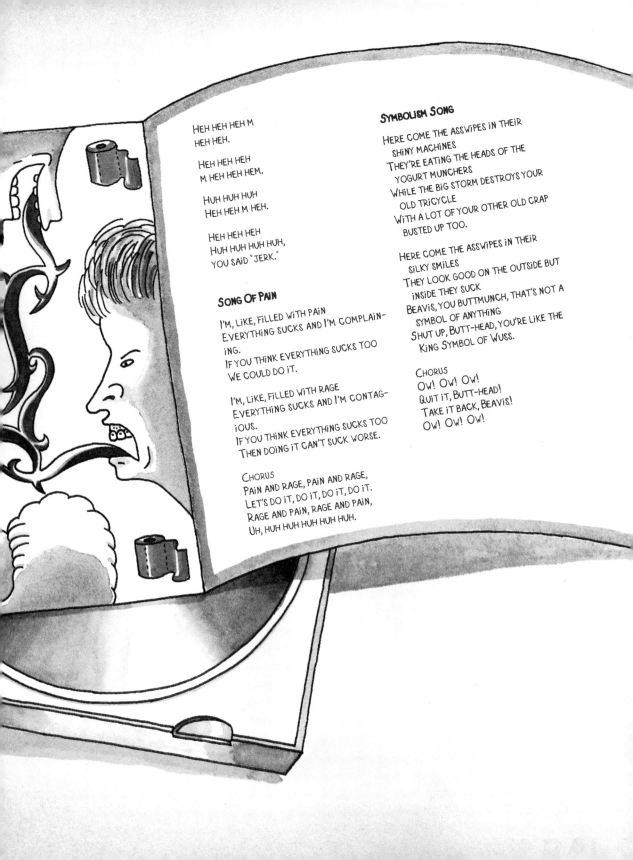

HEH HEH HEH M
HEH HEH.

HEH HEH HEH
M HEH HEH HEM.

HUH HUH HUH
HEH HEH M HEH.

HEH HEH HEH
HUH HUH HUH HUH,
YOU SAID "JERK."

SONG OF PAIN

I'M, LIKE, FILLED WITH PAIN
EVERYTHING SUCKS AND I'M COMPLAIN-
ING.
IF YOU THINK EVERYTHING SUCKS TOO
WE COULD DO IT.

I'M, LIKE, FILLED WITH RAGE
EVERYTHING SUCKS AND I'M CONTAG-
IOUS.
IF YOU THINK EVERYTHING SUCKS TOO
THEN DOING IT CAN'T SUCK WORSE.

CHORUS
PAIN AND RAGE, PAIN AND RAGE,
LET'S DO IT, DO IT, DO IT, DO IT.
RAGE AND PAIN, RAGE AND PAIN,
UH, HUH HUH HUH HUH HUH.

SYMBOLISM SONG

HERE COME THE ASSWIPES IN THEIR
SHINY MACHINES
THEY'RE EATING THE HEADS OF THE
YOGURT MUNCHERS
WHILE THE BIG STORM DESTROYS YOUR
OLD TRICYCLE
WITH A LOT OF YOUR OTHER OLD CRAP
BUSTED UP TOO.

HERE COME THE ASSWIPES IN THEIR
SILKY SMILES
THEY LOOK GOOD ON THE OUTSIDE BUT
INSIDE THEY SUCK
BEAVIS, YOU BUTTMUNCH, THAT'S NOT A
SYMBOL OF ANYTHING
SHUT UP, BUTT-HEAD, YOU'RE LIKE THE
KING SYMBOL OF WUSS.

CHORUS
OW! OW! OW!
QUIT IT, BUTT-HEAD!
TAKE IT BACK, BEAVIS!
OW! OW! OW!

HORSES CAN TAKE A DUMP WHILE THEY'RE WALKING, BUT THEY HAFTA STAND IN ONE PLACE TO PEE.

IT'S FIZZICALLY IMPOSSIBLE TO CHOKE YOUR CHICKEN MORE TIMES IN ONE DAY THAN THE NUMBER OF YEARS OLD YOU ARE. BEAVIS CAN'T WAIT UNTIL HIS FIFTEENTH BIRTHDAY.

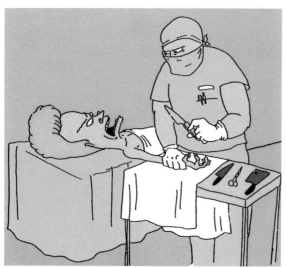

IF YOU AMPUTATE AN INSECT'S LEG, IT'LL KEEP MOVING, EVEN THOUGH IT'S NOT ATTACHED TO THE INSECT ANYMORE. HUH HUH HUH! AND IF YOU, LIKE, AMPUTATE BEAVIS'S HAND? IT'LL PROBABLY KEEP SPANKING HIS MONKEY.

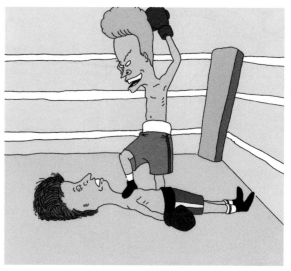

BEAVIS SAYS HE KICKED MY ASS ONCE. IT MUSTA BEEN WHILE I WAS ASLEEP, OR I WOULDA KICKED HIS ASS INSTEAD.

BUTT TRUE

SOME DUDES ACKSHULLY FREEZE THEIR SPERM.
BEAVIS PREFERS TO MAKE HIS FRESH DAILY.

THERE'S, LIKE, THESE CHICKS THAT'LL DO IT WITH YOU
IF YOU PAY THEM ENOUGH MONEY. EVEN BEAVIS.

A HUNDRED YEARS AGO, IN, LIKE, THE DARK AGES,
PEOPLE'S BATHING SUITS COVERED PRACTICALLY
THEIR WHOLE BODIES. EVEN CHICKS' BATHING
SUITS. THE DARK AGES SUCKED!

ONE DAY BEAVIS IS GONNA GROW UP TO BE A MAN.
BELIEVE IT OR NOT, HE MIGHT EVEN SCORE THEN.
UH, SEE ABOVE.

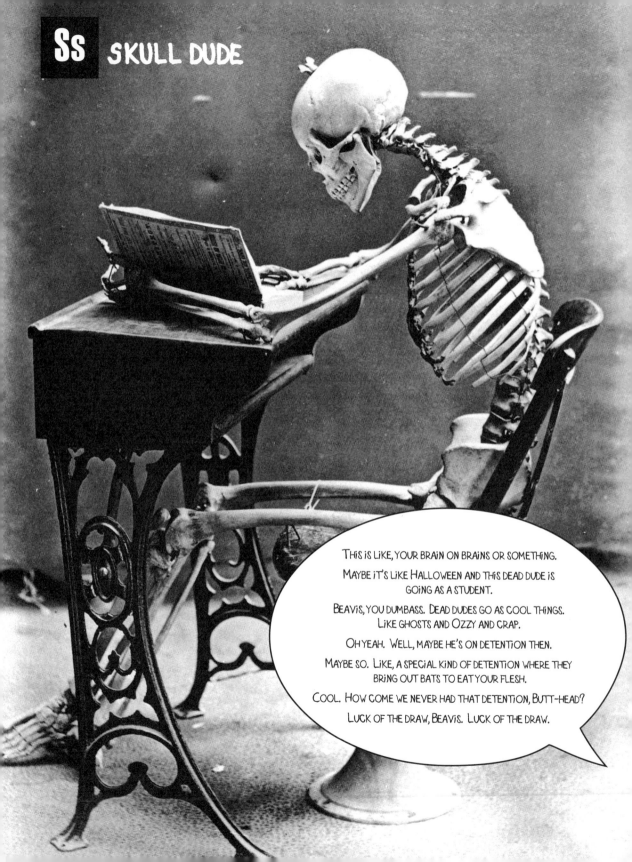

TESTIES

TEST SHEET
Mr. Van Driessen's Class
Week Seven Test
Subject: The U.S. and Central America.

C-

Good Work, Beavis I sense that you're really making some progress

List the states of Central America.

Mississississippi, Houston, England AND Nicaragua. Nicaragua! Aqua!)

Which overly aggressive American leader summed up his belligerent policy towards Central America with the phrase, "Speak softly and carry a big stick"?

THAT WAS PROBLY ME OR SOMETHING ESPESHULLY THE PART ABOUT THE BIG STICK.

What were President Kennedy's interventionist goals in going forward with the disastrous "Bay of Pigs" invasion in 1961?

UH, ME AND BUTT-HEAD FOUND A PIG, ONCE ON SOME OLD DUDES FARM. IT WAS EATING A BUNCH OF GARBAGE. WE WERE, UH, WORRIED ABOUT THE PIG, HAVING ALL THAT BAD FOOD IN IT, AND STUFF? SO WE FED IT SOME LEFTOVER CHOCLAT LACKSATIVES FOR, LIKE SIENCE.

What was the outcome?

A BIG TURD. ITS OUTCOME WAS SO FAST I GOT SPLATTERED. THAT SUCKED!

Compare and contrast the soaring rhetoric of America's "Good Neighbor" policy towards Central America with the grim reality of "Dollar Diplomacy."

UH, COULD YOU REPEAT THE QUESTION?

List a few ways in which the United States could truly be a "Good Neighbor" to other countries in this hemisphere.

WE COULD SET OUR TAZERS ON STUN, UNLESS WE WERE, LIKE, REALLY ANGRY. WE COULD SEND THEM MORE AMERICUNS, TO HELP THEM OUT SO THEY WOULDN'T BE SO FULL OF FOREINURZ. AND WE COULD DO IT WITH THEIR CHICKS. THAT'D BE COOL!

CLARK COBB'S TOOL CHEST

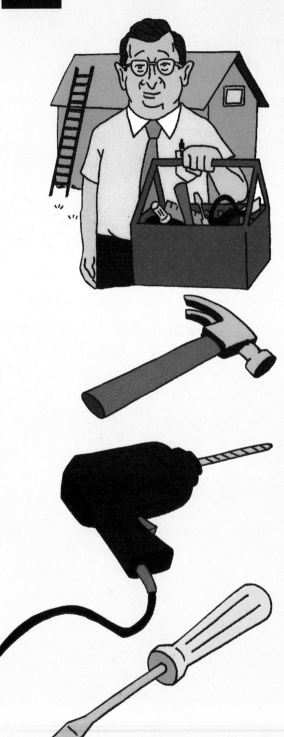

Hello, young students. I'm Clark Cobb of Cobb Family Hardware. Did you know Christ was a carpenter? That's right. And you better believe He took good care of his tools. At Cobb Family Hardware, we believe that a man who's got his toolbox in order is a man who's got his soul in order—just so long as he keeps in mind the words of Psalm 127: "Unless the Lord builds the house, those who build it labor in vain" (Verse 1). But you should also keep in mind the tenth Psalm, "Break thou the arm of the wicked and evil-doer." (Verse 15). Which is why in my book, like the Good Book, if a fella gets into your tools, you got the God-given right to break some arms.

Hammer Just as the Lord may use a tractor-trailer brake failure to pound a little faith into a car full of joyriding young people, so I use my hammer to pound nails into boards of wood. And like nails, faith holds this House of Man together. I call my hammer Big Rig.

Drill Folks, don't go to a job without the right tools. Sometimes, hammer and nails aren't enough. Many times I have gathered with my brethren CBs to assemble a large scaffold or stage from which to celebrate the occasion of a recently paroled minister or Businessman only to find that there are still those who have not heard the good news about drills, bolts and nuts. Listen up folks: get a drill.

Screwdriver Jesus once said to the Pharisees, "He who does not enter the sheepfold by the door but climbs in by another way, that man is a thief and a robber" (John 10:1). But you know what? Sometimes the door is broke! But with your screwdriver, you can take off the hinges, move the door, and go right in. Incidentally, I'm sure you'll all agree that in the above statement the Lord makes pretty damn clear his opinion of your so-called alternative lifestyles.

Level Sometimes in life, you need to step back and ask, "Am I on the level? Is my life straight and true?" As a guide, we may turn to our pastor, or to a fellow Christian Businessman. And that Christian Businessman may say, "Clark, you're sagging—let's get on our knees and get you straightened out." Well, think of a level as a Christian Businessman who's got a little bubble instead of a mouth.

Laminated Copy of the Christian Businessmen's Association Oath "I swear to do my best to spread the God's Report® while building business opportunities in the community. For as faith nourishes the soul, so good business nourishes the community in which the soul and its body live. I will not be unfair in my business, and I will profitshare with the Lord."

®God's Report is a registered trademark of the Christian Businessmen's Association. The Christian Businessmen's Association is a chartered member of Christworks, Inc., a division of the Wormwood Industries Group.

Extension Cord When I see a church steeple, I think of it as an extension cord to heaven, bringing the "juice" of the Lord right down into the little people like me. In a way, I think of myself as a little tiny robot man who gets his battery charged every Sunday down at First Highland Methodist. Then I run around all week like a robot until I start to wind down on Saturday. Sunday, I'm good as new.

Socko II Meet my friend, Socko II. He lives in my toolbox. It's good having a friend with you when you do your work. Because even though the Lord is always with you, sometimes, as in the book of Revelations, "there was silence in heaven" (Chapter 8, Verse 1). But if you put a friend in your toolbox, you can strike up a conversation any time you want. Socko II's brother, Socko, lives in the glove compartment of my vehicle. I take him out to talk to young students like you. And, sometimes, to me when I drive.

Pamphlets Often when I'm working with my tools, young people gather round to watch. That's why I keep these important youth-orientated pamphlets: "Help Me, Lord, My Body Is Changing"; "666 is Satan in Digital—CD's Every Youngster Should Avoid"; "God's Expectations For Dating"; "The Seven Warning Signals of Hell"; "Onan, Girls, and God—Where Do I Fit In?"; "Dear Jesus, Why Did Daddy Leave?—Children's Letters to Christ."

THE ILLUSTRATED TOILET

BEFORE THE TOILET WAS INVENTED, PEOPLE HAD NO PLACE TO GO TO THE TOILET.

THAT'S NOT TRUE, BUTT-HEAD. SOMETIMES THEY WENT OUTSIDE. WHEN PEOPLE ASKED THEM WHERE THEY WERE GOING, THEY SAID, LIKE, "I HAVE TO GO TO THE FOREST," OR, "I HAVE TO GO TO THE SIDEWALK."

OR IF THEY WERE LIKE YOU, BEAVIS, THEY SAID, "I HAVE TO GO TO MY PANTS." HUH HUH.

SHUT UP, BUTT-HEAD!

TODAY EVERYONE USES THE TOILET BUT NO ONE KNOWS HOW THEY WORK. EXCEPT ME AND BEAVIS. WE DID LIKE RESEARCH IN THE LIBRARY. IN THE TOILET SECTION. THE FIRST THING WE LEARNED WAS, WHEN YOU FLUSH A TOILET, IT MAKES THE TURD DISAPPEAR. HUH HUH. THAT WAS COOL! WE'RE GONNA START DOING THAT.

NOT ME.

BUT WE LEARNED MORE. WE WROTE IT ALL DOWN ON A DIAFRAM OF A TOILET SO YOU CAN LEARN IT TOO. ALL THIS STUFF IS TRUE. IF YOU DON'T BELIEVE IT, TRY FLUSHING A TOILET SOMETIME. THEN LIFT UP THE SEAT. LIKE, PRIESTO OR SOMETHING!

TOILET SEAT: PLACE YOUR BIG BUTT HERE.

TOILET BOWL: WHERE THE CRAP AND VOMIT GO. OH YEAH, AND WEE-WEE.

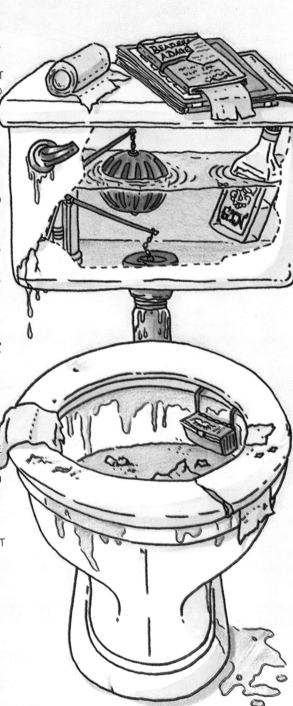

FLUSHER THINGIE: TURN THIS AND IT MAKES THE TURD GO AWAY. IF YOU KNOW ONLY ONE THING ABOUT A TOILET, THIS SHOULD BE IT. OR TO LIFT THE SEAT COVER.

REFRIGERATOR SECTION: THIS IS WHERE BEAVIS'S MOM KEEPS HER MEDICINE COLD.

BIG COPPER BALL: THIS IS LIKE KEY TO THE WHOLE OPERATION. AS THE WATER RUSHES IN, SCIENTIFIC STUFF MAKES THIS BALL RISE TO THE TOP. IT'S LIKE WHEN BEAVIS WETS THE BED, SOMETIMES HE ALSO GETS A WOODROW.

PIPES AND STUFF: WE'RE NOT SURE WHAT THIS STUFF DOES CAUSE IT'S SO DARK IN THERE. THEY SHOULD PUT A LIGHT IN THE TOILET SO YOU CAN SEE WHERE THE CRAP GOES.

FART RECYCLER (OPTIONAL): THIS DEVICE IS FOUND SOME-TIMES IN YOUR FINER TOILETS. IT LIKE COLLECTS FART GAS AND CONVERTS IT TO CHEAP FUEL THAT THEY CAN SELL TO POOR COUNTRIES. YEAH, HEH HEH. THE TURD WORLD.

READING MATERIAL: IT'S GOOD TO HAVE LOTS OF MAGAZINES WITH CLEAR PICTURES OF INTERESTING PEOPLE WHO LIKE TO, YOU KNOW, DO IT. MAKE SURE THEY'RE THE KIND YOU CAN READ WITH ONE HAND, IN CASE YOU NEED YOUR OTHER HAND TO LIKE UH...HUH HUH...PULL YOUR FLUSHER.

Uu URANUS

URANUS IS LIKE THE FUNNIEST OF ALL THE
PLANETS. LIKE, JUST SAYING THE NAME
URANUS WITHOUT LAUGHING IS PROBLY THE
HARDEST PART ABOUT BEING ONE A THOSE
ASSNAUTS. HUH HUH, URANUS. HEH HEH
HEH. BUT IT'S ALSO DANGEROUS, CAUSE
ONE TIME WE WERE LAUGHING AT IT AND
BUZZCUT MADE US LIKE, GIVE A REPORT
ABOUT IT. HE SAID HE WISHED HE COULD
GIVE US CORPORAL PUNISHMENT, BUT LIKE,
I DON'T THINK HE'S ALLOWED TO CAUSE HE
NEVER GOT THAT FAR IN THE MARINES.

FACTS ABOUT URANUS

SIZE: IT'S BIG. BUT LIKE, NOBODY KNOWS EXACKLY HOW BIG CAUSE, LIKE, IF YOU TRY
TO MEASURE IT, THE GRAVITY SUCKS YOU INTO URANUS. URANUS. HUH HUH HUH HUH
HUH. M HEH HEH HEH. THAT'S LIKE THE OPPOSITE AS ON EARTH. CAUSE LIKE HERE ON
EARTH, WHEN YOU'RE ON THE TOILET OR WHATEVER, GRAVITY SUCKS EVERYTHING <u>OUT</u>
OF URANUS. HUH HUH HUH. HEH HEH M HEH HEH.

ATMOSPHERE: IT HAS THIS THING CALLED METHANE ON IT, WHICH DARIA TOLD US
COMES FROM FARTING. SO IT'S LIKE, CALLED THE SBD PLANET. THAT'S JUST ITS
NICKNAME, THOUGH.

NAME: THE BOOK SAYS IT'S NAMED FOR THIS GREEK DUDE. RIGHT.

MOONS AND RINGS: THERE'S MOONS AND RINGS ON URANUS. HUH HUH HUH HUH.
HEH HEH M. JUST LIKE BEAVIS'S MOM. IT'S LIKE, SOMETIMES, IF YOU LOOK AT HER
WHEN SHE'S ASLEEP, LIKE AT AROUND NOON, AND THE SHEETS ARE ALL OVER THE
PLACE, SHE'LL BE MOONING YOU, HUH HUH. THEN BEAVIS GETS ALL PISSED, HUH HUH.
AND THEN, ALL THOSE DUDES SHE KNOWS, SHE SAYS THEY'RE HER COUSINS. BUT THEY
GIVE HER RINGS AND STUFF. THEN SHE GIVES THE RINGS TO THE DUDE AT THE PAWN
SHOP AND SHE GOES OUT AND LIKE, BUYS SOME HAIR SPRAY OR LIKE GOVERMENT
CHEESE OR WHATEVER. BEAVIS'S MOM HAS A LOT IN COMMON WITH URANUS.
URANUS. HUH HUH HUH HUH HUH HUH. HEH HEH HEH HEH M HEH HEH. WAIT. WAIT.
SHUT UP, BUTT-HEAD. FARTKNOCKER.

PRACTICE SENTENCES:
URANUS IS A DARK AND MYSTERIOUS PLACE. HUH HUH HUH HUH HUH.
I DON'T THINK CIVILIANIZED PEOPLE WILL EVER GO TO URANUS. HEH HEH HEH. HEH.
BEAVIS, IF YOU PISS ME OFF ONE MORE TIME I'M GOING TO RIP URANUS IN HALF. HUH HUH.
BUZZCUT SUCKS.

Patrick Henry, Patriot and Orifice

The fondling fathers who started this country spent all their time giving speeches, but the greatest orifice of them all was Patrick Henry. He could talk about anything -- chicks, dogs, your weiner, why the world sucks. You know, important stuff.

Patrick Henry loved the sound of his own voice. And he loved the sound of his own butt. That's because he ate lots of bean burritos. Everywhere he went, you could hear him talking and farting, talking and farting. He talked so much and farted so much, he made like uh...a *reputation*.

So one day all the fondling fathers like George Washing and Abraham Lincoln and the Jeffersons were standing around talking about what kind of country this should be. Some wanted a demonocracy, where everyone could do what they want like it says on the Statue of Liberty. Others wanted a *dorkocracy*, huh huh, where one asswipe runs everything like in Buzzcut's class.

Finally Patrick Henry got up and made a famous speech. He said, "Give me liberty or pull my finger!" So everyone chose liberty because they didn't want to pull Patrick Henry's finger and release some of that reputation.

BILLY THE KID'S VIRGIN

"PULL MY FINGER" HAS BEEN PLAYED
THRU THE AGES BY PEOPLE OF MANY LANDS
AND LANGUAGES. THAT IS BECAUSE YOU DON'T
HAVE TO BE, LIKE, DEVELOPED TO PLAY IT.
BEAVIS COULD FART BEFORE HE COULD WALK.

YEAH, HEH HEH. I COULD DUMP, TOO.

IN MEXICO THEY SAY, "PULL MY FINGER,
ÉSE." IN FRANCE THEY SAY, "POOL MY FEENGER,
SHEREE." IN GERMANY THEY SAY, "YA! YA!
PULL MY FINGER! YA! YA!" HUH HUH. HUH HUH.
ASSWIPES.

SOME PEOPLE PLAY DIFFERENT VIRGINS
OF THE GAME. BILLY THE KID LIVED IN THE
OLD WEST AND HE INVENTED AN INTERESTING
VIRGIN. HE'D GO UP TO SOME DUDE ON THE
STREET AND SAY, "PULL MY FINGER." AND WHEN
THE GUY DID, BILLY FILLED HIM FULL OF LEAD.
THAT WAS COOL. EVENTUALLY BILLY THE KID
WAS KILLED BY PAT GARRETT. ACCORDING TO
HYSTERIANS, GARRETT USED TWO FINGERS.

BEAVIS IN THE LIBRARY

BEAVIS IS PRETTY FUNNY. ONE DAY
BEAVIS AND ME HAD TO GO TO THE SCHOOL
LIBRARY BECAUSE WE FORGOT TO STAY HOME.

WHILE WE WERE AT THE LIBRARY, OUR
TEACHER MRS. DICKEY, HUH HUH, GOT MAD AT
THE CLASS CAUSE IT WAS HER PERIOD. SHE
SAID, "EVERYBODY SHUT UP!"

SO THEN IT WAS QUIET FOR A WHILE.
THEN BEAVIS SAID, "PULL MY FINGER."
I PULLED HIS FINGER AND HE LET A REAL LOUD
FART. IT WAS REALLY COOL.

YOU'RE PRETTY FUNNY, BEAVIS.

YEAH, HEH HEH, I KNOW. REMEMBER
THAT TIME I CUT ONE IN THE LIBRARY?

IF WE MADE, LIKE, A VIDEO

ABOUT 108% OF ALL VIDEOS SUCK, NO MATTER HOW LOUD YOU TURN UP THE TV. THAT'S BECAUSE LIKE MOST PEOPLE DON'T KNOW HOW TO DO IT RIGHT. THEY'RE TOO BUSY LIKE, MAKING VIDEOS THAT ARE LIKE SPOSED TO

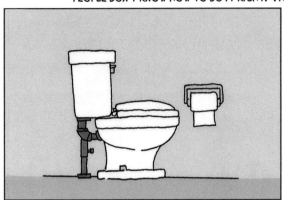

1. THE INTRODUCTION. LIKE THE INTRODUCTION HAS TO BE SO COOL THAT PEOPLE WATCH THE REST OF THE VIDEO. LIKE, WE'D PROBLY PUT A TOILET IN THE INTRODUCTION. AND THAT WAY PEOPLE WOULD GO, "UH, THIS LOOKS COOL. I WONDER IF THEY'RE GONNA FLUSH IT. HEY, WHAT IF A FAT GUY SITS ON IT? INSTRESTING. I GUESS I'LL JUST KEEP WATCHING TO SEE WHAT HAPPENS."

2. EXPLOSION. ANY TIME IS THE RIGHT TIME FOR AN EXPLOSION. IT WOULD BE COOL TO SEE LIKE A GUY ON A MOTORCYCLE EXPLODE. BUT LIKE, THE TV COMPANIES GET WUSSY ABOUT SHOWING THAT KIND OF STUFF, CAUSE THEY'RE AFRAID PEOPLE WILL DO IT? SO, LIKE, AS A COMPROMISE, JUST EXPLODE THE GUY AND LEAVE THE MOTORCYCLE ALONE.

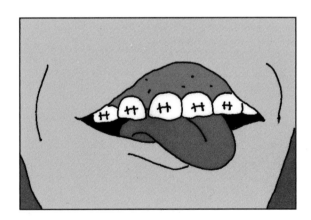

5. UH, LIKE, IF WE HAD FANS, THEY'D PROBLY BE MOSTLY CHICKS. HUH HUH. SO LIKE, WE'D NEED TO PUT SOME PICTURES OF ME IN THE VIDEO. LIKE, I THINK IT'D BE GOOD TO HAVE A CLOSEUP OF MY MOUTH AND TONGUE, HUH HUH. THAT'S LIKE ONE OF THE PARTS OF MY BODY THAT TURNS CHICKS ON THE MOST, HUH HUH HUH.

6. UM, THIS IS A GOOD PLACE FOR ANOTHER EXPLOSION. IF YOU ONLY HAVE ONE EXPLOSION, YOU CAN PUT IT ANYWHERE, CAUSE YOUR VIDEO WILL PROBLY SUCK. BUT IF YOU HAVE MORE THAN ONE, DON'T PUT 'EM ALL AT THE BEGINNING, OR PEOPLE'LL FEEL GYPPED. AND LIKE, IN A LOT OF VIDEOS, THEY JUST BLOW UP BUILDINGS AND STUFF, WITH LIKE A TOTAL DISREGARD FOR INCLUDING HUMAN LIFE. THAT WON'T BE A PROBLEM IN OUR VIDEO, HEH HEH.

MEAN SOMETHING. BUT ALL A VIDEO'S SPOSED TO MEAN IS THAT TV DOESN'T SUCK FOR THREE MINUTES. SO LIKE, WE'VE MADE IT SIMPLE FOR PEOPLE TO DO A COOL VIDEO. SPECIALLY CAUSE IT STARS US.

3. CHICKS REALLY GIVE A VIDEO SOMETHING, AND THAT SOMETHING IS CHICKS. CERTAIN KINDS OF DANCING CHICKS ARE GOOD TO HAVE IN A VIDEO. BUT ONLY CERTAIN KINDS. HUH HUH. SLUTS, MOSTLY. UH, IF YOU HAVE LIKE QUESTIONS, ME AND BEAVIS CAN PERSONALLY CHECK OUT EACH CHICK TO MAKE SURE SHE'S THE RIGHT KIND OF DANCING CHICK, HUH HUH.

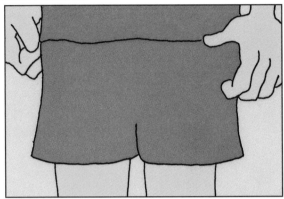

4. UM, LIKE, A VIDEO IS FOR ALL PEOPLE TO ENJOY, BUT MOSTLY IT'S FOR THE FANS, HEH HEH. SO LIKE, SINCE WE'RE THE STARS, WE WANNA SHOW US IN WAYS WE'VE NEVER BEEN SEEN BEFORE. LIKE A GIANT CLOSEUP OF MY CROTCH WOULD BE PRETTY COOL. HEH HEH. THEY'D BE LIKE, "I'LL BE DAMNED. NEVER SAW THAT BEFORE." HEH HEH.

7. IF YOUR SONG'S ABOUT LOVE, YOU SHOULD PROBLY SYMBOLIZE THAT WITH SOME PICTURES OF PEOPLE DOING IT, HUH HUH. PROBLY ME AND ONE OF THE DANCER CHICKS ARE DOING IT. OR LIKE, WE'RE JUST ABOUT TO DO IT. YOU CAN TELL WE'RE JUST ABOUT TO CAUSE SHE HASN'T LEFT THE ROOM YET. HUH HUH. SHE WANTS ME.

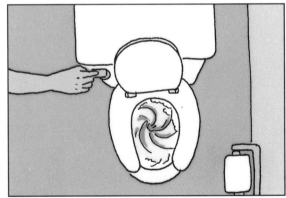

8. LIKE, AT THE END OF THE VIDEO, YOU'D PROBLY WANNA PUT THE TOILET BACK IN AGAIN, BECAUSE RIGHT NOW EVERYBODY'S GOING, HEY, WHATEVER HAPPENED TO THAT TOILET. AND YOU'D GO, FUNNY YOU SHOULD ASK. IT'S BEING FLUSHED, HEH HEH. THAT'S OUR STORY, THANKS VERY MUCH. HEH HEH.

HUH HUH. I GUESS NOW IT'S TIME TO PICK A COOL SONG TO GO WITH THE VIDEO.

NO WAY! A SONG WOULD, LIKE, RUIN IT.

OH YEAH. VIDEOS RULE. SONGS SUCK.

HOW TO LIKE WORK AT BURGER WORLD

THEY SAY THAT WORKING AT THE WORLD IS SPOSED TO BE LIKE, UH, CHALLENGING OR SOMETHING. BUT LIKE, WHAT THEY DON'T TELL YOU IS THAT IT'S LIKE A JOB.

So LIKE IF YOU'RE WORKING AT THE WORLD, HERE'S SOME TIPS TO GET THROUGH YOUR SHIFT SO YOU CAN GET PAID. THEN YOU CAN GO BUY SOME REAL FOOD, LIKE NACHOS.

PUNCHING IN
UH, HUH HUH. GET IT?

Rong ~~Right~~ Way

Cool Way

GREETING THE CUSTOMER
UH, LIKE CUSTOMERS ARE ALWAYS AROUND TRYING TO MESS UP YOUR DAY. SO IT'S LIKE IMPORTANT THAT THE CUSTOMER GETS A REAL CLEAR IDEA OF WHAT TO EXPECT. IT'S LIKE TREAT THEM THE WAY YOU WANT THEM TO TREAT YOU IF YOU LIKE SUCKED OR SOMETHING.

Hi, welcome to Burger World. How may I ~~help~~ you today?

HUH HUH HUH HUH. YOU'RE OLD.

MAKING THE CUSTOMER GO AWAY

THEY KEEP TELLING YOU THAT IT'S LIKE IMPORTANT FOR THE WORLD TO LIKE LIVE UP TO THE NAME "FAST FOOD," EVEN THOUGH FAST FOOD ISN'T EVEN IN THE NAME. ASSWIPES. SO YOU SHOULD MAKE THEM WANT TO LIKE LEAVE FAST, HUH HUH.

TALK ABOUT GROSS STUFF.

SCREW UP THE ORDER.

DON'T TAKE ANY CRAP FROM PEOPLE.

HANDLING THE MEAT, HUH HUH

LIKE, HANDLING THE MEAT IS FUN, HEH HEH. IT'S LIKE, TIME TO HANDLE THE MEAT, I'M GOING ON BREAK. BUT ALWAYS WASH YOUR HANDS AFTER YOU DO IT.

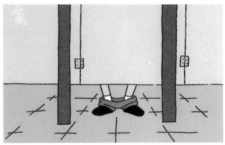

USING THE GRILL AND STUFF

WITHOUT THE GRILL, BURGER WORLD WOULD JUST BE, LIKE, UH, WORLD. BUT IT'S NOT JUST LIKE A GRILL OR SOMETHING. IT'S, UH, A BIG FLAT HOT THING YOU CAN COOK CRAP ON TOO.

CHECK TO SEE IF THE GRILL IS HOT. A GOOD WAY IS TO TELL BEAVIS THAT IF HE LOOKS REAL CLOSE HE CAN SEE A NAKED CHICK IN THE GREASE.

IT'S FUN TO FRY THE HEADSET CAUSE PEOPLE THINK IT'S LIKE STATIC, HUH HUH.

IF YOU'RE MELTING SOMETHING PLASTIC, LIKE SOMEBODY'S CREDIT CARD, DON'T LET IT BURN UNLESS YOUR SUPERVISOR'S TOO FAR AWAY TO SMELL IT.

DEALING WITH LEFTOVERS

BURGER FRISBEE

F-TIPS

SHAKE GLUE

FIRST AID

LIKE, IF SOMEBODY HURTS THEMSELVES ON THE GRILL OR SOMETHING, TELL THEM TO QUIT SCREWING AROUND AND GET BACK TO WORK. IF THEY BLEED ON THE FOOD AND STUFF, TELL PEOPLE IT'S LIKE A NEW KETCHUP WE'RE TESTING OR SOMETHING.

CLEANING THE BATHROOMS

IT'S COOL TO CLEAN THE BATHROOMS CAUSE, LIKE, YOU CAN WATCH PEOPLE COME IN AND TRY TO PINCH A LOAF AND DRAIN THEIR WEINERS AND STUFF AND THEY LIKE, GET NERVOUS. TRY TO LIKE RELAX THEM BY SAYING, "HEY, IT'S COOL, PINCH YOUR LOAF IN PEACE." IF NOBODY COMES IN, THOUGH, YOU CAN JUST SLEEP AND STUFF.

PUNCHING OUT

HUH HUH. I BET YOU GET IT NOW.

VANDALISM – These are those guys. The ones who pray on TV. The TV Vandalist guys. They tell you that they want you to become like a Full Faith Partner in the Ministry Foundation, and then they cry, so you send them money, and then the TV Vandalist gets you into heaven. He's like a bouncer or something. But can TV vandalism get those dudes into heaven who, uh, egged Anderson's house last night? Huh huh. That's where like faith or something comes in, dude.

VEGETABLES – These are those things they say you're sposed to eat. But like, if they're not on the Burger World menu, how important can they be? The best thing to do with vegetables is throw them at city buses and Anderson.

VIETMOM – Vietmom is a country in China, but it's also a war. And cause we had it during the 60s, the only soldiers we could get were hippies and stuff, so naturally we got our ass kicked. But then we invented Rambo, and he went back and won the war, and it was called Operation Desert Nam. So even though we really won, sometimes we call it a tie to make the people in Vietmom feel better.

VIRGIN – Huh huh huh huh huh. This is like a dude or a chick who's never done it.
For more information, see Beavis.

WAR OF THE WORLDS – This is a war that happened a long time ago, when Anderson was a young dude. Like, a hundred pounds ago, or something. So what happened was, the Chinese bombed Pearl Harbor, and so we had to fight both the Germans and the Nazis. Then there was D-Day, and they say this dude ran around saying, "The British are coming!" But he probly wasn't Anderson cause the dude never said anything about wanting a beer.

WEDGIE – There are like different kinds of wedgies. There's like the normal everyday wedgie, like when Beavis pisses you off for no reason. Then there's like the first-class wedgie, like the ones the seniors give on Torture Day, and you have to like walk around with it all day or get an atomic wedgie, which really deserves its own definition.

WEDGIE, ATOMIC – Heh heh. When, like, Butt-head says he can kick Todd's ass, and Todd hears him? And when you see Butt-head a little later hanging from the top of a locker by his underwear? And he's talking all choked up? That's like an atomic wedgie.

WEINER – There's like two different meanings for this word, which like, proves how messed up the English language is. But the definition for weiner that most people use is uh, huh huh huh, your thing. The other meaning is hardly ever used anymore but, like, they used to say a weiner was a hot dog. One time Stewart's dad was grilling stuff and he goes, "Who wants a weinie?" And like, Stewart went, "Me!" That whole family's like, messed up.

WOOD – Wood is the best part about being a dude, practically. It's like, you could take away all my money and my clothes and my TV, and I'd probly live. But if you took away my wood, it's like, why would I even want to?

WUSS – This is a person who's like so pathetic and weak and sorry that if you gave him a baseball bat and like, a big chain with spikes in it, and some knives, and then you put him in a little tiny room with that dude from the B-52s, the B-52 dude would still kick his ass. Huh huh. For more information, write to Beavis, 1515 Wussy Avenue, Wussburg, Wussylvania, 029wuss4. Huh huh.

WW THE SEVEN WONDERS OF THE WORLD

STONEHEDGE
CAUSE EVERYBODY WONDERS WHAT THE HELL IT IS. LIKE, I WONDER WHAT KIND OF STUPID DILLHOLE WOULD HAUL A BUNCH OF ROCKS UP A HILL AND LIKE, NOT GET PAID CAUSE THEY DIDN'T INVENT MONEY YET? HEY, THAT MAKES STONEHEDGE TWO WONDERS.

THE GREAT WALL OF CHINA
UHHH, PINK FLOYD MADE A PRETTY COOL MOVIE ABOUT IT. BUT I GUESS THEY TORE IT DOWN AT SOME CONCERT IN GERMONEY.

WUNDER BREAD
LIKE, YOU CAN SQUEEZE IT AND WONDER IF THAT'S WHAT A CHICK FEELS LIKE.

BEAVIS
I WONDER IF HE'S EVER GONNA GET ANY! HUH HUH HUH.

ALGEBRA
Huh Huh Huh Huh Huh.

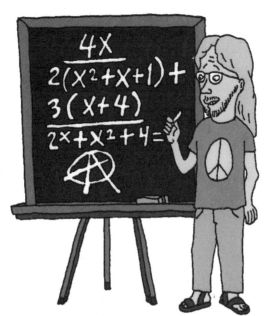

CIRCLES
Those circles that Led Zeplin put in fields. Those stupid farmers don't even know who's putting them there! What a bunch of dumbasses!

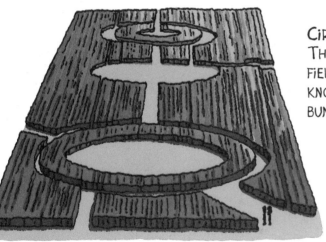

STEVIE WONDER
He can, like, defect bullets with his magic braces.

Editorial Director: Mike Judge
Editor: Glenn Eichler

Art Direction: Roger Gorman, Reiner Design Consultants, Inc.
Illustration Supervisor: Dominie Mahl.
Illustrators: Mike Judge, Kevin Lofton, Miguel Martinez-Joffre, and Bryon Moore
Colorists: Masako Kanayama and Robert Charde

Special thanks at MTV to: John Andrews, Jonathan Cropper, Howard Handler, Joy Marcus, Jeffrey Marshall, Judy McGrath, Ed Paparo, Renee Presser, Lisa Silfen, Robin Silverman, Sabrina Silverberg, Donald Silvey, Abby Terkuhle, and Van Toffler

Special thanks at Pocket Books to: Lynda Castillo, Gina Centrello, Amy Einhorn, Jack Romanos, Bill Siebert, Jennifer Weidman, Kara Welsh, and Irene Yuss

Cover Illustration from *The Joy of Knowledge* by Mitchell Beazley courtesy of Reed Consumer Books.
Photo credits: Cover photographs, clockwise from top left: Bettmann Archive, Bettmann Archive, Archive Photos, Bettmann Archive, Bettmann Archive, Archive Photos, Archive Photos, Archive Photos, Bettmann Archive, Bettmann Archive, Archive Photos, Archive Photos, Bettmann Archive, Bettmann Archive, Bettmann Archive, Archive Photos, Archive Photos, Bettmann Archive, Bettmann Archive, Archive Photos, Archive Photos, Bettmann Archive, Archive Photos, Archive Photos and Bettmann Archive. Interior photos: Frank Micelotta/Retna Ltd.: pp. 16,17; Archive Photos: pp. 15, 27, 28, top right 33; Bettmann Archive: pp. 26, top right 32, 72, 73, 80; UPI/Bettmann; pp. 8, 9, bottom left 32, far left and insert 33, 42; AP/Wide World Photos: pp. top left 32, bottom right 33, 51, 64, 65; p. 58, from left to right, top row: AP/Wide World Photos; second row: Bettmann Archive, AP/Wide World Photos, AP/ Wide World Photos; third row: Archive Photos, AP/Wide World Photos, AP/Wide World Photos; fourth row: AP/Wide World Photos; p. 59: top row: AP/Wide World Photos; second row: Wide World Photos, Bettmann Archive, AP/Wide World Photos, Archive Photos; third row: AP/Wide World Photos; fourth row: AP/Wide World Photos, AP/Wide World Photos, AP/Wide World Photos, Reuters/Bettmann, Bettmann Archive; p 85

HUH HUH
FOR
HOLLYWOOD

CREATED BY MIKE JUDGE
WRITTEN BY LARRY DOYLE

Beavis and Butt-head are not role models. They're not even human. They're cartoons.
Some of the things they do would cause a real person to get hurt, expelled, arrested, possibly deported.
To put it another way: don't try this at home.

Editor: Glenn Eichler
Art Direction: Roger Gorman/Design: Leah Sherman, Reiner, NYC
Production Supervisor: Dominie Mahl
Art Supervisor: Patrick Worlock
Artists & Inkers: John Allemand, Brad MacDonald, Bryon Moore
Artists: Mike Baez, Willy Hartland
Background Painter: Bill Long
Color Designers, Cel Painters: Lisa Klein, Monica Smith
Cel Painter: Marty Polansky
Air Brush Artist: Sophie Kittredge
Production Assistant: James Wood
Production Coordinator: Sara Duffy

Special thanks at MTV to: Cindy Charles, Ed Paparo, Renee Presser, Robin Silverman,
Donald Silvey, and Van Toffler.

Special thanks at Pocket Books to: Lynda Castillo, Gina Centrello, Kendra Falkenstein, Felice Javit, Eric Rayman,
Dave Stern, Kara Welsh, and Irene Yuss. Also thanks to Al Travison at Stevenson.

Photo Credits: Photofest p. 5, 6, 11, 12, 13, 18, 19, 34, 35, 40, 54, 56, 58, 69, 74, 84, 85;
Everett Collection p. 14, 16, 19, 20, 24, 29, 30, 34, 35, 38, 42, 50, 78, 79, 82, 86, 88, 90;
Celebrity Photo p. 76, 77, 92; AP/Wide World Photos p. 79; Globe Photo p.93.
Thanks also to KoCo Cards Hollywood CA.

HOW TO BECOME FAMOUS

UH, THEY ONLY PUT FAMOUS PEOPLE IN MOVIES, SO, LIKE, IF YOU WANT TO BE A BIG MOVIE STAR, YOU HAVE TO BE FAMOUS FIRST.

Name: Butt-Head, a.k.a. Dr. Juice, That Handsome Dude, El Diablo Macho, The Satisfier, Peter Johnson.

Name: Beavis, a.k.a. Dillhole, Buttmunch, Bumwipe, Chicken Choker, The Skid Mark Kid, Big Wuss, Richard Wadd

FIVE SURE WAYS TO GET FAMOUS

1. DO IT WITH SOMEBODY FAMOUS. LIKE THAT DUDE THAT DID IT WITH MADONNA. HE'S FAMOUS.

2. KILL SOMEBODY FAMOUS. LIKE ABRAHAM LINCOLN. HE KILLED SOME FAMOUS DUDE.

3. KILL TEN PEOPLE WHO AREN'T FAMOUS.

   ER, BUTT-HEAD, I THINK, UM, IT'S LIKE TWENTY PEOPLE NOW.

   UH, MAYBE. SO YOU SHOULD PROBABLY KILL LIKE FIFTY PEOPLE JUST TO BE ON THE SAFE SIDE.

   EH, BUT IF ONE OF THEM IS SORT OF FAMOUS, LIKE THAT DUDE WHO CRIES FOR BEER ON TV, THEN YOU DON'T HAVE TO KILL AS MANY, RIGHT?

   UH. I DUNNO. I GUESS YOU JUST HAVE TO TRY IT AND SEE. JUST KEEP KILLING PEOPLE, LIKE TWO OR THREE AT A TIME, UNTIL YOU'RE FAMOUS.

4. DO GOOD DEEDS UNTIL YOU'RE LIKE 106 OR SOMETHING.

5. GET YOUR NAME IN THE PAPERS.

GETTING YOUR NAME IN THE PAPERS

IT'S EASY TO GET YOUR NAME IN THE PAPERS. YOU JUST, LIKE, DO STUFF AND, UH, THEN REPORTERS COME TO YOUR HOUSE AND DON'T GO AWAY UNTIL YOU TALK TO THEM. AND THEN, LIKE, YOU'RE FAMOUS.

Highland Times-Item

Weather
Hot and dry, with increased tumbleweed activity and scattered tornadoes

Highland's Only Newspaper Since 1956

AREA TEENS FOUND NAKED, PROBED

By Ruth Davis
Highland Times-Item reporter

In a story bearing an eerie resemblance to last summer's blockbuster movies, two 14-year-old boys found naked and disoriented in a wheat field told police yesterday they were abducted by extraterrestrials who sucked the boys into their spacecraft using an artificial tornado and then forced them to perform an erotic striptease.

A shaved dog and strange crop markings found in the area were also the work of the aliens, the boys said. One of the boys claimed the aliens had performed invasive medical tests on him.

Police Chief Billy Bratton said he was not surprised by the boys' story. "We've had a number of alien abductions in the area, and this is consistent with what other victims have told us," Bratton said. "Except for the erotic striptease. Though I wouldn't put nothing past these extraterrestrials. They're not God-fearing like human Christian beings."

The two boys were found early Saturday in Sam Johnson's wheat field, just north of the Greased Palm Video Parlor and Package Liquors on Route 3. Police at the scene said the two youths, who were laughing uncontrollably and had trouble speaking coherently, were only able to give their names as "Beavis" and "Butt-Head." By late yesterday police had still not determined the boys' actual identities, though Bratton said no teenagers had been reported missing.

"Butt-Head" partially regained his senses first, police said. He told authorities that the boys were walking through the field discussing "algebra and poetry and Spanish" when a funnel cloud suddenly appeared before them.

"We were pulled into the suck zone," the boy said, becoming hysterical again. Over the next several hours, police were able to piece together the events that followed. The boys found themselves inside an alien ship, described as a long cigar-shaped craft with two large orbs at its base which the aliens called "nads." Inside the ship, the aliens, who said they were from Uranus (see police sketch, left), forced the youths to dance naked over their laps. "Beavis"

said the aliens then strapped him to a table and inserted a medical probe into his rectum. The device "hummed" for a few minutes, the boy said. He said the aliens then thanked him and said they had "learned a lot about our civilization."

The other boy vigorously denied being probed.

The shaved dog found with the teens was identified as being a poodle owned by Tom Anderson, a retired veteran. Anderson confirmed that the dog disappeared Friday evening, shortly after he had heard a banging and strange wail emanating from his tool shed. The boys speculated that the aliens had shaved the poodle in order to "see if it was really a dog."

The wheat field where the boys and dog were found was also marked by several areas where the wheat had been trampled into unusual shapes, including one matching the boys' description of the ship. In addition, one figure included a pair of large circles above a triangle, and numerous pairings of twin crescent moons.

The area showed no other sign of disruption, or of the tornado the boys said spirited them to the ship. Asked about this, "Butt-Head" explained that after the aliens deposited the youths back in the field, an elite government team arrived on a secret mission to eliminate any trace of the alien visit. The team leader then confiscated their clothes and told them, "You have been erased."

Police Chief Bratton dismissed this part of the boys' story, calling it "the product of surging hormones and an anti-American educational system."

YOUTH VIRTUE PLEDGE CANNED

The Highland Young People Pledge of Virtue planned for this day has been cancelled because of disagreement among its sponsors what constitutes virtue.

Clark Cobb, of the Christian Businessmen's Association, said his was withdrawing its support of the refusal of pledge founder Van Driessen to add masturbation to the list of activities youth are pledging to avoid.

"There are no self-abuse on the highway to he—" explained. "But the road paved with the seed of—"

"Self-pleasuring is you give yourself," Driessen, a social studies teacher at Highland High School said. "... masturbation only ... closet."

The two had ... over whether masturbation belongs on the "no" list. "Cowardly ..." insisted. "Cowardly ... gift from God ..." countered, "God lo..."

GETTING ON TV

WHEN YOUR NAME IS IN THE PAPERS, THE PEOPLE ON TV FIND OUT SOMEHOW.

> HEY, D'YA HEAR ABOUT THIS *BEAVIS AND BUTT-HEAD*? YEAH, THE *TEENAGERS* WHO WERE AB*DUCTED* BY **ALIENS**. THESE *CHARACTERS* SAID THE ALIENS TOOK ALL THEIR CLOTHES, *PERFORMED* **ANAL PROBES** ON THEM, AND **SHAVED** THEIR **POODLE**. YEAH. BUT, Y'KNOW, THEY WERE **LUCKY**. ON *HOLLYWOOD BOULEVARD*, THAT WOULDA COST 'EM TWO HUNDRED **BUCKS**!

HUH HUH HUH HE SAID "ANAL." HUH HUH. YEAH. HEH HEH. AND "POO." THIS GUY'S A LOT FUNNIER THAN THAT OTHER GUY.

X-Files—Drama *1:00* "Suck Zone" Mulder doubts boys' story of alien abduction

THIS DUO VOWED IF THEY EVER ENCOUNTERED THE ALIENS WHO ABDUCTED THEM AGAIN, THEY WOULD "KICK THEIR URANUSES."

Sally—Discussion *1:00* Boys abducted by aliens give advice to mothers of daughters who dress like sluts.

Ricki—Discussion *1:00* "I want a date with those boys who were abducted by aliens."

MAD TV (CC)—Comedy *1:00* Sketches include, "Beavis and Butt-Master," "E.E.T. Extraterrestrial Entertainment Tonight," and "Aliens XXII: Man from Uranus"

Entertainment Tonight (CC) "Will Hollywood Abduct Beavis and Butt-Head?" An exclusive E.T. probe.

ER, UM, "WHO ARE BATMAN AND ROBIN?"
BEAVIS, YOU DUMBASS. THAT'S US.
WE'RE BATMAN AND ROBIN? HOLY THAT'S COOL, BATMAN!

GETTING THE CALL FROM HOLLYWOOD

SO, UH, THEN THIS DUDE FROM HOLLYWOOD CALLS AND SAYS, "YOU GUYS ARE *E.T.* MEETS THE *WIZARD OF OZ* MEETS *DELIVERANCE*!" AND THEN YOU TALK TO HIM FOR A WHILE AND THEN HE SAYS, "MEETS *DUMB AND DUMBER*!" AND THEN YOU ASK HIM TO SEND YOU MONEY, AND HE SAYS, "WE'LL BREAK BREAD," WHICH SUCKS BECAUSE IF YOU WANTED TO BREAK BREAD, YOU COULD JUST GO DOWN TO THE KWIK FOOD, AND NOT ALL THE WAY TO HOLLYWOOD.

UH, THIS IS IMPORTANT: WHEN A HOLLYWOOD DUDE SAYS "CHOW," IT MEANS HE HAS TO GET OFF THE PHONE TO GO EAT SOME NACHOS OR SOMETHING.

GO HOLLYWOOD, YOUNG MAN

So, uh, once you're famous you have to go to Hollywood because that's like where the chicks go to meet famous people.

BUSES

BUSES SUCK, AND LIKE THE PEOPLE ON THEM SMELL BAD.

YEAH, AND LIKE, THERE'S NO PLACE TO POOP. YOU HAVE TO, LIKE, POOP IN YOUR PANTS.

BEAVIS, THERE IS TOO A PLACE TO TAKE A DUMP ON THE BUS. IT'S IN THE BACK, NEXT TO WHERE THE FAT GUY SITS.

REALLY? UM. BUT BUSES STILL SMELL PRETTY BAD.

AIR MAIL

THIS IS LIKE FLYING IN A PLANE, EXCEPT YOU'RE IN A BOX.

UM, THEY LIKE SHOOT YOU OUT OF A CANNON OR SOMETHING.

UH, THIS IS IMPORTANT: YOU HAVE TO LIKE PUT HOLES IN THE BOX.

ER, WHY?

BECAUSE, BUTTMUNCH, SO THEY CAN FEED YOU NACHOS IF YOU GET HUNGRY.

PLANES

PLANES ARE FASTER THAN BUSES, BECAUSE THEY DON'T HAVE TO LIKE PICK PEOPLE UP AND STUFF.

PLUS THERE'S THESE CHICKS WHO BRING YOU SNACKS.

HUH HUH. IT'S LIKE HAVING A GIRLFRIEND.

YEAH, EXCEPT THEY WON'T DO IT WITH YOU.

BEAVIS, THAT'S A DIFFERENT KIND OF GIRLFRIEND. GIRLFRIENDS WHO DO IT WITH YOU NEVER BRING YOU SNACKS.

HM. I GUESS IF I HAD TO CHOOSE, I'D PICK A GIRLFRIEND WHO BRINGS ME SNACKS.

GOOD CHOICE, BEAVIS. CAUSE EVEN GIRLFRIENDS WHO DO IT WITH YOU WOULDN'T DO IT WITH YOU.

YEAH, SO THIS WAY AT LEAST I GET A SNACK.

HITCHHIKING

HITCHHIKING IS SPECIAL.

YEAH. CAUSE THE GUY WHO PICKS YOU UP MIGHT BE, LIKE, A INSANE MANIAC, AND UH, HE CAN TELL YOU ABOUT ALL THE PEOPLE HE'S KILLED AND LIKE WHAT HE DID TO THEM AFTERWARDS.

UH, YEAH. PLUS IT'S FREE.

HOLLYWOOD SIGHTS TO SEE

UH, WHEN YOU GET TO HOLLYWOOD AND YOU CALL THE HOLLYWOOD DUDE WHO CALLED YOU, AND THEN THEY SAY HE DOESN'T WORK THERE ANYMORE, YOU MIGHT AS WELL GO SEE THE SIGHTS.

UM, THIS IS THE LA BRA TAR PITS. THERE'S SUPPOSED TO BE DINOSAURS HERE.

YEAH, BUT YOU CAN'T SEE 'EM BECAUSE THE WATER IS, LIKE, REALLY DARK. AND STICKY.

BEAVIS, YOU DILLHOLE. THE REASON THERE'S NO DINOSAURS HERE IS THEY'RE OUT MAKING THAT *JERSEY PARK* SEQUEL.

OH, OH YEAH.

IN THIS ONE, THEY'RE GOING TO EAT THOSE STUPID KIDS FROM THE FIRST ONE.

HEH HEH HEH. HEY, BUTT-HEAD, I'LL BET IF THEY DID THAT IN THE FIRST ONE, IT WOULD HAVE BEEN, LIKE, A BIG HIT.

BEAVIS, YOU'RE BEGINNING TO TALK LIKE ONE OF THOSE HOLLYWOOD DUDES ALREADY.

THIS IS THAT CHINESE MOVIE THEATER NAMED AFTER HO CHEE MANN.

HEH HEH. YOU SAID 'HO.

HUH HUH. YEAH. HUH HUH.

HEY, BUTT-HEAD, IF THIS THIS THE HO THEATER, HOW COME ALL THE 'HOS ARE DOWN THE STREET?

BEAVIS, I'M SURE SOME OF THESE CHICKS ARE 'HOS. WHY DON'T YOU ASK THEM?

UH, THESE LETTERS ARE A LOT BIGGER THAN THEY LOOK.

YEAH, UM, AND HEAVY. THEY, LIKE, DON'T MOVE AT ALL.

BEAVIS, I'LL BET THESE LETTERS WERE LEFT HERE BY ANCIENT ASTRONAUTS.

There's this museum in Hollywood that has just movie stars in it.

Hey, Butt-Head, wouldn't it be cool if like all museums just had movie stars and not like Indian blankets and stuffed ocelots and crap?

That would be too cool to be true.

Um, this Rambo dude hasn't moved in a while. Maybe he's hypnotized or something.

You dumbass, Beavis. He's made of wax.

Really? Er, um, I thought movie stars were made of plastic.

No, asswipe, he's just like a statue. I mean, the real Rambo is like, twice as big as this.

Oh. Oh yeah.

This is, like, the drawer where Marilyn Monroe lives.

Um, she was, like, the fifth president or something.

No Buttmunch, she was like that chick who was the first chick who was ever naked.

Really?

She was, like, a pioneer. Hey, Beavis, I think she's still naked in there.

Urh! Urh! How do you open this thing? C'mon, Butt-Head, gimme a hand here!

Uh, this is important: In Hollywood, even dead people have burglar alarms.

CHEAP SOUVENIRS

Souvenirs in Hollywood are like really expensive.
Yeah, like, "I went to Hollywood and spent 25 dollars and all I got was this dumb t-shirt."
I told you not to buy it, dumbass.
Well, I didn't know they were going to charge me, like, 40 dollars for it.
That's because you didn't shop around. There's like lots of cheap stuff just lying around Hollywood.
Yeah, like bums and stuff.
Beavis, that dude wasn't a bum. Remember, he said he was, like, an independent producer or something.
Yeah, he was like producing a bad smell.

DOLLS
These are the official Planet of the Hollywood Apes dolls. The guy gave us a special deal cause he liked us.

MEMORY-O-BEELIA
This is like a piece of the dress that Marilyn Monroe wasn't wearing when she posed naked, and it only cost a dollar!

HEADS
In back of the wax museum there's like free heads. You can use them to go bowling.

1-555-32?-523
MAKE THIS FAT LADY SING
Call Now
TUB O' LUV
FUNTIME

TRADING CARDS
Everywhere you look, there's these free Hollywood chick trading cards all over the sidewalk and in the gutter and in the garbage and in the bottom of urinals. Beavis collected like a hundred of them.

Er, actually 7,302, Butt-Head. Not counting the ones that are stuck together.

STARS
There's like these stars on the sidewalk in Hollywood, and there's these guys who for like $10 will give you one. This star is from that MTV dude who, like, was in *Encino Man* and then like died or something.

COOL PARTS

BIG GUNS ARE COOL.
   AND LIKE, THE BIGGER THE GUN IS, THE COOLER
IT IS. BECAUSE CHICKS GO FOR THE DUDES WITH THE
BIGGEST GUNS.
   YEAH, LIKE, "IS THAT A LEG IN YOUR PANTS, OR
DO YOU HAVE A REALLY BIG GUN?"
   "HEY, BABY, THEY CALL ME BAZOOKA JOE."
   EH, BUTT-HEAD, I THOUGHT YOUR NAME WAS
BUTT-HEAD.
   I WAS JUST PLAYING A CHARACTER, DILLHOLE!
HIS NAME IS BAZOOKA JOE AND HE'S GOT A
BAZOOKA THAT DRIVES THE CHICKS WILD.
   EH, I THOUGHT BAZOOKA JOE HAD A BASEBALL
CAP. AND I'VE NEVER SEEN HIM WITH ANY CHICKS.
   BEAVIS, YOU'RE JUST LUCKY MY BAZOOKA IS IN
THE SHOP.

MAP OF THE MOVIE STARS' HOMES

ONE OF THE COOL THINGS ABOUT HOLLYWOOD IS LIKE IF YOU'RE FAMOUS YOU CAN JUST STOP BY OTHER FAMOUS PEOPLE'S HOUSES AND WATCH THEIR TV AND STUFF. SO HERE'S WHERE ALL THE FAMOUS PEOPLE LIVE. BUT DON'T GO THERE IF YOU'RE NOT FAMOUS, BECAUSE, LIKE, IN HOLLYWOOD IT'S LEGAL FOR FAMOUS PEOPLE TO KILL YOU.

1. ARNOLD SCHWARZENEGGER. HE MUST OF USED UP ALL HIS WEAPONS AND EXPLOSIVES AND STUFF IN HIS LAST MOVIE, CAUSE ALL HE HAD WERE THESE OLD GOLF CLUBS, WHICH EVEN SUCKED FOR SWORDFIGHTING.

2. WHOOPI GOLDBERG. SHE SURE SCREAMS AND SWEARS A LOT, FOR A NUN.

3. ROSEANNE. SHE'S, LIKE, ONLY FIVE FEET TALL AND THREE FEET WIDE, BUT SHE STILL HITS PRETTY HARD.

4. O.J. SIMPSON. THIS IS THAT DUDE WHO STARRED IN THAT MOVIE ABOUT THAT WHITE CAR THAT WOULD EXPLODE IF IT WENT, LIKE, OVER 15 MILES AN HOUR. HE BOUGHT US BURGERS AND ASKED US IF WE WANTED TO COME LIVE WITH HIM CAUSE WE REMINDED HIM OF SOMEONE. BUT, UH, HE WAS KIND OF CREEPY SO WE SAID NO, AND THEN HE LIKE GAVE US A BAG OF HIS DIRTY CLOTHES.

5. LEONARD NIMOY. SO, UH, I GUESS VULCANS ONLY SHOW EMOTIONS WHEN YOU WALK IN ON THEM SITTING ON THE TOILET.

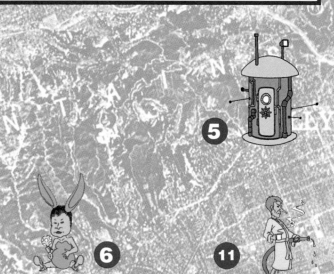

HOLLYWOOD

5

6

11

BEVERLY HILLS

10

9

13

Culver City

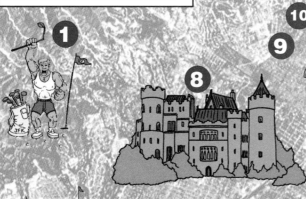

1

8

4

3

BEWARE OF DOGS OF THE STARS

FREDERICK OF HOLLYWOOD

WARNING: FILM STUDENTS

6. PLAYBOY MANSION. <u>WARNING: IT SUCKS.</u> THERE'S SUPPOSED TO BE ALL THESE NAKED CHICKS STUFFED IN ALL THESE LITTLE GROTTOS, BUT MRS. PLAYBOY MADE THEM ALL PUT ON THEIR CLOTHES AND GO OUT AND GET REAL JOBS. SO THERE WEREN'T ANY BUNNIES, JUST BABIES, AND MRS. PLAYBOY WOULD EVEN LET US WATCH HER FEED 'EM.

7. RONALD REAGAN. THIS GUY WAS COOL. HE USED TO BE LIKE KING OF COWBOYS. HE TOOK US FOR A RIDE ON HIS HORSE, AND TOLD US STORIES ABOUT HOW HE DROPPED ALL THESE H-BOMBS ON RUSSIA AND HOW HE GOT HIS LEGS CUT OFF ONCE. BUT THEN HIS MOM SHOWED UP AND MADE US LEAVE.

8. THE SPELLING ESTATE. THIS IS THE HOUSE WHERE THEY BUILT TORI SPELLING.

9, 10. CHARLETON HESTON AND EDDIE VAN HALEN. MOSES AND THAT VAN HALEN DUDE LIVE, LIKE, RIGHT, ACROSS THE STREET FROM ONE ANOTHER. WE SAW THEM JAMMING TOGETHER.

11. STEVE MARTIN. HE'S NOT THAT WILD AND CRAZY AT SIX IN THE MORNING.

12. HEIDI FLEISS, THE HOLLYWOOD MADAME. WE WENT TRICK OR TREATING HERE, BUT THE MAID SAID THE MADAME OF THE HOUSE WASN'T GOING TO BE BACK FOR THREE TO FIVE HALLOWEENS.

13. THE MENENDEZ HOUSE. THIS IS THE HOUSE WHERE THOSE TWO DUDES KILLED THEIR PARENTS FOR MAKING THEM WEAR STUPID WIGS.

14. JULIETTE LEWIS. SHE WAS LIKE THE ONE CHICK IN DUSK TILL DAWN WHO DIDN'T GET NAKED OR TURN INTO A VAMPIRE. SHE MUST OF FELT PRETTY GUILTY, CAUSE SHE DIDN'T WANT TO TALK ABOUT IT.

15. BILLY IDOL. THIS IS WHERE THE "WHITE WEDDING" DUDE WAS SUPPOSED TO BE, BUT HE WASN'T HOME, WHICH IS WEIRD CAUSE IT'S NOT LIKE HE HAS ANYTHING BETTER TO DO.

16. MADONNA'S "CASTILLO DEL LAGO" ("CASTLE MADE OUT OF LEGOS"). MADONNA LIVES IN THIS GIANT CASTLE, ONLY SHE WAS LIKE OUT HAVING A BABY WHEN WE GOT THERE. BUT, LIKE, IN THE BASEMENT, THERE WAS THIS HUGE DUNGEON FILLED WITH YOUNG MUSCLE DUDES WEARING ONLY, LIKE, SPEEDOS. THEY LOOKED REALLY SCARED.

MOMENTS THAT SUCK

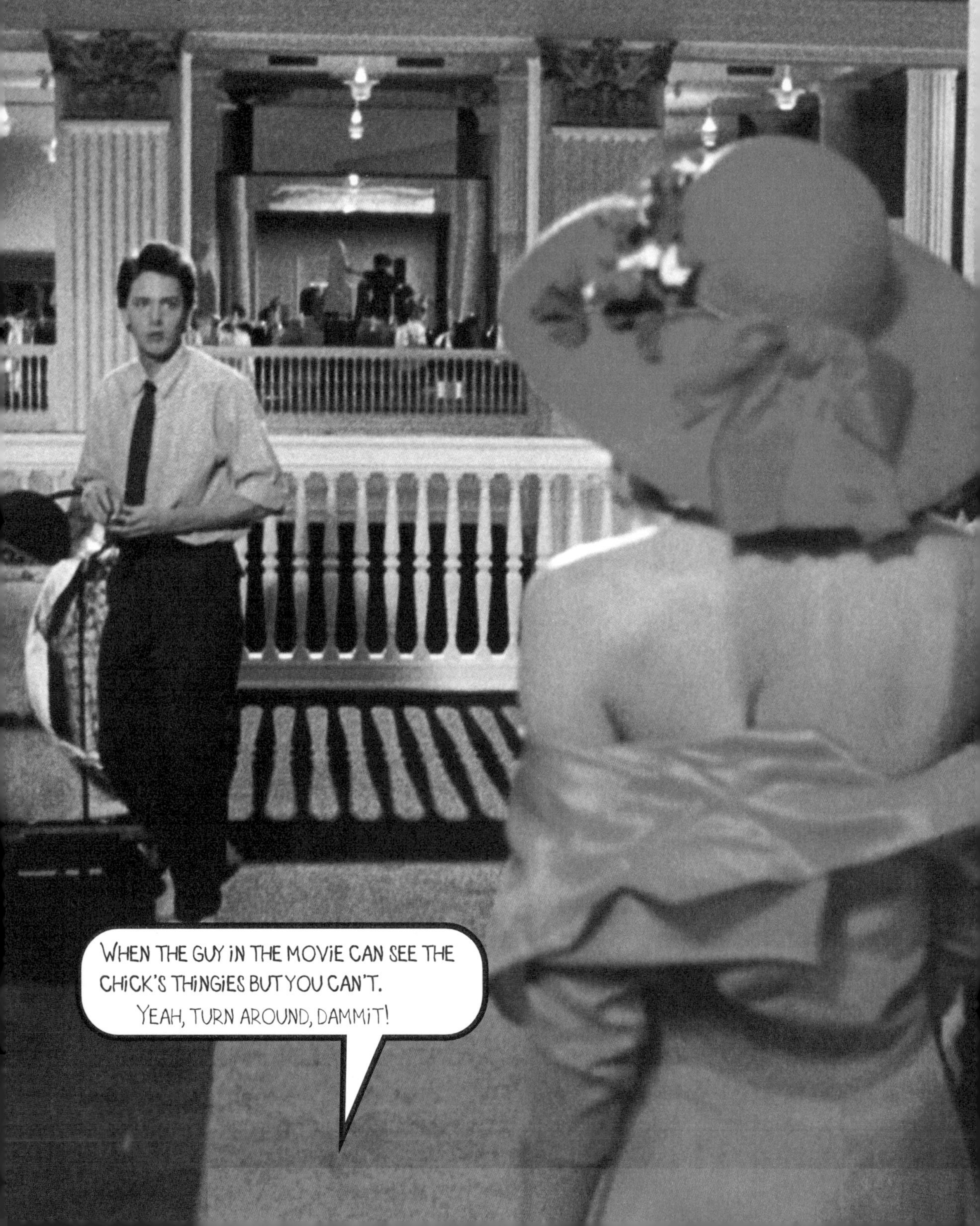

HOLLYWOOD PEOPLE WHO SUCK

NOT EVERYBODY IN HOLLYWOOD IS COOL.

CHICKS WITH NAMES LIKE DICK

THERE'S THESE OTHER CHICKS ON HOLLYWOOD BOULEVARD WHO WILL LIKE DO IT WITH YOU FOR LIKE ONLY TEN BUCKS, BUT THERE'S A CATCH.

YEAH! THEY WANT YOU TO GIVE *THEM* THE TEN BUCKS.

NO, DUMBASS, THE CATCH IS THAT THEY'RE, LIKE, REALLY GUYS.

WHAT?!

YEAH, THEY'RE CHICKS WITH MONKEYS, BEAVIS.

NOOO! YOU'RE KIDDING, RIGHT, BUTT-HEAD? ER, TELL ME YOU'RE KIDDING.

FAMOUS OLD BAGS

SHE LIKE TELLS YOU SHE'S A BIG FAMOUS STAR, BUT LIKE WHEN YOU GET TO HER HOUSE SHE JUST SHOWS YOU A BUNCH OF OLD BLACK AND WHITE MOVIES STARRING SOME YOUNG CHICK WHO YOU'VE NEVER SEEN BEFORE.

YEAH, AND SHE'S GOT THIS PET MONKEY, AND SHE WON'T LET YOU PLAY WITH IT.

BEAVIS, THAT MONKEY WAS DEAD.

RIGHT. SO WHAT'S THE HARM?

JAPANESE SCAM ARTISTS

THEY, LIKE, GIVE YOU A CAMERA, AND THEN WHEN YOU LIKE TRY TO WALK AWAY, THEY LIKE START SCREAMING AT YOU AND MAKE YOU GIVE IT BACK.

INDEPENDENT PRODUCERS ON PARK BENCHES

THIS SMELLY DUDE ASKS IF YOU WANT TO BE IN THE MOVIES AND YOU SAY, "UH, DO WE LOOK LIKE DUMBASSES OR SOMETHING? SURE WE WANT TO BE IN THE MOVIES." AND SO THEN YOU LIKE GO TO HIS OFFICE, WHICH IS LIKE IN A COOL ABANDONED BUILDING, AND ALL OF A SUDDEN HE SAYS YOU HAVE TO LIKE AUDITION, WHICH SOUNDS LIKE IT SUCKS BUT IT TURNS OUT YOU JUST HAVE TAKE OFF YOUR PANTS. SO THEN HE SAYS HE'LL BE RIGHT BACK AND HE LEAVES, BUT HE NEVER COMES BACK WITH ANY CHICKS, OR YOUR PANTS, OR ANYTHING.

AGENTS

UH, WHEN YOU GO TO HOLLYWOOD, PEOPLE ALWAYS ASK YOU, "WHO'S YOUR AGENT?" AND WHAT'S COOL IS TO SAY, "BOND. JAMES BOND."

YEAH, BUT BUTT-HEAD, SOMETIMES THEY SLAP YOU WHEN YOU SAY THAT.

THAT'S WHEN YOU KNOW IT'S TIME TO GET AN AGENT, SO THEY CAN, LIKE, SLAP HIM INSTEAD. THERE'S FOUR KINDS OF AGENTS TO CHOOSE FROM:

OLD AGENT DUDE
HE, LIKE, KNOWS EVERYBODY WHO'S DEAD NOW.

YOUNG AGENT DUDE
HE'S ALWAYS TALKING TO DUDES WHO AREN'T THERE.

OLD AGENT CHICK
SHE, LIKE, DID EVERYBODY WHO'S DEAD NOW.

SCARY AGENT CHICK
SHE KEEPS SAYING SHE HAS BIG NADS.

DEALS

WHEN YOU GET AN AGENT, THEY CAN LIKE GET YOU DEALS.
YEAH, AND MONEY AND CHICKS!
THAT'S WHAT A DEAL IS, DUMBASS.

all other compensation, monetary or other monies, notwithstanding, STUDIO agrees to provide BEAVIS AND BUTT-HEAD, for the duration of this contract and thereafter, additional compensations and perquisites inclusive of, but not limited to, those enumerated herein.

1. A trailer of equal or greater size to any other in the PRODUCTION, previously designated as the "Those Boys Who Were Abducted By Aliens Project," though not to be less than thirty-six (36) feet in length, and to be equipped and decorated in a manner deemed acceptable to BEAVIS AND BUTT-HEAD, cost of such decoration not to exceed $100,000. Trailer shall be equipped with
   i. A commercial nacho machine similar to those employed in movie theaters and convenience stores, to be replenished three times daily.
   ii. Three (3) color television monitors, not less than twenty (20) inches in diameter, all operation from a single remote, and dedicated as follows: one (1) shall be connected to a cable system that shall include at least 99 channels and all premium services, now known or which may be known in the future in all media, currently existing or not yet invented, throughout the universe; one (1) shall be connected to a state of the art stereo-video center, and supplied with not less than ten (10) videos daily of current first run movies, each rated not less that PG-13; and one (1) shall be connected to a state-of-the-art security surveillance system, installed in each of the other trailers in the PRODUCTION.
   iii. A shower with dual Shower Massage™ adjustable shower heads and sufficient water pressure to achieve pounding, pulsating action.
2. Four (4) female production assistants, to be equipped and decorated in a manner deemed acceptable to BEAVIS AND BUTT-HEAD, whose duties shall be inclusive of, but not limited to

UH, THIS IS IMPORTANT: WHEN YOUR AGENT ASKS YOU TO DO LUNCH, YOU'RE NOT SUPPOSED TO, LIKE, DO HIS LUNCH.

COOL PARTS

WHEN OLD ASIAN DUDES SAY COOL STUFF, THAT'S COOL.
    LIKE, "GRASSHOPPER, YOU MUST SPRING FORWARD AND FALL BACK."
    YEAH, AND LIKE, "DON'T BUY A POKE WITH A PIG."
    NO, BEAVIS, I WAS THE ONE WHO TOLD YOU THAT.
    YOU ARE WISE, OLD MASTER.

MOVIES THROUGHOUT HISTORY

So, like, you get a movie deal, so then it's a good time to learn some stuff about the movies.

1 MILLION B.C. The first movie is about naked cave chicks fighting dinosaurs. It sets the standard that all other movies must be judged by.

2001 B.C. Cave monkeys discover how to turn bones into space ships.

ANCIENT TIMES Romans feed Baptists to the Lions. It's the first summer blockbuster!

Jason kills skeletons. The first *Friday the 13th* movie, only it doesn't count because the skeletons didn't do it before Jason chopped them up.

1941 Mr. Van Driessen says *Citizen Kane* is the best movie ever, but it sucks, except for the part where, uh... No, I guess the whole thing sucks.

1967 *Planet of the Apes.* As part of all the social upchuck in the sixties, monkeys win the right to make their own movies.

1969 *Deep Throat* and *Easy Rider*, the first two porno movies, come out. They're huh huh Coming Attractions huh huh huh huh. In the first one, this chick does it with anyone, even dudes with Village People mustaches. In the other one, these two dudes ride hogs.

1971 Cool dudes invented.

1980 *Friday the 13th.* Dead hockey player kills dudes and chicks right after they do it. The Age of Cool Movies begins.

1981 *Friday the 13th, Part 2.* Just like the first one, only different dudes and chicks get killed.

1982 *Friday the 13th, Part 3 .* Like the first one and the second one put together, then cut in half.

1984 *Friday the 13th: the Final Chapter.* Since it had the word "chapter" in it, we thought it might be a book so we didn't go.

1985 *Friday the 13th, Part V: A New Beginning.* Corey Feldman gets killed in this one, making it the best Jason movie ever.

1986 *Friday the 13th, Part VI: Jason Lives.* He gets hit by lightning and turns into a Frankenjason.

1988 *Friday the 13th, Part VII: The New Blood.* Actually, it looked like some of the same blood from before.

1989 *Friday the 13th, Part VIII: Jason Takes Manhattan.* He, like, kills that Woody dude. Huh huh Woody huh huh. Then he like climbs the Empire State building and does battle with a giant monkey.

1991 Beavis sees *Backdraft* 27 times.

1993 *Friday the 13th, Part IX: Jason Goes to Hell.* They must of, like, gotten Beavis's letter.

THE PRESENT People stop seeing movies until, like, our movie comes out because they know that any movie they see now will suck when they think about it after seeing our movie.

WHEN SOMEBODY GETS SCARED AND YOU THINK THEIR EYEBALLS ARE ABOUT TO GET SUCKED OUT, BUT IT'S JUST A DAMN CAT BEHIND THE DOOR. THAT SUCKS.

YEAH, EH, LIKE, UNLESS THE CAT IS A ZOMBIE.

CATS CAN'T BE ZOMBIES, BEAVIS. UNLESS YOU KILL THEM, LIKE, NINE TIMES OR SOMETHING.

EH, OH YEAH. BUT WHAT IF YOU LOSE COUNT?

THEN YOU HAVE TO START OVER. CAUSE, LIKE, YOU CAN'T TELL THE DIFFERENCE BETWEEN A LIVE CAT AND A ZOMBIE CAT.

HEY, BUTT-HEAD, MAYBE ALL CATS ARE ZOMBIES.

NOT ANY CATS I EVER MET. HUH HUH.

THE DIFFERENCE BETWEEN REAL LIFE AND MOVIES

In real life, everything sucks. In the movies, everything is cool.
Even things that suck, suck in a cool way in the movie.

REAL LIFE   MOVIES

Tom Anderson
He's a old dork.

Tommy Ray Anderson
He's a scary old dork.

Coach Buzzcut
He's, like, a gym teacher who can do one-armed push-ups.

Sgt. Karl "Coach" Buzzcut
He's, like, a gym teacher who fought in the Franco-American wars where Nazi gorillas bit off his arm and so now he can only do one-armed push-ups.

Stewart
He's a fat kid.

The Fat Kid
He's dead.

THE COOLEST MOVIES OF ALL TIME THAT WE DIDN'T MAKE

IF YOU'RE GOING TO MAKE MOVIES, THESE WOULD BE COOL MOVIES TO MAKE.
YEAH, BUT BUTT-HEAD, SOMEBODY, LIKE, ALREADY MADE THESE MOVIES.
BEAVIS, YOU'RE NEVER GOING TO GET ANYWHERE IN THIS BUSINESS.

BARBWIRE (1996)

IT STARTS LIKE WITH PAMELA ANDERSON LEE, THE LIFEGUARD CHICK WHO'S MARRIED TO BRUCE LEE, THE DUDE WHO'S LIKE A KARAOKE EXPERT, AND SHE'S, UH, WEARING THIS RUBBER DRESS AND...

THEY'RE SPRAYING HER WITH A GIANT HOSE!

LET ME TELL IT, BUTTWIPE. THEY'RE SPRAYING HER WITH THIS GIANT HOSE AND...

HER THINGIES POP OUT!

BEAVIS, DON'T MAKE ME SPRAY YOU WITH MY GIANT HOSE. SO, LIKE, HER THINGIES POP OUT. THEY'RE LIKE A LOT BIGGER THAN ON THE TV, AND, HUH HUH, THEY'RE SLIPPERY WHEN WET. AND THEN SHE SEES THIS GUY STARING AT HER, AND SHE LIKE, TAKES OFF HER HIGH HEEL SHOES AND SHE LIKE THROWS IT...

AND THE SPIKE GOES RIGHT IN HIS FOREHEAD!

AND THEN, LIKE, THE MOVIE'S OVER. THEY TURN ON THE LIGHTS AND MAKE YOU LEAVE THE THEATER.

YEAH, IT'S SHORT, BUT COOL.

INDEPENDENCE DAY (1996)

THESE ALIENS COME AND THEY BLOW UP THE WHITE HOUSE AND, UH, SOME MONUMENTS AND OTHER HISTORY THINGS.

SO RIGHT THERE YOU KNOW THESE ALIENS ARE COOL. CAUSE NOW KIDS DON'T HAVE TO MEMORIZE ALL THAT STUFF ANYMORE.

UH, YEAH. SO THEN THEY BLOW UP A BUNCH MORE CITIES AND PEOPLE AND STUFF, GIVING US NO CHOICE BUT TO KICK THEIR PESKY ALIEN ASSES.

YOU KNOW, BUTT-HEAD, I THOUGHT THE MOVIE WAS PRETTY REALISTIC, EXCEPT FOR THE PART WHERE THE ALIENS DIDN'T STICK ANYTHING UP ANYBODY'S BUTT. CAUSE YOU KNOW, REAL ALIENS DO THAT. THEY DID THAT TO ME.

BEAVIS, EVERYBODY ALREADY KNOWS ALL ABOUT THE LITTLE BUTT GAMES YOU PLAYED WITH THOSE ALIENS. WE WERE ON JERRY SPRINGER, REMEMBER?

THE ROCK (1996)

UH, I'M NOT SURE WHAT HAPPENS IN THIS MOVIE, BUT LOTS OF STUFF EXPLODES.

STRIPTEASE (1996)

THIS IS DEMI MOORE AT HER BUTT-NAKEDEST. YOU GET TO SEE HER THINGIES MOVING, AND WITHOUT PAINT ON THEM OR ANYTHING. AND LIKE THERE'S THIS OTHER CHICK, PANDORA PEAKS, WHO MUST HAVE BEEN INVOLVED IN SOME KIND OF FREAK RADIOACTIVE LABORATORY ACCIDENT BECAUSE SHE'S GOT AMAZING COLOSSAL THINGIES.

YEAH, AND, LIKE, BURT REYNOLDS'S DAD IS IN IT.

THE NUTTY PROFESSOR (1996)

HUH HUH HUH HUH HUH HUH HUH HUH. THEY ALL FARTED HUH HUH HUH.

HEH HEH HEH HEH HEH HEH. YEAH, I LAUGHED UNTIL I FARTED HEH HEH.

HUH HUH. AND THEN I LAUGHED SOME MORE HUH HUH HUH.

MISSION: IMPOSSIBLE (1996)

YOUR MISSION, IF YOU DECIDE TO ACCEPT IT, IS TO BLOW UP EVERYTHING AND MAKE TOM CRUISE NOT SUCK FOR ONCE. MISSION ACCOMPLISHED.

YOU KNOW WHAT WOULD BE COOL, BUTT-HEAD? WHAT IF THEY MADE THIS, LIKE, INTO A TV SHOW AND LIKE, THEY COULD HAVE A DIFFERENT MISSION AND WEAR COOL DISGUISES AND BLOW UP DIFFERENT STUFF EVERY WEEK. WOULDN'T THAT BE COOL?

DON'T GET YOUR HOPES UP, BEAVIS. NOTHING THAT COOL WOULD EVER BE ON TV.

ERASER (1996)

ARNOLD SCHWARZENEGGER LIKE ERASES AND KILLS PEOPLE. DIFFERENT PEOPLE, I MEAN. LIKE HE ERASES THAT CHICK WHO WAS MISS AMERICA, THE ONE WHOSE TALENT WAS POSING NAKED. AND HE LIKE KILLS, UH, EVERYBODY ELSE.

TWISTER (1996)

HUH HUH HUH. THIS MOVIE REMINDED ME OF THAT TIME WE ALMOST DID IT WITH THOSE TWO CHICKS IN THE TRAILER DURING THE TORNADO.

YEAH. HEH HEH HEH. EVERY TIME I SEE A TORNADO I GET LIKE, EH, A WARM FEELING.

PLUS IN THIS MOVIE, THEY MAKE A COW FLY. WHICH IS, LIKE, REALLY HARD TO DO.

DUSK TIL DAWN (1996)

STRIPPERS TURN INTO VAMPIRE ZOMBIE CHICKS WHO GET BLASTED, DECRAPITATED, FLAME-THROWED AND THEN EXPLODED.

IT'S THE PERFECT MOVIE.

WEEKEND AT BERNIE'S 2 (1993)

THIS SEQUEL SURPASSES THE ORIGINAL IN EVERY WAY. BECAUSE, LIKE, IN THE FIRST ONE, BERNIE IS JUST DEAD, AND IN THIS ONE, HE'S LIKE DEAD BUT HE'S ALSO A VOODOO ZOMBIE DUDE WHO LIKE GOES TO THE BAHAMAS AND PERFORMS THE LAMBADA — THE FORBIDDEN DANCE.

AND BUTT-HEAD, DON'T FORGET, HE'S ALSO GOT A SPEAR THROUGH HIS HEAD.

YEAH, HE'S A WILD AND CRAZY ZOMBIE.

TOP SUCKING MOVIES OF ALL TIME

MOST MOVIES SUCK, BUT THESE MOVIES SUCK IN A VERY SPECIAL WAY.

THE CABLE GUY (1996)

THAT PET DETECTIVE DUDE IS IN IT, BUT HE DOESN'T TALK WITH HIS BUTT.

YEAH, HE THINKS HE'S LIKE TOO BIG OF A STAR OR SOMETHING.

UH, YEAH. UH, YOU KNOW, BEAVIS, NO MATTER HOW BIG OF A STAR I GET TO BE, I WON'T FORGET MY BUTT.

ME NEITHER. MY BUTT IS GOING TO HAVE A BIG SPEECH IN EVERY MOVIE. ER, I MEAN, JUST AS SOON AS I CAN TEACH IT HOW TO TALK.

BEAVIS, YOU MEAN YOUR BUTT CAN'T TALK?

ER, EH, NO. IT JUST, ER, KIND OF MUMBLES.

BEAVIS, IT SOUNDS LIKE YOU'VE GOT A BUTT IMPEDIMENT.

JAMES AND THE GIANT PEACH (1996)

IN THE POSTER IT LOOKED LIKE IT MIGHT BE A CHICK'S BUTT OR SOMETHING. BUT IT'S REALLY A PEACH. SO DON'T WASTE YOUR MONEY.

DEAD MAN WALKING (1995)

HE'S NOT EVEN DEAD UNTIL, LIKE, THE END.

THAT PART WAS PRETTY COOL.

YEAH, BUT THEN HE DOESN'T WALK AFTER THAT. HE'S JUST, LIKE, "DEAD MAN SITTING."

YEAH, IT WAS FALSE ADVERTISING.

ELEPHANT MAN (1980)

VAN DRIESSEN MADE US WATCH THIS ONE. THE GUY IS SUPPOSED TO BE AN ELEPHANT BUT HE DOESN'T HAVE A TRUNK OR BIG EARS AND CAN'T FLY OR ANYTHING. AFTER WE WATCHED IT, VAN DRIESSEN ASKED US IF WE LEARNED ANYTHING. AND BEAVIS SAID, "YEAH, SOME PEOPLE ARE FREAKS!" AND THEN VAN DRIESSEN MADE US WATCH THE WHOLE THING AGAIN, AND IT SUCKED EVEN WORSE THE SECOND TIME BECAUSE YOU KNEW THE WHOLE TIME THE ELEPHANT DUDE WASN'T GOING TO STAMPEDE OR ANYTHING.

NAKED CITY (1948)

WE LIKE STAYED UP UNTIL FOUR O'CLOCK IN THE MORNING TO SEE THIS MOVIE AND THERE WASN'T EVEN A SINGLE NAKED PERSON, NOT EVEN FOR A SECOND, NOT EVEN LIKE A CHICK LEANING OVER.

ER, I SAW LOTS OF NAKED PEOPLE. AND THEY WERE WRITHING AROUND IN HELL.

BEAVIS, YOU WERE DREAMING AGAIN.

OH. OH YEAH. THAT'S ONE OF MY FAVORITE DREAMS.

BUT THE PART THAT SUCKED THE MOST WAS THAT IT WAS IN BLACK AND WHITE.

NO IT WASN'T. EVERYTHING WAS LIKE RED AND ORANGE.

THE MOVIE, BUTTMUNCH.

THE WIZARD OF OZ (1939)

YOU'D THINK THAT A MOVIE THAT HAS BOTH FLYING MONKEYS AND MIDGETS IN IT COULDN'T SUCK, BUT IT DOES.

CHANGES AND CHALLENGES (LIKE 1 MILLION B.C.)

THEY MADE US WATCH THIS IN GYM CLASS. IT WAS SUPPOSED TO BE, LIKE, SEXY, OR SOMETHING, BUT IT'S JUST ABOUT GUYS' NADS.

YEAH, GUYS' NADS SUCK.

BUT BEAVIS, YOU GAVE IT A "THUMBS UP."

ER, I DID NOT! I WAS THINKING ABOUT SOMETHING ELSE.

I SAW YOU STARING AT THOSE NAD DIAGRAMS.

YEAH, UM, BUT I WAS THINKING ABOUT CHICKS' NADS.

BEAVIS, CHICKS DON'T HAVE NADS. I THINK MAYBE YOU BETTER SEE THIS FILM AGAIN. YOU'D LIKE THAT, WOULDN'T YOU?

MOVIE LAWS

BAD DUDES ARE ALWAYS UGLIER THAN GOOD DUDES.

Unless it's an Arnold Schwarzenegger movie. Then they make an exception.

Yeah, but Butt-Head, bad chicks are always hotter than good chicks, right?

Sometimes. Other times bad chicks are fat old German Nazis who want to attach electrodes to your nads.

Yeah! Make me talk! Make me talk!

WHAT THE RATINGS MEAN

 IT STANDS FOR "GOO-GOO." THESE MOVIES ARE JUST FOR BABIES. YEAH, IT'S JUST LIKE MOVIES OF BOUNCING BALLS AND CRAP.

 THEY USED TO MAKE PG MOVIES, BUT THEY ALL SUCKED, SO THEY DON'T MAKE THEM ANYMORE.

 IT MEANS, "PRETTY GOOD UP UNTIL YOU'RE 13." KIDS KIND OF LIKE THESE MOVIES BECAUSE THEY CAN STILL SEE PEOPLE GET KILLED AND STUFF, AND SOMETIMES CHICKS' BUTTS. BUT THE CHICKS DON'T STAY NAKED LONG ENOUGH FOR YOU TO DO ANYTHING ABOUT IT, AND NOBODY USES THE F-WORD.

YOU CAN'T SAY "FART" IN A PG-13 MOVIE?

NO, THE OTHER F-WORD, DUMBASS.

THERE'S ANOTHER F-WORD?

NEVER MIND, BEAVIS, YOU'LL NEVER NEED TO KNOW IT.

Y'KNOW, BUTT-HEAD, IT'S A GOOD THING YOU CAN SAY FART IN A PG-13 MOVIE, CAUSE IT WOULD JUST BE A SHAME IF KIDS COULDN'T ENJOY FARTS AT THE MOVIES. I MEAN, LIKE, FARTS ARE ALL THAT KIDS HAVE.

 IT MEANS IT'S A REGULAR MOVIE, WITH ALL THE REGULAR STUFF. YOU'RE NOT SUPPOSED TO SEE THEM WITHOUT YOUR PARENT OR GUARDIAN, BUT IF YOU JUST TELL THEM YOUR PARENTS ARE DEAD, THEY'LL LET YOU IN.

 THESE ARE MOVIES THAT ARE SO COOL THAT THEY CAN'T LET TEENAGERS SEE THEM CAUSE THEN THEY MIGHT NOT GO TO SCHOOL AND JUST GO SEE MOVIES ALL THE TIME.

YEAH, IT SUCKS. INSTEAD YOU HAVE TO NOT GO TO SCHOOL AND, LIKE, WAIT FOR THEM TO COME OUT ON VIDEO.

THERE'S ANOTHER THING YOU CAN DO. WHEN THEY ASK YOU HOW OLD YOU ARE, JUST LIKE LAUGH AND SAY, "MAN, YOU JUST MADE MY DAY. I'M 37." THIS WORKS BETTER IF YOU'RE A CHICK.

THEY HAD TO STOP SHOWING THESE AT REGULAR THEATERS, BECAUSE THERE WERE STAMPEDES AND STUFF.

XCITING, XPOSING AND XTRA LARGE.

TITLES
THE FIRST THING YOU DO WHEN MAKING A MOVIE IS COME UP WITH A COOL TITLE. THEN YOU'LL, LIKE, KNOW WHAT THE MOVIE IS ABOUT AND STUFF.

SONGS

A LOT OF MOVIES ARE THE NAMES OF SONGS, LIKE "STAR WARS" AND "FRANKENSTEIN." BUT THERE'S STILL PLENTY OF COOL SONGS THAT HAVEN'T BEEN MADE INTO MOVIES YET.

"BEAT IT"

"DOIN IT"

"SEXORCISTO"

"HIGHWAY TO HELL"

"BITCH SCHOOL"

"PLEASURE DOME"

"BURNING LOVE"

"DUDE LOOKS LIKE A LADY"

"VASELINE"

"FIRE"

"KILLER QUEEN"

"LOVE IN AN ELEVATOR"

"I'M ON FIRE"

"SMOKIN' IN THE BOYS ROOM"

"DIRTY DEEDS DONE DIRT CHEAP"

"LIGHT MY FIRE"

LEGAL SAYINGS

MOVIES ABOUT LEGAL STUFF ARE NAMED AFTER THINGS LEGAL DUDES SAY, LIKE "BURDEN OF INNOCENCE." USUALLY LEGAL MOVIES SUCK, BUT THEY MAKE A BUTTLOAD OF MONEY, SO HERE'S SOME OTHER LEGAL SAYINGS.

CAUGHT IN THE ACT

ASSUME THE POSITION

URINE TEST

CAVITY SEARCH

JUVENILE DETENTION

TRIED AS AN ADULT

PREDATORS, TERMINATORS, AND ERASERS AND STUFF

THE BEST MOVIES ARE JUST OTHER NAMES FOR PEOPLE WHOSE JOBS IT IS TO KILL STUFF. HERE'S SOME NEW ONES WE'RE GOING TO MAKE (SO YOU CAN'T HAVE THEM):

THE ELIMINATOR

THE SNUFFER

THE ASSASSINATOR

THE EUTHANASIATOR

THE CUISINARTER

THE RUBBER OUTER

THE BUCKET KICKER

THE KIBOSHER

THE SCHWARZENEGGER

SAYINGS

UH, SOME OTHER MOVIE TITLES ARE NAMED AFTER COMMON SAYINGS, LIKE "SPANKING THE MONKEY" AND "EATING RAOUL." HERE'S SOME OTHER SAYINGS THAT WOULD MAKE COOL MOVIE TITLES.

GROOMING THE POODLE

WETTING THE WEASEL

WORM WRESTLING

STARTING A SPERM FARM

MONKEY SHINING

WHITTLIN' DIXIE

BURNING THE CANDLE AT ONE END

FLIPPING THROUGH THE SEED CATALOG

MAKING TOILET PAPIER MACHE

CROWNING KING RICHARD

TONING THE FLUTEOUS MAXIMUS

Their purple hearts have worms in them.

MADE-UP NAMES

UH, IF ALL ELSE FAILS, YOU CAN LIKE MAKE UP AN ORIGINAL TITLE. THIS WORKS THE SAME AS LIKE WITH BAND NAMES EXCEPT IT SORT OF HAS TO MAKE SENSE AT THE END.

PICK ONE	THEN	PICK ANOTHER ONE	THEN	PICK ONE OF THESE
SCREAMING		VAMPIRE		PALS
FLAMING		ARMY		SCHOOL
CANNIBAL		(ZOMBIE)		ACADEMY
DEADLY		BIMBO		NURSES
WILD		BRAIN		PARTY
AMAZON		SEX		KILLERS
BLOOD-SUCKING		CYBORG		GIRLS
INSANE		VICE		HUNTERS
(NAKED)		VIRGIN		MANIACS
THE LAST		COED		SLAUGHTER
HOT		JUNGLE		MAMAS
EVIL		BEAST		HOOKERS
SLIMEBALL		TEENAGE		HIGH
HOLLYWOOD		MOVIE		PEOPLE
TINY		FLESH		(FORCE)

COOL PARTS

WHAT'S COOL IS WHEN A GUY FIGHTS WITH A DEADLY CHICK.

YEAH, AND THEN THEY, LIKE, DO IT.

NO, DUMBASS, THEY DO IT BEFORE HE FIGHTS WITH HER. AFTER HE FIGHTS WITH HER, SHE'S DEAD.

OH, YEAH. I GUESS THEY COULDN'T DO IT THEN. NOT UNLESS SHE'S A ZOMBIE. HUH HUH.

HEH HEH. I LIKE DOING IT WITH ZOMBIE CHICKS BECAUSE THEY CAN'T LIKE SAY, "I'D RATHER DIE THAN DO IT WITH YOU."

BEAVIS, YOU COULDN'T EVEN SCORE WITH A ZOMBIE CHICK, EVEN IF HER HEAD WAS CUT OFF. YOU WOULD, LIKE, STRIKE OUT WITH BOTH PIECES.

MOMENTS THAT SUCK

MOVIES WITH WORDS SUCK.
    IT'S LIKE PAYING MONEY TO GO SEE A BOOK.
    HEY, BUTT-HEAD, Y'EVER NOTICE THAT IN
MOVIES WITH WORDS YOU CAN NEVER UNDERSTAND
WHAT PEOPLE ARE SAYING?
    YOU BUMWIPE, THAT'S BECAUSE THEY'RE
SPEAKING IN ASIAN OR HISPANISH OR SOMETHING.
    WELL, IF THEY CAN'T SPEAK ENGLISH THEY
SHOULD, LIKE, LOVE IT OR LUMP IT.
    BEAVIS, YOU'RE NOT SPEAKING ENGLISH.
    THAT'S DIFFERENT. I'M A U.S.-AMERICAN.

Var snäll och tala om för mig var är nächøs?

IDEAS

IT'S EASY TO MAKE IDEAS FOR MOVIES BECAUSE THEY HAVE TO BE 25 WORDS OR LESS.

A PACK OF RENEGADE STRIPPERS GO AROUND TAKING THEIR CLOTHES OFF IN CHURCHES AND HIGH SCHOOL SOCIAL STUDIES CLASSES. ONLY ONE MAN CAN STOP THEM.

ALIENS TRAVEL BACK TO CAVEMAN TIME CAUSE THEY THINK WE CAN'T KICK THEIR ASSES BACK THEN. BUT THE CAVEMEN TRAVEL TO MODERN TIMES AND ESCAPE.

THIS CITY MAKES ALL THE COPS MONKEYS, CAUSE THEY DON'T COST ANYTHING. BUT THEN THE MONKEY COPS START SHOOTING EVERYBODY, EVEN IF THEY'RE NOT ILLEGAL.

A DUDE BUILDS A HOUSE ON SECRET ALIEN BURIAL GROUNDS. THE HOUSE MULTIPLIES AND PRETTY SOON IT'S THE SUBURBS. ONLY ONE MAN CAN STOP IT.

THIS SCIENTIST DEVELOPS A TOP SECRET FORMULA FOR THE BEST POSSIBLE NACHOS. BEAVIS IS ASSIGNED TO PROTECT HIM, BUT WITHOUT EATING HIS NACHOS.

BEAVIS EATS RADIOACTIVE NACHOS AND TURNS INTO EL NACHO, WHO SPITS MOLTEN CHEESE AND SHOOTS DEADLY NACHI THROWING CHIPS. ONLY ONE MAN CAN STOP HIM.

THIS DUDE IS ACCUSED OF A CRIME HE DIDN'T COMMIT. SO HE KILLS EVERYBODY AND ESCAPES.

ONE DAY THE ANIMALS IN THE ZOO START TALKING. BUT NOBODY GOES, SINCE ALL THE ANIMALS DO IS COMPLAIN. ONLY ONE MAN CAN STOP THEM.

THERE'S A NEW LAW WHERE ALL CHICKS HAVE TO BE NAKED. AND SOME OTHER STUFF HAPPENS.

THERE'S THIS BAD ASSASSIN CHICK WHO EATS SECRET AGENTS AND THEN SENDS HER POOP TO THE WHITE HOUSE. ONLY ONE MAN CAN STOP HER UP.

TWO DUDES GET PAID TO DO IT WITH THIS CHICK. BUT FIRST THEY HAVE TO TAKE A BUS RIDE WITH OLD PEOPLE AND SEE HISTORY.

IT'S THE FUTURE, AND EVERYTHING SUCKS.

THE DEAD WALK THE EARTH. ONLY ONE MAN CAN STOP THEM, SO THEY EAT HIM. THEN THEY THROW UP AND HE COMES BACK TO LIFE.

UH, THIS IS IMPORTANT: THESE ARE OUR IDEAS. IF YOU, LIKE, STEAL THEM, WE'LL HIRE LAWYERS WHO WILL GO OVER TO YOUR HOUSE AND KICK YOUR ASS.

THE SCRIPT

THE PART THAT SUCKS THE MOST ABOUT MOVIES IS YOU HAVE TO WRITE IT ALL DOWN FIRST.

YEAH, BUT, LIKE, THE COOL PART IS, NO MATTER HOW MANY ANSWERS YOU GET WRONG, THEY DON'T MAKE YOU DO IT OVER. THEY MAKE SOMEONE ELSE DO IT.

UH, YEAH. THEY SAY, "EXCELLENT FIRST DRAFT" AND THEN THEY SAY THEY WANT TO GET SOMEBODY ELSE TO "DO A POLISH." HUH HUH HUH.

HEH HEH HEH. YEAH, LIKE, SO YOU SAY, "I, EH. I'M A REALLY GOOD POLISHER." BUT THEY SAY THIS GUY IS, LIKE, A LOT BETTER. AND, LIKE, WHEN YOU MEET HIM, YOU CAN SEE WHY. HUH HUH. HE'S PROBABLY HAD A LOT OF PRACTICE.

Title too long. How about "Wild Thing"? "Night Moves?"

MAYBE - 'SPACE COWBOY' 'PURPLE PEOPLE EATER' 'TICKET TO RIDE' 'ROCKET MAN'

OK.. FATAL JUCTION? ALIEN PROPOSAL? INVASION of PRIVACY? BAD BOYS II?

Leaving PG- territory

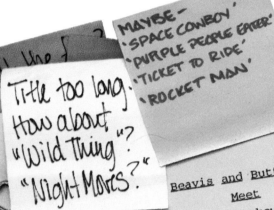

Beavis and Butt-Head
Meet
The Alien Butt-Monkeys from Uranus

START HERE

Beavis and Butt-head, like, doing it. With two chicks. With Big Thingies. And they're naked. You can see their thingies.

Butt-Head

Hey, baby. Nice Thingies.

Then the chicks heads explode.

Beavis

Ahhh! My chick's head exploded!

Butt-Head

I just wrote that, Butt-Munch.

Then these two alien heads pop out where the chicks'es heads was. But they're still naked chicks, except for the heads part.

Alien Naked Chick

We will suck you now.

Butt-Head

Whoa.

Beavis

Hey, Butt-Head, this is just like in the movies!

Butt-Head

This is the movies, dumbass. And you're slowing everything down with all this talking!

Beavis

sorry. You alien chicks, ...through. Suck

$$$!!! SUGGEST RATHER THAN SHOW?

PROMO → LINE POTENTIAL

Do we need this dialogue?

THE CASTING COUCH

SO IF A CHICK WANTS TO BE AN ACTRESS IN YOUR MOVIE, SHE HAS TO GET YOU TO SAY YES. HUH HUH. UH, THINK ABOUT IT.

EH. UM. ER, BUTT-HEAD, I'M THINKING ABOUT IT, BUT NOTHING'S HAPPENING.

BEAVIS, NOTHING EVER HAPPENS WHEN YOU THINK. ALL SYSTEMS ARE NORMAL.

OH. OH, GOOD. I WAS AFRAID SOMETHING WAS WRONG THERE FOR A SECOND.

SURE-FIRE CASTING COUCH PICK-UP LINES

"SO, UH, THAT SHIRT LOOKS HEAVY."

"WE'RE LOOKING FOR AN ACTRESS WHO HAS THINGIES. DO YOU KNOW ANY?"

"OH, YEAH? PROVE IT."

"IT'S ESSENTIAL FOR THE PLOT AND STUFF THAT YOUR CHARACTER SHOW US HER THINGIES. IT'S REALLY, REALLY ESSENTIAL."

"IN THIS SCENE, YOUR CHARACTER TAKES OFF ALL HER CLOTHES IN FRONT OF THE MIRROR. SO, UH, JUST PRETEND I'M THE MIRROR."

"ALL RIGHT. NOW, IN THIS SCENE, I'M A BAR OF SOAP..."

"SO, UH, LET'S DO AN ACTING EXERCISE. YOU'RE LIKE A TREE. AND IT'S FALL."

"I SEE ON YOUR RESUME YOU WERE IN 'THE MIRACLE WORKER.' SO, UH, IF A CHICK EVER DID IT WITH BEAVIS, THAT WOULD BE A MIRACLE."

"SO, UH, DO YOU YOU WANT TO BE IN THIS MOVIE OR NOT?"

UH, THIS IS IMPORTANT: IT'S AGAINST THE LAW FOR YOU TO TELL A CHICK SHE HAS TO DO IT WITH YOU IF SHE WANTS TO BE IN YOUR MOVIE.

YEAH, IT'S LIKE LITTERING. EXCEPT INSTEAD OF THROWING CRAP ON THE GROUND, YOU'RE SEXUALLING HER ASS, OR SOMETHING LIKE THAT.

OH, AND LIKE THIS IS REALLY IMPORTANT: IT'S NOT AGAINST THE LAW IF, LIKE, SHE JUST REALLY WANTS TO DO IT WITH YOU.

YEAH, UNLESS THEN SHE, LIKE, WANTS 300 BUCKS OR SOMETHING, AND YOU HAVE TO GO STEAL IT.

COOL ACTORS

If you could put all these people in one movie, it would be, like, cooler.

Jean-Claude Van Damme

He kicks ass. That's all he does.

Arnold Schwarzenegger

He kicks ass just as hard as Van Damme, only he uses missiles. Plus you can sort of understand what he's saying.

And he like kills people all day long but he still has time to teach kindergarten and have his own babies.

Yeah, but he's still cool.

Pamela Anderson Lee

They should put her in movies more.

Yeah, either that, or let her take her top off on  Baywatch.

Whoa. Huh huh. That would be even cooler.

Yeah, because, like, they can't make you leave your couch just because you take your pants off.

Charleton Heston

This guy has kicked ass throughout the universe. Like once, he landed on this planet that was ruled by chimps, and he kicked their monkey asses. And then like this other time, he was on this planet with all these  diseased zombies, and he kicked their undead asses. And then he was on this planet where everybody was eating these little green snackcakes made out of people, and he kicked their cannibal asses.

Yeah, and remember, this other time, he was on this planet called Egypt, and he turns a whole river into blood, and he makes all these frogs to do his evil bidding, and he, like, talks to this bush that's on fire.

You know what, Beavis. I heard that movie was based on a book.

No way, Butt-Head. No book would ever be that cool.

Sir Anthony Hopkins

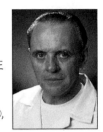

He eats people, and he doesn't wait for them to come out in snackcake form, either. He says they're delicious just the way they are. Plus he bombed a bunch of people over in Vietland, like, when he was the president. Now he's like a knight so you have to like call him Sir or he takes out his sword and cuts off your fava beans.

Sigourney Weaver

He really kicks alien ass, even if he does look a little like a chick.

Pandora Peaks

Based on seeing her in only one  movie, I can safely say this actress has got a lot of talent.

Yeah, heh heh. She's like, bursting with talent. I predict she's going to go places.

And I predict, not with you, Beavis.

That Chick in Dusk Till Dawn

She, like, strips on a table and then, like, turns into a blood-sucking vampire zombie. Enough said.

The Dead Guy

He, like, plays dead guys  better than real dead guys. If you need a dead guy for your movie, there's no point in killing anybody. This is your guy.

ACTORS WHO SUCK

SOMETIMES YOU HAVE TO PUT THESE PEOPLE IN YOUR MOVIES BECAUSE, LIKE, EXECUTIVES ARE DUMBASSES WHO SAY, LIKE, AT LEAST A COUPLE OF THE PEOPLE IN YOUR MOVIE HAVE TO BE ABLE TO ACT.

TOM HANKS

FIRST HE WAS IS THIS MOVIE WHERE HE WAS SUPPOSED TO BE REALLY DUMB, BUT HE DIDN'T KNOCK STUFF OVER OR TALK WITH HIS BUTT-CHEEKS OR DO ANY COOL DUMB STUFF. THEN HE WAS A SPACE DUDE BUT HE DIDN'T EVEN FIGHT ANY ALIENS. AND NONE OF THE CHICKS HE'S WITH EVER GETS NAKED.

SEAN PENN

HE WAS COOL IN THAT MOVIE ABOUT HIGH SCHOOL, AND HE LIKE, DID IT WITH MADONNA BACK WHEN THAT WAS COOL. BUT NOW HIS FACE IS SCRUNCHED UP ALL THE TIME, LIKE HE'S CONSTIPATED OR SOMETHING. AND HE CRIES AND STUFF.

I DON'T KNOW, BUTT-HEAD. I WOULD CRY IF I WAS CONSTIPATED ALL THE TIME.

BEAVIS, IF YOU WERE CONSTIPATED, YOU WOULD BECOME, LIKE, A GENIUS.

HARVEY KEITEL

HE'S ALWAYS SHOWING HIS WEINER IN MOVIES. IF HE DID THAT IN REAL LIFE, HE WOULD GET ARRESTED.

YEAH, AND, EH, HE'D HAVE TO PICK UP LITTER AT THE PARK FOR 12 WEEKENDS.

MERYL STREEP

SHE TALKS FUNNY.

CLINT EASTWOOD

HE USED TO BE COOL. THEN HE WAS IN THIS MOVIE ABOUT SOME BRIDGES SOMEPLACE, AND HE DANCED WITH THIS CHICK, BUT IT WAS LIKE A REGULAR DANCE, NOT ONE OF THOSE DANCES WHERE IT LOOKS LIKE YOU'RE DOING IT.

YEAH, AND INSTEAD OF A GUN, HE HAD A CAMERA. BUT HE DIDN'T TAKE ANY DIRTY PICTURES OR ANYTHING. AND HE DIDN'T BLOW UP ANY OF THE BRIDGES, EITHER.

AND THEN HE, LIKE, CRIED.

OH, AND OH, YEAH, WHEN HE TOOK OFF HIS SHIRT, HE HAD THINGIES.

YOU KNOW A MOVIE SUCKS WHEN THE ONLY THINGIES YOU SEE ARE A GUY'S.

THE DORK GUY

THIS GUY IS, LIKE, HOLLYWOOD'S TOP DORK.

YEAH, BUT HE ONLY PLAYS A DORK. THAT DOESN'T MEAN HE'S A DORK IN REAL LIFE.

OF COURSE HE'S A DORK, BEAVIS. NOBODY WOULD ACT LIKE A DORK IF THEY DIDN'T HAVE TO. WOULD YOU BE SUCH A DILLHOLE IF YOU'D DIDN'T HAVE TO?

ER, NO, I GUESS NOT. HEY, BUTT-HEAD, DOES THAT MEAN I CAN MAKE MILLIONS OF DOLLARS PLAYING A DORK IN THE MOVIES?

UH, NO. THIS GUY IS THE DESIGNATED DORK. HE'S GOT, LIKE, A DORKOPOLY.

THAT GORILLUFFALO CHICK

SHE'S ALWAYS THE CHICK IN THE MOVIE WHO, LIKE, SHOULD BE PLAYED BY A CHICK WITH BIG THINGIES BUT INSTEAD IT'S HER.

YEAH, AND SHE REALLY DOESN'T HAVE BIG THINGIES AT ALL.

NOT EVEN WHEN SHE WAS FAT.

PLUS, SHE NEVER LETS YOU SEE THEM.

THE MAKING OF THE MOVIE PART

MAKING MOVIES ISN'T AS EASY AS IT LOOKS. THERE'S LIKE ALL THESE PEOPLE, AND THEY MUST BE DOING SOMETHING.

FAT DUDES

THERE'S LIKE ALL SORTS OF MACHINES AND DEVICES AND WIRES AND TECHNICAL STUFF IN MOVIES, AND, LIKE, FAT DUDES ARE THE ONLY PEOPLE WHO KNOW HOW TO USE THEM. SO YOU END UP HAVING TO HIRE FAT DUDES, AND YOU KNOW WHAT THAT MEANS: LESS NACHOS FOR YOU.

1. CAMERA JOCKEY. HE'S THE DUDE RIDING THE CAMERA, AND HE'S A DILLHOLE CAUSE HE WON'T LET YOU RIDE IT JUST BECAUSE OF, LIKE, ONE TIME.

2. GRIP. HE, LIKE, HOLDS ONTO STUFF. AND HE FIXES STUFF THAT GETS BROKEN SOMEHOW. HE'S KINDA CRANKY.

3. GAFFER. HE, LIKE, DOES COOL ELECTRICAL STUFF, BUT HE WON'T LET YOU NEAR IT WHILE HE'S AROUND. WHICH IS LIKE TOO BAD CAUSE HE KNOWS WHICH WIRES ARE SUPPOSED TO GO BACK WHERE.

4. GOFFER. THIS IS, LIKE, THE MOST IMPORTANT DUDE ON A MOVIE, CAUSE IF YOU WANT SOMETHING, LIKE A SPECIAL MAGAZINE, YOU JUST TELL HIM AND HE FETCHES IT. AND THEN IF YOU YELL AT HIM, "NO, DAMMIT, I SAID I WANTED *CHICKS WITH DIPS!* THE ONE WHERE THEY'RE SLATHERED WITH NACHO SAUCE!" HE, LIKE, APOLOGIZES ALL OVER THE PLACE AND GOES OUT AND GETS IT RIGHT AWAY. UH, BUT HE GETS, LIKE, REALLY INSULTED IF YOU CALL HIM A DOGGY.

MOVIE LAWS

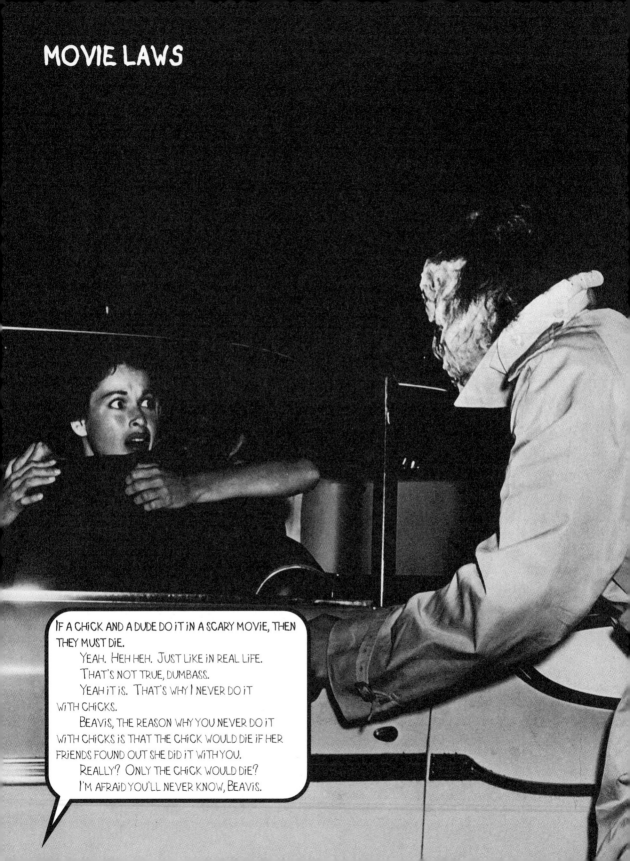

IF A CHICK AND A DUDE DO IT IN A SCARY MOVIE, THEN THEY MUST DIE.

YEAH. HEH HEH. JUST LIKE IN REAL LIFE.

THAT'S NOT TRUE, DUMBASS.

YEAH IT IS. THAT'S WHY I NEVER DO IT WITH CHICKS.

BEAVIS, THE REASON WHY YOU NEVER DO IT WITH CHICKS IS THAT THE CHICK WOULD DIE IF HER FRIENDS FOUND OUT SHE DID IT WITH YOU.

REALLY? ONLY THE CHICK WOULD DIE?

I'M AFRAID YOU'LL NEVER KNOW, BEAVIS.

DIRECTING

In a movie, the director is the dude who used to do videos but then he did like that Weezer video so they wouldn't let him do anymore, so he had to make movies instead. Or sometimes the director used to be an actor, but then Madonna broke up with him so he was like crying all the time, so he could only be in movies about dudes who cry all the time, so he had to do something else the rest of the time. Or like Mel Gibson became a director so that they couldn't sneak up behind him and show his butt anymore. Oh, and this one director is a chick, because of some law or something.

DIRECTIONS	MEANS
"ACTION"	GO
"CUT!"	STOP
"CAN WE TRY THAT AGAIN?"	GO
"WHAT THE HELL!?"	STOP
"KEEP ROLLING. C'MON, GUYS."	GO
"I'LL BE IN MY TRAILER."	STOP

ANGLES

Uh, when you shoot your movie, you have to show stuff from different angles all the time so that people don't think they're watching a play and walk out.

Yeah, and plus another good thing is like, when you're starring in the movie, and the camera angle is on the other guy you're talking to, you can go out and poop if you need to. Or, like, just want to

LOOKING DOWN ANGLE
This is, like, an angle looking down at something.

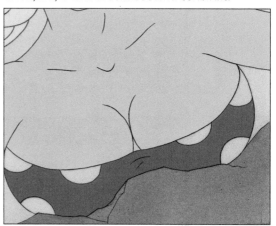

ZOOM! ZOOM!
This is a close-up of what's important.

VICE VERSA SHOT
This is who's looking at what.

SPECIAL FX

SO, UH, IT TURNS OUT THAT MOST OF THE COOL PARTS IN MOVIES ARE TOTALLY FAKE.

THAT SUCKS! IF I'M GOING TO PAY NINE BUCKS TO SEE THE WHITE HOUSE EXPLODE, I WANT TO SEE THE REAL WHITE HOUSE EXPLODE, DAMMIT!

BEAVIS, YOU NEVER PAY NINE BUCKS. YOU ALWAYS TELL THEM YOU'RE ELEVEN.

THAT'S EVEN WORSE! FOOLING A LITTLE KID LIKE THAT!

THIS IS NOT, LIKE, A REAL BLIMP EXPLODING. IT'S JUST A BALLOON ANIMAL OR SOMETHING.

HOW THEY DO STUFF

AIRPLANES, EXPLODING THEY'RE NOT EVEN REAL PLANES. THEY'RE LIKE FROM CANADA OR SOMETHING.

ARMS, RIPPING OFF THEY JUST GET PEOPLE WITH THEIR ARMS ALREADY RIPPED OFF AND PUT FAKE ARMS ON THEM.

BLOOD IT'S NOT REAL. AND IT TASTES TOO SWEET.

BOMBS, ATOMIC SINCE IT NEVER REALLY EXPLODES, THEY JUST KEEP USING THE SAME ONE OVER AND OVER.

BUILDINGS, BURNING DOWN THE BUILDINGS ARE JUST LIKE MADE OUT OF OLD WOOD, AND LIKE, ANYBODY COULD MAKE THAT KIND OF BUILDING BURN DOWN. PLUS THEY ONLY USE BUILDINGS THAT SOMEBODY WANTED TO BURN DOWN ANYWAY, SO IT DOESN'T REALLY COUNT.

FIGHTS, WITH FISTS THE PUNCH EACH OTHER ON THE PARTS OF THE FACE WHERE IT DOESN'T HURT.

FIGHTS, WITH GUNS IT LOOKS LIKE THEY'RE SHOOTING AT EACH OTHER, BUT THEY'RE REALLY AIMING TO, LIKE, MISS THE OTHER GUY BY AN INCH. AND IF THEY DO LIKE HIT A GUY, EVERYBODY STOPS AND THEY CALL A DOCTOR AND THE GUY, LIKE, CRIES, WHICH WOULD NEVER HAPPEN IN A REAL GUNFIGHT.

HEADS, EXPLODING THEY MAKE THE DUDES PUT A WHOLE CAN OF DOG FOOD IN THEIR MOUTHS BEFORE THEY EXPLODE THEIR HEADS, CAUSE REAL EXPLODING HEAD DON'T LOOK THAT COOL ALL BY THEMSELVES.

RAYS, LASER DEATH THEY DON'T KILL YOU; THEY JUST BURN A LITTLE.

THINGIES THEY SEW THESE BAGS FULL OF SILLY PUTTY INSIDE CHICKS' REAL THINGIES SO THEY'LL SHOW UP BETTER ON CAMERA.

ZOMBIES THEY JUST USE ACTORS PRETENDING TO BE ZOMBIES, CAUSE REAL ZOMBIES WON'T DO WHAT THEY'RE TOLD.

SOUND FX

THE SOUNDS YOU HEAR IN MOVIES ARE USUALLY SOMETHING ELSE BECAUSE, UHHH...

ER, MAYBE SOMEBODY FORGOT TO TURN ON THE TAPE RECORDER WHEN THEY WERE DOING IT THE FIRST TIME.

UH, PROBABLY.

SOUND	HOW THEY MAKE IT
SQUEAKY DOOR OPENING	THEY TAKE A REGULAR DOOR AND ADD MICE.
HORSES GALLOPING	THEY TIE MONKEYS ON THE BACKS OF DOGS AND RUN THEM IN A GYMNASIUM.
DOG BARKING	THEY HIRE ACTORS TO DO IT, CAUSE THEY'RE CHEAPER THAN REAL DOGS.
CHICK SCREAMING	IT'S JUST A CHICK SCREAMING FOR NO GOOD REASON AT ALL.
SOMEONE BEING DECRAPITATED	THEY HAVE AN OLD TAPE FROM FRENCH TIMES WHEN THEY DID IT ALL THE TIME.
CHOPPING HEAD OF CABBAGE IN HALF	THEY USE THE DECRAPITATION TAPE

MAKE-UP

MOVIE MAKE-UP CAN LIKE MAKE YOU LOOK LIKE A MONKEY, OR AN ALIEN, OR LIKE EVEN THE PRESIDENT.
IT CAN EVEN MAKE BEAVIS LOOK HUMAN.

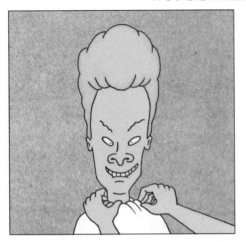
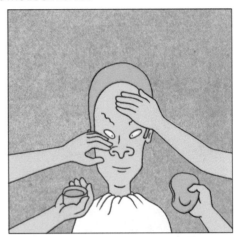
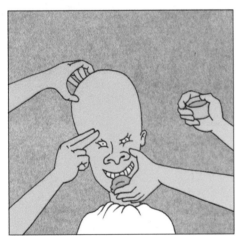
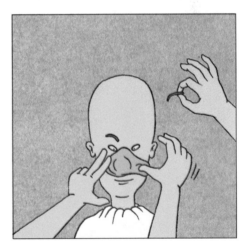
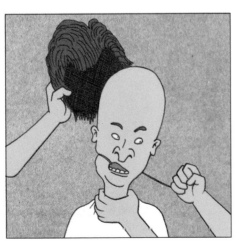

COOL PARTS

IT'S COOL WHEN THE GUY GIVES THE OTHER
GUY A CHOICE OF HOW HE'S GOING TO DIE.
    YEAH, LIKE, "I COULD SHOOT YOU, OR YOU CAN
JUMP OUT THE WINDOW, OR MY DOG WILL EAT YOUR
NADS, OR YOU COULD JUST, LIKE, SPONTANEOUSLY
EXPLODE. YOUR CHOICE."
    HUH HUH. WITH THAT MANY CHOICES, IT MAKES
YOU ALMOST WANT TO DIE, DOESN'T IT, BEAVIS?
    EH, NOT REALLY.
    C'MON, BEAVIS, YOU HAVE TO CHOOSE.
    ER. OKAY. IF I HAD TO DIE, IT WOULD BE LIKE IN
A THOUSAND YEARS, AND THEN I GUESS IT WOULD BE
COOL IF I JUST EXPLODED.
    GOOD CHOICE. HUH HUH. IT WOULD BE COOL IF
MORE OLD DUDES EXPLODED.
    YEAH. I'LL BET PEOPLE WOULD LIKE VISIT OLD
DUDE HOMES ALL THE TIME THEN. YOU COULD, LIKE,
CHARGE ADMISSION.
    BEAVIS, I THINK YOU JUST MADE ME A RICH MAN.

STUNTS

STUNTS SHOULD BE COOL. LIKE, THEY SHOULD BE SO COOL THAT IF YOU TRIED THEM AT HOME, IT WOULD LIKE COST A MILLION DOLLARS AND YOU WOULD STILL GET KILLED INSTANTLY. SO THAT KIDS DON'T GET THE IDEA THAT THEY COULD DO IT THEMSELVES AND SAVE THE EIGHT BUCKS.

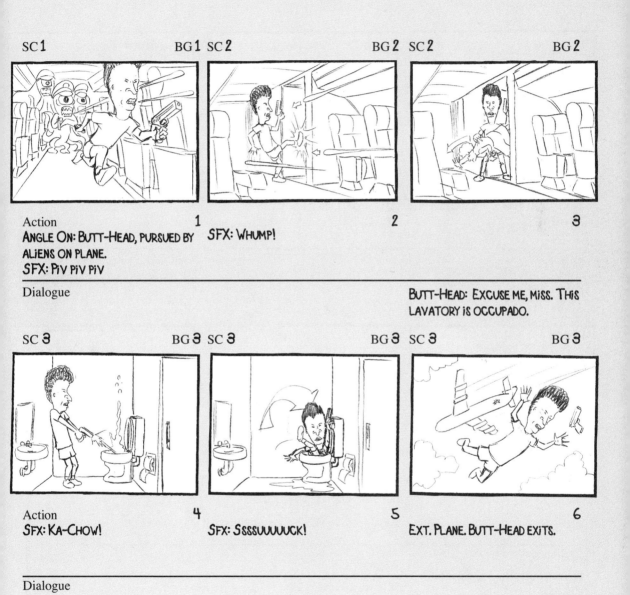

SC 1   BG 1   SC 2   BG 2   SC 2   BG 2

Action   1   2   3
ANGLE ON: BUTT-HEAD, PURSUED BY   SFX: WHUMP!
ALIENS ON PLANE.
SFX: PIV PIV PIV

Dialogue

BUTT-HEAD: EXCUSE ME, MISS. THIS LAVATORY IS OCCUPADO.

SC 3   BG 3   SC 3   BG 3   SC 3   BG 3

Action   4   5   6
SFX: KA-CHOW!   SFX: SSSSUUUUUCK!   EXT. PLANE. BUTT-HEAD EXITS.

Dialogue

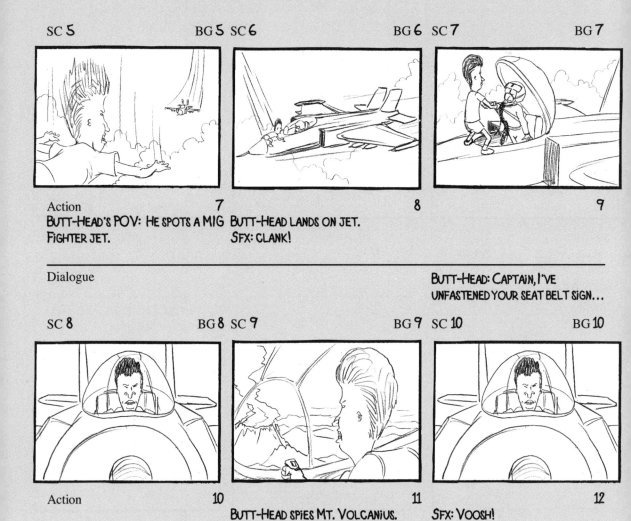

SC 5   BG 5   SC 6   BG 6   SC 7   BG 7

Action   7   8   9

BUTT-HEAD'S POV: HE SPOTS A MIG
FIGHTER JET.

BUTT-HEAD LANDS ON JET.
SFX: CLANK!

Dialogue

BUTT-HEAD: CAPTAIN, I'VE
UNFASTENED YOUR SEAT BELT SIGN...

SC 8   BG 8   SC 9   BG 9   SC 10   BG 10

Action   10   11   12

BUTT-HEAD SPIES MT. VOLCANIUS.   SFX: VOOSH!

Dialogue

BUTT-HEAD: OKAY, YOU BUTT-
MONKEYS. LET'S PLAY.

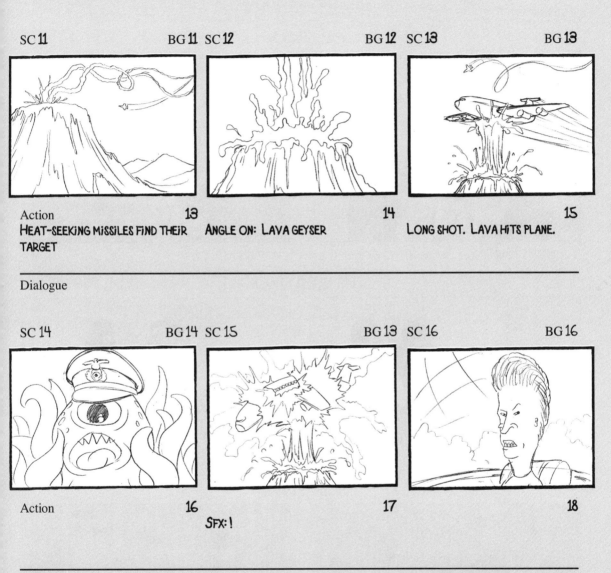

SC 11   BG 11   SC 12   BG 12   SC 13   BG 13

Action   13   14   15

HEAT-SEEKING MISSILES FIND THEIR   ANGLE ON: LAVA GEYSER   LONG SHOT. LAVA HITS PLANE.
TARGET

Dialogue

SC 14   BG 14   SC 15   BG 13   SC 16   BG 16

Action   16   17   18

SFX: !

Dialogue

ALIEN: ØΠ¥ΣΔΩ!   BUTT-HEAD: HOPE IT'S HOT ENOUGH
                                             FOR YOU—IN <u>HELL</u>.

FIGHT SCENES

THERE'S ALL KINDS OF WAYS TO KICK ASS. LIKE, I'VE KICKED BEAVIS'S ASS ELEVEN DIFFERENT WAYS SO FAR.

EH, BUTT-HEAD? EXCUSE ME, BUT, EH, REALLY, I THINK IT'S ONLY, LIKE, TEN.

UH, OKAY.

OW! HEY! EEE! YOWK! OW! OW! OW!

SO, LIKE I WAS SAYING, I'VE KICKED BEAVIS'S ASS ELEVEN DIFFERENT WAYS SO FAR, BUT NONE OF 'EM WERE COOL ENOUGH TO PUT IN A MOVIE. NOT LIKE THESE THREE.

"DEAD DUDES WALKING"

TWO AGAINST ONE? WELL, PARDNERS, THERE'S ONLY ONE THING TO SAY—

—WATCH YOUR STEP.

"HEART ATTACK"

TWO AGAINST ONE? ISN'T THAT KINDA UNFAIR? I MEAN, C'MON, GUYS—

—HAVE A HEART!

"GOIN' FISHIN'"

TWO AGAINST ONE? PLUS YOU GUYS HAVE HARPOONS. I GUESS I'M GONNA HAVE TO SAY—

—GO FISH!

UH, THIS IS IMPORTANT: THESE MOVES ONLY WORK IN THE MOVIES. DON'T TRY THIS WITH REAL LIFE BAD DUDES, OR THEY WILL KICK YOUR ASS.

NAKED CHICKS

IT'S GOOD TO HAVE NAKED CHICKS IN YOUR MOVIE, CAUSE THEN PEOPLE HAVE A REASON TO RENT THE VIDEO.

EH, RIGHT. AND IT SHOULD SAY ON THE VIDEO BOX: "WARNING: NAKED CHICKS INSIDE."

BEAVIS, YOU DUMBASS. THE NAKED CHICKS ARE ON THE TAPE; THEY'RE NOT INSIDE THE DAMN BOX.

ER, YEAH. BUT I'LL BET, YOU KNOW, BUTT-HEAD, I'LL BET IF THEY DID PUT NAKED CHICKS IN A BOX, I'LL BET THEY'D SELL A LOT.

BEAVIS, THIS IS A BOOK ABOUT HOW TO MAKE MOVIES. SAVE THAT FOR OUR BOOK ABOUT HOW TO MAKE A MILLION DOLLARS.

RIGHT. IF YOU MADE LIKE A MILLION DOLLARS, YOU COULD BUY A JUMBO SIZE BOX OF NAKED CHICKS.

BEAVIS, I'M GOING TO KICK YOUR ASS JUST AS SOON AS THIS PAGE IS OVER. OKAY, SO, UH, WE WERE TALKING ABOUT NAKED CHICKS IN MOVIES. UH, UM, WELL, EVERY MOVIE CAN HAVE TWO SEX SCENES, AND THE CHICKS HAVE TO BE NAKED FOR THAT, BUT THEN—

HEY, BUTT-HEAD, WHY CAN'T A MOVIE HAVE LIKE ALL SEX SCENES?

BECAUSE YOU HAVE TO HAVE EXPLOSIONS TOO, DILLHOLE.

EH, OH YEAH. BUT WHAT IF IT WAS ALL SEX SCENES, ONLY THE PEOPLE LIKE EXPLODED AT THE END?

BEAVIS, IF A MOVIE HAS ALL SEX SCENES, THEN THEY CAN'T SHOW IT IN REGULAR THEATERS.

WHY NOT?

CAUSE IT'S TOO HARD TO MOP UP A WHOLE THEATER. THEY HAVE TO LIKE SHOW IT IN PRIVATE BOOTHS.

I LIKE PRIVATE BOOTHS. NO ONE STEALS YOUR POPCORN.

YEAH, BUT IF YOU SHOW YOUR MOVIE IN A PRIVATE BOOTH, YOU CAN ONLY LIKE CHARGE A QUARTER. THAT'S WHY YOU NEVER SEE ANY REALLY BIG STARS IN THOSE MOVIES; THEY'RE TOO EXPENSIVE.

HEH HEH. I'D BE IN ONE OF THOSE MOVIES FOR FREE.

I'LL BET YOU WOULD, BEAVIS. BUT THEY'D HAVE TO PAY EVERYBODY ELSE SO MUCH MONEY, IT WOULDN'T BE WORTH IT. UH, SO ANYWAY, YOU HAVE TO THINK OF OTHER WAYS THAT AREN'T SEX SCENES TO GET NAKED CHICKS IN YOUR MOVIE.

WHAT IF ALL THE CHICKS, EH, JUST LIKE WALKED AROUND NAKED?

NO, THERE HAS TO BE A REASON. LIKE IT'S HOT OUT, OR SOMETHING.

YEAH, LIKE THE MOVIE IS SET IN HELL. WHICH MEANS LIKE ALL THE CHICKS ARE BAD, TOO. AND YOU HAVE TO, LIKE, SPANK 'EM.

UH, SURE, BEAVIS. AND LIKE ANOTHER WAY TO HAVE NAKED CHICKS IN YOUR MOVIE IS LIKE, IF YOU HAVE TO MEET SOMEBODY TO TALK ABOUT SOMETHING, THEN YOU LIKE MEET THEM IN A STRIP CLUB.

YEAH, BUT IF YOU MEET IN A STRIP CLUB, WHAT'S THERE TO TALK ABOUT, EXCEPT ALL THE NAKED CHICKS?

IT DOESN'T MATTER. NOBODY LISTENS ANYWAY.

THE BUTT-HEAD ACTING METHOD

SO YOU DON'T HAVE TO ACT IF YOU'RE A MOVIE STAR BUT IT'S A GOOD THING TO KNOW FOR LATER, FOR CAR COMMERCIALS AND STUFF.

FACE EXPRESSIONS

UH, VAN DRIESSEN SAYS YOU'RE SUPPOSED TO, LIKE, TALK ABOUT YOUR FEELINGS, WHICH IS WHY HE'S JUST A TEACHER AND ONLY GETS CHICKS WHO SMELL LIKE HUMMUS. CAUSE WHEN MOVIE STARS WANT YOU TO KNOW WHAT THEY'RE FEELING, THEY, LIKE, JUST MAKE FACES.

Acting Exersize: Pretend Your Cool

I'M FEELING PERFECTLY NORMAL.

I'M FEELING LIKE SOMETHING SUCKS.

I'M FEELING FRISKY.

I'M FEELING LIKE THERE'S THIS THING ON THE TV I'M WATCHING.

I'M FEELING LIKE I'M THINKING ABOUT POOR PEOPLE, OR DISEASES, OR SOMETHING.

I'M FEELING LIKE HAVING SOME NACHOS, WITH EXTRA CHEESE.

I'M FEELING LIKE YOU'RE NOT TALKING IN ENGLISH, EVEN THOUGH THOSE SEEM TO BE ENGLISH WORDS.

I'M FEELING LIKE YOU CAN ALMOST SEE THAT CHICK'S LEFT THINGIE BETWEEN THE SECOND AND THIRD BUTTON OF HER SHIRT.

I'M FEELING LIKE A DUMBASS.

DIALOGUE

DIALOGUE IS STUFF YOU SAY WHEN YOU'RE NOT KICKING SOMEONE'S ASS, OR LIKE DOING A CHICK. UH, SO IF THE STUFF YOU'RE SAYING HAS NOTHING TO DO WITH KICKING SOMEONE'S ASS, OR DOING A CHICK, THEN YOU'RE LIKE WASTING EVERYBODY'S TIME.

COOL STUFF TO SAY...

BEFORE KICKING SOMEONE'S ASS

"YOU REALIZE, OF COURSE, THAT THIS MEANS I'LL HAVE TO KICK YOUR ASS."

"I'M SORRY, DID YOU SAY, 'PLEASE KICK MY ASS?'"

"CONGRATULATIONS. YOU'VE JUST WON AN ALL-EXPENSE-PAID ASS KICKING."

"ALLOW ME TO INTRODUCE YOUR ASS TO MY FRIENDS, THE FIVE TOES OF DEATH."

"YOU WANT TO KICK MY ASS? WELL, YOU'LL HAVE TO GET PAST ME FIRST."

WHEN MEETING A CHICK

"WHAT'S A NICE CHICK LIKE YOU DOING NOT DOING IT WITH ME RIGHT NOW?"

"YOU REMIND ME OF MY DEAD WIFE. WE USED TO DO IT ALL THE TIME."

"YOU MAY HATE ME NOW, BUT BEFORE THIS IS OVER, YOU'RE GOING TO HATE YOURSELF."

"DO ME NOW." (THIS WORKS BEST IF YOU'RE LIKE ARNOLD SCHWARZENEGGER, OR LIKE ONE OF THOSE VERY SPECIAL CHALLENGED ACTOR DUDES.)

"BOND. JAMES BOND." (UH, THIS ONLY WORKS IF YOU'RE LIKE REALLY JAMES BOND. IF YOU'RE NOT, JAMES BOND WILL PROBABLY SHOW UP AND KICK YOUR ASS FOR DOING CHICKS THAT WERE RIGHTFULLY HIS.)

INTERLUDES

HERE'S SOME SEX SCENE ACTING TIPS.

YOU MUST REFRAIN FROM SPANKING YOUR MONKEY FOR AT LEAST 30 SECONDS BEFORE EACH BIG LOVE SCENE. OR YOU MIGHT GET CRAMPS.

YOU SHOULD LIKE PRACTICE EVERY SEX SCENE LIKE AT LEAST TWENTY TIMES BEFORE EVERYBODY GETS THERE. AND, LIKE, TEN TIMES AFTER THEY LEAVE.

IF YOU'RE SUPPOSED TO BE DOING IT, YOU SHOULD PROBABLY JUST DO IT, BECAUSE THEN YOU, LIKE, GET TO SCORE.

IF THE CELEBRITY CHICK YOU'RE SUPPOSED TO BE DOING USES A BODY DOUBLE, OFFICIALLY YOU CAN STILL TELL PEOPLE YOU DID IT WITH HER.

AFTER KICKING SOMEONE'S ASS

"I HOPE THIS ISN'T YOUR BLOOD ALL OVER MY NEW SHOES."

"THIS IS YOUR BRAIN. ANY QUESTIONS?"

"SO IF THE DOCTOR ASKS WHERE YOUR NADS ARE, TELL HIM TO LOOK IN YOUR EARS"

"HUH HUH HUH HUH HUH."

"UH, SORRY, I THOUGHT YOU WERE SOMEBODY ELSE."

AFTER DOING IT WITH A CHICK

"UH, I GOTTA GO."

MOMENTS THAT SUCK

WHEN THE MOVIE REVIEW SAYS THERE'S LIKE BRIEF NUDITY, BUT IT'S A GUY'S BUTT.

YEAH, IF I WANTED TO SEE GUYS' BUTTS, I'D GO TO GYM CLASS OR SOMETHING.

YOU _DO_ GO TO GYM CLASS, BEAVIS.

YEAH, UH, BUT, UH, NOT TO SEE GUYS' BUTTS. I GO THERE TO WORK OUT MY, UH, UH...

WEINER?

NOOOO! I WORK OUT, UH, UH, THOSE MUSCLES IN MY ARMS.

BEAVIS, YOU DON'T HAVE ANY MUSCLES IN YOUR ARMS.

NO, THEY'RE CALLED BISEXUALS OR SOMETHING.

BEAVIS, YOU DILLHOLE, BISEXUALS ARE THE MUSCLES IN YOUR BUTT.

OH, OH, YEAH. I LIKE TO WORK THOSE OUT, BECAUSE IN GYM, YOU NEVER KNOW WHO MIGHT BE LOOKING AT 'EM.

EDITING

No matter how much a movie sucks, you can always "fix it in the editing." An editor dude told us that. That's why all movies have cool endings now. Cause before, when movies sucked, all the editors weren't born yet or something. So anyway, here's how you could fix some old movies that still suck.

It's a Wonderful Life That George Bailey dude has to go to jail, and then like that angel dude comes back and busts him out using his new wings, which are like loaded with missiles.

The Wizard of Oz They all make a getaway in the balloon, but then they're attacked by flying monkeys out for revenge, and, like, the lion bites their heads off and the tin man makes, like, a cannon out of his arm, and blasts them. But then they're out of hot air, so the scarecrow sets his head on fire and sticks it up in there. And then when they get back, it turns out it wasn't all a dream at all and like there's no place at home. So they all go off on another adventure.

Citizen Kane It turns out that Rosebud is, like, a stripper. Or like, an elite team of strippers.

Star Trek: The Motion Picture They all get killed for good in the first one.

Director's Uncut

Sometimes when they make the video, they let the director put back in all the naked chicks they made him take out before, cause they wanted, like, kids to be able to see it. But when it's a video, kids can see it no matter what, so they can put everything back in. And like sometimes they change the name, so kids know there's new naked chicks they haven't seen yet.

Movie Title	Special Director's Uncut Title
The Nutty Professor	The Slutty Professor
Mission: Impossible	Mission: Posterior
The Hunchback of Notre Dame	The Hunchfront of Notre Dame
Independence Day	In the Underpants Day
Striptease	Stripteens
From Dusk Til Dawn	From Dusk on Dawn
Flipper	Floppy
Ace Ventura, Pet Detective	Bob Guccione, Pet Detective
Bordello of Blood	Bordello of Chicks
A Time to Kill	A Time to Do It
Beavis and Butt-Head Do America	Beavis and Butt-Head Do Americans

MOVIE DIARY

UH, YOU SHOULD WRITE DOWN EVERYTHING THAT HAPPENS WHEN YOU'RE MAKING A MOVIE, SO THAT, LIKE, IF THERE'S LEGAL THINGS, YOU WON'T HAVE TO WRITE DOWN YOUR SIDE AGAIN LATER.

YEAH, AND SOMETIMES STUFF HAPPENS, LIKE THE DIRECTOR STARTS CRYING, AND YOU CAN CALL THOSE NEWSPAPERS, THE ONES FROM THE KWIK FOOD, AND THEY'LL PAY YOU IF YOU CAN MAKE A DOCUMENT OUT OF IT.

AND, UH, ALSO YOU SHOULD WRITE DOWN EVERYTHING, SO LIKE LATER WHEN YOU GO ON TV SHOWS YOU'LL BE ABLE TO REMEMBER THE FUNNY PARTS AND NOT JUST SIT THERE SAYING YOU HAVE TO POOP, LIKE BEAVIS DID.

ER, WELL, EVERYBODY THOUGHT IT WAS FUNNY.

UH, YEAH. HUH HUH. UNTIL YOU POOPED.

I SAID I HAD TO POOP! NOBODY WOULD LISTEN! THEY JUST KEPT LAUGHING AT ME!

CALM DOWN, BEAVIS. I'M ALL OUT OF DIAPERS.

DAY ONE
SO LIKE THIS DUMBASS GUARD WOULDN'T LET US IN, EVEN WHEN WE SAID WE WERE BIG MOVIE STARS. SO WE WENT TO THE BEACH TO SEE IF WE COULD GET CHICKS TO AUDITION FOR OUR MOVIE, BUT THEY ALL SAID THEY WERE IN MOVIES ALREADY.

DAY TWO
THE SAME DUMBASS GUARD WAS THERE, BUT HE WAS ALL SCARED. HE SAID WE WERE, LIKE, DEAD. BUT HE LET US IN ANYWAY. WHAT GOOD IS A GUARD IF HE CAN'T EVEN STOP ZOMBIES?

SO, LIKE, EVERYBODY WAS SURPRISED TO SEE US, ESPECIALLY THESE TWO DUDES NAMED COREY THEY HIRED TO PLAY US IN THE MOVIE INSTEAD OF US. THE PRODUCER STARTED YELLING, SAYING, "THIS LITTLE STUNT YOU PULLED COST US $800,000!"

AND THEN I SAID, "WHOA. THAT MUST OF BEEN A COOL STUNT."

YEAH, AND I SAID, "ER, CAN WE DO IT AGAIN? SO WE CAN SEE IT THIS TIME?"

SO THEN THE PRODUCER LIKE STARTED TO LIGHT UP A CIGARETTE, AND I SAID, "UH, SMOKING IS, LIKE, BAD FOR YOU."

EH, YEAH, AND I SAID, "EH, YEAH. AND SO ARE CIGARETTES."

SHE, LIKE, JUST STARED AT US FOR LIKE A MINUTE.

YOU KNOW, BUTT-HEAD, WHEN SHE WAS STARING AT US LIKE THAT, I THOUGHT OUR HEADS WERE GONNA EXPLODE, BUT THEY DIDN'T. I GUESS SHE DIDN'T HAVE HER EYES TURNED UP ALL THE WAY.

UH, YEAH, I GUESS. SO THEN, LIKE, EVERYBODY HAD LUNCH. IT WAS LIKE A SMORGASBOARD WHERE YOU COULD GO BACK AS MANY TIMES AS YOU WANT, BUT IT WAS ALSO LIKE A SMORGASBOARD BECAUSE ALL THE FOOD SUCKED. EXCEPT THERE WEREN'T ANY MEATBALLS, WHICH MADE IT SUCK MORE THAN A SMORGASBOARD, WHICH ISN'T SO EASY TO DO.

YEAH, ER, SO SINCE THERE WEREN'T ANY MEATBALLS, WE TRIED THE MULTI-GRAIN ROLLS, BUT, EH, THEY DIDN'T GO AS FAR.

UH, YEAH. AND WHEN THEY HIT SOMEONE IN THE HEAD, THEY JUST KIND OF BOUNCE OFF.

SO THEN WE SAT AROUND THIS TABLE AND ALL HAD TO READ OUT LOUD, LIKE WE WERE IN FOURTH GRADE OR SOMETHING. AND YOU COULD TELL THE SCRIPT THEY HAD WASN'T THE ONE WE WROTE CAUSE IT DIDN'T HAVE ANY OF THE DRAWINGS. SO WE ACTUALLY HAD TO, LIKE, READ IT.

ER, YEAH, SO I, LIKE, SAID, "THIS DOESN'T LOOK LIKE SOMETHING I WOULD SAY."

AND THE DIRECTOR SAID THAT BEAVIS DIDN'T HAVE TO SAY THAT. IT WAS JUST DIRECTIONS. AND THEN BEAVIS SAID, "I NEVER FOLLOW THE DIRECTIONS. THAT'S FOR WUSSES."

BUTT-HEAD, LET ME SAY WHAT I SAID. I SAID, ER, "MAKE MY DAY. YOU'RE ERASED."

UH, YEAH. SO THEN THE PRODUCER, SHE WAS LIKE GRABBING ONTO HER HAIR, AND A BIG CLUMP CAME OUT. AND SHE STARED AT IT FOR, LIKE, THREE MINUTES, AND THEN WE ALL GOT TO GO HOME.

DAY THREE
WHEN WE GOT TO WORK EVERYBODY ALREADY ATE LUNCH, AND THERE WASN'T ANY FOR US, AND THE PRODUCER WAS SCREAMING AND COUGHING, AND SO WE WENT INTO OUR TRAILER. HUH HUH. JUST LIKE MOVIE STARS. HUH HUH.

YEAH, BUT WHEN WE GOT IN THERE, THOSE TWO COREY DUDES WERE STILL THERE, PLAYING WITH OUR NACHO MACHINE. I SAID, "HALT! DROP THOSE NACHOS!"

UH, AND I SAID, "WHAT ARE YOU DUDES STILL DOING HERE? DON'T YOU, LIKE, HAVE JOBS?" THEN THEY SAID THE PRODUCER TOLD THEM TO STAY AROUND "JUST IN CASE." AND I SAID, "JUST IN CASE WHAT? JUST IN CASE I WANT TO KICK YOUR ASS?"

THEN THE SCARY COREY CAME UP AND STUCK HIS FACE, LIKE, RIGHT WHERE A CHICK WHO WANTS YOU TO KISS HER WOULD STICK IT, AND HE SAID, "DON'T YOU KNOW WHO I AM?"

AND I SAID, "UH, NO." AND THAT MADE HIM REALLY MAD. HE STARTED THROWING CRAP AROUND ALL OVER THE TRAILER, AND BREAKING STUFF, SO WE, LIKE, GOT OUT OF THERE, SO WE'D HAVE AN ALIBI.

DAY FOUR

UH, TODAY BEAVIS BECAME A WOMAN.

I DID NOT.

BEAVIS, STOP DENYING YOUR FEMININE HYGIENE SIDE.

I AM NOT A WOMAN!

GO AHEAD AND SING YOUR LITTLE WOMEN SONGS, BEAVIS. I'VE GOT A DIARY TO KEEP HERE. SO, LIKE, IN THE MORNING WE WENT DOWN TO THE BEACH TO SEE IF ANY OF THE CHICKS WANTED US TO AUDITION TO BE IN THEIR MOVIES, BUT THEY HAD THESE BIG DUDES WITH THEM, AND THEY LIKE BURIED US UP TO OUR NECKS, AND THEN THEY KICKED SAND IN OUR FACES.

YEAH, I WAS GONNA KICK THEIR ASSES. ER, EXCEPT I WAS, LIKE, BURIED AND I COULDN'T MOVE.

UH HUH HUH HUH. BEAVIS, IF YOU TRIED TO KICK THOSE DUDES' ASSES, THEY WOULD HAVE LIKE CRUSHED YOUR TOES BETWEEN THEIR POWERFUL BUTT CHEEKS.

EH, WELL, THAT'S WHY I WAS GOING TO, YOU KNOW, AIM AWAY FROM THE CRACK PART.

UH, YEAH, THAT WOULD WORK, I GUESS. SO THEN LATER, THE TIDE CAME IN AND BEAVIS GOT A BAD CASE OF THE CRABS.

DAY FIVE

THIS BAYWATCH DUDE FOUND US AND DUG US OUT, BUT THEN HE WOULDN'T TAKE US TO THE SECRET BAYWATCH CHANGING PLACE, SO WE WENT TO WHERE THE MOVIE WAS.

THE PRODUCER CHICK WAS SCREAMING AT US, LIKE EVEN BEFORE WE GOT THERE, EXCEPT ONLY A SQUEAK WAS COMING OUT. AND LIKE THE DIRECTOR WAS YELLING, TOO, AT THE WRITER DUDE, SCREAMING, "I SAID I WANTED A DIET COKE!" AND THE OLD CINEMATOGGLER WAS SCREAMING AT THE DIRECTOR, "YOU WANT BEAUTIFUL PICTURE? I GIVE YOU BEAUTIFUL PICTURE. BUT IT WILL STILL BE BEAUTIFUL PICTURE OF EXCREMENT." THEN HE LOOKED AT US, AND WE THOUGHT HE WAS, LIKE, GOING TO THROW HIS TEETH AT US OR SOMETHING, SO WE WENT INTO THE TRAILER.

WE WERE, LIKE, IN THERE FOR ONLY AN HOUR WHEN THE PRODUCTION ASS CHICK KNOCKED ON THE DOOR AND WANTED TO KNOW WHAT OUR DEMANDS ARE. AND I WAS LIKE, WE'RE HOLDING OURSELVES FOR RANSOM. COOL.

YEAH, SO I DEMANDED FIFTY POUNDS OF M&MS, BUT WITH THE CANDY COATING ON ALL THE RED ONES LICKED OFF AND REPLACED WITH CANDY COATING FROM BROWN ONES. AND LIKE THE OTHER WAY, TOO.

AND, UH, I DEMANDED THAT FROM NOW ON, EVERYBODY HAD TO CALL ME SIR BUTT-HEAD. AND THEY HAD TO CALL BEAVIS "MILADY."

EH, YEAH, THAT WAS COOL. AND I DEMANDED THAT THE PRESIDENT RELEASE ALL THE PRISONERS IN THE PRISONS WHO WERE UNFAIRLY PRISONED FOR SPANKING THEIR MONKEYS, ER, BECAUSE THAT'S A CAUSE I CARE DEEPLY ABOUT.

THEN I LIKE, UH, DEMANDED AN ACTING COACH JUST FOR MY BUTT, LIKE JIM CARREY HAS. AND THAT, LIKE, MY BUTT WOULD GET IN THE CREDITS BEFORE THE MOVIE, BEFORE BEAVIS, LIKE, "BUTT-HEAD AND HIS BUTT AND BEAVIS STAR IN—"

ER, RIGHT, THEN I DEMANDED THAT THE MOVIE INCLUDED AT LEAST SIX SCENES WHERE I KICK BUTT-HEAD'S ASS FOR DEMANDING THAT.

HUH HUH. THEN I SAID, "BEAVIS, YOU COULDN'T KICK MY ASS, EVEN, LIKE, MY STUNT ASS." AND THEN I DEMANDED THAT BEAVIS BE PLAYED BY A CHICK WITH BIG THINGIES.

AND I SAID, "OKAY. BUT IF A CHICK PLAYS ME, SHE CAN'T LIKE DO IT WITH BUTT-HEAD, BECAUSE THEN THAT WOULD BE LIKE ME DOING IT WITH BUTT-HEAD. BUT SHE COULD LIKE DO IT WITH ME, THOUGH, CAUSE I ALWAYS DO IT WITH MYSELF."

HUH HUH. YOU SPEAK THE TRUTH, BEAVIS. HUH HUH. SO, THEN, WE WERE GOING TO MAKE MORE DEMANDS, BUT WE WERE OUT OF NACHOS, SO WE WENT OUT AND MADE THE DAMN MOVIE.

UH, THIS IS IMPORTANT: YOU SHOULD MAKE A TAPE RECORDING OF EVERYTHING YOU PUT INTO YOUR DIARY. THAT WAY, LATER, IF YOU CAN'T READ WHAT YOU WROTE, YOU CAN JUST TELL YOURSELF.

REVIEWS

"Execrable!..Obscene!"
Janet Pablum, BLURBWORKS

"An Unmitigated Disaster...Movie!"
Harold Squib, HI BROW JOURNAL

"The Thing That Sucked Does Indeed!"
Reginald Pole III, LONDON VIDEO EXPRESS

"We laughed until we realized it wasn't a comedy!"
Sam and Chris, K-OOS 15-SECOND MOVIE RUDE-VIEW

"The Movie We Always Knew
Beavis and Butt-Head Would Make!"
Norman Vanamee, HIGHLAND TIMES-ITEM

The Thing That Sucked

IN SPACE, NOBODY CAN HEAR YOU SQUEAL

UH, THIS IS IMPORTANT: REVIEWS ARE SUPPOSED TO BE TEN WORDS OR LESS, NOT COUNTING EXPLANATION MARKS.

SELLING IT

SOMETIMES WHEN YOUR MOVIE COMES OUT, YOU HAVE TO GET PEOPLE TO GO SEE IT AND NOT LISTEN TO THOSE DUMBASS ASSWIPES ON TV WHO SAID IT SUCKED.

HEY, BUTT-HEAD, WE OUGHTA KICK THEIR ASSES.

UH, THAT'S NOT VERY PROFESSIONAL, BEAVIS. THE PROFESSIONAL THING IS TO, LIKE, MAKE A BLOCKBUSTER AND THEN TAKE THAT MONEY AND BUY THE TV STATION WHERE THE ASSWIPE CRITICS WORK, AND THEN, LIKE, ORDER THEM TO KICK EACH OTHER'S ASSES.

PROMOTION

YOU GO ON TV AND TALK ABOUT HOW COOL YOUR MOVIE IS. AND, LIKE, THEY ALWAYS AGREE WITH YOU. BUT ALSO IT'S GOOD TO LIKE CREATE A CONTROVERSY, SO PEOPLE WILL THINK YOU'RE COOL. LIKE YOU COULD GET ARRESTED BEFORE THE SHOW, UH, OR EVEN BETTER, YOU COULD GET ARRESTED <u>ON</u> THE SHOW.

MERCHANDISE-ING

YOU CAN LIKE PUT THE NAME OF THE MOVIE ON STUFF AND PEOPLE WILL LIKE PAY YOU MONEY FOR IT, AND LIKE WALK AROUND FOR FREE. BECAUSE PEOPLE ARE, LIKE, STUPID.

MOMENTS THAT SUCK

IT SUCKS LIKE WHEN A MOVIE TRIES TO MAKE YOU CRY.

YEAH, IT SUCKS. AND PLUS IT DOESN'T WORK.

BEAVIS, YOU CRY ALL THE TIME AT MOVIES.

I DO NOT, BUTT-HEAD.

YOU CRIED WHEN ALL THOSE PEOPLE CAME OVER AND GAVE THAT GEORGE BAILEY GUY A WONDERFUL LIFETIME SUPPLY OF MONEY.

YEAH, WELL, THAT WAS JUST BECAUSE THEY WEREN'T GIVING IT TO ME.

AND WHEN THAT OLD YELLOW DOG GOT ALL FOAMY AND THEN THAT KID HAD TO SHOOT HIM, YOU CRIED THEN.

YEAH, WELL, THAT'S CAUSE I WANTED THEM TO LET HIM GO SO HE COULD GO ON A RAMPAGE OR SOMETHING.

AND THEN LIKE WHEN THAT TERMINATOR DUDE WAS LOWERING HIMSELF INTO THE STEEL LAVA—

THAT ONE DOESN'T COUNT! I WAS SITTING ON SOME NACHOS, AND THEY WERE, LIKE, EXTRA SPICY.

BEAVIS, YOU'RE A BIG CRYBABY.

YEAH, WELL, BUTT-HEAD, YOU CRIED AT THAT PART WHERE THAT LITTLE LION KING DUDE'S DAD DIED.

THOSE WERE TEARS OF JOY, BEAVIS.

SEQUELS

Once you made a movie once, it's easy to make it again, and uh, it's a good idea, especially if you have a lot of leftover t-shirts.

Yeah, and, like, people like it when you make the same movie all over. Because then there's, like, no nasty surprises.

Uh, this is important: When you make the same movie again, you have to change the name for some reason. If you can't think of anything, you can just put a number on the end, so people will know what order to see them in.

But don't use those numbers that Roman dudes use. Unless you just want Roman dudes seeing your movie.

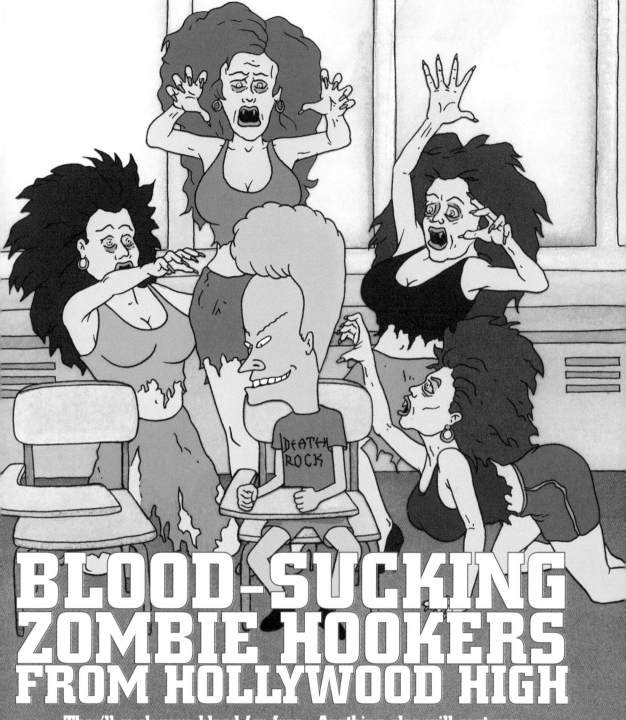

BLOOD-SUCKING ZOMBIE HOOKERS FROM HOLLYWOOD HIGH

They'll suck your blood for free. Anything else will cost you.

Starring **PAMELA ANDERSON**, **JASMINE BLEETH**, and **PANDORA PEAKS**.
Co-starring **BUTT-HEAD** as "Principal Wang." With **BEAVIS** as "First Sucked Dude."

A TOTALLY COOL PRODUCTION

MOMENTS THAT SUCK

WHEN ONE DUDE IS SHOOTING ANOTHER DUDE AND THEY
SHOW THE DUDE WHO IS SHOOTING THE OTHER DUDE
AND NOT THE OTHER DUDE BEING SHOT, THAT SUCKS.

THAT'S A SURE SIGN THE MOVIE IS, LIKE, RATED PG.

OR LIKE MAYBE THEY RAN OUT OF BLOOD OR
SOMETHING.

BEAVIS, YOU CAN'T RUN OUT OF BLOOD. UH, NOT UNLESS
A VAMPIRE SUCKS IT ALL OUT.

YOU KNOW, IF THEY'RE LIKE SHOOTING A GUY, AND, UH, AT
THE SAME TIME A VAMPIRE IS SUCKING OUT ALL HIS BLOOD, AND
THEN THEY DON'T EVEN SHOW IT, THAT WOULD TOTALLY SUCK.

UH, I THINK IF LIKE THE VAMPIRE SUCKED OUT ALL THE
BLOOD, THEN WHEN THE DUDE SHOT HIM, THERE LIKE WOULDN'T
BE ANY BLOOD.

EH. OH YEAH.

MAYBE THEY SHOULD LIKE SHOOT HIM AND THEN THE
VAMPIRE COULD START SUCKING AND THEN THE BLOOD WOULD
LIKE GET SUCKED BACK INTO THE HOLES.

THAT WOULD BE COOL!

YEAH, BUT THEY'D NEVER SHOW SOMETHING THAT
COOL. CAUSE THEN PEOPLE WOULD NEVER GO SEE ANY
OTHER MOVIES.

BEING A CELEBRITY

WHEN YOU'RE A CELEBRITY YOU CAN DO STUFF THAT IF YOU WERE JUST LIKE REGULAR, PEOPLE'D SAY, "WHO DO YOU THINK YOU ARE, A CELEBRITY OR SOMETHING?"

IF YOU...	AND YOU'RE A CELEBRITY	AND YOU'RE JUST A PERSON
WALK OUT OF A RESTAURANT WITHOUT PAYING	THEY PUT YOUR PICTURE UP ON THE WALL.	THEY PUT YOUR PICTURE UP NEXT TO THE CASH REGISTER.
SNEAK INTO A MOVIE AFTER IT'S STARTED	THEY START THE MOVIE OVER SO YOU DON'T MISS ANYTHING.	COMMUNITY SERVICE, AFTER THE THIRD TIME.
WRITE YOUR NAME ON STUFF	THEY SAY YOU'RE A GREAT CELEBRITY.	COMMUNITY SERVICE, PLUS YOU HAVE TO WASH IT OFF.
KICK STEWART'S ASS WHEN HE WON'T STOP FOLLOWING YOU JUST BECAUSE YOU'VE GOT HIS TV	THEY'D PROBABLY GIVE YOU A MEDAL OR SOMETHING.	COMMUNITY SERVICE, PLUS YOU HAVE TO SAY YOU'RE SORRY.
KILL SOME DUDES	THEY GIVE YOU YOUR OWN TV CHANNEL.	UH, UM, COMMUNITY SERVICE FOR LIKE A HUNDRED WEEKENDS, PROBABLY.

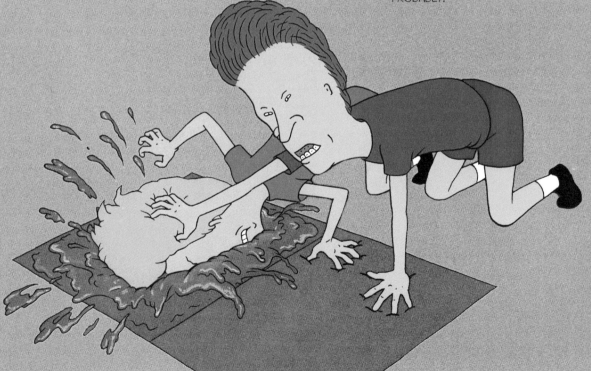

LIKE IF YOU WEREN'T A CELEBRITY AND YOU LIKE DID SOMETHING LIKE THIS, YOU WOULD PROBABLY HAVE TO DO COMMUNITY SERVICE. UH, IF, LIKE, YOU GOT CAUGHT.

TV Shows

Celebrities can just like walk on a TV show if they feel like it. That's why most TV shows suck.

Larry King: We're talking to Kooch from Beaver Hole, Virginia.
Butt-Head: Huh huh he said Virginia huh huh huh.

Very Specials

Very Specials are like regular TV shows only they suck in some very special way.

Beavis was in this one where this Barbara chick made him cry.
    She did not! My eyeballs were sweating.
    She was like talking about how your mom was a slut and your dad was like from another planet probably, and you were crying like a baby wuss.
    Er, no. Eh, when nobody was looking, she like poked me in the eye.

Tips

Celebrities always give big tips.

Butt-Head: Hey, baby, thanks for the date. Here's, like, ten dollars.

On Tourage

When you're a celebrity, no matter where you go, you're, like, a celebrity. So it's like being on tour. That's why you have an on tourage. They're like roadies except they don't carry your stuff and you have to get THEM chicks. But the cool part is that if you like tell them to kiss your butt, it's not just a saying.

Uh, this is important: It's probably a good idea to have one of the dudes in your on tourage be a cop, just in case.

GETTING RICH

UH, THE REASON WHY BIG CELEBRITIES ARE RICH IS BECAUSE PEOPLE ARE LIKE ALWAYS GIVING 'EM MONEY.

YEAH, LIKE, "HEY, YOU'RE A CELEBRITY! HERE'S A MILLION DOLLARS."

IT'S NOT THAT EASY, BUTTMUNCH. SOMETIMES YOU HAVE TO, LIKE, ASK.

OH, YOU MEAN, LIKE, "HELLO, YOU MAY RECOGNIZE ME AS A CELEBRITY. THAT WILL COST YOU ONE MILLION DOLLARS."

UH, YEAH.

MEMORY-O-BEELIA

PEOPLE WILL BUY STUFF WITH YOU ON THEM SO THAT THEY CAN, LIKE, REMEMBER WHO YOU ARE AFTER YOU'RE LIKE NOT FAMOUS ANYMORE.

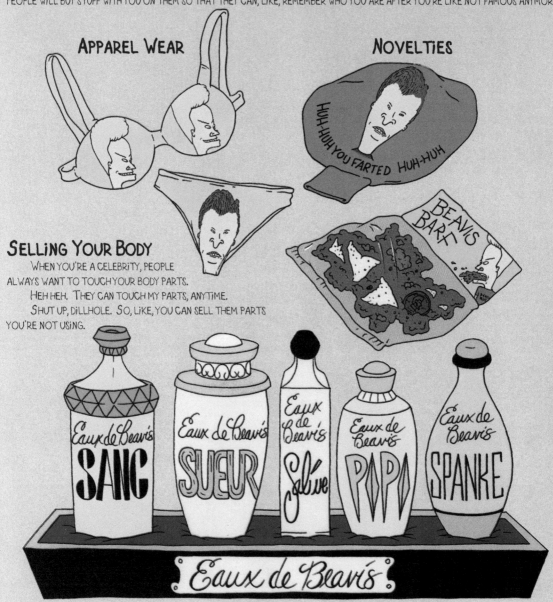

APPAREL WEAR

NOVELTIES

HUH-HUH YOU FARTED HUH-HUH

BEAVIS BARF

SELLING YOUR BODY

WHEN YOU'RE A CELEBRITY, PEOPLE ALWAYS WANT TO TOUCH YOUR BODY PARTS.

HEH HEH. THEY CAN TOUCH MY PARTS, ANYTIME.

SHUT UP, DILLHOLE. SO, LIKE, YOU CAN SELL THEM PARTS YOU'RE NOT USING.

Eaux de Beavis
SANG

Eaux de Beavis
SUEUR

Eaux de Beavis
Salive

Eaux de Beavis
PIPI

Eaux de Beavis
SPANKE

Eaux de Beavis

UH, THIS IS IMPORTANT: THERE'S PARTS OF YOUR BODY YOU SHOULDN'T SELL EVEN IF PEOPLE LIKE OFFER YOU A HUNDRED DOLLARS. ASK YOUR DOCTOR.

DOING STUFF

WHEN YOU'RE A CELEBRITY, THERE'S PEOPLE WHO WILL LIKE PAY YOU TEN DOLLARS TO TAKE A DUMP IN THEIR TOILET.
YEAH, BUT LIKE IF I REALLY HAVE TO GO, I ONLY CHARGE THEM, LIKE, FIVE DOLLARS.
UH, AND LIKE THERE'S OTHER STUFF YOU CAN DO, TOO, ONLY IT'S NOT AS MUCH FUN.

SIGNINGS

ONLY CELEBRITY SUCKERS SIGN STUFF FOR FREE ANYMORE.

CELEBRITY APPEARANCES

YOU JUST SHOW UP PLACES AND ACT LIKE A CELEBRITY.

INFOMERCIALS

THESE ARE, LIKE, REGULAR COMMERCIALS, EXCEPT WITHOUT ANY SUCKY SHOWS INTERRUPTING THEM.

MOVIE LAWS

IF A CHICK KISSES AN ACTION DUDE, SHE MUST GET NAKED. OR DIE.

Or, like, both. Heh heh. That would be my vote.

Beavis, you don't get a vote in the movies. If people got to vote in the movies, then all the chicks would be naked all the time.

Y'know, Butt-Head, in the future, like, you will get to vote. I saw this thing on TV about it. You'll get to, like, push a button next to your seat. It'll be like, "If you would like to see Demi Moore naked, press one now."

"You have pressed one. Please deposit $12 million."

SPENDING MONEY

WHEN YOU'RE RICH IT'S COOL CAUSE YOU NEVER HAVE TO PAY FOR ANYTHING. BUT IF YOU DO FEEL LIKE PAYING FOR STUFF, THERE'S LIKE A LOT OF WAYS TO SPEND MONEY, AND LIKE LOTS OF PEOPLE WHO WILL HELP YOU SPEND IT.

DESIGNERED CLOTHES

THERE'S THESE CLOTHES THAT COST LIKE A MILLION DOLLARS. THEY'RE LIKE REAL CLOTHES, EXCEPT THEY DON'T FIT.

YEAH, AND THEY DON'T HAVE THAT REAL CLOTHES SMELL.

UH, YEAH. BUT THE THING IS, CHICKS KNOW THAT DESIGNERED CLOTHES COST A MILLION DOLLARS, SO IT'S A WAY OF TELLING A CHICK, "I'VE GOT LIKE A MILLION DOLLARS, OR LIKE, I USED TO."

GORMAY QUEASINE

ANYTIME YOU WANT, YOU CAN LIKE HAVE FRESH NACHOS FLOWN TO YOUR HOUSE FROM MEXICO CITY, WHERE THEY'RE MADE BY PROFESSIONAL NACHO CHEFS AT A MAXIMART DOWN THERE.

ART

YOU'RE SUPPOSED TO BUY FAMOUS PAINTINGS AND STUFF WHEN YOU'RE RICH. BUT LIKE FOR THE SAME MONEY, YOU CAN GET SOME DUDE TO PAINT YOU EVEN BETTER ONES.

ELECTRONICS STUFF

BEAVIS BOUGHT THIS REALLY EXPENSIVE VIRTUAL REALITY BELT, BUT THEN IT TURNS OUT THAT IT ONLY WORKS ON PEOPLE WHO HAVE NADS.

ANYTHING YOU WANT

LIKE, IF YOU SEE SOMETHING YOU WANT IN A STORE OR IN SOMEBODY'S HOUSE, YOU JUST SAY, "HOW MUCH?"

UH, THIS IS IMPORTANT: THIS DOESN'T ALWAYS WORK IF THE THING YOU WANT AT SOMEBODY'S HOUSE IS A CHICK.

MANSIONS

YOUR MANSION IS WHERE YOU LIVE WHEN THEY'RE CLEANING YOUR MOVIE TRAILER. IT, LIKE, COSTS A BILLION DOLLARS, BUT IT'S WORTH IT.

NACHORIUM

THIS IS THE NACHOS ROOM. IT'S LIKE ONE OF THOSE NACHOS MACHINES AT THE MOVIES, ONLY IT'S A WHOLE ROOM. THE NACHOS ARE, LIKE, TWO FEET DEEP, AND THERE'S, LIKE, A MACHINE IN THE CEILING THAT DRIZZLES MOLTEN CHEESE ON THEM, LIKE 24 HOURS A DAY. YOU HAVE TO, LIKE, WEAR A SPECIAL SUIT WHEN GO IN THERE, SO YOU CAN EAT ALL THE NACHOS YOU WANT WITHOUT SUFFERING SEVERE CHEESE BURNS.

LIBRARY

YOU CAN SCREAM AS MUCH AS YOU WANT AND NOBODY CAN DO ANYTHING ABOUT IT. UH, BUT THAT'S ABOUT IT.

BARFORIUM

THEY USED TO HAVE THESE IN OLDEN ROMAN TIMES, WHERE YOU WOULD GO AND BARF AFTER EATING TOO MANY LIONS OR SOMETHING. AND THEN YOU COULD GO BACK AND EAT MORE LIONS. THIS IS LIKE THE SAME THING, EXCEPT IT'S NACHOS YOU'RE BARFING INSTEAD OF LIONS. WHICH IS, LIKE, NOT AS COOL, BUT IF LIONS TASTE AS BAD AS THEY SMELL AT THE ZOO, NOBODY WANTS TO BE THAT COOL.

POOL

YOU CAN LIKE PUT THOUSANDS OF SNAKES IN THE POOL, ONLY THEY DON'T SWIM REAL WELL. SO THEN YOU CAN LIKE THROW SOME MONKEYS IN THERE TO EAT THE SNAKES, ONLY THEY DON'T EAT SNAKES, EVEN IF YOU TELL THEM THEY'RE REALLY LONG BANANAS. PLUS, THEN WHEN YOU TRY TO SWIM, THE MONKEYS WILL BITE YOU. PLUS, THEY PEE IN THE POOL. SO IT'S PROBABLY BEST TO JUST PUT THE SHARKS IN THERE FIRST THING, CAUSE THEN YOU DON'T WASTE ALL THOSE SNAKES AND MONKEYS AND YOU CAN STILL SEE THE BOTTOM OF THE POOL.

MASTER BEDROOM
This is the BEDROOM WHERE YOU'RE THE MASTER. HUH HUH.

HEH HEH I'M THE MASTER OF MY WEINER.

SURE THING, BEAVIS. THEN WHY DON'T YOU TELL IT TO GET DOWN?

EH. ER. IT'S NOT VERY OBEDIENT.

TENNIS COURT
THERE'S A MACHINE THERE THAT SHOOTS TENNIS BALLS AT STUFF, LIKE TRESPASSERS. AND IT'LL ALSO SHOOT OTHER STUFF, EXCEPT DEAD SNAKES DON'T FLY VERY FAR.

MASTER BATHROOM
THIS IS WHERE YOU MASTER BATHE. HUH HUH HUH.

HEH HEH. THERE'S A LOT OF COOL STUFF IN HERE, BUTT-HEAD. LIKE, THERE'S THIS LEVER YOU PUSH AFTER YOU POOP? AND LIKE THIS WATER SHOOTS UP AND LIKE HOSES OFF YOUR BUTT.

UH, BEAVIS. I THINK THAT LEVER IS FOR CHICKS ONLY.

NO! THAT'S NOT FAIR! WHY DO CHICKS GET ALL THE DEVICES?

KITCHEN
THIS IS JUST LIKE IN THE BACK OF BURGER WORLD, WHERE THEY MAKE FOOD AND STUFF, ONLY INSTEAD OF HAVING TO BE 15 YEARS OLD TO WORK THERE YOU HAVE TO BE, LIKE, 90. THE OLD DUDE IN CHARGE IS COOL, THO'. LIKE WHEN YOU TELL HIM TO MELT SOME CHEESE ON WHATEVER HE MAKES, HE STARTS SWEARING IN FRENCH, AND IF IT'S SO BAD HE HAS TO SAY IT IN FRENCH, THEN HE MUST BE COOL. PLUS HE'S BALD, SO HE DOESN'T HAVE TO WEAR ONE OF THOSE DORKY HAIRNETS.

BUTTLER'S QUARTERS
WHEN YOU LIKE NEED SOMETHING, LIKE SOMEBODY TO GET THE REMOTE OFF THE TV, YOU CAN LIKE RING THIS BELL AND THIS DUDE COMES OUT OF HERE AND DOES WHATEVER YOU WANT. HE'S CALLED A BUTTLER CAUSE YOU CAN LIKE KICK HIM IN THE BUTT AND HE'LL JUST GO, "VERY WELL, SIR."

COOL PARTS

WHEN PEOPLE'S HEADS GET CUT OFF, THAT'S COOL.
YEAH, EVERY MOVIE SHOULD HAVE A
DECRAPITATION. IN FACT, BUTT-HEAD, I'LL GO ONE
STEP FURTHER: AT THE END OF EVERY MOVIE,
EVERYBODY IN THE MOVIE SHOULD BE DECRAPITATED.
WHOA. THAT WOULD BE COOL.
WAIT, HEH HEH, EVEN BETTER, EVERYBODY IN THE
MOVIE, AND LIKE EVERYBODY IN THE THEATER
WATCHING THE MOVIE, SHOULD BE DECRAPITATED.
THAT WOULD BE COOL, TOO. BUT MESSY.

PLASTIC SURGERY

THERE'S SOME SORT OF RULE THAT iF YOU'RE A HOLLYWOOD STAR, YOU HAVE TO BE AT LEAST 50 PERCENT PLASTIC.
IT'S SOME KIND OF GOVERNMENT REGULATION.

IMPLANTS

REGULAR CHiCK   HOLLYWOOD CHiCK

SUPPOSEDLY iN HOLLYWOOD, LiKE, ALL THE CHiCKS ARE SUPPOSED TO HAVE NEW, iMPROVED THiNGiES. IT'S, LiKE, PART OF GETTiNG YOUR DRiVER'S LiCENSE OR SOMETHiNG.

I DON'T WANT THiNGiES! I MEAN, iN ME, I MEAN.

BEAViS, ONLY CHiCKS HAVE TO GET THiNGiE iMPLANTS. FOR DUDES, iT'S TOTALLY VOLUNTARY.

OH. THAT'S A RELiEF. I JUST DiDN'T WANT TO, LiKE, STRETCH OUT ALL MY T-SHiRTS.

YOU KNOW, BEAViS, MAYBE YOU SHOULD GET YOUR OWN THiNGiES. THEN YOU WOULD LiKE BE ABLE TO TOUCH THiNGiES SOME TIME BEFORE YOU DiE.

ER, YEAH. GOOD iDEA.

FACE LiFTiNG

IF YOU WASH YOUR FACE TOO MANY TiMES, iT GETS ALL WRiNKLED. SO WHAT THEY DO iS THEY PULL THE SKiN iN YOUR FACE UP OVER YOUR HEAD AND TiE iT iN A KNOT OR SOMETHiNG.

HEY, BUTT-HEAD, THAT SOUNDS LiKE A WEDGiE.

UH, YEAH. THAT'S THE OFFiCiAL MEDiCAL NAME: CRANiUS WEDGiMUS. ONLY THEY DON'T TELL PEOPLE THAT, CAUSE, LiKE, WHO WANTS TO PAY SOMEONE $15,000 TO GiVE THEM A WEDGiE?

PEELS

WHEN YOUR F ACE GETS ALL USED-UP LOOKiNG, THEY, LiKE, PEEL iT OFF.

REALLY? YOU MEAN, LiKE, YOU CAN SEE THEiR SKULL?

UH, I THiNK SO.

EH, THAT SOUNDS KiNDA SCARY.

YEAH, BUT I GUESS iT LOOKS BETTER THAT WAY.

RHiNO PLASTiCS

IN HOLLYWOOD, EVEN THE RHiNOS HAVE TO BE BEAUTiFUL. SO THEY, LiKE, CUT OFF THEiR BiG NOSES.

TUCKS

WHEN YOUR BUTT GETS TOO BiG, THEY LiKE TUCK PART OF iT UP YOUR CRACK.

LiP-O-SUCTiON

THiS iS WHERE THEY SUCK FAT OUT OF YOU, WiTH THEiR LiPS.

SO, ER, BUTT-HEAD, DOES THAT MEAN iF YOU HAVE, LiKE, A CHUBBY...

BEAViS, YOU KNOW THEY'RE NEVER GOiNG TO LET THAT GO iN. NOW WE HAVE TO, LiKE, START OVER.

THiS iS WHERE THEY SUCK FAT OUT OF YOU, WiTH THEiR LiPS.

HEH HEH I THiNK I'VE GOT A CHUBBY HEH HEH.

BEAViS, DON'T MAKE ME KiCK YOUR ASS. OKAY, SO LiP-O-SUCTiON, TAKE THREE.

THiS iS WHERE THEY SUCK FAT OUT OF YOU, UH, WiTH THEiR LiPS.

YEAH, EH, THEY'RE LiKE VAMPiRES, EXCEPT THEY LiKE FAT iNSTEAD OF BLOOD.

UH, YEAH, THEY'RE LiKE VAMPiRES WiTH BAD DiETS.

PUBLICITY

CELEBRITIES ARE ALWAYS IN THE PAPERS BECAUSE THEY HAVE THESE CHICKS WHO CALL PEOPLE UP AND TELL THEM STUFF THEY DID.

YEAH, SHE'S A SNITCH. WE SHOULD KICK HER ASS, BUTT-HEAD.

BEAVIS, THAT PUBLICITY CHICK WOULD KICK YOUR ASS SO HARD YOU'D BE LICKING HER BOOT FROM THE INSIDE. HUH HUH I'LL BETCHA THAT WOULD GET US ON THAT DAVE SHOW HUH HUH STUPID BUTT TRICKS HUH HUH HUH.

NO WAY! MY BUTT STILL HURTS FROM THAT MAGIC TRICK YOU SAID WAS GOING TO MAKE US FAMOUS.

'BUTT'-ING HEADS The decidedly un-Boffo B.O. for "The Thing that Sucked" hasn't stopped newcomers **Beavis** and **Butt-Head** from quickly becoming Hollywood's latest bad boys. At **The Viper Room** last night, the Brat Pair were acting like they owned the place, much to the dismay of actual owner **Johnny Depp**. Sources say Depp fumed as Butt-Head repeatedly called him **Keanu**, and opined that Keanu/Depp's band should be called "Dogsuck." Beavis, meanwhile, cornered Depp galpal **Kate Moss**, entreating the supermodel to slip away and "pull his finger." Said the source: "It reminded me of back in the days when **Charlie** and **Emilio** used to hang out here."

VANITY FAIR

BUTT HOT!

HE'S GOT THAT JAMES DEAN LOOK. NOW IF ONLY HE COULD LOSE THE SIDEKICK...

GQ

Real Beavis

Butt-Head's darker half reveals that beneath that maddeningly inscrutable veneer, there lies a simple man.

UH, THIS IS LIKE, REALLY, IMPORTANT: WHEN YOUR PUBLICITY CHICK TELLS YOU SHE WANTS TO TOUCH BASE WITH YOU, SHE DOESN'T MEAN SECOND BASE.

JERRY LEWIS TIMES *DEUX*: Never mind the homegrown box office, the French love **Beavis** and **Butt-Head**. While *The Thing That Sucked* isn't exactly packing them in at American multiplexes, at the *Cinema Dingue* in Paris, lines start forming at 6 a.m.—for the midnight show. "They are so very American," opined one young French cineaste as he waited to see *Thing* for the nineteeth time. "They are like **Jerry**, only so much more of the American." And, of course, the unprecedented 23 scenes set in strip clubs don't hurt.—*James Seymour*

COOL PARTS

WHEN A TIED-UP CHICK SPITS IN A BAD DUDE'S FACE, THAT'S COOL.

YEAH, AND SHE SPITS ACID, AND HIS FACE, LIKE, MELTS.

BEAVIS, IF SHE CAN SPIT ACID, THEN SHE'S A DEMON, NOT A CHICK.

UM, I THOUGHT ALL CHICKS WERE DEMONS. OH.

LIKE WHEN I HAVE DREAMS, CHICKS ARE ALWAYS POKING ME WITH PITCHFORKS AND LIKE TEARING OFF MY FLESH, AND THEN THEY ALL SPIT ON ME.

BEAVIS, MAYBE YOU SHOULD GO TO THE COUNSELOR'S OFFICE.

YEAH, BUT THEN I MIGHT NOT HAVE THOSE DREAMS ANYMORE.

VALLEY PARKING

CELEBRITIES ARE SO COOL THAT THEY LET OTHER PEOPLE DRIVE THEIR CARS ALL THE TIME. LIKE, WHEN YOU GO TO A RESTAURANT OR SOMETHING, YOU LEAVE THE KEYS IN THE CAR, AND SOME DUDE JUST DRIVES OFF WITH IT AND PARKS IT IN THE VALLEY SOMEPLACE.

BUT IF WE WERE VALLEY PARKING DUDES, WE WOULD PROVIDE, LIKE, OTHER SERVICES:

- ADJUST THE PRE-SETS ON YOUR RADIO SO YOUR DATE DOESN'T THINK YOU'RE A DORK.
- TEST YOUR BRAKES UNDER HIGH SPEED CONDITIONS.
- TEST THE ABILITY OF YOUR CAR TO PICK UP CHICKS.
- TAKE THE CHICKS TO YOUR HOUSE, SO THEY'LL KNOW WHERE TO GO NEXT TIME.
- CLEAN OUT YOUR REFRIGERATOR, SO THERE'S ROOM FOR YOUR DOGGY BAG.
- PUT YOUR DOGGY IN A BAG IF HE WON'T STOP BITING US.
- TEST THE ABILITY OF YOUR CAR TO BEAT SOME PUNKS WHO THINK THEY HAVE A REALLY HOT CAR OR SOMETHING.
- RETURN YOUR CAR WITHIN THREE TO FIVE BUSINESS DAYS.

DOING IT WITH CELEBRITY CHICKS

CELEBRITIES ONLY LIKE DO IT WITH OTHER CELEBRITIES, SO WHEN YOU'RE A CELEBRITY, CELEBRITY CHICKS HAVE TO DO IT WITH YOU IF LIKE CHRISTIAN SLATER IS BUSY.

EH, YEAH. OR LIKE SOMETIMES THEY CAN'T DO IT WITH YOU BECAUSE THEY HAVE TO READ A SCRIPT THAT NIGHT, OR LIKE, PAINT THEIR TOENAILS, OR WASH THEIR CAT, OR SOMETHING.

SO, LIKE, WHEN YOU DO IT WITH A CELEBRITY CHICK, YOU'RE NOT SUPPOSED TO TELL ANYBODY, EVEN THOUGH THAT'S THE BEST PART. SO, UH, I DIDN'T DO IT WITH THESE CELEBRITY CHICKS, NO MATTER WHAT THEY SAY.

HEY, BUTT-HEAD, WHAT ABOUT ME?

OH, YEAH. AND, UH, BEAVIS WASN'T THERE WATCHING, EITHER.

HEH HEH. YEAH, I WASN'T IN THE CLOSET, AND I WAS WEARING MY PANTS THE WHOLE TIME.

BUT IF, LIKE, I DID DO IT WITH THESE CELEBRITY CHICKS (AND, LIKE, I NEVER SAID I DID) I, UH, HYPOTENUSE, IT WENT A LITTLE SOMETHING LIKE THIS:

CHER

SO ONE TIME LET'S PRETEND I WAS WITH CHER, HUH HUH HUH, IN HER BEDROOM. AND SHE LIKE WANTED TO DO IT, BECAUSE SHE REALLY DIGS YOUNGER DUDES.

HEY, I'M YOUNGER THAN YOU ARE, BUTT-HEAD!

I SAID "DUDES," BEAVIS. SO ANYWAY, SHE SAYS, "HEY, BABY, YOU KNOW WHAT TURNS ME ON?"

AND I SAID, "THIS?"

AND SHE SLAPPED ME AND SAID NO. SHE SAID, "WHAT WOULD BE REALLY SEXY IS IF YOU WOULD WEAR THIS FOR ME."

AND THEN SHE TOOK OUT THIS MID-ELVIS SUIT OF ARMOR SHE HAD, LIKE, UNDER THE BED. I GUESS SHE'S LIKE REALLY INTO, YOU KNOW, PROTECTION. SO LIKE I GOT INSIDE THE ARMOR, AND THEN WE LIKE DID IT, I THINK.

DREW BARRYMORE

SO I WENT TO THAT RESTAURANT WHERE ONLY THE CELEBRITIES GO, PLANET HOLLYWOOD? AND DREW BARRYMORE WAS THERE. SHE SAID I REMINDED HER OF A CHICK SHE KNEW, AND THEN WE WENT OUT TO HER CAR AND LIKE DID IT, RIGHT ON THE HOOD, JUST LIKE IN THAT MOVIE, POISON IVY. OR AT LEAST THAT'S HOW SHE SAID WE WERE GONNA DO IT, ONLY ANDERSON'S VISA CARD WAS EXPIRED OR SOMETHING.

SO, LIKE, I CALLED DREW BARRYMORE THE NEXT DAY TO SEE IF SHE LIKE TOOK AMERICAN EXPRESS, ONLY HER MAID OR SOMETHING SAID NOT TO CALL AGAIN.

ELIZABETH SHUE

She's like that hooker, in that movie? So I was on Sunset Boulevard and I saw her working there. She looked, like, a little fatter than she was in the movie, and like, she had these holes in her face. So I said, "Hey, aren't you that chick in that movie?" And she said, "Sure, baby, whatever you want."

But like Beavis spent our last $20 on some special chick rubbing oil from Fred and Rick's of Hollywood, which is stupid if, like, then you don't have any money to buy the chick.

Hey, Butt-Head, it works without the chick.

Well, that's certainly good news for you, Beavis.

PAMELA ANDERSON LEE

Didya ever notice how much that baby looks like me?

Me with my various celebrity conquests.

COURTNEY LOVE

She was at this place called Ralph's, which is where all the celebrities buy their food. And I like followed her until, like, she got to the produce section, and then like at exactly the right second, I said, "Say, could I see your melons so that I know these ones are the right size?"

And so then she told me to, like, do myself. So I went right home and did, so that sort of counts.

PANDORA PEAKS

It was like climbing Mount Everest. And then, just as I was about to reach the peak, I lost my footing and started to fall. And then I woke up. It was all a dream. A sweet, beautiful, incredible, but kind of messy dream.

FILM FESTIVALS

MOVIE STARS ARE ALWAYS FLYING TO FOREIGN LANDS WHERE THERE'S LOTS OF PARTIES WITH NAKED CHICKS, AND SOMETIMES JUST NAKED CHICKS OUT ON THE STREET, AND THEY TAKE YOUR PICTURE A LOT, ESPECIALLY IF YOU'RE STANDING NEXT TO A NAKED CHICK. AND, LIKE, IF YOU GET TIRED OF LOOKING AT NAKED CHICKS OR JUST WANT TO GO SOMEPLACE DARK, YOU CAN GO SEE A MOVIE OR SOMETHING.

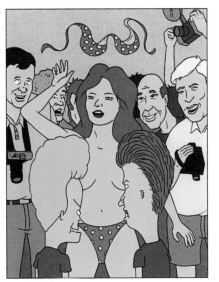

CANNES

THERE'S A PLACE IN FRANCE WHERE THE CHICKS WEAR NO TOPS, AND YOU CAN LIKE SEE IT ALL. HUH HUH HUH.

ER, BUTT-HEAD, I THINK, AT THAT PLACE IN FRANCE? THE CHICKS WEAR NO PANTS. I KNOW, CAUSE I SING THAT SONG ALL THE TIME.

THAT'S A DIFFERENT PLACE IN FRANCE, DUMBASS. THAT'S GAY PANTS-FREE. THIS PLACE IS CALLED CANS, CAUSE ALL THE CHICKS HAVE LIKE, REALLY BIG CANS.

ER, YEAH, BUT, EH, I THINK CANS ARE BUTTS. SERIOUSLY.

NOT IN FOREIGN LANGUAGE ARTS. IN FRANCE, DUDES CALL THINGIES CAN-CANS.

REALLY? WHAT DO THEY CALL BUTTS?

WHAT DO I LOOK LIKE, BEAVIS? A FRENCH GUY?

HELPFUL FRENCHISH PHRASES

"HELLO. MAY I TOUCH YOUR THINGIES?" *VOO LOOVOO TOO SHAY BOO COO?*

"GIVE ME SOME NACHOS." *VOO LEE VOO NACHOS DAMMIT.*

"WHERE ARE ALL THE FROGS ANDERSON TOLD US ABOUT?" *VOO LEE VOO COO SHAY ASS ESS SWAH?*

VENICE

THIS IS THAT UNDERWATER PLACE WHERE THEY MADE THAT SWIMMING WITH WOLVES MOVIE.

YEAH, EXCEPT THERE AREN'T ANY BUFFALOS. THEY MUST NOT FLOAT OR SOMETHING.

UH, YEAH. AND INDIANS MUST LIKE ITALIAN FOOD. BECAUSE THAT'S LIKE ALL THE RESTAURANTS SERVE.

HELPFUL NATIVE ITALIAN PHRASES

"GIVE ME SOME NACHOS." *TEE PEE NACHOS MOZZARELLA, KEMOSABE.*

"WITH EXTRA CHEESE." *HOW NOW PARMAGIANA.*

"HELP, I CAN'T SWIM." *WOO WOO WOO MAMA MIA!*

SUNDANCE

UH, THIS IS A NEW COUNTRY UP IN THE MOUNTAINS. THEY'RE TRYING TO MAKE YOU THINK IT'S REALLY A REAL COUNTRY, CAUSE THE BUILDINGS ARE ALL BRAND NEW BUT THEY LOOK LIKE THEY'RE FROM WILD WEST HISTORY. PLUS THEY HAVE THEIR OWN LANGUAGE, BUT IT'S JUST A RIP-OFF OF ENGLISH.

HELPFUL SUNDANCER PHRASES

"GIVE ME SOME NACHOS." *GREEN LIGHT THOSE NACHOS, DOUBLE ESPRESSO.*

"TAKE OFF YOUR CLOTHES. NOW, DAMMIT." *PUT THAT BACK END IN TURNAROUND, BABE.*

"LET'S, LIKE, DO IT." *I'D LOVE TO HEAR YOUR PITCH.*

COOL PARTS

MONKEYS ARE COOL.
  IF A MOVIE HAS A MONKEY, THEN IT SHALL BE
COOL. IT IS WRITTEN.
  YEAH, AND IT'S REALLY COOL IF, LIKE, THE
MONKEY PUNCHES SOMEONE OR LIKE SHOOTS A GUN
OR PLAYS BASEBALL OR SOMETHING.
  THOSE MONKEYS HAVE A LOT OF RANGE.
  BUTT-HEAD, YOU KNOW THE OTHER COOL
THING ABOUT MONKEYS? THEY'RE ALWAYS NAKED.
  UH, SO? DOGS ARE NAKED ALL THE TIME, TOO.
  OH. OH YEAH. HEY, THAT REMINDS ME OF A
JOKE. DO YOU KNOW WHY DOGS, LIKE, LICK
THEMSELVES?
  UH, BECAUSE YOU BITE?

THE LITTLE PEOPLE

IT'S, UH, IMPORTANT WHEN YOU'RE A BIG STAR TO, LIKE, REMEMBER WHO THE LITTLE PEOPLE ARE.

YEAH, YOU'RE NOT SUPPOSED TO, LIKE, MAKE FUN OF PEOPLE WHO ARE DIFFERENT. EH, EVEN IF THEY ARE, YOU KNOW, DIFFERENT AND STUFF.

NOT THOSE LITTLE PEOPLE, BUNGHOLE. THE LITTLE PEOPLE WHO LIKE YOU KNEW BEFORE YOU WERE A BIG STAR.

I DON'T REMEMBER US KNOWING ANY LITTLE PEOPLE, BUTT-HEAD. EXCEPT FOR THAT ONE KID. BUT HE WOULDN'T OF BEEN THAT LITTLE, IF HE, LIKE, HAD LEGS AND STUFF.

NEVER MIND, BEAVIS, JUST LICK THESE STAMPS. AND DON'T GET ANY CHUNKS OF FOOD ON 'EM, LIKE LAST TIME.

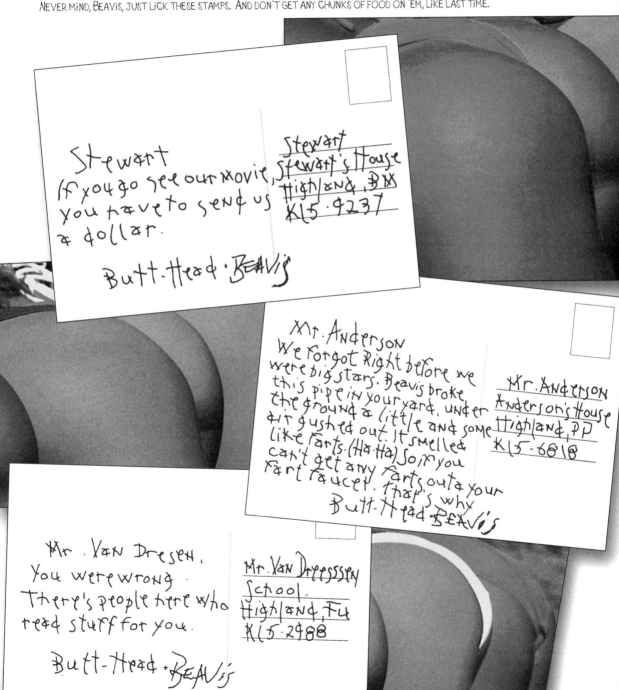

It sucks when people in the movie are watching TV.

They're never watching anything cool. It's always, like, "It's a Wonderful Life" or some other stupid TV show.

Yeah, and you can't tell them to change it. Hey, Butt-head, you know what would be cool, if like in the future you could like have a remote and you could change what they're watching on TV, you know, in the movie. Then if the movie sucked, you could just watch TV.

That would be cool.

PROBLEMS

CELEBRITIES HAVE PROBLEMS, TOO, ONLY THEY'RE COOLER.

GETTING FAT

STARS DON'T WANT TO BE FAT BECAUSE NOBODY LIKES TO SEE FAT PEOPLE WHEN THEY GO TO THE MOVIES.

YEAH, WHEN PEOPLE SEE FAT PEOPLE IN MOVIES, THEY BUY LESS POPCORN.

SO, LIKE, WHEN STARS GET FAT, THEY HAVE TO GO TO A FARM, WHERE THEY PULL PLOWS AND STUFF.

GETTING OLD

IF A STAR DOESN'T DIE AT THE RIGHT TIME, THEY END UP GETTING OLD. WHICH IS BAD, CAUSE THERE'S ONLY JOBS IN HOLLYWOOD FOR ONE COOL OLD DUDE AND ONE COOL OLD CHICK. SO YOU'VE GOT ALL THESE OLD STARS, LIKE, PUSHING EACH OTHER DOWN STAIRS AND STUFF.

HEY, BUTT-HEAD, THAT WOULD BE A COOL MOVIE.

BEAVIS, THAT IDEA TOOK NEARLY FIFTY WORDS TO EXPLAIN. HAVEN'T YOU LEARNED ANYTHING I'VE TAUGHT YOU?

ER, EH, HOW ABOUT THAT MONKEY SPANKING THING?

OKAY, SO ONE THING. IT'S ABOUT TIME YOU LEARNED A NEW TRICK, INSTEAD OF DOING THAT ONE ALL THE TIME.

DRUGS AND STUFF

SOME CELEBRITIES END UP TAKING A LOT OF DRUGS AND STUFF, BECAUSE, LIKE, THEY WEREN'T PAYING ATTENTION IN SCHOOL.

PAYING ATTENTION TO WHAT?

BEAVIS, DON'T YOU REMEMBER WHEN THAT COP DUDE CAME TO SCHOOL AND HE TOLD US, UH, SOMETHING ABOUT DRUGS AND STUFF?

EH, YEAH, HE HAD A GUN. THAT WAS COOL.

Beavis's sad confession:

"I'M A PYRO"

Will the star's brave admission help other young people deal with their fiery obsessions?

SKIN CANCER

SKIN CANCER IS, LIKE, WHEN YOU HANG OUT AT THE BEACH UNTIL YOUR FACE LOOKS LIKE A WALLET.

EH, YEAH, THAT'S COOL. WHEN YOUR FACE LOOKS LIKE A WALLET, I MEAN. BUT I GUESS CANCER ISN'T COOL. MM. BUT HANGING OUT AT THE BEACH IS COOL, SO I GUESS THAT'S TWO OUT OF THREE.

UH, YEAH, BUT WHEN YOU HAVE CANCER, THEY HAVE TO, LIKE, CUT OFF YOUR NOSE TO SPIT IN YOUR FACE.

EH, BUTT-HEAD, THAT DOESN'T SOUND RIGHT.

YEAH, IT'S AN ANCIENT CHINESE SECRET OR SOMETHING.

OH, WELL, THEN, ER, OKAY. BUT I STILL THINK IF YOUR FACE LOOKS LIKE A WALLET, YOU SHOULD JUST LEAVE IT ALONE. CAUSE IT LOOKS COOL.

SURE, IF YOU'RE A DUDE. BUT IF YOU'RE LIKE A CHICK AND YOUR FACE LOOKS LIKE A WALLET, NOBODY'LL DO IT WITH YOU.

I DUNNO, BUTT-HEAD. I WOULD DO IT WITH A WALLET-FACE CHICK, YOU KNOW, IF SHE WAS NICE.

BEAVIS, YOU WOULD, LIKE, DO IT WITH AN ACTUAL WALLET.

THE OSCARS

These are like the Academy Awards, except they're named after that slobby dude on reruns, even though it doesn't look anything like him. Like, everybody wants to win one of these because, uh, it really impresses the chicks.

Ways to Win an Oscar

1. Play a very special dude. Like if Beavis wasn't really Beavis, he could of won an Oscar for playing Beavis, cause like the Academy would feel sorry for him since people might think he really is a Beavis.

2. If you're like a hot chick, play an ugly chick.

3. If you're an ugly chick, become a director.

4. Make a movie out of a book nobody read cause then everybody will be surprised at what happens, and you can change anything you want, cause nobody's gonna go back and read the book, that's for sure.

5. Buy everybody in Hollywood some nachos.

Oscars They'd Give Out If They Let Somebody Cool Think Up The Damn Oscars For Once

| Best movie in which no animals were harmed in the filming, but it sure looked like they were | The Jim Carrey Award for Finest Achievement in Fartography | Movie trailer that was the most times better than the real movie | Best Explosion where they really blew something up, not just a damn toy |

OSCAR SPEECH

OSCAR SPEECHES ARE SUPPOSED TO SUCK, BUT THEY DON'T HAVE TO. YOU DON'T HAVE TO LIKE THANK GOD OR LIKE EVEN THE DILLWEED WHO LIKE WIPED YOUR BUTT CLEAN EVERY MORNING.

ER, BUT BUTT-HEAD, I DON'T THINK I COULD HAVE DONE IT WITHOUT HIM. THE BUTT WIPER, I MEAN.

UH, BEAVIS, THERE'S A SPOT THERE ON YOUR BUTT.

WHAT?! HE'S FIRED! FIRED! *FIRED!* HE'LL NEVER WIPE BUTTS IN THIS TOWN AGAIN!

HUH HUH HUH HUH HUH.

HEH HEH TESTES TESTES HEH HEH.

BEAVIS, THEY CAN HEAR YOU. JUST LOOK AT 'EM OUT THERE.

I KNOW, I JUST LIKE TO SAY THAT. TESTES. *TESTES.* TES-TEEES.

WELL, SHUT UP, ASSWIPE. YOU CAN PLAY WITH YOUR TESTES LATER. HUH HUH. I'M GIVING A SPEECH HERE. SO, UH, FOUR SCORES AND SEVEN CHICKS AGO HUH HUH HUH. I'D LIKE THE THANK THE SEVEN CHICKS WHO I SCORED WITH FOUR TIMES ON THIS MOVIE. HUH HUH. AND I'LL BET THEY WOULD LIKE TO THANK ME. HUH HUH. ANY TIME, BABES.

ER, BUTT-HEAD, THAT DOESN'T MAKE SENSE. HOW CAN YOU SCORE FOUR TIMES WITH SEVEN CHICKS? YOU MUST OF BEEN ABSENT FROM MATH THAT DAY, BEAVIS.

ER, OH YEAH, PROBABLY.

SO, UH, WHERE WAS I? OH YEAH, I WAS SCORING WITH SEVEN CHICKS. THAT'S WHY IT WAS SO COOL MAKING THIS MOVIE, EVEN THOUGH, LIKE, NOBODY WHO SPEAKS ENGLISH SAW IT. SO, LIKE, I DON'T WANT TO THANK ANYBODY ELSE, BECAUSE YOU BUTTMUNCHES DIDN'T VOTE FOR US OR GIVE US ANY OSCARS, WHICH IS WHY WE HAD TO KNOCK DOWN THAT OLD CHICK TO GET UP HERE. AND WE'RE GOING TO LIKE KEEP THIS OSCAR UNTIL WE GET ONE FOR REAL, PLUS, UH, A MILLION DOLLARS.

EH, ER, BUTT-HEAD, CAN I SAY SOMETHING NOW?

UH, SURE. THEY SHUT OFF THE MICROPHONE ANYWAY.

ER, EH, AHEM. SO IF THERE'S ANY CHICKS OUT THERE WHO WOULD LIKE TO SCORE WITH ME, I'LL BE, EH, BACKSTAGE. THANK YOU AND DRIVE THROUGH.

UH, THIS IS IMPORTANT: DON'T LIKE GIVE THIS SPEECH IF YOU EVER LIKE WANT ANYBODY TO DO YOU FOR LUNCH AGAIN.

THE UNTOLD EXPOSE

SO, LIKE, THEN, AFTER YOU'RE NOT FAMOUS ANYMORE—

WHAT? WE'RE NOT FAMOUS ANYMORE?

BEAVIS, DON'T YOU REMEMBER WHEN THAT DUDE SHOWED UP AND GAVE US BACK ALL THAT STUFF WE PUT ON THE WALLS AT PLANET HOLLYWOOD?

EH, OH, YEAH. HEH HEH. BUT THAT WAS GOOD, CAUSE, EH, THAT WAS MY ONLY PAIR OF UNDERPANTS.

AND THEN, REMEMBER, ALL THE CHICKS LEFT?

ER, THEY SAID THEY WERE JUST GOING OUT TO SHOPLIFT SOME MAKE-UP OR SOMETHING.

NO, DUMBASS. WHAT THEY SAID WAS THEY WERE TAKING A POWDER. AND, LIKE, HOW LONG COULD THAT TAKE?

MAYBE THEY GOT ARRESTED, AND NOW THEY'RE IN JAIL AND TAKING SHOWERS TOGETHER AND SWEATING UP THEIR PRISON UNIFORMS, AND SO, LIKE, MAYBE WE SHOULD, YOU KNOW, WAIT FOR THEM. SO THEY COULD TELL US ABOUT IT.

BEAVIS, WE CAN'T DO THAT. REMEMBER, THOSE BIG GHOST DUDES CAME AND SAID THEY WERE GOING TO, UH, POSSESS OUR MANSION, AND THAT WE HAD TO LEAVE?

YEAH, THEY WERE PRETTY STRONG FOR GHOSTS. YOU KNOW, BUTT-HEAD, WE SHOULD CALL OUR AGENT AND HAVE HIM PUT US IN ANOTHER MOVIE, AND THEN, LIKE, WE COULD HIRE THOSE GHOST EXTERMINATOR DUDES AND GET OUR MANSION BACK.

WE DID CALL OUR AGENT, DILLHOLE. REMEMBER, HE WAS, LIKE, IN THE BATHROOM FOR SIX HOURS?

EH HEH. HE MUST OF BEEN TRYING TO BREAK MY RECORD.

NO, BEAVIS, I THINK HE JUST DIDN'T WANT TO TALK TO US. REMEMBER, THEN THEY TOLD US HE WAS DEAD, BUT THEN WE SAW HIM ON THE STREET, AND HE RAN AWAY FROM US?

YEAH, HE WAS PRETTY FAST, FOR A ZOMBIE.

AND REMEMBER, WE WERE LIKE ON THE STREET AND LIKE NOBODY RECOGNIZED US, EXCEPT FOR JAPANESE PEOPLE.

SO THEN WE MUST BE PRETTY FAMOUS IN JAPAN.

BEAVIS, ALL AMERICAN PEOPLE ARE FAMOUS IN JAPAN. THAT'S HOW YOU KNOW YOU'RE NOT FAMOUS ANYMORE, WHEN YOU'RE FAMOUS IN JAPAN.

WE'RE NOT FAMOUS ANYMORE?! BUTT-HEAD, WHAT ARE WE GONNA DO?

BEAVIS, WE'RE GONNA DO THE SAME THING ALL CELEBRITIES DO WHO USED TO BE FAMOUS BUT AREN'T FAMOUS ANYMORE. WE'RE GONNA WRITE A BOOK.

AND THEN WE'LL BE FAMOUS AGAIN?

UH, NO.

HAPPY ENDINGS

HEY BEAVIS, OUR MOVIE IS ON SHOWTIME AGAIN.

OUR MOVIE SUCKS. CHANGE IT.

BEAVIS, IF OUR MOVIE SUCKS SO MUCH, WHY WOULD THEY SHOW IT, LIKE, EVERY THREE HOURS?

I SAID, CHANGE IT. CHANGE IT, BUTT-HEAD.

UH, WAIT. HERE COMES THAT PART WHERE YOU MAKE FRIENDS WITH THE ALIENS.

BUTT-HEAD, IF YOU DON'T CHANGE IT, I'M GONNA KICK YOUR ASS, LIKE RIGHT NOW.

HEY THERE, BEAVIS, WHAT'S THAT ALIEN HAVE IN HIS HAND?

CHANGE IT!

SAY, IS THAT SOME KIND OF...PROBE?

BUTT-HEAD, PLEASE! THIS SUCKS! THIS SUCKS!

HUH HUH. OPEN UP AND SAY, "AH," BEAVIS.

YAAAAAAAAAAAAAAHHHH!!!!

HUH. YOU'RE A GOOD ACTOR, BEAVIS. YOU SHOULD BE IN THE MOVIES.

THE BUTT-FILES

BEAVIS & BUTT-HEAD'S GUIDE
TO SCI-FI AND THE UNKNOWN

CREATED BY MIKE JUDGE
WRITTEN BY GREG GRABIANSKI AND AIMEE KEILLOR

UHH, I'D LIKE TO DEADIKATE THIS BOOK TO MY BUTT, HUH-HUH-HUH-HUH!
YEAH, HEH-HEH-HEH, UMM, I'D LIKE TO DEFICATE THIS BOOK TO MY NADS, HEH-HEH-HEH. WITHOUT WHO
I'D, UMM, HAVE NO NADS, HEH-HEH-HEH-HEH.

Beavis and Butt-Head created by Mike Judge
Written by: Greg Grabianski and Aimee Keillor
Edited by: Kristofor Brown
Art Direction: Roger Gorman/Leah Sherman, Reiner, NYC
Senior Art Supervisor: Dominie Mahl
Art Supervisor: Sharon Fitzgerald
Production Coordinator: Sara Duffy
Illustrators: Mike Judge, John Allemand, Karen Disher, Bryon Moore, Mike Baez
Ink and Paint: Monica Smith, Lisa Klein
Background Painters: Bill Long, Sophie Kittredge
Additional Illustrators: Brad MacDonald, Willy Hartland, Eugene Salandra
Production Assistants: James Wood, Tati Nguyen, Matt LaBarge

Special Thanks: John Andrews, Christine Friebely, Andrea Labate, Ed Paparo, Renee Presser, Robin Silverman, Donald Silvey,
Abby Terkuhle, and Van Toffler.

Special thanks at Pocket Books to: Lynda Castillo, Gina Centrello, Kendra Falkenstein, Max Greenhut, Felice Javit,
Eric Rayman, Dave Stern, Kara Welsh, and Irene Yuss. Also thanks to Al Travison at Stevenson, and Paula Trotto.

INTRODUKSHUN

SO IT'S, LIKE, ME AND BEAVIS KEEP SEEING ALL THESE MOVIES AND TV SHOWS ABOUT THE SUPPERNATURAL AND THE UNKNOWN AND STUFF. WHERE DUDES ARE LIKE, "UHH, THIS IS A MYSTERY. NOBODY CAN EXPLAIN IT! IT IS BEYOND ALL HUMAN COMPREHENSION!" HUH-HUH-HUH! DUMB-ASSES! IT'S LIKE, THEY CAN'T EXPLAIN THIS STUFF 'CAUSE THEY'RE, YOU KNOW, STUPID OR SOMETHING. HUH-HUH-HUH!

HEH-HEH-HEH! YEAH! STUPID BUTTHOLES! HEH-HEH!

SO WE, LIKE, CHECKED OUT A BUNCH OF THIS SUPPERNATURAL AND UNKNOWN CRAP FOR OURSELVES AND DID SOME EXPERAMINTS. AND THEN WE DID THIS BOOK TO EXPLAIN ALL THIS STUFF AND MAKE LOTS OF MONEY. HUH-HUH!

YEAH, HEH-HEH- HEH! AND ALL THESE SCIENTIFIC DUDES ARE GONNA BUY THIS BOOK AND GO, "OHHH, YEAH. I SEE NOW. I GUESS I WAS JUST A DUMB-ASS!" HEH-HEH-HEH-HEH-HEH!

AND, UHH, SOME OF OUR BOOK IS ABOUT SCIENCE FRICTION. LIKE, A LOT OF STUFF ABOUT THE UNKNOWN HAS TO DO WITH OUTER SPACE AND THE FUTURE AND STUFF. AND THERE'S A LOT OF SCI-FI MOVIES AND TV SHOWS THAT ARE ABOUT THAT KIND OF CRAP TOO, SO WE THOUGHT WE'D CHECK SOME OF THEM OUT. MAYBE SOME OF THIS SCI-FI STUFF'LL HELP YOU UNDERSTAND THE UNKNOWN BETTER, IN CASE YOU'RE, LIKE, SLOW OR SOMETHING. LIKE THOSE SCIENTIFIC DUDES. HUH-HUH-HUH!

HEH-HEH-HEH! YEAH! STUPID BUTTHOLES! HEH-HEH!

SO, LIKE, HERE WE GO. JUST TURN OFF THE LIGHTS, GET SOME NACHOS, SIT BACK, RELAX, AND UH, TAKE OFF YOUR PANTS (ESPESHULLY IF YOU'RE A CHICK). HUH-HUH-HUH!

LIFE AFTER DEATH

EVERYONE'S ALWAYS LIKE, "UMM, IS THERE LIFE AFTER DEATH?" IT'S LIKE THIS BIG MYSTERY AND NOBODY KNOWS THE ANSWER. SO, LIKE, ME AND BUTT-HEAD WANTED TO DO AN EXPEARMINT TO FIND OUT THE TRUTH. WE FOUND THIS COOL DEAD THING IN THE ROAD. HEH-HEH!! I THINK IT WAS A GOAT. THEN WE WATCHED IT TO SEE IF THERE WAS LIFE AFTER DEATH. I TOOK A BUNCH OF NOTES AND STUFF. CHECK IT OUT.

DAY 1: WE WATCHED THIS DEAD GOAT. HEH-HEH. ALL DAY. HEH-HEH. IT WAS PRETTY COOL 'CUZ IT WAS ALL SMASHED AND YOU COULD SEE ITS GUTS AND STUFF. IT WAS DEAD, HEH-HEH-HMM-HEH-HEH.

DAY 2: UMM, THE GOAT STILL DIDN'T MOVE OR ANYTHING BUT IT WAS STILL COOL, 'CUZ WE GOT TO SEE A LOT OF FLIES AND ANTS CRAWLING ON IT, HEH-HEH-HEH, I STEPPED ON SOME, HEH-HEH-HEH.

DAY 3: UMM, THIS DEAD THING IS STARTING TO SMELL. THAT'S COOL! BUTT-HEAD POKED IT WITH A STICK AND SOME JUNK LEAKED OUT OF ITS BUTT! HEH-HEH-HEH!

DAY 4: HEH-HEH-HEH. TRUCKS KEEP RUNNING OVER THE GOAT, AND NOW IT'S ALL FLAT AND KIND OF LOOKS LIKE THE HAIR AND STUFF IN MY BATH-TUB. HEH-HEH-HEH! I SPIT ON IT, BUT, UMM, IT STILL DIDN'T MOVE!

DAY 5: UMM, THIS EXPEARMINT SUCKS! IT'S, LIKE, WE KEEP WATCHING AND WATCHING, AND NOTHING HAPPENS! NYAAAAHHHHH! MOVE, DAMMIT! I'M GONNA KICK YOUR ASS, YOU SON OF A BITCH!

CONCLOOSHUN: WE DON'T KNOW WHY PEOPLE THINK LIFE AFTER DEATH IS SUCH A MYSTERY. THERE IS NO LIFE AFTER DEATH! AFTER DEATH, YOU JUST LAY THERE AND STINK AND GET ALL ROTTEN AND CROWS EAT YOUR EYES AND GUTS OUT. HEH-HEH!

MAGGOT-ALIENS FROM MARS

UMM, THIS IS A PICTURE OF ALIENS FROM MARS! SOME SCIENTIFIC DUDE ON TV SAID THAT THESE MAGGOTS CAME FROM SOME ROCK THAT FELL FROM MARS. HEH-HEH! IT WAS ALL OVER THE NEWS AND STUFF. IT FREAKED US OUT CUZ ME AND BUTT-HEAD SEE THESE THINGS ALL THE TIME, BUT WE NEVER KNEW THEY WERE ALIENS!

SO ME AND BUTT-HEAD DECIDED TO FIND SOME OF THESE MAGGOT-ALIENS AND KILL THEM TO PROTECT EARTH'S WOMEN AND STUFF. HEH-HEH! WE KNEW WHERE THEY HUNG OUT. IT'S LIKE, THEIR SECRET ALIEN HIDE-OUT OR SOMETHING.

YEAH, HUH-HUH. WE TIPPED OVER ANDERSON'S GARBAGE CAN AND FOUND A BUNCH OF THESE MAGGOT-ALIENS IN THERE, CRAWLING AROUND ON SOME OLD MEAT, HUH-HUH-HUH. THEY WERE LIKE ALL TOGETHER AND I THINK THEY WERE PLANNING ON HOW TO TAKE OVER THE WORLD AND STUFF. WE TOOK THE LEADER OF THE MAGGOT-ALIENS HOSTAGE AND WE TIED IT UP AND ASKED IT A BUNCH OF QUESTIONS. WE ASKED IT WHAT THEY WERE GONNA DO WITH EARTH AND WHEN THE INVASION WAS GONNA START. BUT IT JUST KEPT QUIET, SO BEAVIS STOMPED ON IT AND SQUISHED IT. HUH-HUH-HUH. SO THEN WE WENT BACK AND SCREAMED AT THE MAGGOT-ALIENS TO SURRENDER. BUT, LIKE, THEY IGNORED US, SO WE STOMPED ON ALL OF THEM TOO. HUH-HUH-HUH!

YEAH, HEH-HEH! UMM, THE WOMEN OF EARTH ARE SAFE NOW. SO AS AN AWARD, THEY SHOULD COME DO IT WITH US! HEH-HEH! THAT WOULD RULE!

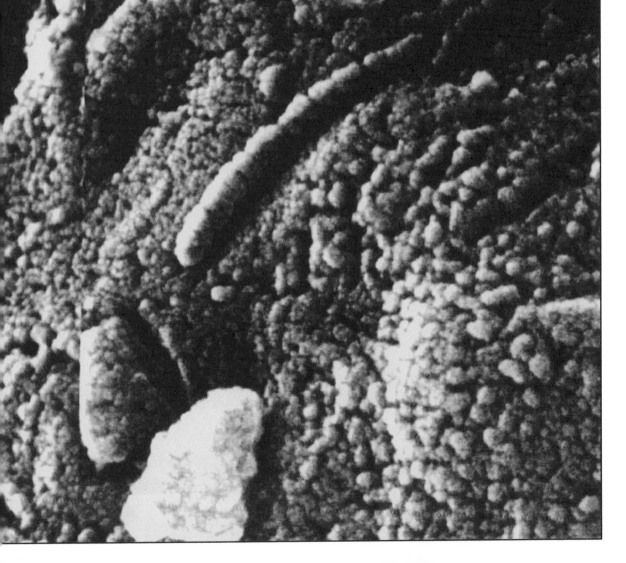

VOODOO DOLLS

SO, LIKE, VOODOO DOLLS ARE COOL. WHEN YOU HAVE A VOODOO DOLL OF SOMEONE, YOU HAVE, LIKE, TOTAL POWER OVER THEM. CUZ WHEN YOU DO SOMETHING TO A VOODOO DOLL, IT, LIKE, REALLY HAPPENS IN REAL LIFE. LIKE, IF I TOOK A VOODOO DOLL OF MCVICKER AND THREW IT OFF A CLIFF, MCVICKER WOULD REALLY FALL OFF A CLIFF, HUH-HUH-HUH.

YEAH! HEH-HEH! AND, LIKE, IF I HAD A VOODOO DOLL OF PAMELA ANDERSON AND TOOK OFF ITS CLOTHES, THEN SHE'D BE NAKED IN REAL LIFE! HEH-HEH-HEH!

COOL! HUH-HUH. SO, UHH, THE WAY YOU MAKE A VOODOO DOLL IS YOU TAKE A DOLL FROM A LITTLE CHICK OR AN ACTION FIGURE FROM BEAVIS (HUH-HUH, HE STILL PLAYS WITH THEM). THEN YOU TAKE PIECES OF BODY STUFF FROM THE PERSON YOU WANNA DO VOODOO TO. LIKE, I WAS MAKING A VOODOO DOLL OF BEAVIS. SO I RIPPED A CHUNK OF HIS HAIR OUT OF HIS HEAD. THEN I TAPED IT TO A DOLL. THEN WHEN YOUR DOLL'S READY, YOU RAISE YOUR ARMS AND GO, "UGGAH-BUGGA-BLUH-BLUH-BUTT!"

NOW THE DOLL WAS ALL FULL OF MAGIC VOODOO POWER AND I HAD CONTROL OVER BEAVIS. HUH-HUH! I STARTED STABBING THE DOLL IN THE HEAD AND THAT GOT BEAVIS PISSED, SO HE TRIED TO GRAB THE DOLL. BUT HE TRIPPED AND FELL DOWN AND BASHED HIS HEAD ON THE EDGE OF A TABLE. SO VOODOO KICKS ASS.

STUFF TO DO WITH A VOODOO DOLL OF SOMEONE THAT SUCKS

* THROW IT AT A WALL, OVER AND OVER.
* STAB IT IN THE FACE WITH A NAIL.
* HIT IT WITH A HAMMER.
* STICK IT IN YOUR BUTT.
* MELT ITS WEINER.
* POOP ON IT.
* FLUSH IT DOWN THE TOILET.
* THROW IT UP ON SOMEONE'S ROOF.
* LET A DOG RIP ITS HEAD OFF.
* PUT IT ON A BUS THAT'S GOING TO ANOTHER TOWN.

PHONE PSYKICKS

PHONE PSYKICKS ARE THESE PEOPLE WHO, LIKE, ARE SUPPOSED TO KNOW WHAT'S GONNA HAPPEN AFTER IT HAPPENS, OR, UHH, SOMETHING. WE CALLED A PHONE PSYKICK TO SEE IF THEY'RE FOR REAL. HUH-HUH. THIS WAS LIKE, OUR CONVERSASHUN:

Welcome to the Psychic Pals Network.

HEY, BABY. UH-HUH-HUH.

Hi, would you like me to predict your future?

NO, HUH-HUH. BUT, UHH, DO YOU HAVE BIG BOOBS? HUH-HUH-HUH!

Excuse me? This is a psychic hot-line, not a sex line.

UHH, OKAY. HUH-HUH. CAN YOU, UHH, PREDICT IF YOU'VE GOT BIG BOOBS? HUH-HUH-HUH-HUH!

I don't understand.

YEAH, HEH-HEH-HEH!
CAN YOU, UMM,
PREDICT IF YOU'RE NAKED?
HEH-HEH-HEH-HEH!
HUH-HUH! HUH-HUH-HUH!
HEH-HEH-HEH-HEH! CAN YOU
PREDICT IF I HAVE A STIFFY?
HEH-HEH-HEH-HEH!

(CLICK)

CONCLOOSHUN: SHE WAS A REAL GOOD PHONE PSYKICK. AND SHE WAS PRETTY HOT. HUH-HUH. UHH, I CAN PREDICT STUFF TOO. I PREDICT STEWART'S GONNA GET HIS ASS KICKED WHEN HIS DAD GETS THE PHONE BILL. HUH-HUH-HUH!

DEMONIC POZE SHUN

UHH, HUH-HUH. WHEN SOMEONE'S POZESSED BY THE DEVIL, YOU GOTTA, LIKE, DO THE SAME THINGS THAT THE PRIEST DUDE IN THAT ONE "EXORCIST" MOVIE DID:

UHH, HOW'S IT GOING, DEVIL? UHH, BE GONE OR SOMETHING, UH-HUH-HUH. UHH, OKAY, DEVIL DUDE, IF YOU'RE NOT GONNA LISTEN, I'M GONNA THROW HOLY WATER ON YOU. UH-HUH-HUH. BUT, LIKE, I DON'T GOT ANY, SO, UHH, I'LL THROW A FREEZY WHIP ON YOU, HUH-HUH-HUH.

UHH, OKAY, DEVIL. I'M GONNA PRAY. HUH-HUH. UHH, I PLEDGE A LEGION TO THE FLAG OF THE UNITED AMERICAS, OR SOMETHING. HMM. OKAY, THAT DIDN'T WORK. HOW ABOUT THIS. UHH, TAKE ME! HUH-HUH-HUH! TAKE ME INSTEAD AND STUFF! HUH-HUH-HUH. THAT WOULD BE COOL!

WHOA! HUH-HUH. SOMETHING'S HAPPENING.

I AM THE GREAT CORNHOLIO! I NEED T.P. FOR MY BUNGHOLE!

YOU DORK, YOU WEREN'T SUP-POSED TO DRINK THE FRUITY WHIP! NOW GET OUT OF BED, YOU LAZY DILL-WAD!

ARE YOU THREATENING ME?! YOU MUST BOW DOWN TO THE ALMIGHTY BUNGHOLE!

HOW DID THE DINASORES DIE?

UMM, THESE STUPID SCIENTISTS THINK THAT SOME BIG ROCK FROM OUTER-SPACE CRASHED INTO THE EARTH AND THAT'S WHY ALL THE DINASORES DIED. BUT THAT'S STUPID. HOW COULD ONE ROCK KILL ALL 100 DINASORES? THIS IS THE WAY IT REALLY HAPPENED.

LIKE, ONCE UPON A TIME, ALL DINASORES LIVED IN JAPAN. IT WAS PRETTY COOL 'CUZ, LIKE, THESE DINASORES WOULD EAT THE JAPAN PEOPLE AND KICK OVER THEIR BUILDINGS AND EAT THE BUILDINGS TOO, HEH-HEH-HEH. AND THEY'D BREATHE RADIASHUN AND FRY EVERYONE! YEAHHHHH! OOOO-AHHHH! HEH-HEH-HMM-HEH-HEH! AND JAPANESE DUDES WOULD BE RUNNING AROUND SCREAMING! AND SOMETIMES THE DINASORES WOULD FIGHT EACH OTHER AND RIP EACH OTHER'S ARMS OUT AND SPLASH BLUE BLOOD ALL OVER THE PLACE AND THROW EACH OTHER AROUND THESE JAPAN CITIES AND WRECK EVERYTHING! HEH-HEH-HEH!

SO FINALLY THESE JAPAN ARMY DUDES GOT ALL PISSED, HEH-HEH, AND THEY SENT OUT TANKS AND JETS AND STUFF. HEH-HEH-HEH! THEY SHOT BOMBS INTO THE DINOSORE'S HEADS AND KICKED THEIR ASSES! HEH-HEH-HEH! AND THEN THE DINASORES STARTED SPEWING BLUE BLOOD OUT OF THEIR GUTS AND SCREAMING AND MOST OF THEM DIED.

A FEW DINASORES DIDN'T WANNA GET KILLED, SO THEY GAVE UP. THEN THE JAPAN DUDES ROUNDED THEM UP AND SHOVED THEM IN MUSEUMS AND LOCKED EM IN. THE DINASORES, LIKE, LIVED THERE FOR AWHILE BUT THEY GOT TIRED OF WALKING AROUND THE MUSEUM LOOKING AT STUPID THINGS, SO THEY FELL DOWN AND DIED OF BOREDOM. AND YOU CAN STILL SEE THEIR BONES THERE. THAT'S COOL.

JURASSICK PARK

THIS MOVIE WAS PRETTY COOL, BUT, LIKE, IF ME AND BEAVIS DIRECTED IT, IT'D BE MUCH BETTER. CHECK IT OUT, HUH-HUH-HUH.

TAROT CARDS

HEH-HEH, WE FOUND SOME OF THESE, UMM, TAROT CARDS IN VAN DRIESSEN'S GARAGE, HEH-HEH. PEOPLE CAN USE THESE TO, YOU KNOW, TELL YOUR FUTURE OR SOMETHING IF YOU JUST PULL OUT SOME CARDS. HEH-HEH-HEH! "PULL OUT." UMM, THESE ARE THE ONES I PULLED AND LIKE, BUTT-HEAD TOLD ME MY FUTURE. IT WAS AMAZ-ING! HE KNEW ALL THIS JUST BY LOOKING AT THESE CARDS:

(1) UHH, OKAY, BEAVIS. THIS CARD MEANS THAT IN THE FUTURE, A DUDE WEARING A BATH ROBE AND A MASK IS GONNA JUMP OUT AT YOU. THEN HE'S GONNA TAKE OFF HIS MASK AND HE'S GONNA BE A COOL SKULL DUDE UNDERNEATH. THEN HE'S GONNA TAKE THIS BIG KNIFE THAT'S ON A STICK AND HE'S GONNA CHOP YOU IN HALF AND WATCH YOU SQUIRM AROUND AND DIE. HUH-HUH-HUH!

(2) THIS CARD MEANS THAT IN THE FUTURE, YOU'RE GONNA SEE SOME FUNNY-LOOKING CHICK WITH A BUNCH OF ARMS WALKING DOWN THE STREET AND SHE'S GONNA BE TOP-LESS AND FEELING HER OWN BOOBS. HUH-HUH! THAT'S A COOL FUTURE!

(3) UHH, THIS CARD MEANS THAT IN THE FUTURE SOME UGLY HUNCHED-UP DUDE IS GONNA RUN BY YOU WAVING AROUND A BUNCH OF TOILET PAPER OR SOMETHING. UHH, I GUESS THAT'S A PRETTY COOL FUTURE, TOO.

CONCLOOSHUN: HEH-HEH! TAROT CARDS ARE AMAZING! MY FUTURE RULES! IT'S, LIKE, I CAN HARDLY WAIT OR SOMETHING! UMM, EXCEPT FOR THAT SKULL DUDE. HEH-HEH. WHEN I SEE HIM, I THINK I'M JUST GONNA TELL HIM THAT BUTT-HEAD'S REALLY THE ONE WHO PULLED THAT CARD!

AINCHENT EGYPT: THE SPHINXTER & THE GREAT PEERAMIDS

IN EGYPT, THERE'S A BUNCH OF MYSTERIOUS STUFF. BUT EVERYONE'S LIKE, REALLY CONFUSED ABOUT THESE THINGS CALLED THE GREAT PEERAMIDS AND THE SPHINXTER. HUH-HUH. IT'S, LIKE A BIG MYSTERY ABOUT WHAT THE HELL THEY ARE AND WHY THEY'RE THERE. SO, UHH, WE CHECKED IT OUT FOR OURSELVES, AND WE SOLVED THE MYSTERY.

A LONG TIME AGO, THE SPHINXTER WAS, LIKE, THE GOD OF BUTTS, HUH-HUH-HUH. IT'S LIKE, IF YOU HAD A PROBLEM WITH YOUR BUTT, YOU'D GO PRAY TO THE SPHINXTER, HUH-HUH-HUH. YOU'D BE, LIKE, "UHH, ALMIGHTY SPHINXTER. HUH-HUH-HUH. MY BUTT'S GOT PROBLEMS. FIX IT, DUDE." AND THEN, LIKE, YOU'D HAVE TO GO AROUND BACK AND SMELL THE SPHINXTER'S BUTT AND YOU'D BE OKAY. HUH-HUH-HUH-HUH!

ALL THESE PEOPLE KEPT COMING TO THE SPHINXTER AND COMPLAINING ABOUT THEIR ITCHY BUTT-CRACKS. HUH-HUH. THE SPHINXTER GOT SICK AND TIRED OF HEARING ABOUT IT, SO HE COMMANDED THEM TO BUILD THESE THINGS CALLED THE GREAT PEERAMIDS. AND HE ORDERED THAT WHEN SOMEONE HAD A ITCHY BUTT-CRACK THEY HAD TO CLIMB UP TO THE TOP OF A GREAT PEERAMID TO WHERE IT GOT ALL POINTY, HUH-HUH, THEN CROUCH DOWN AND ITCH THEIR BUTT-CRACKS WITH THE POINTY PART. HUH-HUH-HUH!

BEAVIS SHOULD BUILD ONE OF THOSE GREAT PEERAMIDS CUZ HE KEEPS USING THE EDGE OF THE KITCHEN TABLE AND, LIKE, NOW IT SMELLS FUNNY.

MUMMIES & KING BUTTUNCOMMON

MUMMIES ARE, LIKE, THESE DEAD DUDES FROM, LIKE, 100 YEARS AGO, THAT LIVED IN THE GREAT PEERAMIDS AND LIKED TO WRAP THEMSELVES UP IN TOILET PAPER AND HAD THEIR BRAINS PULLED OUT THROUGH THEIR NOSES, HEH-HEH-HEH. THEY WERE COOL.

SO, UHH, THE GREATEST MUMMY WHO EVER LIVED WAS THIS DUDE NAMED KING BUTTUNCOMMON, HUH-HUH-HUH. HE WAS PRETTY COOL LOOKING. UHH, SCIENTIFIC DUDES FOUND OUT STUFF ABOUT HIM FROM THESE DRAWINGS THEY FOUND ON A WALL. I THINK THEY CALL IT, UHH, HYDROGLIBICS OR SOMETHING. WE FOUND THIS IN SOME SCIENCE BOOK:

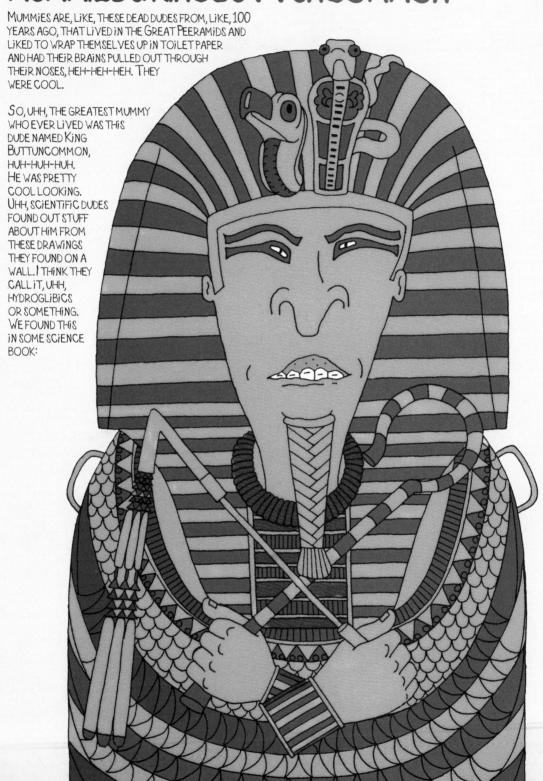

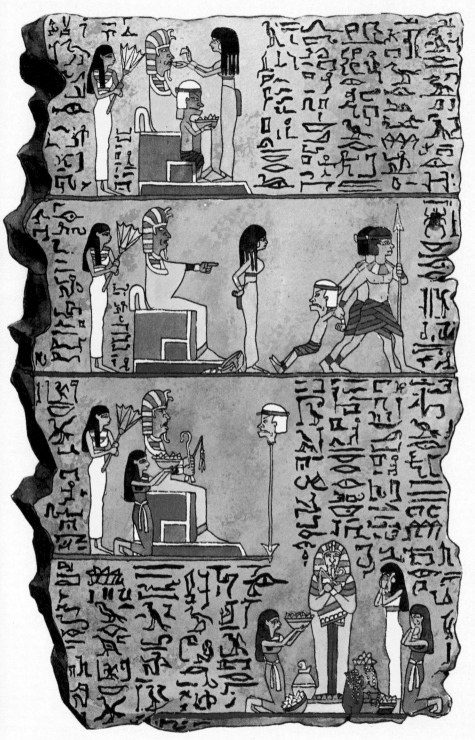

A strict and much-feared ruler, King Buttuncommon (1284-1269 B.C) had already reached the peak of his power and glory by age 14. As a result of a self-imposed law, King Butt was the only male in the kingdom allowed to have sexual relations. Thus, he enjoyed constant female attention. Besides women, King Butt always kept one loyal male slave, called a "Dum-as" at his side.

Any mistakes on the part of the slave were met with swift and terrible punishment, as shown here after the "Dum-as" had apparently dropped a bowl of the royal food. A replacement "Dum-as" would be found immediately.

King Butt died of what can only be called excessive intercourse. A study of his well-preserved remains revealed unusual wear on his genitalia. Thousands of women, now doomed by law to a life without sexual intercourse, mourned his death. King Butt was buried with items the Egyptians believed would serve him in the afterlife: gold, jewels, and several urns of flattened, baked-corn wedges mixed with a cheese-like substance.

THE ABDOMINAL SNOWMAN

HEY BUTTHEAD, ISN'T THIS, LIKE, THAT GIANT HAIRY THING THAT LIVES IN SOME MOUNTAINS?

UHH, I'VE GOT A GIANT HAIRY THING THAT LIVES IN MY PANTS, HUH-HUH-HUH-HUH.

OH, YEAH. HEH-HEH-HEH-HEH! ME TOO.

THIS THING IS CALLED THE, UHHH, ABDOMINAL SNOWMAN 'CUZ IT'S STOMACH IS ALL BUFF AND HARD, HUH-HUH-HUH. KINDA LIKE MINE. HE'S ALWAYS, YOU KNOW, WORKING OUT, GOIN' TO THE GYM AND STUFF.

THEN HE GOES TO THE MALL TO THAT ONE HEALTH STORE AND HE GETS THAT POWDER THAT'S SUPPOSED TO MAKE YOU ALL MUSCULAR.

YEAH-YEAH! HEH-HEH. I TRIED THAT STUFF! REMEMBER, BUTTHEAD? IT DIDN'T WORK TOO GOOD.

YEAH, YOU OPENED IT IN THE STORE AND ATE, LIKE, HALF THE CAN. HUH-HUH. THEN YOU STARTED CHOKING AND PUKING, HUH-HUH-HUH.

SHUT-UP, BUTTHEAD!

UH-HUH-HUH-HUH-HUH. SO, LIKE, HARDLY ANYBODY'S SEEN THE ABDOMINAL SNOWMAN, BUT, LIKE, IF YOU'RE A CHICK AND YOU SEE HIM, YOU GET ALL HORNY, HUH-HUH-HUH, AND, LIKE, YOU GOTTA, YOU KNOW, HAVE IT, HUH-HUH-HUH-HUH.

PSYKICK INVESTGATORS

THERE'S THESE PEOPLE WHO STAND WHERE SOMETHING, YOU KNOW, HAPPENED. THEN THEY GET THESE, UHHH, PICTURES IN THEIR HEADS ABOUT WHAT WAS GOING ON IN THAT SPOT...HUH-HUH-HUH-HUH..."SPOT." I THINK THEY CALL IT, UHH, "PSYKICK FLASHES." THIS IS LIKE WHAT HAPPENS TO THAT DUDE ON THAT "MILLENNIUM" SHOW.

SO, ME AND BUTT-HEAD WATCHED THAT SHOW A BUNCH OF TIMES. AND IT SUCKED. HEH-HEH. BUT, UMM, WE LEARNED HOW TO DO THOSE "PSYKICK FLASHES."

YEAH. HUH-HUH. IT WAS COOL. WE, LIKE, WALKED ALL OVER TOWN AND THIS IS WHAT WE, YOU KNOW, SAW IN OUR HEADS. IT'S, LIKE, A GIFT OR SOMETHING. SO, UHH, WE DECIDED TO USE IT FOR MANKIND AND STUFF. HUH-HUH-HUH.

GIRL'S LOCKER-ROOM: HUH-HUH-HUH! WE, LIKE SNUCK IN, CLOSED OUR EYES AND SAW ALL THESE NAKED CHICKS EVERYWHERE! HUH-HUH-HUH! THIS RULES!

YEAH! YEAH! CHECK IT OUT! BARE CHICK ASS! HEH-HEH-HEH-HEH! BOOBS EVERYWHERE! LOOK! AHHHHH! WET HOOTERS!

SIDEWALK: WE FOUND A SPOT WHERE WE SENSED THAT ONCE A DOG WAS TAKING A DUMP, HEH-HEH-HEH! I, LIKE, SAW IT REAL CLEAR IN MY MIND AND STUFF. HEH-HEH! EVEN THOUGH I WAS KINDA DISTRACTED AND STUFF CUZ I WAS STANDING IN A TURD AND IT STUNK.

THE COOLER AT BURGER WORLD: UMM, HEH-HEH. THIS WAS WHERE I SENSED SOME DUDE WAS ONCE JUST STANDING AROUND WITH HIS SHLONG HANGING OUT OF HIS PANTS, HEH-HEH-HEH. UMM, OHHH YEAH. HEH-HEH-HMM-HEH-HEH. THAT WAS ME.

THE ALLEY: WE WENT IN THIS DARK ALLEY AND THERE WAS ALL THESE COPS RUNNING AROUND AND THERE WAS A DRAWING OF A DUDE ON THE GROUND. THERE WAS ALL THIS YELLOW TAPE ALL OVER THE PLACE AND A BURNED-UP CAR THAT WAS FULL OF LITTLE HOLES. WE, LIKE, STOOD THERE AND CLOSED OUR EYES AND WE SENSED THAT ONE TIME, A GARBAGEMAN WAS THERE AND HE HOCKED A BIG LOOGIE! HEH-HEH-HEH! THAT RULED!

BEAVIS' KITCHEN: THIS WAS WHERE WE SENSED SOME GUY WITH A MOUSTACHE SCORING WITH BEAVIS' MOM, HUH-HUH-HUH-HUH. OH, YEAH. AND SOME DUDE WITH A PONY-TAIL. AND A FAT GUY WITH A BUNCH OF TATTOOS, HUH-HUH-HUH. SOME MEXICAN GUY, THEN A TALL DUDE WITH A COWBOY HAT, AND A COUPLE OF COPS. HUH-HUH! HUH-HUH-HUH-HUH!

HEH-HEH-HEH. SHE'S A SLUT.

YEAH. HUH-HUH. IT WAS PROBABLY ALL IN ONE NIGHT. HUH-HUH-HUH!

WITCHCRAFT

UHH, THIS IS, LIKE, THE ONLY KNOWN PICTURE OF WITCHES...IN THE WORLD AND STUFF. HUH-HUH. JUST THE CHICKS, THOUGH. THAT DUDE ISN'T A WITCH, HUH-HUH-HUH. HE'S JUST A DORK.

HEY, BUTT-HEAD, ISN'T THIS THAT SHOW THAT'S ON, UMM, NICKIMMODIUM?

SHUT-UP, BEAVIS! IT'S, LIKE, YOU HAVE TO RUIN EVERYTHING! BUNGHOLE! HUH-HUH. SO, ANYWAY, LIKE THIS WITCH DOES SOMETHING WITH HER NOSE....UHH, I THINK SHE PICKS IT, HUH-HUH, AND THEN MAGIC CRAP HAPPENS.

BUT, LIKE, IF YOU'RE A WITCH AND THE COPS CATCH YOU, THEY, UMM, BURN YOUR STEAK.

UHH, WHAT?

IT'S PROBABLY, LIKE, ONE OF THE COPS HOLDS YOU DOWN AND THE OTHERS MESS UP YOUR KITCHEN AND THE FRIDGE LOOKING FOR SOME STEAK, THEN THEY FRY IT UP UNTIL IT'S ALL BLACK AND BURNED, SO NO ONE CAN EAT IT. HEH-HEH-HEH. IT'S LIKE, REALLY MEAN.

NO, DUMBASS. HUH-HUH. I THINK THE ONLY WAY YOU KILL A WITCH IS TO THROW WATER ON HER. THEN SHE LIKE, MELTS AND TURNS INTO A BUNCH OF PUKE AND STUFF. HUH-HUH-HUH.

YEAH! YEAH! HEY, BUTT-HEAD, IF A WITCH WAS CHASING ME, I'D, LIKE, STOP AT THE WATER FOUNTAIN AND DRINK SOME WATER REAL FAST, HEH-HEH. THEN I'D TURN AROUND AND SPIT IT ON HER, HEH-HEH-HEH. SHE'D BE, LIKE, "AGGGHHH!" AND I'D JUST BE STANDING THERE, GOING "YOU'RE LUCKY I DIDN'T BURN YOUR STEAK, BEE-OTCH!"

UHH, SOME WITCHES DO THESE THINGS CALLED MAGIC SPELLS, WHERE THEY MIX UP SOME STUFF IN A BIG POT AND SAY SOME MAGIC WORDS OR SOMETHING AND THEN STUFF THEY WANT TO HAPPEN COMES TRUE! ME AND BEAVIS THOUGHT THAT WAS A PRETTY COOL IDEA, SO WE MADE SOME MAGIC SPELLS, TOO. I GUESS YOU CAN USE THEM IF YOU WANT.

MAGIC SPELL FOR GETTING MONEY
FIRST, YOU GET A BIG POT OR SOMETHING. THEN YOU GET THIS STUFF AND, LIKE, THROW IT IN THE POT:

WINGS OF FLY.
EARS OF MOTH.
MUD.
BUTT OF CENTIPEED.
TURD OF DOG.
WEINER OF GRASSHOPPER.
LEFTOVER RAT GUTS FROM BIOLOGY CLASS.

THEN YOU, LIKE, MIX IT ALL UP AND THROW IT AT STEWART'S WINDOW UNTIL HE COMES OUT. HUH-HUH-HUH. SO THEN, LIKE, WHEN HE COMES OUT YOU HAVE TO, UHH, SAY THESE MAGIC WORDS OR SOMETHING: "STEWART, I'LL, LIKE, LET YOU HANG OUT WITH ME IF YOU GIMME FIVE BUCKS." HUH-HUH-HUH. IT'S A PRETTY COOL SPELL 'CUZ IT ALWAYS WORKS.

Magic Spell For Being Cool

For this spell to work, you need money. So, umm, do the "Magic Spell To Get Money" first. Then, you need to mix-up these magic ingredients:

Puke of cat.
Leftover frog guts from biology class.
Dead squirrel.
A fish brain.
Turd of Beavis.

Umm, heh-heh, then you take all this and leave it in Anderson's mailbox, heh-heh-heh! After that you, like, find Todd. First you tell him what you did to Anderson, heh-heh. Then you say these magic words: "Umm, hey man, can I be in your gang? Heh-heh, I got money." Then he'll say something like "Gimme that money or I'll rip your head off." When you give Todd the money he'll, like, drive away. But you'll be pretty cool now, heh-heh, see, 'cuz Todd talked to you and he didn't kick your ass.

A Magic Spell To Get Food

Mix-up these magic things:

1 dead, rotten bird
Stomped-on worm guts
12 cockroaches.
Head of cricket.
Turd of cat.

So then, like, put all this stuff in your hands and, umm, take it to the food cort at the mall, heh-heh. Then walk up to some chicks that are eating and, like, show it to them. Heh-heh-heh-heh! Lots of times, they'll scream and run away. Heh-heh-heh. Then you can sit down and eat their food! If you go wash your hands, the chicks might change their minds and come back for their food, so better wait 'til you're done eating.

Magic Spell For Beavis To Score

This is, like, a spell that only works on Beavis. If Beavis messes up, huh-huh-huh, he won't score. First, he has to, like, eat all these things:

A handful of worms.
Some dirt.
Junk from the grease trap at Burger World
A stick.
Buzzcut's jock-strap.

After Beavis, like, eats all this stuff, huh-huh-huh, tell him he can't watch TV or spank his monkey or eat nachos or take a dump for a week. Huh-huh-huh-huh! Only then will he score.

Huh-huh-huh! This spell rules cuz it's cool to watch Beavis try and eat all that stuff.

STONE HENDGE

WHOA! UMM, ISN'T THIS THAT THING? THE EYEFULL TOWER?

UHH, NO, DUMBASS. THE EYEFULL TOWER IS THAT THING IN FRANCE THAT'S JUST, LIKE, A BUNCH OF GIRDERS AND CRAP. AND LIKE, NOBODY IN FRANCE WANTS TO FINISH BUILDING IT BECAUSE THEY'RE A BUNCH OF LAZY, WHINING BUTT-HOLES, HUH-HUH-HUH-HUH!

OH, YEAH, HEH-HEH-HEH-HEH!

THESE ARE JUST A BUNCH OF BIG ROCKS IN NEW ENGLAND THAT SOME AINCHENT DUDES PUT UP. IT'S SUPPOSED TO BE AN OLD CALENDER OR SOMETHING. HUH-HUH. BUT THIS CALENDER SUCKS AND THE AINCHENT DUDES THAT MADE IT MUST'VE BEEN STUPID OR SOMETHING.

IT'S LIKE, THE AINCHENT DUDES WOULD GET UP EVERY MORNING AND GET SOME COFFEE AND BRUSH THEIR TEETH AND GO LOOK AT THIS STONE HENDGE CALENDER TO SEE WHAT DAY IT WAS AND THEY'D JUST STARE AT THE ROCKS AND BE LIKE, "UHH, THERE'S NO NUMBERS OR DAYS OR ANYTHING! IT'S JUST A DAMN BUNCH OF ROCKS! THIS SUCKS! I DON'T KNOW IF IT'S SATURDAY OR IF I GOTTA GO TO WORK! DAMMIT! I HATE THIS STUPID CALENDER!"

YEAH, REALLY! IT'S, LIKE, IF IT WAS A NORMAL CALENDER, IT'D HAVE NUMBERS ON IT AND PICTURES OF BARE-ASS CHICKS LAYING ALL OVER CARS! HEH-HEH!

MENTAL TELEPATHY

UHH, HUH-HUH, ME AND BEAVIS SAW SOME DUDE ON TV READING PEOPLE'S MINDS. SO, LIKE, I READ SOME PEOPLE'S MINDS TOO. AND THIS IS WHAT THEY WERE, UHH, THINKING:

ANDERSON: "I'M OLD. AND I SUCK."

STEWART: "I LIKE WINGER AND I SUCK MORE THAN ANYONE HAS SUCKED BEFORE."

VAN DRIESSEN: "I'M A WUSSY. SOMEONE SHOULD KICK MY ASS."

STEWART'S MOM: "BUTT-HEAD RULES. I WANT HIM. OH YEAH, AND STEWART SUCKS!"

BUZZCUT: "STEWART AND VAN DRIESSEN SUCK. I SHOULD KICK THEIR ASS. I SUCK, TOO. I SHOULD KICK MY OWN ASS."

BEAVIS: "HEY, HOW'S IT GOIN'?"

BUTT-HEAD: "I'M THE COOLEST DUDE EVER. I CAN EVEN, LIKE, READ MY OWN MIND. THIS IS COOL."

U.F.O. SIGHTINGS

U.F.O STANDS FOR, UHH, UNDER-IDENTIFIED FLYING CRAP. THERE'S ALL THESE PEOPLE WHO SAY THEY SAW U.F.O'S, AND THERE'S EVEN, LIKE, PICTURES OF THESE THINGS. CHECK "EM OUT.

THESE PICTURES SUCK, HEH-HEH-HEH. THEY'RE, LIKE, FAKE! HEH-HEH-HEH.

YEAH, REALLY. WHAT A DAMN RIP-OFF! SO, LIKE, WE TOOK SOME REAL PICTURES OF U.F.O'S. HUH-HUH-HUH. CHECK THIS OUT.

UMM, ME AND BUTT-HEAD TOOK THIS PICTURE. HEH-HEH. OUT OF A MAGAZINE, HEH-HEH. I WAS, LIKE, WHOA! WHAT THE HELL IS THAT THING!! I'M, LIKE, PRETTY SURE THIS A U.F.O OR SOMETHING.

UHHH, IT KINDA LOOKS LIKE A DOG, BUT IT'S, LIKE, DOGS DON'T FLY. HUH-HUH.

YEAH! YEAH! SEE WHAT I MEAN? HEH-HEH. THIS PICTURE SCARED THE CRAP OUT OF ME!

UHH, ME AND BEAVIS TOOK THIS PICTURE IN THE PARK. THIS U.F.O THING WAS, LIKE, FLOATING AROUND UP IN THE AIR AND STUFF.

YEAH, HEH-HEH, IT WAS CHASING DOWN SOME DUDE. HE WAS TRYING TO RUN AWAY FROM IT BUT, LIKE, IT KEPT FOLLOWING HIM WHEREVER HE WENT. HEH-HEH-HEH. ME AND BUTTHEAD GOT AWAY, BUT THAT GUY PROBABLY GOT KILLED WITH A DEATH RAY OR SOMETHING. HEH-HEH-HEH.

UHH, THIS IS A REAL QUIET U.F.O. SO IT CAN SNEAK UP ON YOU. WHEN IT WENT BY, WE SAW IT HAD A HUMAN PRISONER. HE WAS WAVING AT US, PROBABLY FOR US TO SAVE HIM. BUT, LIKE, WHEN ME AND BEAVIS CHUCKED SOME ROCKS AT THE U.F.O, THE PRISONER GUY STARTED SWEARING AT US. WHATEVER, DUDE. HUH-HUH. SOME PEOPLE JUST DON'T APPRECIATE HELP.

HOW TO FAKE A U.F.O. SIGHTING

UMM, SOME DUDES TAKE, LIKE, FAKE PICTURES OF UFO'S AND, LIKE, SELL IT TO THE GOVERMINT AND NEWSPAPERS AND STUFF! HEH-HEH-HEH! IF YOU WANNA, LIKE, MAKE MONEY, HERE'S HOW TO, UMM, TAKE FAKE UFO PICTURES AND STUFF. YOU NEED A CAMERA AND, LIKE, A GARBAGE CAN LID OR SOMETHING. HEH-HEH-HEH.

CHECK IT OUT, HEH-HEH-HEH! YOU'RE, LIKE, PROBABLY SCARED THAT IT'S A UFO. HEH-HEH-HEH! WUSSY! UMM, THAT'S AKSHULLY ONE OF OUR FAKE PICTURES. HEH-HEH-HEH-HEH!

NEXT YOU NEED TO, UMM, GET SOME PICTURES OF THE UFO FLYING AROUND AND STUFF. LIKE, THROW THE GARBAGE LID IN THE AIR AND TAKE A PICTURE OF IT. HEH-HEH-HEH!

HEH-HEH. WHEN PEOPLE SEE THESE PICTURES, THEY'LL BE ALL FREAKED OUT AND RUNNING AROUND, SCREAMING AND STUFF. THEY'LL BE LIKE: "AHHHHHGH! UFO'S, OR SOMETHING!" IT'LL BE ON THE NEWS AND WE'LL BE RICH, HEH-HEH-HEH-HEH!

INDEPENDUNCE DAY

HUH-HUH! THE FIRST PART OF THIS MOVIE RULED!

YEAH! YEAH! HEH-HEH! EVERYTHING JUST BLEW UP! YAHHHHHH! HOOOOWAHHH! HEH-HEH-HEH-HEH-HEH!

UMM, IT'S, LIKE, I USED TO THINK ABOUT CHICKS WHEN I SPANK MY MONKEY. HEH-HEH-HEH. BUT NOW WHEN I DO IT, UMM, I THINK ABOUT THAT PART OF THE MOVIE, HEH-HEH-HEH-HEH-HEH!

BUT THEN, LIKE, THE REST OF THE MOVIE SUCKED. HUH-HUH-HUH. THERE WAS, LIKE, NO ALIENS. IT WAS JUST A BUNCH OF DORKS GOING "BLAH-BLAH-BLAH-BLAH!" SO, UHH, I THINK THE POINT WAS THAT WHEN ALIENS BLOW UP THE WORLD, THEY'RE ONLY GONNA LET BORING, STUPID ASS-MUNCHES LIVE. HUH-HUH-HUH. LIKE BEAVIS.

YEAH. YEAH, THAT'D BE NICE OF THEM. HEH-HEH. IF I DID THIS MOVIE, AND I HAD A GIANT SPACESHIP LIKE THAT, I'D LIKE BLOW UP OUR SCHOOL, HEH-HEH-HEH-HEH! THEN I'D BLOW UP BURGERWORLD! HEH-HEH! THEN I'D BLOW UP THE STUPID BUTTHOLES WHO MADE THIS PIECE OF CRAP MOVIE! HEH-HEH!

YEAH, HUH-HUH! THE ONLY GOOD THING ABOUT THIS MOVIE IS THAT THEY TOTALLY RIPPED-OFF EVERY SCI-FI MOVIE EVER MADE AND STUCK IT IN ONE MOVIE. SO, LIKE, NOW YOU DON'T HAVE TO RENT ALL THOSE SCI-FI MOVIES, YOU CAN JUST WATCH THIS ONE AND SAVE YOUR MONEY FOR SOMETHING COOL, LIKE PORN.

CURSES

IN THE OLD DAYS IF YOU PISSED SOMEONE OFF, THEY'D PUT A CURSE ON YOU. THEY'D BE, LIKE, "MAY ALL YOUR GUTS BLOW UP." AND SO YOUR GUTS WOULD JUST BLOW UP ALL OVER THE PLACE AND YOU'D JUST BE LAYING THERE, DEAD. HUH-HUH.

YEAH, HEH-HEH. WE FIGURED OUT WHY IT WORKED. IT'S CUZ IF YOU SAY THE WORD "MAY," YOU'RE BEING ALL POLITE TO THE POWERS OF DARKNESS OR SOMETHING. SO THE POWERS OF DARKNESS LIKE IT WHEN YOU KISS THEIR BUTT. HEH-HEH. THEN THEY DO WHAT YOU ASK TO THE PERSON YOU'RE PISSED AT.

ONE TIME I WAS, LIKE, "BUTT-HEAD, MAY YOU TURN INTO A BIG GIANT DOG TURD! HEH-HEH!"

YEAH. HUH-HUH. THEN I WAS LIKE, "BEAVIS, MAY YOU TURN INTO A STUPID LITTLE PRE-SCHOOL CHICK. HUH-HUH-HUH!"

SO, LIKE, THAT WORKED PRETTY GOOD AND STUFF. HUH-HUH. THEN I WAS, LIKE, "BEAVIS, MAY YOUR BUNGHOLE RIP UP IN, LIKE, A HUNDRED PIECES AND ALL THE REST OF YOUR SKIN, TOO! HUH-HUH-HUH!"

AND I WAS, LIKE, "BUTT-HEAD, MAY YOU SUCK MORE THAN ANYBODY HAS EVER SUCKED BEFORE!" HEH-HEH-HMM-HEH! AND IT WORKED CUZ BUTT-HEAD TURNED INTO KENNY G!

EASTER ISLAND

UMM, EASTER ISLAND IS THE PLACE WHERE THE EASTER BUNNY LIVES! HEH-HEH! HE, LIKE, RULES THE ISLAND AND ALL THE PEOPLE THAT LIVE THERE ARE HIS SLAVES AND HAVE TO BOW DOWN AND WORSHIP HIM OR HE THROWS EGGS AT THEIR HOUSE, HEH-HEH-HEH!

BUT, LIKE, THE BIG MYSTERY ABOUT EASTER ISLAND IS THESE, UMM, GIANT STATUES THAT ARE ON THE ISLAND. UMM, I FIGURED IT OUT. THE EASTER BUNNY'S SLAVES MADE THESE GIANT BUNNY STATUES OUT OF CHOCOLATE TO HONOR THE EASTER BUNNY AND STUFF. ONE TIME, SOME DUDE GOT HUNGRY AND ATE THE EARS OFF ALL THE STATUES AND THEN THE EASTER BUNNY GOT PISSED AND SHOVED A EGG UP HIS BUTT. HEH-HEH-HEH! IT WAS PRETTY COOL!

ALL THE SCIENTIFIC DUDES ALL OVER THE WORLD DON'T UNDERSTAND HOW THOSE GIANT STATUES GOT ERECTED. HEH-HEH-HEH-HEH-HEH! ERECTED. UMM, I SAID IT BEFORE AND I'LL SAY IT AGAIN: THOSE SCIENTIFIC DUDES ARE A BUNCH OF STUPID BUTTHOLES! HEH-HEH. IT'S, LIKE, THE SLAVES TOOK A GIANT CRANE AND SOME BULLDOZERS AND THEY PUT UP THE STATUES. I MEAN, LIKE, WHAT'S THE BIG MYSTERY? HEH-HEH. IF I EVER SEE SOME OF THOSE SCIENTIFIC DUDES, I'M GONNA KICK THEIR ASSES!

GHOSTS

THERE WAS THIS SHOW ON TV WITH PEOPLE TALKING ABOUT GHOSTS AND SAYING HOW GHOSTS SLAPPED THEM AND SCREAMED AT THEM AND THREW EVERYTHING ALL OVER THEIR HOUSE. HEH-HEH! GHOSTS ARE COOL! BUT, UMM, THEY'RE STILL PRETTY FREAKY. HEH-HEH. UMM, HEY BUTT-HEAD. DO YOU, LIKE, BELIEVE IN GHOSTS?

UHH, YEAH, BUTT-GHOSTS, HUH-HUH-HUH-HUH!

OHHH YEAH, HEH-HEH. BUT, UMM, I MEAN REAL GHOSTS. CUZ, UMM, LIKE LAST NIGHT I HEARD THESE BIG FOOT-STEPS, AND SLAMMING DOORS, AND SOME GHOST DUDE LAUGHING.

WHOA! THAT'S PRETTY COOL, HUH-HUH-HUH.

YEAH, AND THEN A LITTLE LATER, HEH-HEH-HEH, THERE WAS THIS BANGING AND MOANING, AND I KEPT HEARING THIS CREAKY SOUND OVER AND OVER. IT WAS PRETTY SCARY, BUTT-HEAD.

UHH...HUH-HUH-HUH, YOU BUTT-MONKEY! THAT WAS YOUR MOM AND HER BOYFRIEND. HUH-HUH-HUH-HUH!

OHHH YEAH, HEH-HEH-HEH. SHE'S A SLUT.

GHOSTS ARE COOL 'CUZ THEY'RE LIKE, INDIVISIBLE OR SOMETHING. THEY CAN DO ANYTHING THEY WANT AND NOBODY SEES THEM. HERE'S SOME COOL STUFF WE'D DO IF WE WERE GHOSTS, HUH-HUH-HUH:

HEH-HEH-HEH-HEH-HEH-HEH. PLOP!

HEH-HEH-HEH, PEEK-A-BOO!

WHOA! HUH-HUH-HUH, THIS IS THE COOLEST THING EVER!

UHH, THIS IS, LIKE, THE BEST THING ABOUT BEING A GHOST.
YEAH! TV! HEH-HEH-HEH! TURN ON BAYWATCH!

OTHER STUFF THAT'S PRETTY COOL TO DO WHEN YOU'RE A INDIVISIBLE GHOST:

* LOOK AT PORN AT MAXI-MART.
* SPEND ALL NIGHT HANGING AROUND IN THE PARKING LOT AT MAXI-MART.
* WHEN YOU GO TO SCHOOL, YOU CAN SLEEP IN CLASS AND NOBODY'LL WAKE YOU UP, HUH-HUH-HUH.
* WHEN YOU GO TO THE MOVIES, CUT TO THE FRONT OF THE LINE AND BUY YOUR TICKETS BEFORE EVERYONE ELSE.
* HANG OUT AT THE MALL AND FOLLOW CHICKS AND THINK ABOUT WHAT THEY LOOK LIKE NAKED.

THE BERMUDA TRIANGLE

UHH, THE BERMUDA TRIANGLE, HUH-HUH-HUH, IS THIS PLACE IN, UHH, VIRGINIA, UH-HUH-HUH-HUH-HUH-HUH-HUH! AND
IT'S, LIKE, THE COOLEST PLACE ON EARTH. HUH-HUH-HUH! STUDS LIKE ME ARE ALWAYS GOING THERE, HUH-HUH-HUH!

WHOA! REALLY?!

AND THERE'S ALWAYS THESE THINGS THAT GET LOST IN IT, HUH-HUH-HUH, LIKE ROCKETS AND SUBMARINES, HUH-HUH-
HUH, AND TRAINS AND SNAKES, UH-HUH-HUH-HUH-HUH-HUH! HUH-HUH-HUH-HUH-HUH-HUH-HUH!

WHOA! THAT SOUNDS LIKE A PRETTY SCARY PLACE! LIKE, UMM, YOU CAN DIE! WHY THE HELL WOULD ANYONE GO THERE?

HUH-HUH-HUH! YOU DORK. THE BERMUDA TRIANGLE IS LIKE A BIG MYSTERY FOR BUTT-MUNCHES LIKE YOU, BEAVIS.
YOU'LL PROBABLY NEVER SEE IT IN YOUR WHOLE LIFE, HUH-HUH-HUH-HUH!

WELL GOOD, DAMMIT! IT SOUNDS LIKE IT'D SUCK ANYWAYS! YOU CAN GO THERE. BUT NOT ME. NO, SIR. HEH-HEH. I'M JUST
GONNA STAY RIGHT HERE AT HOME.

HUH-HUH-HUH! DUMBASS!

THE SHROUD OF TURIN

THE SHROUD OF TURIN IS THIS REALLY OLD PIECE OF CLOTH IN A MUSEUM SOMEWHERE. IT'S GOT THIS PICTURE OF SOME DUDE'S FACE ON IT. SOME GUY ON TV SAID IT'S LIKE, THAT ONE RELIGIOUS DUDE, JESUS, THAT DIED A LONG TIME AGO. THEY SAY THAT WHEN JESUS DIED HE GOT, LIKE, WRAPPED UP IN THIS OLD SHEET, AND AFTER A WHILE YOU COULD SEE HIS PICTURE ON IT. BUT, UHH, SOME OTHER PEOPLE THINK IT'S FAKE. HUH-HUH.

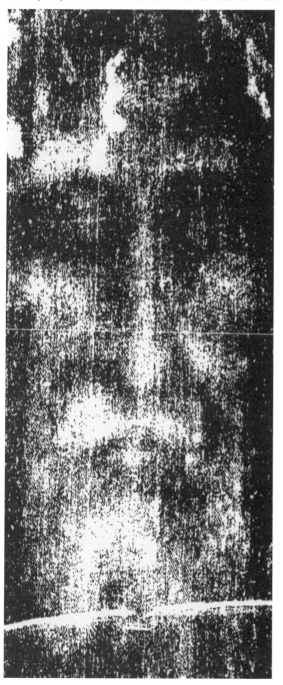

ME AND BEAVIS TRIED TO COPY WHAT HAPPENED TO THAT RELIGIOUS DUDE. WE WANTED TO SEE IF WE COULD MAKE A PICTURE OF BEAVIS ON A SHEET TOO, TO PROVE THAT THE SHROUD OF TURIN IS REAL. HUH-HUH. SO, UHH, I KICKED BEAVIS' ASS UNTIL HE LOOKED LIKE HE WAS DEAD AND STUFF.

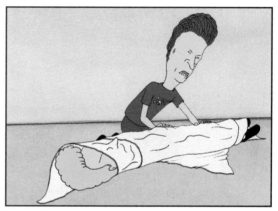

AFTER THAT, I ROLLED-UP BEAVIS IN A BEDSHEET.

LIKE, A FEW DAYS LATER, I UNROLLED BEAVIS AND THERE WAS A PICTURE OF HIM ON THE SHEET! IT, LIKE, REALLY WORKED!

PSYKICK LINKS

PSYKICK LINKS IS WHEN, UHH, SOMETHING HAPPENS TO ONE PERSON AND SOME OTHER PERSON WHO'S, LIKE, SOMEWHERE FAR AWAY GETS THIS FEELING THAT SOMETHING HAPPENED TO THAT OTHER PERSON, OR SOMETHING.

UMM...WHAT?

UHH, I THINK THIS HAPPENED TO ME AND BEAVIS ONCE. I WAS AT HOME TAKING A DUMP AND BEAVIS WAS OUT RIDING HIS BIKE. ALL OF A SUDDEN I STARTED LAUGHING, FOR NO REASON. I WAS, LIKE, "I BET BEAVIS JUST WIPED OUT, HUH-HUH-HUH! WIPED."

WHOA! HEH-HEH-HEH!

SO, LIKE, A COUPLE MINUTES LATER BEAVIS SHOWED UP AND HE WAS ALL BLOODY AND LIMPING AND STUFF. HUH-HUH-HUH!

OHHH, YEAH. HEH-HEH! AND I HAD A PSYKICK LINK, TOO. CUZ WHEN I WIPED OUT, I WAS FALLING AND I WAS THINKING, "I BET BUTT-HEAD IS TAKING A DUMP, HEH-HEH-HEH!"

NOCTURNAL MISSIONS

THERE'S THIS, LIKE, BEAUTIFUL MIRACLE THAT HAPPENS TO DUDES, HUH-HUH-HUH-HUH, CALLED "NOCTURNAL MISSIONS", UH-HUH-HUH-HUH-HUH! IT'S, LIKE, HUH-HUH-HUH, WHEN YOU, LIKE, HUH-HUH-HUH-HUH-HUH, WAKE-UP AND YOU JUST, UH-HUH-HUH-HUH, INOCULATED. HUH-HUH-HUH-HUH-HUH-HUH!

HEH-HEH-HEH-HEH-HEH-HEH-HEH! IT'S THE MOST AMAZING THING EVER! IT'S, LIKE, YOU DON'T EVEN HAVE TO SPANK YOUR MONKEY! HEE-HEE-HEH-HEH! AND, HEH-HEH-HEH, IT HAPPENS ANYWAY! SOMETIMES, HEH-HEH-HEH, THAT HAPPENS WHEN I FALL ASLEEP IN CLASS, HEH-HEH-HEH-HEH! YOU WAKE-UP AND YOU'RE, LIKE, "WHOA!! HEH-HEH!"

HUH-HUH, YEAH. THEN YOU'RE, LIKE, "UHH, EXCUSE ME, I GOTTA, LIKE, GO TO THE BATHROOM! HUH-HUH!"
OHHH, YEAH! HEH-HEH. THEN I HAFTA LIKE, FLUSH MY UNDERWEAR, HEH-HEH-HEH.
HUH-HUH-HUH-HUH! SO, UHH, ME AND BEAVIS THINK IT HAS TO DO WITH WHAT YOU'RE DREAMING ABOUT AND STUFF. WE DID A STUDY
OR SOMETHING. CHECK IT OUT. HERE'S SOME OF THE DREAMS THAT CAUSED OUR, HUH-HUH-HUH, "NOCTURNAL MISSIONS."

LOCKNESS MONSTER

THERE'S THIS OTHER PLACE CALLED SCOTCHLAND OR SOMETHING, WHERE ALL THE DUDES ARE A BUNCH OF DRUNKS WHO WEAR DRESSES, HEH-HEH-HEH! WUSSIES! AND THEY MAKE MUSIC BY SQUEEZING THEIR BAGS, HEH-HEH-HEH! I'M GONNA TRY THAT—OWW! HEH-HEH-HEH! HEY, THAT KINDA SOUNDED LIKE BUSH, HEH-HEH-HEH!

SO, LIKE, IN SCOTCHLAND, THERE'S THIS POND WHERE THE LOCK NESS MONSTER LIVES. SOME PEOPLE SAY IT'S, LIKE, THIS DINO-SORE THAT NEVER DIED. BUT IT CAN'T BE, CUZ IF IT WAS, JAPAN WOULD'VE ATTACKED IT A LONG TIME AGO. PLUS IT WOULD'VE DROWNED.

NOBODY KNOWS WHAT IT IS OR WHAT IT LOOKS LIKE, CUZ ALL THE PICTURES SUCK. THE BIG MYSTERY IS WHY THESE DORKS IN SCOTCHLAND CAN'T TAKE A DECENT PICTURE. THE PICTURES ARE ALWAYS ALL BLURRY AND FAR AWAY, AND THE MONSTER JUST LOOKS LIKE A BUNCH OF GARBAGE FLOATING IN THE WATER. HEH-HEH! I THINK IT'S CUZ PEOPLE IN SCOTCHLAND ARE TOO DAMN DRUNK TO TAKE A GOOD PICTURE. HEH-HEH!

AND NO ONE IN SCOTCHLAND'LL EVER CATCH THE LOCK NESS MONSTER, CUZ THE DUDES ARE SUCH WUSSIES THAT THEY'RE AFRAID TO GET THEIR DRESSES WET. PLUS THEY'RE TOO BUSY SITTING AROUND SQUEEZING THEIR BAGS. HEH-HEH-HEH! IF THE LOCK NESS MONSTER WAS IN AMERICA, WE'D JUST DRAIN ALL THE WATER OUT OF THE POND AND PULL THE MONSTER OUT AND KICK ITS ASS. HEH-HEH-HEH! NONE OF THAT WUSSY CRAP!

IS ELVIS ALIVE?

UHH, LOTS OF YEARS AGO, THERE WAS THIS YOUNG, SKINNY DUDE THAT USED TO PLAY ELVIS. HE WAS PRETTY COOL. HE PLAYED GUITAR AND ACTED IN MOVIES ABOUT THE BEACH AND GOT LOTS OF CHICKS. HE EVEN SCORED WITH LISA MARIE PRESLEY. HUH-HUH-HUH.

THEN SOMETHING HAPPENED TO THE COOL ELVIS. I THINK HE QUIT. ANYWAY, THEN THIS OLDER, FAT DUDE STARTED PLAYING ELVIS. HE SUCKED. HE JUST RAN AROUND IN A WHITE CAPE, EATING DONUTS AND SINGING SONGS THAT STILL SUCK TODAY.

THE ONLY REASON THE FAT ELVIS WAS FAMOUS IS CUZ HE SHOT HIS TV WITH A GUN. HUH-HUH! OH, YEAH, AND HE WAS FAMOUS CUZ HE DIED ON THE TOILET. HE WAS TRYING TO TAKE A DUMP, HUH-HUH, AND HE PUSHED TOO HARD AND DIED. HUH-HUH-HUH!

NOW THERE'S LIKE, ALL THESE TV SHOWS AND NEWSPAPERS AND STUFF SAYING THAT IT'S, LIKE, A BIG MYSTERY IF ELVIS IS REALLY DEAD AND STUFF. SO, UHH, ME AND BEAVIS DUG UP HIS GRAVE TO FIND OUT FOR SURE. HUH-HUH-HUH.

ELVIS' GRAVE WAS COOL! IT SMELLED REAL BAD, BUT THERE WAS, LIKE, BONES AND OLD CLOTHES AND STUFF. BEAVIS KEPT THE SKULL. HE PUT IT ON HIS TOILET TO REMIND HIM NOT TO PUSH TOO HARD. HUH-HUH-HUH!

CONCLOOSHUN: UHH...YEAH, HE'S DEAD.

E.T.: THE EXTRA-TESTICLE

IT WAS COOL WHEN E.T. MADE THAT KID'S BIKE FLY AND STUFF. SO WE TRIED THAT. WE DROVE MY BIKE OFF BEAVIS' GARAGE. HUH-HUH. WE FLEW FOR, LIKE, A SEC-OND. THEN WE FELL AND BROKE A BUNCH OF BONES AND STUFF. HUH-HUH. "OUUUCH."

THIS MOVIE DIDN'T MAKE SENSE. IT'S, LIKE, E.T. COULD MAKE THINGS FLY. SO WHY DIDN'T HE JUST MAKE HIMSELF FLY UP INTO SPACE TO HIS OWN PLAN-ET IF HE WANTED TO GO HOME SO DAMN MUCH. HUH-HUH.

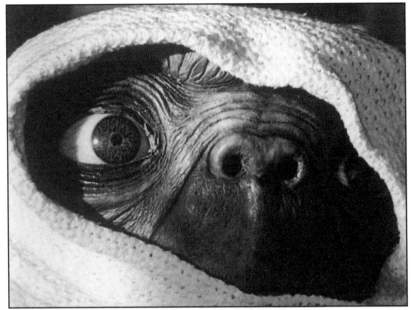

E.T WAS THIS MONKEY FROM OUTER SPACE. AND, LIKE, ALL THESE ASTRONAUT DUDES WANTED TO KILL IT BECAUSE IT HAD A EXTRA TESTICLE, HUH-HUH-HUH! IT'S, LIKE, THEY WERE JELOUS AND STUFF. OH, YEAH, AND THIS MOVIE MADE BEAVIS CRY, HUH-HUH-HUH-HUH!

SHUT-UP, BUTT-HEAD! I WAS CRYING CUZ I LIKE, HAD SOME POPCORN IN MY EYE. BESIDES, IT MADE YOU CRY TOO, BUTT-KNOCKER!

NO WAY! I WAS CRYING CUZ, UHH, I WAS SAD TO SEE THAT YOU WERE SUCH A WUSS, HUH-HUH.

CHECK IT OUT, HEH-HEH. THIS IS THAT PART WHERE THE OTHER ALIEN DUDES ARE LIKE, "LET'S DITCH THAT E.T DUDE. HEH-HEH. HE SUCKS."

YEAH, HUH-HUH. SOMETIMES, E.T'S STOMACH STARTED BURNING UP. HEH-HEH. IT WAS ALL, LIKE, RED. I THINK HE HAD A ULCER OR SOMETHING. LIKE, HANGING AROUND THAT STUPID ELIOT KID JUST MADE IT WORSE, HUH-HUH.

WHEN THAT KID CUT HIS FINGER E.T.'D GO "OUUUCH" AND TOUCH THE KID'S FINGER AND THEN THE KID WAS OKAY. HEH-HEH! IF ME AND E.T HUNG OUT, I'D, LIKE, JUMP INTO A VOLCANO WITH SOME DYNAMITE STRAPPED ON ME AND JUST BEFORE I HIT THE LAVA, I'D BLOW MYSELF UP AND THEN MY BODY PARTS WOULD GET ALL BURNED UP IN THE LAVA, HEH-HEH-HEH. AND THEN E.T'D TOUCH ME AND I'D BE OKAY AGAIN, HEH-HEH. IT WOULD RULE!

ALIEN AUTOPSY

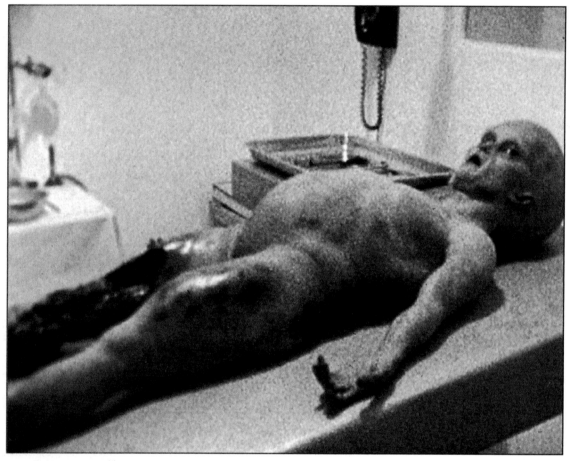

THERE WAS THIS COOL TV SHOW THAT WAS, LIKE, FOR REAL, WHERE A COUPLE OF SCIENTIFIC DUDES GOT THIS DEAD ALIEN AND STARTED CHOPPING ITS GUTS OUT! HEH-HEH-HEH! IT RULED!

YEAH, HUH-HUH-HUH. EVERYONE KEPT ASKING IF IT WAS REAL AND STUFF. BUT LIKE, IF IT WASN'T REAL, IT WOULDN'T HAVE BEEN ON TV.

THESE DUDES THAT CUT UP THE ALIEN DIDN'T DO IT RIGHT. THIS IS WHAT ME AND BEAVIS THINK THEY SHOULD'VE DONE:

THEY SHOULD'VE TURNED THE ALIEN OVER AND LOOKED AT ITS BUTT, HUH-HUH-HUH!

THEY SHOULD'VE STUCK ITS FINGER IN ITS NOSE, SO IT LOOKED LIKE THE ALIEN WAS PICKING IT, HEH-HEH-HEH!

AFTER THEY CUT IT OPEN ONE DUDE SHOULD'VE CLIMBED INSIDE IT, AND LIKE, CRAWLED AROUND INSIDE THE ALIEN FOR AWHILE. THEN HE SHOULD'VE STUCK HIS HEAD OUT ITS BUTT AND WENT "PEEK-A-BOO!"

THEY SHOULD'VE CUT ITS HEAD OFF, THEN FLUSHED IT DOWN THE TOILET, HUH-HUH-HUH!

THEY SHOULD'VE PUT ITS HAND ON ITS SCHLONG, SO IT LOOKED LIKE IT WAS CHOKING ITS CHICKEN! HEH-HEH-HEH!

THEY SHOULD'VE STUFFED A BUNCH OF GARBAGE IN ITS MOUTH THEN JUMP UP AND DOWN ON ITS STOMACH AND LIKE, WATCH ALL THE CRAP SHOOT OUT OF ITS MOUTH.

ONE OF THEM SHOULD'VE MADE THE ALIENS MOUTH MOVE AND SAY "I SUCK" AND "I'M A DORK." HUH-HUH-HUH! AND "I CRASHED THE UFO CUZ I WAS DRUNK."

THE TOOTH FAIRY

ME AND BEAVIS WANTED TO PROVE IF THERE REALLY WAS A TOOTH FAIRY. HUH-HUH. WE HAD A PLAN, OR SOMETHING. SO, LIKE, FIRST WE NEEDED SOME TEETH, HUH-HUH-HUH. BEAVIS' TEETH. HUH-HUH-HUH-HUH.

THEN WE PUT BEAVIS' TEETH UNDER THE PILLOW. HE WAS GONNA PRETEND TO BE SLEEPING AND I WAS GONNA HIDE UNDER THE BED, AND SO, LIKE, WHEN THE TOOTH FAIRY CAME BY, I WAS GONNA JUMP UP AND SPRAY BUG SPRAY ON IT, HUH-HUH!

YEAH, HEH-HEH-HEH-HEH! AND THEN WE WERE GONNA SELL IT TO THE PET STORE. I BET WE'D GET, LIKE, FIVE BUCKS FOR IT! HEH-HEH-HEH.

BUT THEN, UMM, I FELL ASLEEP FOR REAL AND I HAD A "NOCTURNAL MISSION." HEH-HEH-HEH-HEH!

BEAVIS, YOU BUTT-MUNCH, YOU MESSED UP THE PLAN.

OH, YEAH, HEH-HEH. I MESSED-UP THE BED, TOO. HEH-HEH-HMM-HEH-HEH

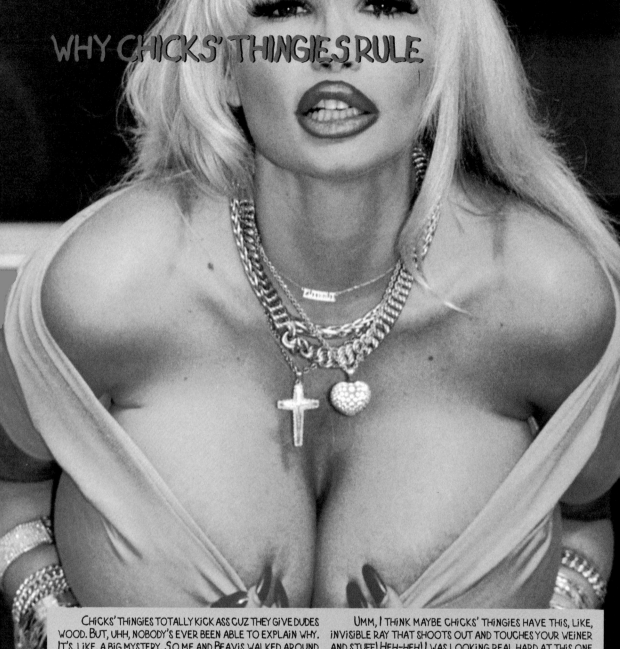

WHY CHICKS' THINGIES RULE

CHICKS' THINGIES TOTALLY KICK ASS CUZ THEY GIVE DUDES WOOD. BUT, UHH, NOBODY'S EVER BEEN ABLE TO EXPLAIN WHY. IT'S, LIKE, A BIG MYSTERY. SO ME AND BEAVIS WALKED AROUND AND LOOKED AT CHICKS' THINGIES AND GOT STIFFYS, ALL IN THE NAME OF SCIENCE OR SOMETHING. HUH-HUH-HUH.

HERE'S SOME IDEAS WE GOT FROM THE EXPEARMINT ABOUT WHY THINGIES GIVE DUDES STIFFYS:

UMM, CHICKS' THINGIES JIGGLE, KINDA LIKE A DUDE'S NADS! SO WHEN A DUDE SEES JIGGLY THINGIES IT REMINDS HIM OF HIS NADS! HEH-HEH! AND SO THE DUDE'S, LIKE, "OHHH, YEAH. I'VE GOT NADS. THAT RULES!"

I THINK THINGIES GIVE DUDES STIFFYS CUZ THINGIES KINDA LOOK LIKE A BUTT THAT'S ON THE CHICKS' STOMACH. HUH-HUH-HUH! THAT'S COOL!

UMM, I THINK MAYBE CHICKS' THINGIES HAVE THIS, LIKE, INVISIBLE RAY THAT SHOOTS OUT AND TOUCHES YOUR WEINER AND STUFF! HEH-HEH! I WAS LOOKING REAL HARD AT THIS ONE CHICK'S THINGIES AT THE MALL AND I SAW A INVISIBLE RAY OR SOMETHING SHOOT OUT OF HER THINGIES RIGHT AT MY WEINER. HEH-HEH! THEN, LIKE, A SECOND LATER MY WEINER FELT SPECIAL! HEH-HEH-HEH! BOIIIIING!

CHICK'S THINGIES USE, UHH, MENTAL TELEPATHY OR SOMETHING TO TALK TO YOUR WEINER. WHEN THINGIES SEE A DUDE THEY'RE LIKE, "HEY, WEINER. HOW'S IT GOING? LET'S PARTY." AND THE DUDE'S WEINER IS KINDA LIKE A ANTENNA OR SOMETHING. HUH-HUH-HUH! IT HAS TO, YOU KNOW, STAND AT ATTENTION SO IT CAN, LIKE, PICK-UP THE MESSAGES THE THINGIES ARE SENDING. HUH-HUH-HUH-HUH!

Deep in the Arctic, they hunt their prey. They're big. They're soft. They're . . . terrifying! Can any man survive the horror of . . .

THE THINGIES

A REALLY COOL PRODUCTION
STARRING ANNA NICOLE SMITH's BOOBS. THE GUY FROM "ESCAPE FROM L.A."
AND BUTT-HEAD AS THE EXPERT ON THINGIES. SPECIAL EFFECTS SUPERVISOR AND GRIP: BEAVIS.

UHH, THIS MOVIE HAD SOME REALLY COOL DIALOG AND STUFF. HERE'S SOME OF THE BEST LINES:

"GENTLEMEN, AFTER MUCH SCIENTIFIC STUDY, I HAVE DETERMINED THAT THEY ARE A GARGANTUAN SET OF MAMMARY GLANDS, HUH-HUH-HUH. IN OTHER WORDS, A HUGE PAIR OF BOOBS."

"LOOK, THE COLD AIR IS DOING SOMETHING TO THEM!"

"WHOA! HUH-HUH-HUH! COME TO BUTT-HEAD!"

"IF WE COULD ONLY HARNESS THEIR POWER, WE COULD FEED THE ENTIRE WORLD!"

"I'D LIKE TO GET A CLOSER LOOK, UH-HUH-HUH, FOR, UH, SCIENTIFIC REASONS."

"DON'T GET BETWEEN THEM! IT'S, LIKE, SUICIDE OR SOMETHING!"

"THE POOR THINGIE EXPERT NEVER HAD A CHANCE. THE THINGIES SMOTHERED HIM, THEN CRUSHED HIM TO DEATH. IT MUST HAVE BEEN A TERRIBLE WAY TO DIE. BUT LOOK AT HIS FACE...IT ALMOST LOOKS LIKE HE'S SMILING."

TWILIGHT ZONE

There's this place called The Twilight Zone where things that suck happen to you. And there's this dude that hangs out there, smoking and saying stuff that doesn't make any sense. One time, me and Butt-Head got trapped in The Twilight Zone for awhile, and it sucked! Check it out

VAN DREISSEN: BEAVIS AND BUTT-HEAD! DON'T YOU @*$% KNOW THAT CLASS BEGINS AT OH-NINE-HUNDRED SHARP?! IT'S 9:01! GET IN YOUR SEATS BEFORE I BREAK YOUR *&#@% NECKS!

BUTT-HEAD: OH, MY GOODNESS! MR. VAN DREISSEN IS QUITE ANGRY. IT FRIGHTENS ME WHEN HE USES SUCH FOUL LANGUAGE.

BEAVIS: HEH-HEH-HEH, WHY BUTT-HEAD, YOU JUST SPOKE IN THE MOST UNUSUAL MANNER. IT WAS QUITE ODD! OH, DEAR! I AM SPEAKING IN THE SAME ERUDITE FASHION!

IMAGINE, IF YOU WILL, TWO TYPICAL, UNDERACHIEVING HIGH SCHOOL BOYS HAVING A DAY THAT'S ANYTHING BUT ORDINARY. BECAUSE WHEN BEAVIS AND BUTT-HEAD ENTERED THEIR CLASSROOM, THEY ALSO STEPPED INTO... THE TWILIGHT ZONE.

BUTT-HEAD: MY NAME "BUTT-HEAD" IS SO VERY CRUDE AND OFFENSIVE. I BELIEVE I WILL CHANGE IT TO THE MORE PROPER GLUTEUS MAXIMUS-HEAD.

STEWART: I'M GONNA CUT YOUR GUTS OUT IF YOU DON'T GIVE ME ALL YOUR MONEY.

BEAVIS: DON'T WORRY GLUTEUS MAXIMUS-HEAD, MY STALWART COMPANION. I WOULD PROTECT YOU WITH MY VERY LIFE. AND AS FOR YOU, STEWART, KNIVES ARE DANGEROUS. AND FURTHERMORE, THEY ARE NOT ALLOWED IN CLASS.

DARIA: SO, GUYS, YOU WANNA MEET ME AT MY PLACE AFTER SCHOOL? WE'LL, LIKE, GET DRUNK AND DO IT ALL NIGHT LONG! HEY, I THINK I CAN SEE YOUR WEINERS, HAW-HAW-HAW! THAT'S COOL!

BUTT-HEAD: DARIA, SOME OF US ARE HERE TO LEARN, NOT TO BE DISTRACTED BY YOUR JUVENILE COMMENTS AND OFFENSIVE BEHAVIOR.

BEAVIS: AND AS FOR YOUR PROPOSITION OF A SEXUAL TRYST, I, FOR ONE, AM CERTAINLY NOT INTERESTED, YOU VILE STRUMPET. PREMARITAL SEX IS SIMPLY WRONG.

BUZZCUT: I HAVE WONDERFUL NEWS FOR YOU, BOYS. YOUR HARD WORK AND SUPERIOR STUDY HABITS HAVE PAID OFF. YOU'VE BEEN ACCEPTED TO OXFORD UNIVERSITY ON A FULL SCHOLARSHIP. I WILL TRULY MISS YOU.

BEAVIS: WHAT JOYOUS NEWS! OUR DREAMS AND ASPIRATIONS HAVE COME TRUE!

BUTT-HEAD: COME WITH US TO COLLEGE, MR. BUZZCUT! YOU ARE OUR FRIEND AND WE LOVE YOU.

AND SO, A VERY UNUSUAL SCHOOL DAY COMES TO AN END, IN A VERY UNUSUAL CLASS ROOM LOCATED SOMEWHERE IN THE FAR CORNERS OF... THE TWILIGHT ZONE.

BUTT-HEAD: THAT GENTLEMAN'S NAME IS ROD. WHAT A FINE NAME!

CONTACTING DEAD PEOPLE

ME AND BUTT-HEAD WANTED TO TALK TO SOME GHOSTS OF DEAD PEOPLE. THE WAY YOU DO IT IS, YOU, LIKE, SIT IN A DARK ROOM AND LIGHT A CANDLE AND THINK OF DEAD PEOPLE. HEH-HEH! BUT, UMM, YOU GOTTA, LIKE, HOLD HANDS OR SOMETHING.

YEAH. THAT BUTT-KNOCKER BEAVIS TRIED TO HOLD MY HAND, SO I KICKED THE LIVING CRAP OUT OF HIM. HUH-HUH-HUH! AND WHILE I WAS BEATING ON BEAVIS A BUNCH OF DEAD DUDES SHOWED UP ANYWAY, HUH-HUH-HUH! THIS IS, LIKE, WHAT THEY SAID:

BEAVIS: WHOA! IT'S SOME OLD DUDE! HEH-HEH!

OLD DUDE: FINALLY! I HAVE BEEN TRYING TO CONTACT THE LIVING FOR SO LONG! I AM ALBERT EINSTEIN. IN DEATH I HAVE LEARNED OF SO MANY WONDERFUL THINGS! SIMPLE ANSWERS TO MYSTERIES THAT HAVE PUZZLED MAN FOR AGES. I CAN TELL YOU IF THERE IS A GOD, OR IF THERE IS LIFE ON OTHER PLANETS. I CAN EVEN TELL YOU THE MEANING OF LIFE! NOW, DO YOU HAVE ANY QUESTIONS?

BUTT-HEAD: UHH, WHAT'S IT LIKE TO SCORE?

BEAVIS: AND, UMM, WHICH EPISODE OF XENA: WARRIOR PRINCESS IS ON TONIGHT? HEH-HEH!

BEAVIS: CHECK IT OUT! SOME AINCHENT DUDE FROM THE 60'S. HEH-HEH!

AINCHENT DUDE: I AM NOSTRODOMUS. LISTEN CAREFULLY! I SHALL REVEAL WHEN AND WHERE TERRIBLE CALAMITIES WILL STRIKE EARTH WITHIN THE NEXT YEARS. WITH THIS KNOWLEDGE YOU MAY SPREAD THE NEWS AND BE ABLE TO SAVE UNTOLD MILLIONS OF LIVES FROM DISASTER.

BUTT-HEAD: YOU SAID "SPREAD." HUH-HUH-HUH!

BEAVIS: WHOA! IT'S BRUCE LEE! HEH-HEH-HEH! HEY, MAN, HOW'S IT GOIN'?

BRUCE LEE: PRETTY GOOD.

BEAVIS: THAT ONE MOVIE WHERE YOU KICKED LIKE, A HUNDRED ASSES RULED, HEH-HEH-HEH! AND THAT TIME YOU PUNCHED THAT BIG GUY IN THE BUTT! HYAAAA! PLOP! HEH-HEH!

BUTT-HEAD: HEY, BRUCE. WE SHOULD HANG OUT, CUZ, YOU KNOW, I LIKE TO KICK DUDE'S ASSES, TOO. HUH-HUH-HUH. IN FACT, I WAS JUST KICKING BEAVIS' ASS. CHECK IT OUT. I'M GONNA DO IT AGAIN.

BEAVIS: NO WAY, BUTT-HEAD! OWW! CUT IT OUT, FART-KNOCKER! AGGGH!

PEOPLE WHO, LIKE, ALL OF A SUDDEN BURN UP FOR NO REASON

CHECK THIS OUT! THERE'S SOME PEOPLE WHO, LIKE, ALL OF A SUDDEN BURN-UP, HEH-HEH-HEH, FOR NO REASON! IT'S, LIKE, THEY'RE JUST WALKING AROUND AND ALL OF SUDDEN THEY'RE LIKE, "AUUGGGHH! I'M ON FIRE!" HEH-HEH-HEH! AND THERE'S NOTHING LEFT BUT THEIR SHOES AND A LITTLE PILE OF DIRT! SCIENTIFIC DUDES CALL IT SPOTANUS HUMAN COMBUSTSHUN OR SOMETHING. HEH-HEH-HEH!

SO LIKE, I WAS IN CLASS TRYING TO MAKE MYSELF SPOTANUSLY HUMAN COMBUST AND STUFF. I WAS TRYING LIKE REALLY HARD, HEH-HEH! AND, LIKE, AFTER A FEW HOURS I BLACKED OUT! HEH-HEH-HEH-HEH! SO IT WAS STILL PRETTY COOL!

UMM, YOU PROBABLY THINK IT WOULD SUCK TO ALL OF A SUDDEN BURN UP FOR NO REASON. BUT SOMETIMES IT MIGHT BE COOL. LIKE, FOR EXAMPUL:

IT'D BE COOL IF YOU'RE STANDING AROUND TALKING TO CHICKS AND ONE OF THEM PUT A CIGARETTE IN HER MOUTH. THEN ALL OF A SUDDEN YOU COMBUSTED,

HEH-HEH-HEH! SHE COULD LIGHT HER CIGARETTE ON YOUR HEAD. HEH-HEH! THAT'D BE PRETTY DAMN SMOOTH.

IT'D BE COOL IF YOU'RE, LIKE, WRESTLING WITH SOME GUY IN GYM CLASS AND ALL OF A SUDDEN YOU BURST INTO FLAMES! HEH-HEH! AND HE, LIKE JUMPS UP AND GOES "AHHH-HGH!" YOU'D WIN FOR SURE!

IF YOU'RE TAKING A TEST AND IT'S REALLY HARD, AND THEN YOU COMBUSTED! HEH-HEH! YOU'D BE, LIKE, "UMM, EXCUSE ME, SIR. I'M ON FIRE." HEH-HEH-HEH!

IF YOU COMBUST WHEN IT'S REALLY COLD OUT. YOU'D BE ALL WARM AND THE CHICKS'LL WANNA STAND CLOSE TO YOU. HEH-HEH!

IF YOU'RE AT WORK, TAKING PEOPLE'S ORDERS AND YOUR FACE SUDDENLY BURNS OFF. IT'D FREAK OUT THE CUSTOMERS AND THEY'D PROBA-BLY GO EAT SOMEWHERE ELSE! HEH-HEH-HEH!

IF YOU'RE STANDING IN LINE FOR THE BATHROOM AND YOU SUDDENLY STARTED BURNING UP, PEOPLE WILL PROBABLY BE LIKE, "IT'S OKAY, MAN, I DON'T HAVE TO GO THAT BAD. YOU GO FIRST."

READING PALMS

There's this place, over by the pawn shop and the porn theatre. When you go there, you pay five bucks and this mysterious old chick that has a lot of necklaces and junk will, like, read your palm. And it's pretty cool cuz she can tell you when you're gonna die and if you're gonna score and stuff just by looking at the lines and stuff on your hand. Beavis wanted to get his palm read, but he didn't have five bucks, so I did it for a dollar. Here's Beavis' palm and what I found out about him:

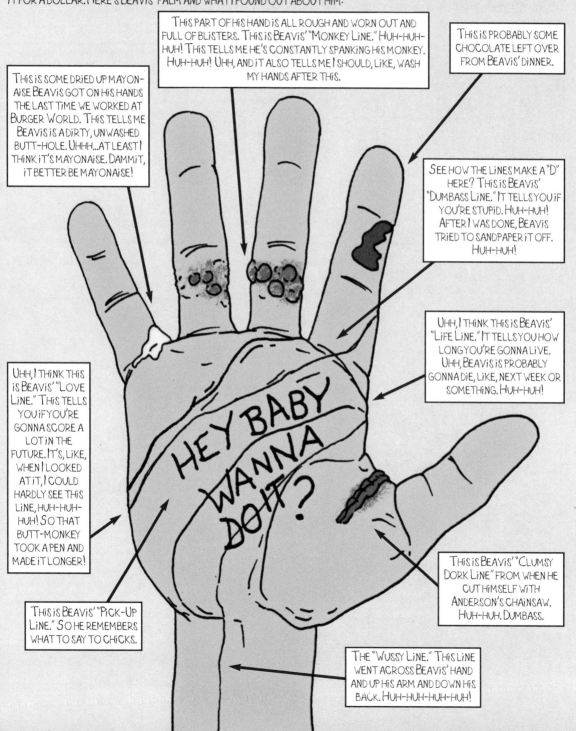

This part of his hand is all rough and worn out and full of blisters. This is Beavis' "Monkey Line." Huh-huh-huh! This tells me he's constantly spanking his monkey. Huh-huh! Uhh, and it also tells me I should, like, wash my hands after this.

This is probably some chocolate left over from Beavis' dinner.

This is some dried up mayonaise Beavis got on his hands the last time we worked at Burger World. This tells me Beavis is a dirty, unwashed butt-hole. Uhhh...at least I think it's mayonaise. Dammit, it better be mayonaise!

See how the lines make a "D" here? This is Beavis' "Dumbass Line." It tells you if you're stupid. Huh-huh! After I was done, Beavis tried to sandpaper it off. Huh-huh!

Uhh, I think this is Beavis' "Life Line." It tells you how long you're gonna live. Uhh, Beavis is probably gonna die, like, next week or something. Huh-huh!

Uhh, I think this is Beavis' "Love Line." This tells you if you're gonna score a lot in the future. It's, like, when I looked at it, I could hardly see this line, huh-huh-huh! So that butt-monkey took a pen and made it longer!

HEY BABY WANNA DO IT?

This is Beavis' "Clumsy Dork Line" from when he cut himself with Anderson's chainsaw. Huh-huh. Dumbass.

This is Beavis' "Pick-up Line." So he remembers what to say to chicks.

The "Wussy Line." This line went across Beavis' hand and up his arm and down his back. Huh-huh-huh-huh!

GENETIC ENGINE-EARRING

UMM, HEH-HEH, GENETIC ENGINE-EARRING IS WHEN SCIENTIFIC DUDES DO EXPEERMINTS ON ANIMALS. THEY LIKE, PUT EM TOGETHER SCIENTIFICULY AND, LIKE, MAKE BRAND-NEW ANIMALS OUT OF EM, HEH-HEH-HEH.

IN SCHOOL, VAN DRIESSEN WAS TALKING ABOUT HOW, UMM, IN THE FUTURE THERE'S GONNA BE A LOT OF THIS GENETIC ENGINE- EARRING. BUT THEN HE SAID THIS STUFF IS, LIKE, REALLY MESSED-UP AND UNNATURAL OR SOMETHING. SO ME AND BUTT-HEAD WANTED TO TRY IT! HEH-HEH-HEH!

1) FIRST YOU GET TWO BUGS YOU WANNA GENETIC ENGINE-EAR. UMM, HERE WE HAVE A SPIDER AND A WORM, HEH-HEH-HMM.

2) THEN YOU SMASH EM TOGETHER, HEH-HEH-HEH!

3) SEE? HEH-HEH. NOW YOU GOT AN ALL-NEW BUG, HEH-HEH-HEH. THEN YOU HAVE TO NAME WHAT KIND OF A BUG IT IS. SO, UMM, SINCE THIS WAS A SPIDER AND A WORM, THIS'LL BE A...UMM...A "SPIRM," HEH-HEH! HEH-HEH-HEH! I'VE GOT "SPIRM" IN MY HANDS, HEH-HEH-HEH-HEH-HEH!

ME AND BUTT-HEAD GENETIC ENGINE-EARED A BUNCH OF OTHER NEW ANIMALS. HEH-HEH-HEH! CHECK IT OUT:

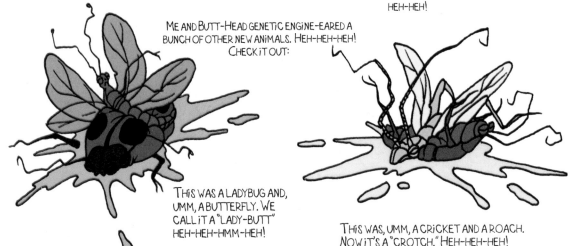

THIS WAS A LADYBUG AND, UMM, A BUTTERFLY. WE CALL IT A "LADY-BUTT" HEH-HEH-HMM-HEH!

THIS WAS, UMM, A CRICKET AND A ROACH. NOW IT'S A "CROTCH." HEH-HEH-HEH!

SOME OF OUR OTHER NEW ANIMALS:
* WE SQUISHED TOGETHER A TERMITE AND A DEAD BIRD. HEH-HEH-HEH! NOW IT'S A "TIRD."
* A DEAD LIZARD AND A DEAD TOAD. WE CALLED IT A "LOAD," HEH-HEH!
* WE MASHED UP A LADYBUG AND A CENTIPEDE. NOW IT'S A "LADY-PEED," HEH-HEH-HEH-HEH!

FAMILIES

Families. Huh-huh-huh.

Families are a mystery cuz it's like when kids hang out with their mom and dad, on purpose. And they, like, do things together, huh-huh-huh! And they're, like, all happy and talking and stuff. What a bunch of dorks! And, uhh, sometimes, the dads live with the family. And they spend "quality time" with their kids. Huh-huh-huh!

Whoa! That's pretty messed up! Heh-heh. It's, like, I feel sorry for them and stuff.

Families suck. Huh-huh. Uhh, nobody knows why, but sometimes you can find a family that's pretty cool. Here's how to tell if your family sucks or if it's cool:

	FAMILIES THAT SUCK	COOL FAMILIES
DADS	One time I heard some kid tell his dad that he loves him, heh-heh-heh! And the dad said "I love you too, son."	Once, I threw a spatula at my mom's boyfriend and he kicked my ass. Heh-heh-heh! He was cool!
MOMS	The mom is always driving the kids everywhere and dropping them off, saying: "Have fun and be careful."	You call your mom to pick you up, and all you hear is a bunch of coughing and then she hangs up.
DINNER	They all eat together and they're always going, "Please pass the potatos." And, uhh, "How was your day?"	You go by yourself and eat a whole bag of marshmallows in the parking lot at Maxi-Mart. Then when you're full you put marshmallows in the street and watch cars run over them, huh-huh-huh!
WHEN SOMEONE DIES	Stewart was crying when his uncle died. Heh-heh!	Umm, when my uncle got shot in prison, they gave me his porn collection. It ruled!
GOING TO BED	The parents are always tucking their kids into bed and saying "sweet dreams." Huh-huh.	You fall asleep on the couch watching TV and your mom and her boyfriend come home drunk and swear at you and tell you to get off the couch so they can do it, huh-huh.

ALIEN ABDUKSHUNS & EXSPEERMINTS ON HUMANS

You know how people are always on those talk shows, saying how aliens took them on their spaceships and then, you know, did it with them? Huh-huh-huh. That's what me and Beavis are gonna do. We're, like, gonna wait here 'til some aliens steal us, huh-huh, and do us, huh-huh-huh-huh.

We're gonna score with aliens, heh-heh-heh! It's, like, probably easier than scoring with chicks on Earth. And it's gonna be cool!

Yeah, huh-huh. And sometimes, after aliens score with you, they do expeermints on your, uhh, equipmint, huh-huh-huh. These are some of the expeermints aliens probably do:

* Take a big death ray and blow up your nut-sack.

* Beam your schlong to another time.

* They take a light saber and fight with your weiner.

* Shoot a freeze bolt at your butt-cheeks.

* Make your public hair radioactive so it glows in the dark.

* Disintegrate your butthole.

* Electrocute your weiner to death.

CLOSE ENCOUNTERS OF THE TURD KIND

THIS IS, LIKE, ANOTHER MOVIE THAT WOULD'VE BEEN COOLER IF ME AND BEAVIS DIRECTED IT. FIRST, WE'D CHANGE THE NAME. BUT, LIKE, YOU ALREADY SAW THAT. HUH-HUH. THEN WE'D MAKE THE ALIENS COOL:

AND LIKE, WE'D CHANGE A FEW SCENES. UH-HUH-HUH.

STATUES THAT CRY

WE SAW ON TV THAT THERE'S THIS STATUE OF SOME FAMOUS HICK IN SOME CHURCH. AND IT'S SUPPOSED TO CRY. BUT NOBODY KNOWS WHY. SO WE DID OUR OWN INVESTIGASHUN AND CHECKED OUT SOME DIFFERENT STATUES TO SEE IF THEY CRIED TOO.

THIS STATUE WAS IN THE ART MUSEUM. WE KEPT SPITTING ON IT, SO IT'D LOOK LIKE IT WAS CRYING. THEN WE STARTED KICKING IT AND A COP CAME BY AND KICKED US OUTTA THERE. HUH-HUH-HUH!

THIS STATUE DIDN'T CRY. SO WE THOUGHT WE'D <u>MAKE</u> IT CRY. BEAVIS GOT ON TOP OF IT AND STARTED BITING IT REALLY HARD. IT DIDN'T WORK ON THE STATUE, BUT AFTER AWHILE BEAVIS STARTED HOLDING HIS MOUTH AND CRYING. HUH-HUH-HUH!

WE FOUND THIS STATUE IN A STORE. IT DIDN'T CRY EITHER. BUT I HEARD SOMEWHERE THAT SMELLING ONIONS MAKES YOU CRY. SO WE GOT A ONION AND HELD IT UNDER THIS STATUE'S NOSE ALL DAY. IT DIDN'T WORK, SO BEAVIS GOT PISSED AND CRAMMED THE ONION IN THE STATUES NOSE, AND THAT KNOCKED THE STATUE OVER AND IT'S HEAD BROKE OPEN. HUH-HUH-HUH! THEN A LADY WHO WORKED AT THE STORE STARTED CRYING.

THIS CHICK STATUE WAS IN THE PARK. IT DIDN'T CRY, BUT WE TOUCHED HER THINGIES. HUH-HUH-HUH! THEN BEAVIS TOOK OFF HIS PANTS AND STARTED RUBBING UP AGAINST IT. IT WAS COLD OUT AND HIS WEINER GOT STUCK TO THE STATUE, HUH-HUH-HUH-HUH! BEAVIS FREAKED OUT AND STARTED CRYING AGAIN BECAUSE HE THOUGHT HE WAS GONNA BE STUCK FOREVER. HUH-HUH!

REINCARNASHUN

SOME PEOPLE THINK THAT THEY WERE ONCE OTHER PEOPLE IN THE PAST. LIKE IN ANOTHER LIFE AND STUFF. THESE ARE SOME OF THE PEOPLE ME AND BEAVIS USED TO BE IN ANOTHER LIFE:

LOTS OF YEARS AGO, ME AND BEAVIS WERE CAVE DUDES. HUH-HUH. IT WAS COOL.

NO. MAN GET EATEN BY TIGER. UGG. WALL IS COOL.

UGG. SUCKS. CHANGE IT.

IN ANOTHER LIFE, ME AND BEAVIS GOT TO DRIVE A BOAT CALLED THE, UHH, TITANIC OR SOMETHING. HUH-HUH. IT HAD A COOL NAME. AT LEAST THE FIRST PART, HUH-HUH!

IN THE 40'S WE RAN SOME RADAR THING JUST BEFORE SOME WAR STARTED OR SOMETHING. IT WAS COOL CUZ WE GOT TO BE IN HAWAII.

THEN, LIKE, IN THE 60'S WE WERE SERVICE DUDES FOR SOME PRESIDENT. I THINK THEY NAMED HIM AFTER THAT ONE ANNOYING CHICK WITH GLASSES THAT'S ON MTV. HUH-HUH. ONE DAY, WE GOT TO HANG OUT AT THIS ONE PARADE IN DALLAS.

BLACK HOLES

UHH, HUH-HUH-HUH. THIS IS, LIKE, A MYSTERY TO SCIENCE DUDES. THEY LIKE, DON'T KNOW WHAT BLACK HOLES ARE OR WHERE THEY ARE. SOME OF THEM EVEN THINK IT'S, LIKE, IN SPACE, HUH-HUH-HUH! THIS IS A PICTURE OF A BLACK HOLE. IF YOU'RE LIKE, SO STUPID THAT YOU STILL DON'T KNOW WHAT THIS IS, HERE'S SOME HINTS OR SOMETHING:

1. SOMETIMES BEAVIS' FINGER GOES THERE.

2. IF YOU, LIKE, DRINK SODA AND LAUGH, THE SODA COMES SHOOTING OUT OF IT.

3. YOU USE IT TO BREATHE.

4. IT GROSSES OUT CHICKS IF YOU STICK FOOD IN IT AND THEN EAT IT.

5. SOMETIMES IF YOU DIG AROUND FOR A WHILE, YOU FIND STUFF IN IT.

6. YOU CAN WALK AROUND WITH PENCILS STUCK IN IT.

7. REALLY COOL PEOPLE GET THIS PIERCED.

ANSWER: A BUTTHOLE, HUH-HUH-HUH! YOU DUMBASS.

THE TERMINATOR

BUTT-HEAD LIKED THIS MOVIE SO MUCH THAT HE TRIED TO COPY IT. HEH-HEH! WHAT A DUMBASS. HEH-HEH!

UHH, I'M A FRIEND OF SARA CONNER, HUH-HUH. CAN I, LIKE, SEE HER?

GET OUT OF HERE, YOU LITTLE MORON. I'M BUSY.

UHH, I'LL BE BACK. HUH-HUH-HUH.

HUH-HUH-HUH. THIS IS GONNA BE COOL. HUH-HUH-HUH.

WHAT THE HELL?

OWW. HUH-HUH.

BIGFOOT

UHH, THIS IS BEAVIS' MOM. HUH-HUH-HUH! AKSHULLY, THIS IS LIKE, SOME WILD DUDE WITH A REALLY BIG FOOT. SOME PEOPLE CALL IT A "SACK-SQUASH," HUH-HUH-HUH! THAT'S CUZ, LIKE, IT KICKS GUYS IN THE NUT-SACK WITH ITS BIG FOOT, HUH-HUH-HUH! THEN BEFORE YOU CAN KICK IT IN THE NADS IN REVENGE, IT RUNS INTO THE WOODS AND HIDES AND PROBABLY, LIKE, LAUGHS ABOUT IT AND STUFF, HUH-HUH-HUH!

OTHER LITTLE-KNOWN BIGFOOT FACTS:

ONE TIME HE FOUGHT THE SIX-MILLION DOLLAR MAN. WE SAW IT ON TV. IT WAS COOL.

HE INVENTED THAT BIG TRUCK WITH THE GIANT WHEELS. HE USED TO DRIVE IT IN THE WOODS, BUT THEN HE NEEDED SOME MONEY SO HE SOLD IT TO SOME GUY AT A MONSTER-TRUCK SHOW.

HOW TO FAKE A BIGFOOT SIGHTING

IT'S LIKE, PRETTY EASY TO TRICK PEOPLE WITH A FAKE BIGFOOT PICTURE THAT YOU CAN SELL FOR LOTS OF MONEY.

TO MAKE A FAKE BIGFOOT PICTURE, YOU NEED TO, LIKE, DO SOME STUFF:

FIRST, YOU GET SOME HAIR. WE BORROWED SOME FROM A POODLE, HUH-HUH-HUH. THEN YOU, LIKE, GLUE IT ON BEAVIS.

AFTER BEAVIS IS ALL HAIRY AND STUFF, MAKE HIM STAND BY A BUSH. HUH-HUH-HUH! UHH, THEN YOU TAKE HIS PICTURE. AND WHEN YOU TRY SELLING THE PICTURE, TELL EVERYONE THAT YOU WERE REALLY SCARED AND STUFF. AND THAT YOU WOULD'VE TAKEN MORE PICTURES, BUT HE KICKED YOU IN THE NADS.

AND ONE MORE THING. YOU NEED SOME BIGFOOT FOOTPRINTS TO PROVE THAT YOU REALLY SAW IT. HERE'S HOW TO MAKE SOME FAKE BIGFOOT FOOTPRINTS:

FIND SOME MUD. THEN, YOU'LL NEED A GIANT FOOT, HUH-HUH. SO LIKE, FIRST, TAKE OFF YOUR SHOE. THEN SMASH YOUR FOOT REALLY HARD WITH A BASEBALL BAT, HUH-HUH-HUH! KEEP SMASHING IT UNTIL YOUR FOOT SWELLS UP BIGGER. THEN WALK AROUND IN THE MUD AND MAKE A BUNCH OF FOOTPRINTS. NOW EVERY-ONE'LL BELIEVE YOU AND YOU CAN SELL THE PICTURE FOR A LOT OF MONEY. HUH-HUH!

SANTA CLAWS

ON CHRISTMAS EVE, SANTA CLAWS GOES AROUND THE WORLD AND GIVES OUT EMPTY BEER CANS AND CIGARETTE BUTTS TO LITTLE KIDS. AT LEAST THAT'S WHAT ME AND BUTT-HEAD ALWAYS GOT, HEH-HEH. CHRISTMAS WAS COOL. BUT, UMM, THERE'S A LOT OF PEOPLE WHO THINK SANTA CLAWS IS LIKE, THIS NICE OLD DUDE WHO LIVES ON A POLE AND WEARS RED PAJAMAS. HEH-HEH. THAT'S LIKE, WRONG. ME AND BUTT-HEAD FOLLOWED SANTA ON CHRISTMAS EVE AND HE DIDN'T KNOW IT. HERE'S SOME SECRET PICTURES WE TOOK:

1. SANTA WAS AT THE MALL AND A BUNCH OF KIDS WERE SITTING ON HIM. LATER, HE WENT IN BACK AND TOOK OFF HIS RED PAJAMAS AND THEN HE, LIKE, RIPPED OFF HIS BEARD. WITHOUT THAT STUFF, YOU COULD SEE HE'S JUST A SWEATY OLD SLOB, HEH-HEH-HEH. INSTEAD OF LOADING UP HIS SACK WITH PRESENTS, HE LOADED UP A PAPER BAG WITH MONEY OUT OF A CASH REGISTER. HEH-HEH! THEN HE TOOK OFF IN A HURRY TO START DELIVERING STUFF TO PEOPLE.

2. SANTA'S SLED MUST'VE BEEN BUSTED OR SOMETHING, CUZ HE RODE OFF ON A BUS. WE SAT BEHIND HIM. HE KEPT TALKING TO HIMSELF AND SWEARING A LOT. IT WAS COOL, HEH-HEH-HEH. THE FIRST PLACE HE STOPPED TO DELIVER PRESENTS WAS A BAR. NOBODY LEFT HIM ANY MILK AND COOKIES, SO THE BARTENDER DUDE GAVE HIM SOME BOOZE AND PRETZELS INSTEAD. SANTA DIDN'T GIVE ANYONE ANYTHING, BUT BEFORE HE LEFT HE PUNCHED SOME GUY. HE MUST'VE BEEN ON SANTA'S "NAUGHTY" LIST, HEH-HEH! THEN SANTA STUMBLED OUTSIDE AND PUKED, HEH-HEH-HEH-HEH!

3. SANTA DOESN'T LIVE ON A POLE, HE LIVES IN A TRAILER PARK. HE HAD LIKE, 10 ELFS THAT LOOKED JUST LIKE KIDS. THEY WEREN'T MAKING TOYS, THEY WERE JUST, LIKE, RUNNING ALL OVER THE PLACE, REFUSING TO GO TO BED AND STUFF. WHEN SANTA CAME HOME FROM THE BAR, HE STARTED SCREAMING AT THE ELFS TO GO TO BED, AND THEN HE SMASHED UP HIS PLACE, HEH-HEH-HEH. THEN MRS. CLAWS CALLED THE COPS AND THEY DRAGGED SANTA TO JAIL. HEH-HEH-HEH-HEH!

HOW CAN SANTA, LIKE, PASS OUT ALL HIS PRESENTS IN ONE NIGHT? WE DID SOME MATH AND STUFF TO FIGURE OUT IF HE COULD REALLY DO IT. CHECK THIS OUT:

SO THERE'S LIKE, MAYBE 100,000 PEOPLE IN THE WORLD. AND THERE'S LIKE, A BUNCH OF HOURS IN A NIGHT. SO TO FIND OUT HOW MUCH TIME SANTA'S GOT, YOU, UHH, TAKE 100,000 AND, UHH, ADD A BUNCH TO THAT:

$$100,000 + A BUNCH = = 100,056$$

HE'S GOT 100,056 MINUTES OR SOMETHING. SO WHEN SANTA DROPS OFF PRESENTS, HE HAS TO GO DOWN THE CHIMNEY AND PUT IT UNDER THE TREE AND THEN CLIMB OUT AGAIN. WE HAD TO KNOW HOW LONG IT TOOK SANTA EACH TIME. SO WE GOT SOME EMPTY BEER CANS AND CIGARETTE BUTTS AND BEAVIS TRIED IT ON ANDERSON'S HOUSE.

FIRST, BEAVIS GOT STUCK IN THE CHIMNEY FOR A HALF HOUR. HUH-HUH-HUH. THEN HE FELL OFF THE ROOF AND SPRAINED HIS BUTT IN 2 PLACES. HUH-HUH-HUH! HE STILL COULDN'T GET IN, SO HE HAD TO BUST THE WINDOW AND THROW THE PRESENTS IN. ANDERSON WOKE UP AND STARTED YELLING THAT HE WAS GONNA CALL 911 OR SOMETHING. THE WHOLE THING TOOK, LIKE, 3 HOURS. SO, LIKE, IF THAT HAPPENS TO SANTA IN EVERY HOUSE IN THE WORLD, THAT WOULD BE, UHH...

$$2 + 911 + 3 = 29,113 \times 3$$
$$THE DIVIDE 29,113 INTO = 29 AND 7113$$

IT'D TAKE SANTA 29 HOURS AND 113 MINUTES. BUT IF YOU DON'T BELIEVE IN SANTA, HE STOPS AT YOUR HOUSE AND LOOKS IN YOUR WINDOW AND FLIPS YOU OFF. HUH-HUH. WHEN WE TRIED IT WITH STEWART'S HOUSE, IT TOOK BEAVIS, LIKE, 8 SECONDS TO WALK UP TO A WINDOW, LOOK INSIDE AND FLIP SOMEONE OFF. STEWART'S DAD WAS PISSED, HUH-HUH-HUH.

SO, UHH, IF THERE'S LIKE 300 PEOPLE THAT DON'T BELIEVE IN SANTA. AND IF IT TOOK SANTA 8 SECONDS TO FLIP THEM OFF EVERY TIME, THAT WOULD BE, UHH, HMM...

$$300 + 8 = 380.$$

UHH, THEN YOU TAKE THE 100,056 HOURS AND, UHHH, YOU DO SOMETHING WITH IT. I THINK YOU ADD THE 29 HOURS. OR MAYBE THE 380. UHHH...DAMN IT, I'M GETTING SICK OF ALL THIS MATH. IT PROBABLY EQUALS, LIKE, 600 OR SOMETHING. HUH-HUH-HUH. THE END.

CONCLOOSHUN: UHH, THIS PROVES THAT SANTA CAN PASS OUT SOME OF HIS PRESENTS IN ONE NIGHT BUT AFTER THAT HE PROBABLY GETS TIRED AND GOES HOME TO DO IT WITH MRS. CLAWS.

OH, YEAH, AND SANTA IS REAL. IF YOU DON'T BELIEVE IN HIM YOU'LL GO TO HELL. HUH-HUH-HUH.

BAYWATCH NIGHTS

BAYWATCH RULES! IT'S LIKE, IF I EVER MISSED AN EPISODE OF BAYWATCH, FOR THE WHOLE WEEK I'D BE PISSED. BUT THEN THEY MADE ANOTHER SHOW CALLED BAYWATCH NIGHTS. SO WHEN I HEARD ABOUT THAT, I HAD A STIFFY FOR A WEEK. HEH-HEH-HMM-HEH! THEN IT CAME ON AND IT SUCKED! IT WAS SUPPOSED TO BE LIKE, PAMELA ANDERSON AND THE OTHER HOT CHICKS FROM BAYWATCH, EXCEPT AT NIGHT, WHEN THEY GET NAKED AND DO IT! YEEEEAH! HEH-HEH-HEH! BUT, UMM, INSTEAD THE WHOLE SHOW WAS ABOUT THAT FLABBY OLD BUNGHOLE, DAVID HASSELHOFF. HE WAS, LIKE, TRYING TO BE LIKE THAT DUDE FROM X-FILES SOLVING ALL THESE SUPPERNATURAL THINGS. WE DIDN'T SEE ANY CHICKS IN BIKINIS, OR EVEN PAMELA ANDERSON! AND ALL THE CHICKS WEAR REGULAR CLOTHES, DAMMIT! AND THERE'S HARDLY ANY SUPPERNATURAL STUFF! BUT, UMM, DAVID HASSELHOFF HAS BOOBS. HEH-HEH! SO I GUESS THAT'S KINDA SUPPERNATURAL. HEH-HEH-HEH!

ME AND BUTT-HEAD WROTE TO THE PEOPLE AT BAYWATCH TO GIVE THEM SOME IDEAS FOR NEW EPISODES:

PAMELA ANDERSON GETS POSSESSED AND FLOATS AROUND NAKED. AND THE REST OF THE EPISODE TURNS INTO ONE OF THOSE LONG MUSIC VIDEO SCENES, WITH ALL THESE SLOW MOTION SHOTS OF HER BUTT!

PAMELA ANDERSON HAS TO FIGHT A GIGANTIC SCHLONG. HEH-HEH! YEAH. HEH-HEH. MINE.

DAVID HASSELHOFF'S BUTT-HAIR COMES TO LIFE AND JUMPS IN HIS EYES WHILE HE'S DRIVING AND HE WRECKS THE CAR. HEH-HEH-HEH!

A GHOST TRIPS DAVID HASSELHOFF AND HE FALLS DOWN SOME STAIRS AND BREAKS HIS BUNGHOLE. HEH-HEH. THAT WOULD BE COOL!

MOVING AND BREAKING STUFF WITH YOUR BRAIN

UMM, WE LEARNED ON TV THAT SOME PEOPLE HAVE THIS COOL MAGIC POWER, CALLED TELEKINEESIS OR SOMETHING. THEY CAN LIKE, MOVE AND BREAK STUFF WITH THEIR BRAIN, HEH-HEH-HEH. LIKE THIS ONE GUY STARED AT A SPOON AND THEN IT BENT AND THEN BROKE! HEH-HEH! I TRIED STARING AT BUTT-HEAD SO I COULD BEND HIM AND BREAK HIM, BUT HE PUNCHED ME IN THE FACE.

TELEKINEESIS IS PRETTY EASY TO DO. YOU JUST, LIKE, STARE AT SOMETHING AND CONSENTRATE FOR A LONG TIME, AND THIS BIG BLUE VEIN STARTS PUFFING UP ON YOUR FOREHEAD, AND THEN ALL THIS COOL STUFF HAPPENS. HERE'S SOME OF THE THINGS I DID WITH TELEKINEESIS:

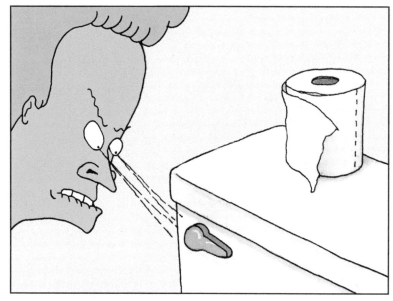

* ONE TIME, MY FREEZY WHIP WAS REAL ICY, AND IT WOULDN'T GO UP THE STRAW. SO, I STARED AT IT REAL HARD TO MAKE IT MELT. IT, LIKE, TOOK AWHILE, BUT THEN IT REALLY DID MELT!

* THIS OTHER TIME, AT BURGER WORLD, THIS DUMBASS CUSTOMER WAS ASKING ME ALL THESE QUESTIONS, SO I LIKE, USED MY POWER TO MAKE HIM GO AWAY. AND IT WORKED, CUZ AFTER I STARED AT HIM FOR FIVE MINUTES, HE LEFT!

* AT THE GROCERY STORE, I DIDN'T FEEL LIKE OPENING THE DOOR WITH MY HANDS, SO I JUST USED MY BRAIN. I WAS STARING AT THE DOOR FOR A LONG TIME, BUT IT DIDN'T WORK. I MUST'VE BEEN TOO FAR AWAY, CUZ WHEN I WALKED UP A LITTLE CLOSER TO THE DOOR IT OPENED ALL BY ITSELF RIGHT AWAY! A LOT OF OTHER PEOPLE GOT THE SAME IDEA AS ME, CUZ I SAW THEM OPENING THE DOOR WITH THEIR BRAINS, TOO.

* ONE TIME, PRINCIPAL MC VICKER ASKED ME A QUESTION, BUT I DIDN'T KNOW THE ANSWER, SO I JUST STARED AT HIM FOR LIKE TEN MINUTES. HE DIDN'T BREAK APART, BUT HE STARTED SHAKING REAL BAD AND HE SCREAMED AT ME TO STOP IT. HEH-HEH. I THINK HE'S SCARED OF ME.

* I WANTED IT TO BE NIGHT SO XENA: WARRIOR PRINCESS WOULD COME ON. SO I WAS STARING AT THE SUN, TRYING TO MAKE IT GO DOWN. AFTER AWHILE, I GOT DIZZY AND ALL OF A SUDDEN IT GOT REALLY, REALLY DARK! I WAS LIKE, "COOL! IT WORKED!" AND I STARTED WALKING AROUND BUMPING INTO THINGS. I MEAN, IT WAS REALLY DARK. IT WAS NIGHT FOR A FEW DAYS AND NOBODY TURNED ON ANY LIGHTS AND I COULDN'T FIND MY WAY HOME. THEN I THINK A CAR HIT ME AND SOMEONE TOOK ME TO THE HOSPITAL AND I HAD A OPERATION ON MY EYES. HEH-HEH. NOW I'M OKAY. BUT I THINK I'M GONNA WAIT AWHILE BEFORE I TRY THAT AGAIN.

MOVING AND BREAKING STUFF WITH YOUR BRAIN (CONT'D.) THERE WAS A PRETTY COOL MOVIE CALLED CARRIE, ABOUT THIS CHICK THAT USED TELEKINEESIS. EVERYONE MADE FUN OF HER AND LAUGHED AT HER AND STUFF. ONE DAY, SHE WAS AT THIS DANCE AND SOME PEOPLE REALLY PISSED HER OFF. SO THEN SHE STARED AT STUFF AND USED HER BRAIN TO GET BACK AT EVERYONE. HEH-HEH-HEH! IT RULED! IF SOMETHING LIKE THAT HAPPENED TO ME, I'D USE TELEKINEESIS TO GET REVENGE TOO. CHECK IT OUT, HEH-HEH-HEH.

CROP CIRCLES

FARMERS ARE ALWAYS FINDING THESE GIANT THINGS CALLED CROP CIRCLES IN THEIR FIELDS. ALIENS COME DOWN IN THE MIDDLE OF THE NIGHT AND DO THESE JUST TO FREAK PEOPLE OUT. HUH-HUH. ME AND BEAVIS MADE OUR OWN CROP CIRCLE TO FOOL MR. ANDERSON. HE'S GONNA LOOK AT IT AND GO, "WHOA! AN ALIEN MUST'VE DONE THIS!" AND THEN HE'LL POOP IN HIS PANTS, HUH-HUH-HUH!

HOW TO SPOT AN ALIEN

UHH, THERE'S THESE PEOPLE THAT THINK ALIENS ARE RUNNING AROUND ON EARTH, LIKE, DISGUISED AS HUMANS. ME AND BEAVIS LOOKED AT THIS PICTURE OF A REAL ALIEN, AND THEN WE, LIKE, TRIED TO FIND SOME UNDERCOVER ONES. WE LOOKED IN SOME MAGAZINES AND FIGURED OUT THAT THERE'S A LOT OF ALIENS THAT PRETEND TO BE THESE CHICKS CALLED SUPERMODELS. SO IF YOU SEE A SUPERMODEL, YOU SHOULD START POINTING AT HER AND SCREAMING FOR HER TO GO BACK TO HER OWN PLANET AND LEAVE US THE HELL ALONE.

OR, UMM, YOU CAN TELL THE SUPERMODEL THAT YOU WON'T TURN HER IN IF SHE LETS YOU TOUCH HER BOOBS. HEH-HEH-HEH!

OUR PROOF:

HEAD: ALIENS HAVE REALLY BIG HEADS. HUH-HUH. JUST LIKE SUPERMODELS. SUPERMODELS' HEADS ARE HUGE, EVEN THOUGH THEIR BRAINS ARE PRETTY SMALL. HUH-HUH. THEY'RE DUMB.

HAIR: UHH, ALIENS ARE REALLY BALD IN REAL LIFE. SO WHEN THEY DISGUISE THEMSELVES LIKE SUPERMODELS THEY WEAR WIGS. IF YOU SEE A SUPERMODEL, PULL HER WIG OFF. IT MIGHT BE ON KINDA TIGHT BUT KEEP PULLING. HUH-HUH.

NECK: ALIENS AND SUPER-MODELS HAVE THESE REALLY LONG, FREAKY-LOOKING STRETCHED OUT NECKS.

EYES: ALIENS AND SUPERMODELS HAVE REAL BIG EYES THAT GIVE OUT DEATH-RAY STARES.

BODY: ALIENS AND SUPER-MODELS BOTH HAVE THESE WEAK, SKINNY LITTLE ARMS AND BODIES. I THINK IT'S CUZ EARTH FOOD MAKES THEM SICK OR SOMETHING.

SKIN: ALIENS AND SUPER-MODELS HAVE REALLY WHITE SKIN. LIKE THEY'RE SICK OR SOMETHING OR ALWAYS PUKING.

UHH...WAIT A MINUTE. YOU CAN SAY SOME OF THIS STUFF ABOUT BEAVIS, TOO. UHHH...LET ME SEE IF YOUR HAIR IS REAL, BEAVIS. HUH-HUH-HUH!

OWW! HEY, WHAT THE HELL? QUIT PULLING MY HAIR, BUTT-HEAD! AGGGH! STOP IT, FARTKNOCKER!

THE GIANT FLOATING BUTT OF HIGHLAND HIGH

THERE'S THIS BIG BUTT THAT FLOATS AROUND OUR SCHOOL SOMETIMES. I THINK IT ONLY COMES OUT DURING FULL MOONS. HUH-HUH. IT'S, LIKE, YOU'LL BE SITTING IN CLASS AND ALL OF A SUDDEN YOU'LL LOOK UP AND THERE'S THIS GIANT GHOSTLY BUTT THAT FLOATS ACROSS THE ROOM REAL SLOW. THEN IT CUTS THE CHEESE AND DISAPPEARS, HUH-HUH-HUH-HUH!

SOME PEOPLE THINK IT COMES FROM THIS KID, WHO, LIKE, YEARS AND YEARS AGO CUT OFF HIS BUTT IN WOOD SHOP. HUH-HUH-HUH! THE KID LIVED AND STUFF, BUT HIS BUTT DIED. AND NOW THE GHOST OF HIS BUTT HAUNTS HIGHLAND FOREVER, OR SOMETHING.

STAR TREK

UMM, STAR TREK WAS THIS SHOW WHERE THESE DUDES IN THEIR PAJAMAS FLY AROUND IN SPACE AND FIGHT STATIC CLING OR SOMETHING. OR MAYBE IT WAS SOME GUY NAMED KLINGER. HEH-HEH. BUTT-HEAD IS SUCH A DILLHOLE, I BET IF HE WAS IN STAR TREK, HE'D PROBABLY BE LIKE THIS, HEH-HEH:

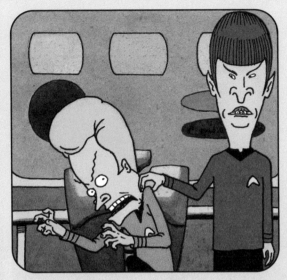

CAPTAIN'S LOG, STARDATE 6969. HEH-HEH-HEH! "LOG"-AGGGH!

THIS VULCAN DEATH GRIP IS COOL, HUH-HUH! SO, LIKE, NOW I'M THE CAPTAIN. I'M GONNA GO TO THE BATHROOM AND MAKE A CAPTAIN'S LOG, HUH-HUH-HUH.

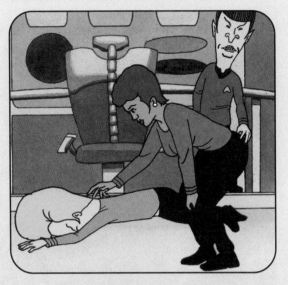

WHAT HAPPENED TO THE CAPTAIN?!

UH-HUH-HUH. HEY, BABY. NICE BUTT. WANNA GO DO IT?

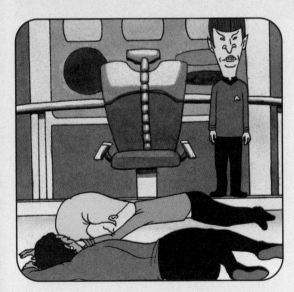

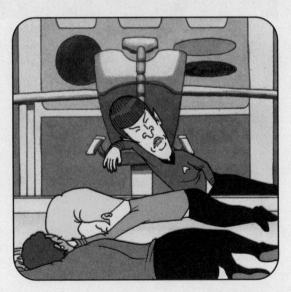

WHOA, HUH-HUH-HUH. SORRY. UHH, I GUESS I'LL JUST HAVE TO, UH-HUH-HUH, SPANK THE MONKEY.

WHY THE BEATLES ARE POPULAR EVEN THOUGH THEY'RE DEAD (AND SUCK)

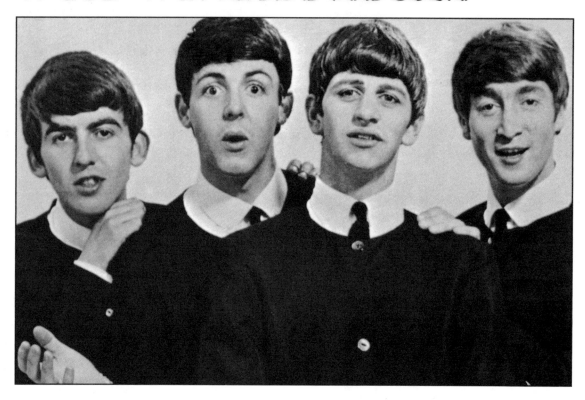

IT'S, LIKE, A BIG ENOUGH MYSTERY WHY THE BEATLES WERE EVER POPULAR. BUT, LIKE, IT'S EVEN A BIGGER MYSTERY WHY THEY'RE POPULAR NOW THAT THEY'RE DEAD. UHH, THE BEATLES WERE JUST THESE WUSSY DORKS FROM ENGLAND AND THEY DID A BUNCH OF CRAPPY SONGS THAT SUCKED. OLD PEOPLE LIKE THE BEATLES CUZ WHEN THEY WERE LITTLE THERE WASN'T ANY OTHER MUSIC. COOL MUSIC WASN'T INVENTED YET OR SOMETHING. HUH-HUH.

AND UMM, IT'S, LIKE, I WAS WATCHING THIS TV SHOW ABOUT THE BEATLES AND THEY SHOWED AN OLD BEATLES CONCERT AND THE AUDIENCE WAS THE UGLIEST BUNCH OF PEOPLE I'VE EVER SEEN IN MY LIFE. HEH-HEH! AND ALL THESE CHICKS WERE SCREAMING IN PAIN AND HOLDING THEIR HEADS. I FELT SORRY FOR THEM.

THEN THEY SHOWED HOW THE BEATLES WERE ALWAYS RUNNING AWAY FROM ALL THESE HORNY CHICKS. HEH-HEH-HEH! STUPID BUTT-HOLES! IF I WAS IN THE BEATLES AND A CROWD OF HORNY CHICKS WERE RUNNING AT ME, I'D LIKE PUT MY GUITAR DOWN, DROP MY PANTS, AND DO EM ALL, RIGHT THERE ON THE STREET! HEH-HEH-HEH!

HUH-HUH-HUH! ME TOO. UHH, BUT THEN THE BEATLES DIED. HUH-HUH. I THINK PANTERA KILLED THEM.

UMM, I THINK THEY'RE STILL ALIVE, BUTT-HEAD. THEY'RE IN HIDING, CUZ COOL BANDS LIKE PANTERA AND METALLICA SCARED EM OFF. I THINK THEY LIVE IN A CAVE NOW, HEH-HEH-HEH! AND THEY'RE ALL SHAKING AND CRYING LIKE WUSSIES CUZ THEY THINK PANTERA IS GONNA FIND THEM AND KICK THEY'RE ASSES.

OH YEAH! HUH-HUH-HUH. ANYWAY, ALL THESE OLD PEOPLE CALLED "BABY BOOMERS" KEEP BUYING BEATLES STUFF CUZ IT PROBABLY MAKES EM FEEL YOUNG, HUH-HUH-HUH! EVEN THOUGH THEY'RE OLD AND THEY'RE ALL GONNA DIE SOON. HUH-HUH-HUH! BABY BOOMERS SUCK!

ALIEN

THIS MOVIE WAS REALLY COOL, BUT, UMM, THERE WAS ONE SCENE THAT I COULDA DONE A LOT BETTER. HEH-HEH!

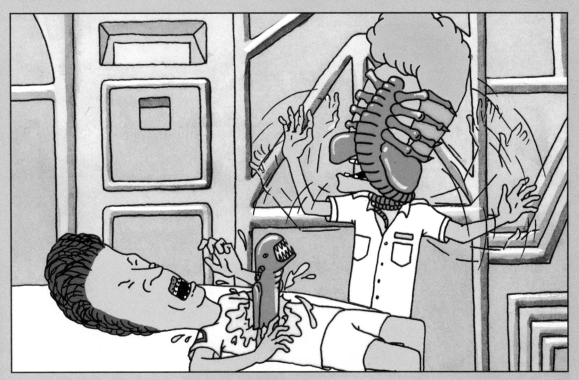

AGGGH! THIS FACE-SUCKER THING'S SUCKING MY FACE! AGGGH!

UMM...WAIT A MINUTE.

YEAH. HEH-HEH-HEH! THAT'S BETTER! HEH-HEH-HEH-HEH! YEAH!

DEJA POO

DID YOU EVER GO SOMEWHERE, AND ALL OF A SUD-
DEN, LIKE, GET THIS FUNNY FEELING THAT ONE TIME
YOU TOOK A DUMP THERE? IT'S CALLED DEJA
POO. HEH-HEH-HEH. AND IT HAPPENS TO ME ALL
THE TIME! HEH-HEH! SO, LIKE, HERE'S A BUNCH OF
PLACES WHERE I FELT DEJA POO. HEH-HEH-HEH!
POOP!

NEAR-DEATH EXPEERIENCES: AN EXPEARMINT

UMM, PEOPLE ON TV KEEP TALKING ABOUT PEOPLE WHO, LIKE, DIE. HEH-HEH-HEH. THEN THEY'RE DEAD. HEH-HEH-HMM-HEH.

THAT'S NOT IT, DUMBASS. IT'S LIKE, THEY'RE DEAD, BUT THEY COME BACK TO LIFE. AND THEN THEY TELL EVERYONE ABOUT ALL THE CRAP THEY SAW WHEN THEY WERE DEAD. HUH-HUH-HUH.

OHHH, YEAH. SO, UMM, ME AND BUTTHEAD WANTED TO HAVE ONE OF THESE NEAR DEATH, UMM, EXPEERIENCES AND, LIKE, TELL EVERYONE WHAT IT WAS LIKE. HEH-HEH.

SO, UHH, THE FIRST THING ME AND BEAVIS HAD TO DO WAS DIE. WE THOUGHT IT'D BE COOL IF TODD, LIKE, KICKED OUR ASSES TO DEATH, HUH-HUH-HUH. SO WE WENT UP TO TODD AND LOOKED AT HIM WHILE HE WAS MAKING OUT WITH HIS CHICK, HUH-HUH-HUH.

THEN TODD BEAT THE LIVING CRAP OUT OF US.

THEN WE WERE DEAD, HEH-HEH, 'CUZ, UMM, I SAW THIS BRIGHT LIGHT! HEH-HEH.
YEAH, ME TOO. HUH-HUH-HUH. AND, UHH, I REMEMBER I WAS, LIKE, FLYING ABOVE EVERYTHING. HUH-HUH-HUH. I, LIKE, LOOKED DOWN AND SAW YOU ON THE GROUND, BEAVIS. IT WAS COOL!

PLANET OF THE APES

BEAVIS IS SUCH A BUTT-MONKEY, THAT HE WOULD'VE BEEN REALLY GOOD IN THIS MOVIE. HUH-HUH! THIS IS PROBABLY WHAT IT'D BE LIKE IF HE PLAYED THAT ONE HUMAN DUDE:

WHY BEAVIS CAN'T SCORE

IT'S LIKE, A SCIENTIFIC FACT, OR SOMETHING, THAT THERE'S NO WAY BEAVIS WILL EVER SCORE. NO MATTER WHAT. UHH, HERE'S SOME REASONS WHY:

JUST LOOK AT HIM. HUH-HUH-HUH-HUH!

HIS VOICE SOUNDS LIKE AN OLD MAN TRYING TO TALK WHILE HE'S TAKING A MASSIVE DUMP.

CHICKS LIKE TATTOOS. SO ONE TIME, BEAVIS TRIED DRAWING A TATTOO ON HIS ARM. HE, LIKE, TOOK A CRAYON AND DREW A NAD ON HIS ARM. THEN HE WALKED UP TO A CHICK AND SHOWED IT TO HER, BUT IT WAS ALL SMEARED AND SHE COULDN'T TELL WHAT IT WAS. HUH-HUH-HUH!

HIS JAW IS ALL STUCK OUT AND UGLY. IT'S, LIKE, HIS FACE LOOKS LIKE AN EEL. HUH-HUH-HUH! A DORKY EEL.

WE SAW ON TV THAT REALLY RICH DUDES BURN MONEY TO SHOW CHICKS THEY'RE RICH. SO ONE TIME, BEAVIS WALKED UP TO A CHICK AND TRIED DOING THAT WITH A QUARTER. BUT IT GOT REAL HOT AND HE DROPPED IT AND STARTED CRYING.

PLUS, BEAVIS DOESN'T KNOW HOW TO TALK TO CHICKS. THESE ARE SOME OF HIS PICK-UP LINES:

"UMM, HEH-HEH-HEH-HEH-HEH!"

"HEH-HEH-HMM-HEH!"

"HMM-HEH-HEH-HEH! UMMM."

"I GOT A STIFFY, HEH-HEH-HEH!"

"HEH-HEH-HEH-HEH! HEH-HEH!"

"POOP."

EVEN IF A CHICK WANTED TO DO IT WITH BEAVIS, HE PROBABLY WOULDN'T KNOW HOW. HUH-HUH. CUZ HE'S STUPID. TO PROVE HOW STUPID HE IS, I STUCK BEAVIS' HEAD UNDER A MICROSCOPE THING IN CLASS, TO LOOK AT HIS BRAIN. AND HIS BRAIN IS SO SMALL, I COULDN'T EVEN SEE IT. HUH-HUH.

2001: A SPACE ODDITY

THIS MOVIE SUCKS. IT'S, LIKE, THE WORST PIECE OF CRAP EVER. IT WAS, LIKE, THERE WAS A BUNCH OF MONKEYS BEATING EACH OTHER ON THE HEAD, AND THAT WAS COOL, BUT THEN THIS ONE MONKEY THREW THIS BONE INTO OUTER SPACE AND IT TURNED INTO A SPACE SHIP. IT'S, LIKE, WHAT THE HELL IS THAT?! ARE WE SUPPOSED TO BELIEVE THAT'S HOW SPACESHIPS WERE MADE?

THEN ALL THIS SUCKY JAZZ MUSIC OR SOMETHING STARTED PLAYING. THEN SOME DUDES ON A SPACESHIP WERE TALKING TO SOME GUY NAMED HAL WHO WAS HIDING BEHIND A WALL. THEN THERE WAS A BUNCH OF COLORS AND SOME OLD DUDE WOKE UP IN BED AND SAW THIS GIANT CANDY BAR AND HE GOT ALL SCARED OF IT AND DIED. HUH-HUH-HUH. IT SUCKED.

YEAH, REALLY. IT'S, LIKE, IF I WOKE UP AND SAW A GIANT CANDY BAR FLOATING IN MY ROOM, I'D START EATING IT. HEH-HEH-HEH!

MOVIES LIKE THIS JUST PISS ME OFF. UHH, I GUESS THE POINT OF THE MOVIE WAS THAT YOU CAN JUST THROW TOGETHER A BUNCH OF CRAP THAT DOESN'T MEAN ANYTHING AND DOESN'T MAKE ANY SENSE, BUT STUPID PEOPLE LIKE SISKEL AND EBERT WILL SAY "TWO THUMBS UP!" HUH-HUH. I'D LIKE TO GIVE THEM TWO THUMBS UP THE BUTT! HUH-HUH! STUPID PEOPLE THINK THEY KNOW WHAT ALL THAT CRAP MEANS AND THEY'RE ALL SERIOUS AND TALK ABOUT IT, BUT THE GUY WHO MADE THE MOVIE DOESN'T EVEN KNOW WHAT THE HELL IT MEANS. HUH-HUH-HUH!

FROZEN DEAD PEOPLE

SOME REALLY RICH DEAD PEOPLE PAY SCIENCE DUDES, LIKE, 25 THOUSAND DOLLARS TO GET THEIR WHOLE BODY FROZEN SO THAT IN THE FUTURE, SOME OTHER SCIENCE DUDE CAN UNMELT THEM AND BRING THEM BACK TO LIFE. ME AND BEAVIS AREN'T RICH OR DEAD, BUT WE THOUGHT IT'D BE PRETTY COOL TO SEE WHAT THE FUTURE WOULD BE LIKE IN 10 YEARS, SO WE TRIED TO GET FROZEN TOO. HUH-HUH. IT WAS WORKING PRETTY GOOD, BUT THEN THE GUY AT MAXI MART TOLD US TO GET THE HELL OUT OF HIS ICE MACHINE BEFORE HE CALLED THE COPS. HUH-HUH. ASSWIPE.

BUT IF YOU'RE NOT TOTALLY RICH, SCIENCE DUDES CAN JUST CHOP YOUR HEAD OFF AND FREEZE IT FOR, LIKE, 5 THOUSAND BUCKS. ME AND BEAVIS ARE SAVING UP FOR IT. AS SOON AS WE GET THE MONEY, SOMEONE'S GONNA CHOP OFF OUR HEADS AND FREEZE THEM.

THEN, IN THE YEAR 6969, OUR HEADS ARE GONNA COME BACK TO LIFE AND FLOAT AROUND IN THESE JET-THINGS AND CHECK OUT ALL THE FUTURE CHICKS. FUTURE CHICKS'LL BE HOT FOR US, CUZ WE'LL PROBA-BLY HAVE GIGANTIC BIONIC SCHLONGS OR SOMETHING. HUH-HUH. I HOPE.

BLADE RUNNER

UMM, THIS MOVIE IS ABOUT THIS GUY THAT WOULD, LIKE, RUN AROUND THE HOUSE WITH SCISSORS, AND HIS MOM'S LIKE "STOP RUNNING WITH SCISSORS!" HEH-HEH-HEH! GET IT, HEH-HEH! BLADE RUNNER?

BEAVIS, YOU BUTT-DUMPLING. JUST SHUT UP. HIS JOB WAS TO FIGURE OUT WHO'S A ROBOT AND WHO WASN'T AND THEN SHOOT EVERYBODY. IF I WAS THAT BLADE RUNNER DUDE AND I WANTED TO TELL IF SOMEONE'S A ROBOT, I'D LIKE, WAIT FOR THEM TO TAKE A DUMP. HUH-HUH. THEN WHEN THEY'RE DONE, I'D GO IN AND CHECK THE TOILET. IF THERE'S JUST A BUNCH OF SCREWS AND NUTS AND BOLTS FLOATING IN THE TOILET, THAT MEANS THAT PERSON'S A ROBOT. HUH-HUH.

IN THE MOVIE, THEY ALSO HAD THESE ROBOTS THAT WERE, UH-HUH-HUH, PLEASURE UNITS. THESE ARE ROBOT CHICKS THAT YOU CAN SCORE WITH.

REALLY? HEH-HEH! WHO'D WANNA SCORE WITH A CHICK THAT'S LIKE, MADE OF PLASTIC AND HER BOOBS ARE FAKE AND HER HAIR ISN'T REAL?

YEAH, REALLY. HUH-HUH. I LIKE REAL CHICKS LIKE PAMELA ANDERSON AND ANNA NICOLE SMITH AND JENNY MCCARTHY.

YEAH, ME TOO. HEH-HEH-HEH!

SUPERMARKET TABLOIDS

Like, the only reason to learn how to read is to check out those cool newspapers at the register in supermarkets and stuff. Heh-heh! They always got cool stories about cool suppernatural stuff and celebrity people. Me and Butt-Head found a bunch of pictures in the garbage and made our own supermarket tabloid. Cuz, umm, I think that's how they really do it. Heh-heh-heh! Check it out:

Was Elvis Ever Really Alive?

THE DAILY SPANK

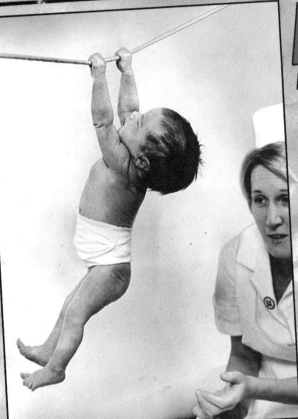

BABY TRIES DARING ESCAPE FROM HOSPITAL!

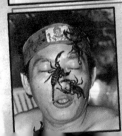

Kitchen Conditions Improving At Burger World

PJ HARVEY AND BILLY CORGAN SEEN LEAVING TRENDY NIGHTCLUB TOGETHER

DOG GROWS FROM DUDE'S HEAD

THE DAILY SPANK

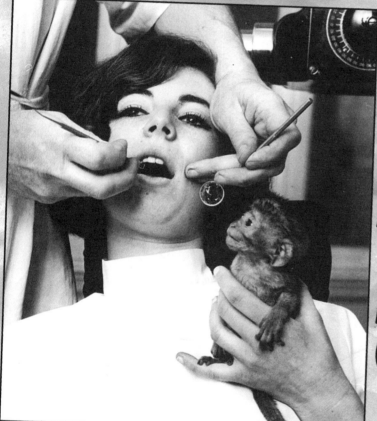

WOMAN SPANKS DENTIST'S MONKEY WHILE HE FILLS HER CAVITY!

ACTRESS SANDRA BERNHARD WEDS!

Dude Chokes His Chicken 500 Times In One Day; Breaks World Record (And Weiner). Says: "Whew! I'm Beat!"

WHY BUTT-HEAD SUCKS

Why Butt-Head sucks. By Beavis. Heh-heh-heh! This is gonna be cool! Umm, it's, like, a mystery why he sucks so much. For as long as I've known him, people have been, like, "Why does Butt-Head suck so much?" Umm, I'm here today to tell you why:

What the hell's with Butt-Head's gums? Heh-heh-heh! They're disgusting! I think when he was a little kid, a dog ripped off his top lip and it never grew back.

He always wears the same clothes. I swear it's, like, he only owns one shirt.

Plus, his breath stinks cuz he's always got food and crap stuck in his braces. And his braces are all rusted and they've been on forever.

His eyes are all crooked and stupid. Umm, I think that's cuz when we were little, I hit him in the back of the head with a shovel.

He thinks he's, um, smarter than, um, me. Or something. I don't know. Maybe. Um, what?

Once, I put this brick in my underwear so when Butt-Head would kick me in the nads, he'd break his foot, heh-heh. But like, that day he didn't kick me! I walked around funny all day with this brick hanging there between my legs, scratching up my nut-sack. Heh-heh. So finally I was like, " So, umm, Butt-Head. You wanna kick me in the nads?" And he was, like, "Uhh, okay." But just then my underwear ripped and the brick fell out and smashed my foot. I was screaming and he kicked me in the nads. The end. Heh-heh-heh!

When we were little, he used to sit on my head all the time and cut the cheese. And, umm, now I'm deaf in one ear.

Oh yeah, and he wants to do it with my mom.

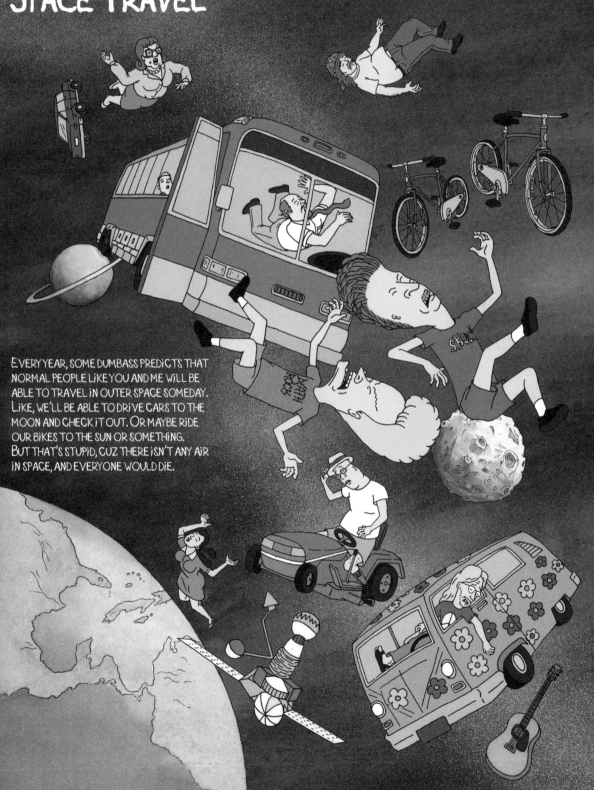

SPACE TRAVEL

EVERY YEAR, SOME DUMBASS PREDICTS THAT
NORMAL PEOPLE LIKE YOU AND ME WILL BE
ABLE TO TRAVEL IN OUTER SPACE SOMEDAY.
LIKE, WE'LL BE ABLE TO DRIVE CARS TO THE
MOON AND CHECK IT OUT. OR MAYBE RIDE
OUR BIKES TO THE SUN OR SOMETHING.
BUT THAT'S STUPID, CUZ THERE ISN'T ANY AIR
IN SPACE, AND EVERYONE WOULD DIE.

STAR WARS

THE STAR WARS MOVIES ALL KICKED ASS. HUH-HUH. DARTH VADER RULED, BUT HE WOULD'VE BEEN EVEN COOLER IF I PLAYED HIM. AND LUKE SKYWALKER WAS A WUSSY, BUT IF BEAVIS PLAYED HIM HE'D BE EVEN MORE OF A WUSS. HE'D PROBABLY BE CALLED LUKE FARTKNOCKER. HUH-HUH-HUH!

UHH, WE HEARD THAT IN THE FUTURE, WHEN THAT LUCAS DUDE GETS OFF HIS LAZY ASS, THERE'S GONNA BE THIS NEW MOVIE ABOUT THE DUDES FROM *STAR WARS*. EXCEPT, LIKE, EVERYTHING IN IT'S SUPPOSED TO HAPPEN BEFORE THE FIRST *STAR WARS* MOVIE OR SOMETHING. IT'LL PROBABLY BE LIKE THIS:

SUPPERNATURAL DUDES

GIBBY HAYNES

THIS DUDE KICKS ASS! HE'S THE SINGER GUY IN THE BUTTHOLE SURFERS. THEY RULE! HE'S SUPPERNATURAL, CUZ THERE IS NONE COOLER. HE IS THE GREATEST SINGER EVER. LIKE, A LOT OF PEOPLE DON'T KNOW IT, BUT, UHH, ALL THAT IS COOL IN THE WORLD COMES FROM GIBBY. HUH-HUH.

YEAH, REALLY! IT'S, LIKE, IF I WAS A MUSIC DUDE I'D BE JUST LIKE GIBBY. HE'S ALWAYS ALL MESSED-UP AND HE'S, LIKE, 10 FEET TALL AND HE SCREAMS A LOT. HEH-HEH! YOU KNOW, UMM, THERE SHOULD BE A HOLIDAY CALLED BUTTHOLE SURFERS DAY. LIKE, ALL THE KIDS WOULD DRESS UP LIKE GIBBY. THEY'D GLUE ON THESE BAD MOUSTACHES AND MESS UP THEIR HAIR AND TAKE OFF THEIR SHIRTS AND THROW CRAP AND PUKE AND BLOOD ON THEMSELVES. HEH-HEH! THEN THEY'D RUN AROUND RINGING PEOPLE'S DOOR-BELLS AND WHEN SOMEONE COMES TO THE DOOR, THE KIDS WOULD, LIKE, TURN AROUND AND PULL DOWN THEIR PANTS AND SCREAM "HAPPY BUTTHOLE DAY!" HEH-HEH-HEH-HEH!

THAT GUY ON WEATHER CHANNEL

THIS GUY IS PRETTY DAMN AMAZING. HE MUST BE SUPPERNATURAL CUZ HE KNOWS WHAT IT'S GONNA BE LIKE OUT-SIDE THE NEXT DAY. HUH-HUH. IT'S, LIKE, I WAS WATCHING WEATHER CHANNEL AND I SAW HIM DO IT. HE WAS, LIKE, "UHH, THERE'S GONNA BE RAIN TOMORROW." I WAS, LIKE, "UHH, OKAY, DUDE." BUT, LIKE, THE NEXT DAY, IT WAS RAINING! HUH-HUH-HUH. I WAS, LIKE, "WHOA! THAT'S COOL!"

YEAH! HEH-HEH! WE SAW HIM AT THE MALL. AND, UMM, I GOT HIS AUTO-GRAPH. HEH-HEH-HEH. I WAS LIKE, "HEY, MAN. HOW'S IT GOIN'? SO, WHAT'S IT GONNA BE LIKE TOMORROW?" AND HE WAS, LIKE, "PROBABLY HOT AND SUNNY." AND, LIKE, THE NEXT DAY IT WAS ALL HOT AND SUNNY! I COULDN'T BELIEVE IT! HEH-HEH-HEH! THIS GUY PROBABLY SCORES CONSTANTLY! YOU KNOW, UMM, THE WAY THIS GUY DOES IT, IS HE TIME TRAVELS TO TOMORROW AND THEN HE LOOKS AROUND AND SEES WHAT THE WEATHER'S LIKE. THEN HE GOES BACK AND TELLS EVERYONE! HEH-HEH! SEE, CUZ HOW ELSE COULD HE KNOW THE WEATHER TOMORROW? HEH-HEH!

OH, YEAH. THAT'S COOL!

UHH, OUR CITY IS CALLED BIG CRACK. UH-HUH-HUH-HUH!

THERE'S THIS GIANT GLASS BUBBLE COVERING THE CITY. I DON'T KNOW WHY, BUT THAT'S WHAT ALL FUTURE CITIES HAVE. PROBABLY SO YOU HAVE SOMETHING TO THROW ROCKS AT WHEN YOU'RE BORED.

IN OUR CITY THERE'D BE THIS ONE GIGANTIC TV SET, SO LIKE, NO MATTER WHERE YOU ARE IN THE CITY, YOU CAN STILL WATCH TV ALL DAY LONG. HUH-HUH. AND I GET THE REMOTE. HUH-HUH-HUH! AND IF SOMEONE TRIES TO CHANGE THE CHANNEL THEY GET KICKED IN THE NADS BY MY SECRET SERVICE DUDES.

ALL THE BUILDINGS WILL LOOK LIKE BUTTS AND BOOBS AND WEINERS. HEH-HEH-HEH-HEH-HEH! AND THE ENTRANCES TO THE UNDER-GROUND SUBWAY THINGS WOULD BE SHAPED LIKE, HEH-HEH-HEH-HEH. YOU KNOW. HEH-HEH-HEH!

THERE WILL BE BARE-ASS NAKED CHICKS LAY-ING AROUND EVERYWHERE, READY TO DO IT WITH MY ROYAL SCHLONG.

SKULL

DEATH ROCK

THE ONLY MUSEUM WOULD BE "THE BEAVIS MUSEUM OF BUTT PORN."

I'D HAVE A COPY OF HIGHLAND HIGH BUILT, HEH-HEH-HEH, THEN I'D GO IN THERE AND WRECK EVERY-THING. THEN I'D TELL THEM TO BUILD IT AGAIN AND I'D WRECK IT OVER AND OVER, HEH-HEH!

THERE'LL BE THIS GIANT TOILET IN THE MIDDLE OF THE CITY, AND IF YOU SUCK, YOU'LL BE THROWN IN THERE AND GET FLUSHED.

1 2 3

STAR TREK: THE NEXT GENERASHUN

THAT DUDE THAT PLAYS CAPTAIN PICCARD IS OLD. HUH-HUH-HUH. WHEN HE DIES, I'LL BET THEY GET ME TO PLAY CAPTAIN PICCARD. HUH-HUH-HUH! PICK HARD. HUH-HUH-HUH! WHEN I TAKE OVER, IT'LL BE LIKE THIS:

CAPTAIN'S LOG. NUMBER TWO HAS BEEN TELEPORTED TO THE PLANET OF LONELY HOT CHICKS. MAYBE HE'LL FINALLY SCORE. HUH-HUH.

WHOA! HEY, JORDY. CHECK OUT THIS CHICK, HUH-HUH-HUH! UHH...WHAT THE HELL'S WRONG WITH YOU, DUDE? DON'T YOU LIKE CHICKS?

DAMMIT, HOW THE HELL DO YOU TURN ON THE TV? HUH-HUH. UH, LIKE, MAKE IT SO, OR SOMETHING

WHOA! IT'S NUMBER TWO. HUH-HUH-HUH! HEY! HEY, WHAT THE HELL'S GOING ON?! I DIDN'T ASK TO BE BEAMED UP YET! DAMMIT, I WAS ABOUT TO SCORE WITH 40 CHICKS! NOOOO!

TIME TRAVEL

IN THE FUTURE, PEOPLE WILL BE ABLE TO GET IN TIME MACHINES AND GO BACK IN TIME. THEN THEY CAN LIKE, CHANGE STUFF IN THE PAST, SO THAT, UMM, IN THE PRESENT, THINGS BECOME DIFFERENT AND STUFF. SO LIKE, IN A DOZEN YEARS OR SOMETHING, ME AND BUTT-HEAD ARE GONNA GO BACK IN TIME TO WHEN SOMEONE FIRST INVENTED CLOTHES FOR CHICKS. HEH-HEH.

WE'D KICK HIS ASS! HEH-HEH! THAT WAY, CLOTHES FOR CHICKS WOULD NEVER BE INVENTED! HEH-HEH-HEH! AND ALL CHICKS WOULD STILL BE RUNNING AROUND NAKED! HEH-HEH. THANK YOU VERY MUCH.

VAN DREISSEN SAID THAT IN THE FUTURE WHEN THERE'S TIME MACHINES, TEACHERS ARE GONNA TAKE US BACK IN TIME TO TEACH US ABOUT HISTORY AND STUFF. WHAT A DUMBASS. IF I WANTED TO LEARN ABOUT HISTORY, I'D WATCH THE HISTORY CHANNEL.

BY THE MIRACLE OF TIME TRAVEL, WE'RE HERE AT THE DAWN OF TIME, TO WITNESS THE MOST IMPORTANT MOMENT IN HISTORY. AS THIS ONE BRAVE CREATURE CRAWLS FORTH FROM THE OCEAN, IT IS THE MOMENT WHEN LIFE ON EARTH TRULY BEGINS. IT'S ANCESTORS WILL DEVELOP OVER THE NEXT MILLIONS OF YEARS, EVENTUALLY EVOLVING INTO HUMAN BEINGS.

I...I'M MOVED TO TEARS BY THIS WONDEROUS SIGHT. UHH, WHAT THE HELL'S HE TALKING ABOUT? HUH-HUH. WHOA, CHECK IT OUT! HEH-HEH! IT'S SOME LITTLE FISH THING!

NO! STOP! IF YOU KILL IT, HUMANS WILL NEVER HAVE EVOLVED AND

MTV's

BEAVIS AND BUTT-HEAD™

CHICKEN SOUP FOR THE BUTT

CREATED BY
MIKE JUDGE
WRITTEN BY
ANDY RHEINGOLD
SCOTT SONNEBORN

Beavis and Butt-Head are not role models. They're not even human. They're cartoons.
Some of the things they do would cause a real person to get hurt, expelled, arrested,
possibly deported. To put it another way: don't try this at home.

Beavis and Butt-Head created by Mike Judge

Art Direction/Reiner Design: Roger Gorman and Leah Sherman

Art Director/MTV: Bryon Moore

Assistant Art Director/MTV: Janet Benn

Writers: Andy Rheingold and Scott Sonneborn

Editor: Kristofor Brown

Production Manager: Sara Duffy

Production Assistant: Laura Murphy

Illustrators: Dino Alberto, John Allemand, Mike A. Baez, Michael C. Breton, Bill Moore, Martin Polansky

Production Assistant: Patrick Intrieri

Background Painter: Bill Long

Color Designer, Cel Painter: Lisa Klein

Special Thanks: Eduardo A. Braniff, Avery Coburn, Janine Gallant, Julie Johns, Yvette Kaplan,
Andrea Labate, George Lentino, Kim Noone, Sue Perrotto, Robin Silverman, Donald Silvey, Machi Tantillo,
Abby Terkuhle, Van Toffler

Special Thanks at Pocket Books to: Brian Blatz, Gina Centrello, Karen Clark, Twisne Fan, Lisa Feuer,
Max Greenhut, Donna O'Neill, Liate Stehlik, Kara Welsh. Also thanks to Paula Trotto.

AP Wide World Photo: p. 37 top left, 64 bottom right, 68; Archive Photo: p. 24 bottom right, 26 bottom right, 36 top
right, 65 top right; Everett Collection: p. 23 top middle & bottom right, 24 top left, top right & bottom left, 25 top
left, top right & bottom left, 26 bottom left, 27 right top & bottom right, 29, 31, 37 bottom left, 48 bottom right, 60,
61, 64 top left, top right & bottom left, 65 top left, middle right, bottom right, 70; FPG International: p. 49 top left,
Globe Photos: p. 18, 26 top right, middle right & top left, 27 top left, 33, 36 bottom left, 40, 51, 53, 72; H.
Armstrong Roberts: p. 37 top middle, 49 bottom left, 65 bottom left; Image Bank: p. 27 middle left, 36 middle top,
37 far right, 48 top left, 49 top right, 52, 64 background; MTV Networks: p. 37 bottom right; Jerry Ohlingers: p. 23
middle bottom row; Photofest, NY: p. 8, 9, 23 top row right, bottom row left, top row left; Tony Stone Images, NY: p.
25 bottom right, 36 top left, 37 middle right; Starfile Photo: p. 37 far left; Paula Trotto: p. 36 bottom middle.

YOU NEED HELP!

UH HUH HUH, IF YOU NEED HELP, YOU NEED **CHICKEN SOUP FOR THE BUTT.**
DOES YOUR LIFE SUCK? THEN LIKE, READ OUR BOOK! CAN'T SCORE WITH CHICKS? READ OUR BOOK!
CAN'T READ? READ OUR BOOK! IT REALLY WORKS. UH, LIKE, GUARANTEED.

YEAH, HEH HEH. YOU KNOW, BUTT-HEAD, THAT'S PRETTY GOOD ADVICE. BUT I BET PEOPLE ARE
WONDERING WHY OUR BOOK IS CALLED **CHICKEN SOUP FOR THE BUTT.** WELL, I'LL TELL THEM.
WHEN PEOPLE FEEL BAD, THEY'RE SUPPOSED TO EAT CHICKEN SOUP OR SOMETHING
SO THEY CAN GET BETTER. NOW I DON'T KNOW ABOUT YOU,
BUT WHEN I FEEL BAD, MY BUTT HURTS.

THAT'S PROBABLY CUZ I KICKED YOUR ASS, DUMBASS.

OH YEAH, HEH HEH. LIKE, THAT'S WHAT **CHICKEN SOUP FOR THE BUTT** IS ALL ABOUT.
IF LIFE IS KICKING YOUR ASS, **CHICKEN SOUP FOR THE BUTT**
WILL MAKE YOUR BUTT FEEL BETTER.

YEAH, SO LIKE, READ OUR BOOK.

THE WORST THINGS IN LIFE ARE FREE

Some people say ,"the best things in life are free."
They're probably the same buttcracks who also say
"buy one get one free" and yell "Freebird!" at concerts.

A kick in the nads, school, Free Willy — those things are
all free. And they all suck.

On the other hand, it costs like, $1,500 or something to buy a
car, or take a chick out to dinner, or have someone killed.

If you think getting kicked in the nads is cooler than having
someone killed, then you must be some kind of a dumbass.

The best things in life cost money. Lots of money.

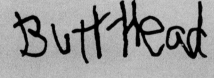

SAY SOMETHING NICE TO EVERYONE YOU SEE TODAY

PERSONALITY TEST

THE SCHOOL COUNSELOR MADE ME TAKE ONE OF THOSE PERSONALITY TESTS. IT HAD A BUNCHA QUESTIONS ABOUT FEELINGS AND CRAP. THE COUNSELOR GUY SAID IF I PASSED IT, I WOULDN'T HAVE TO GO TO HIGHLAND HIGH ANYMORE. I'D GET TO GO TO THIS INSTITUTE. I THINK THAT'S LIKE COLLEGE OR SOMETHING.

BUT HIS TEST SUCKED, CUZ LIKE, I'M STILL AT HIGHLAND. SO I DECIDED TO MAKE UP MY OWN PERSONALITY TEST WITH LIKE, BETTER QUESTIONS.

<u>Directions</u>: Answer every question with a #2 pencil. Huh huh huh number 2.

You see a squashed bug on
the road. Do you...
A. step on it
B. eat it
C. make Beavis eat it

Pick the band that sucks:
A. Gwar
B. Metallica
C. some crappy band from England

It's better to be pissed off,
than...
A. pissed on
B. pissed in
C. angry

If you see a naked chick, you...
A. do her
B. do her again
C. all of the above

Prison is...
A. pretty cool
B. like jail
C. where Beavis goes to try to
   find his dad

Have you ever seen...
A. two monkeys doing it
B. a dead snake
C. that episode of <u>The Newlywed Game</u>
   where they did it "in the butt."

If you have no money do you...
A. get a job
B. dig for change in the couch
C. tell Beavis you're gonna kick
   his ass unless he gives you
   five bucks

Fill in the blanks:

_____ gives me a stiffy.

Explosions are to _____

as blowing stuff up is to _____.

This chick takes off her shirt and I'm like, "hey baby," and she comes
over to me, and we start, you know, doin' it. So I'm doin' her and she's
doin' me and then like, we're done doin' it. So I turn on the TV and watch

_____.

How do you think this dude feels?

SCORE

Uh huh huh, this is how you score. Give yourself one point for every
right answer and like, no points for all the wrong answers. Then add up
your points.

1-5   No Personality
6-7   Borderline Personality (someone who like, lives near the border)
8   Beavis-type Personality (wuss)
9   Getting Cooler-type Personality
10   Butt-Head-type Personality (cool)

INKBLOTS

THERE'S THIS TEST THAT THIS DUDE HORSHACH CAME UP WITH. YOU'RE SUPPOSED TO, LIKE, LOOK AT DRAWINGS AND FIGURE OUT WHAT THEY ARE. WHAT YOU THINK THEY ARE TELLS YOU, LIKE, WHAT'S ON YOUR MIND.

HUH HUH HUH. I SAW THIS IN A MOVIE ONCE. THEN I LIKE REWOUND THE VIDEOTAPE AND LIKE WATCHED IT AGAIN.

I LIKE, SEE THIS DUDE, AND HE'S LIKE, REALLY PISSED OFF BECAUSE HE NEVER GETS TO SCORE. HE'S ALWAYS TRYING TO SCORE AND USE HIS SCHLONG AND HE'S ALWAYS THINKING, "WHEN AM I GONNA GET SOME? I WANT SOME!" BUT HE NEVER GETS ANY! DAMMIT! IT'S NOT FAIR! IT'S NOT FAIR! AHHH!!!

BEAVIS, WHAT THE HELL ARE YOU TALKING ABOUT?

UM, OH YEAH, UM, THAT'S A GOOD DRAWING.

THAT LOOKS LIKE ONE OF THOSE BUTTERFLY BUGS.

OH YEAH. I PULLED THE WINGS OFF A BUTTERFLY BUG ONCE. HEH HEH, THEN IT WAS JUS,T LIKE, THE "BUTT" PART OF THE BUG.

HUH HUH, HEAD. HUH HUH.

YEAH, IT LOOKS LIKE THAT PINOCCHIO BUTTKNOCKER. HE'S GOT A STIFFY ON HIS FACE.

THIS ONE SUCK.

YEAH REALLY. THIS DUDE SHOULD LEARN HOW TO DRAW.

WORLD'S GREATEST SELF-HELP DUDES

SICKMUND FREUD

WE SAW THIS DUDE ON THAT BLACK AND WHITE CHANNEL ON TV. THERE WAS A ROCKUMENTARY ON HIM. I THINK HE'S LIKE FROM AUSTRALIA OR CANADA OR SOMETHING. HE WAS LIKE, ALWAYS TALKIN' ABOUT HIS SCHLONG. FOREIGN DUDES ARE ALWAYS TALKIN' ABOUT THEIR SCHLONGS.

FREUD THINKS THAT THE WORLD IS FULL OF SCHLONGS. LIKE, IF YOU LOOK AT A CIGAR, IT'S REALLY A SCHLONG. OR IF YOU LOOK AT A BUTT, FREUD WOULD SAY IT'S REALLY A SCHLONG. THAT'S PRETTY COOL, HUH HUH.

I THINK HE'S MARRIED TO THAT OLD CHICK, DR. RUTH. SHE ALSO LIKES TALKIN' ABOUT SCHLONGS. THEY SHOULD LIKE, GET A ROOM OR SOMETHING. HUH HUH HUH.

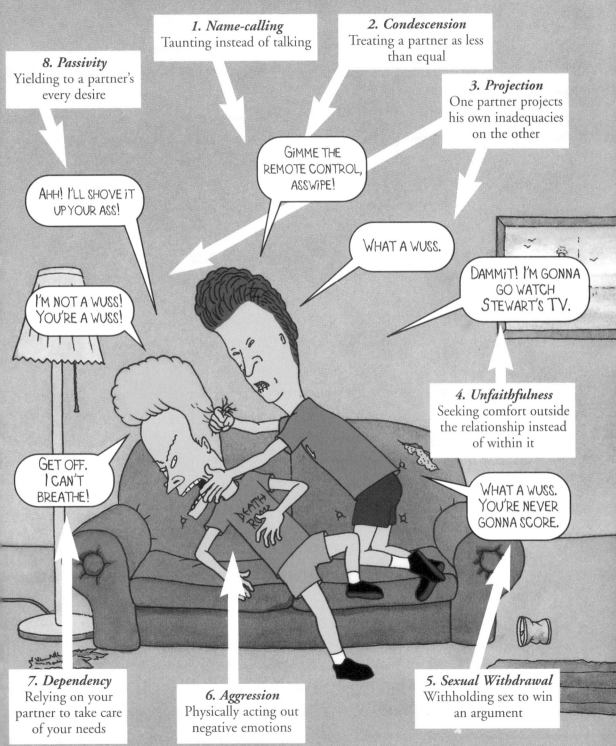

GET IN TOUCH WITH YOURSELF

 BEAVIS IS THE MASTER, HUH HUH, OF LIKE, FEELING HIS INNER CHILD, HUH HUH.

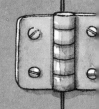

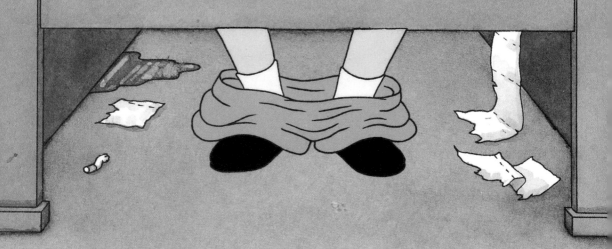

HEH HEH, YEAH. UM, SIT BACK, RELAX. TAKE A FEW DEEP BREATHS. SAY SOMETHING TO SET THE MOOD:
"HEY, HOW'S IT GOING? WHERE YOU FROM, SOLDIER? I'M GONNA HAFTA ASK YOU TO STAND UP
STRAIGHT." THERE'S NEVER A WRONG TIME OR PLACE TO SALUTE THE CAPTAIN, IF YOU KNOW WHAT I
MEAN, HEH HEH HEH. AND UM, IF SOMEONE TELLS YOU TO STOP, IT MEANS THEY DON'T LOVE
THEMSELVES OR SOMETHING. HEH HEH HEH. UMM, I NEED TO BE BY MYSELF FOR A WHILE. I'LL HAFTA
ASK YOU TO TURN THE PAGE NOW. OOOHHH, AAHHH, DO ME, OHHH YEAHHHH...

LETTER TO THE WORLD

Dear World,

Hey. How's it going? It must suck
to be you. You've like, got all these dillweeds
standing on top of you. Beavis stood on top of
me once. That sucked.

You've also, like, got all this crap growing
out of you, like trees and wood and stuff like
that. I've got wood growing out of me too,
huh huh huh.

So uh, world, I guess we're, like, the same
or something. Except I'm not covered with
foreigners.

Butt-Head

WISDOM OF THE ELDERS

Some guy once said that old people know a lot of stuff.
Yeah, heh heh. It was probably some old guy who said that.
So like, we asked some old people to like, tell us something.

Coach Buzzcut told us about war or something.

LISTEN UP MAGGOTS, BECAUSE I'M ONLY GOING TO TELL YOU THIS ONCE! IN THE MILITARY, I LEARNED 5 SIMPLE RULES. I LIVE BY THESE RULES EVERY DAY:

PAIN DOESN'T HURT.

NEVER DEFECATE WHERE YOU EAT.

ALWAYS WASH BELOW THE JIMMY.

THERE'S NO SUCH THING AS SAFE SEX IN THAILAND.

IF YOUR FRIENDS HAVE GUNS, MAKE SURE YOU HAVE A GUN, TOO.

Mr. Van Driessen gave us this crappy poem he wrote. I think it's, like, a love poem.

Give the World a Hug

If I could speak to every hug,
I'd say, Robber, don't you sting,
Cynic, don't you sting,
Drinker, don't you glug,
Just give the World a Hug.

Open your arms and your heart.
Hug a stranger, do your part.
You can't stop once you start.
Just be careful behind Maxi-Mart.

A frightened boy lost in the mall.
A lonely man in a bathroom stall.
Fishing mishap, just one ball.
A hug can cure them all.

Giving hugs gives back to you
The kind of love Greek men once knew.
A hug can reach the many and the few.
Robbers, cynics, and drinkers, too.

So measure your armspan
With a hug for another man.
You'll be following the plan
Of every, sensitive, loving
American.

WE ASKED ANDERSON FOR SOME ADVICE, BUT THE ONLY THING HE TOLD US WAS "GET THE HELL OFF MY LAWN!" THAT WAS PRETTY GOOD ADVICE CUZ SOME DOG POOPED ALL OVER HIS LAWN.

THE CLERK GUY AT THE MAXI-MART WAS LIKE THE SMARTEST OF THEM ALL. HE TOLD US...

YOU CAN'T MAKE CHANGE WITHOUT BREAKING A DOLLAR.

YOU OPEN IT, YOU BUY IT.

NOTHING IN LIFE IS FREE, BUT IF IT FALLS ON THE FLOOR IT'S 50% OFF.

A COLLEGE DEGREE NEVER GOT ANYBODY WHERE I AM TODAY.

ALWAYS KEEP A LOADED WEAPON IN THE REGISTER.

IF YOU'RE GONNA PEE, RETURN THE KEY.

ASK BEAVIS AND BUTT-HEAD

BEAVIS AND I WEREN'T ALWAYS BIG TIME SELF-HELP AUTHORS. WE HAD TO START OUT SMALL, GIVING ADVICE TO DUMBASSES IN THE HIGHLAND HIGH SCHOOL PAPER. IT WAS PRETTY COOL UNTIL WE HAD TO STOP, CUZ ONE OF OUR READERS FOLLOWED OUR ADVICE AND ACCIDENTALLY GLUED HIS HANDS TO HIS NADS.

DEAR BEAVIS AND BUTT-HEAD: My parents recently divorced. I feel that somehow it's all my fault. I'm consumed with loneliness, feelings of abandonment, and guilt. How can I overcome my depression?

FEELING GUILTY

DEAR GUILTY: I understand your feelings and stuff. I felt the same way when Guns N' Roses broke up. I could still see Axel and Izzy, you know, but uh, not together. Sometimes I, like, feel it's all my fault because I didn't buy their last album.

My advice: check out White Zombie. They're a lot cooler than GnR ever were.

BUTT-HEAD

■

DEAR BEAVIS AND BUTT-HEAD: My kid brother Jimmy's pet gerbil just died. How do I tell Jimmy that Fluffy is gone?

CONCERNED SIS

DEAR SIS: Sometimes stuff like this is hard to talk about. So it's better to show it. Take Fluffy and put him in the street. Let Jimmy see how Fluffy doesn't move — even when a truck runs over him and squashes him into a million pieces. That'd be cool.

BUTT-HEAD

■

DEAR BEAVIS AND BUTT-HEAD: My best friend just starting dating this guy, and now I never see her. What should I do? I feel all alone now.

LONELY AND VULNERABLE

DEAR LONELY AND VULNERABLE: Uh, I have no idea what the hell you're talking about, cuz my best friend is Beavis. Like that could never happen to me, cuz Beavis is never gonna score with anybody.

Shut up, fartknocker! You're ruining my chances with this chick. She's like, horny and vulnerable and stuff. I was gonna tell her to come over and do it with me.

Uh huh huh huh yeah, that's a good idea. But my advice is for her to do Big Daddy Butt-Head, not Beavis.

BEAVIS AND BUTT-HEAD

DEAR BEAVIS: I think this might be the end. I failed math. My girlfriend dumped me and I can't remember my locker combination. Now they tell me they are going to cancel *Moesha*. I'm at the end of my rope. Help.

SUICIDAL IN HIGHLAND

DEAR SUICIDAL: Um, I'm sorry but I'm just not in the mood to hear about your problems right now. Butt-Head ruined my chance to do it with that horny and vulnerable chick. He's a fartknocker!

BEAVIS

DEAR BEAVIS: Uh, huh huh, you should let Butt-Head do more of the talking. His advice is much cooler. You suck. Also you should give him three dollars like he told you to this morning.

ANONYMOUS

DEAR ANONYMOUS: That's really weird. Like, how did you know that Butt-Head asked me for...Oh, wait a second. Butt-Head? Butt-Head, is that you?

BEAVIS

DEAR BEAVIS: Dumbass.

BUTT-HEAD

WORLD'S GREATEST SELF-HELP DUDES

ANTHONY ROBBINS

THIS DUDE'S ALWAYS ON TV TELLING
PEOPLE WHAT TO DO AND STUFF. YOU
KNOW HE KNOWS WHAT HE'S TALKING
ABOUT 'CUZ HE'S ALWAYS ON TV. HIS
FILOSOPHY IS REALLY GOOD. IT'S LIKE,
GIVE HIM MONEY AND HE WILL SUCCEED.

AND HE'S GOT REALLY BIG TEETH.

CREATE YOUR OWN PHILOSOPHY

SELF-HELP DUDES ALWAYS HAVE NEW IDEAS ABOUT HOW TO THINK AND LIVE YOUR LIFE. SO LIKE, SELF-HELP YOURSELF BY PICKING SOME WORDS FROM THE LEFT COLUMN AND MATCHING THEM WITH A WORD FROM THE RIGHT.

The best things in life are...

A bird in the hand is...

A penny saved...

Waste not, want...

A stitch in time saves...

Do unto others as you would...

The grass is always greener on...

The golden rule is...

Easy come, easy...

Birds of a feather...

Beggars can't be...

Idle hands make...

Better to have loved than to...

nads

boobs

sucks

t. p.

underwear

wipe

the butt

pee

Ho

pull my finger

Metallica

poop

poop

THE GREAT RELIGIONS OF THE WORLD

BEFORE THERE WAS SELF-HELP, PEOPLE LIKE, HAD TO USE RELIGIONS TO GET HELP WHEN LIFE SUCKED. THERE ARE STILL A COUPLE OF RELIGIONS AROUND TODAY, BUT PEOPLE DON'T USE THEM VERY MUCH. MAYBE RELIGIOUS DUDES SHOULD LIKE, MAKE SOME INFOMERCIALS.

CHRISTIANITY

THE MOST POPULAR RELIGION. IT WAS STARTED BY THIS DUDE CHRIS, A REALLY LONG TIME AGO. LIKE 1940 OR SOMETHING. CHRIS LIKE, CHOPPED DOWN A TREE AND PUT IT IN HIS HOUSE. AND THEN HE DECORATED IT. PEOPLE THOUGHT HE WAS A DUMBASS. BUT THEN LIKE, CHRIS FOUND A BUNCH OF PRESENTS UNDER HIS TREE. SO, LIKE, EVERYBODY THOUGHT HE WAS COOL.

JUDAISM

THE RELIGION OF DADS. IN <u>INDEPENDENCE DAY</u>, THAT DAD IS JEWISH. OR LIKE, ON <u>MAD ABOUT YOU</u>, THAT DAD IS JEWISH. JEWISH DADS SAY THINGS IN A COOL ACCENT LIKE, "OY, MY BACK HURTS." AND THEY LIKE TO PLAY CATCH AND GO FISHIN' AND PLAY WITH THEIR MATZO BALLS. BEAVIS IS STILL HOPING TO FIND HIS JEWISH DAD.

Buddhism
The religion of people who worship Richard Gere. Most famous actors and rock stars are Buddhists, like Michael Stipe, Steven Seagal, and that Dolly Lama chick. "Buddhism" comes from the foreign word "Budd" which means "Butt." Buddhists worship the butt. That's why Richard Gere shows his butt in all the movies he's in.

The Force
The religion of people on other planets. If you use the Force, you can like, move stuff with your mind. You imagine a really sexy chick, and your mind like, makes your wiener move. People on other planets are cool.

Mexican
The religion south of the border. This is the religion of nachos and chimichangas. A lot of people believe nachos are bad for you, but not me and Beavis. I guess we're probably Mexicans, cuz we believe in nachos.

ROLE-PLAYING EXERCISE

GET TO KNOW THE PEOPLE AROUND YOU BY, UH, THINKING ABOUT WHAT IT WOULD BE LIKE TO BE THEM.

UH, IT MUST SUCK TO BE BEAVIS. I DON'T HAVE ANYTHING COOL TO SAY. I LOOK REALLY STUPID AND I'M NEVER GONNA SCORE. IT'S A GOOD THING I HANG OUT WITH BUTT-HEAD. HE'S REALLY COOL. BUTT-HEAD PROBABLY SCORES ALL THE TIME. I WISH I WAS BUTT-HEAD.

UM, HI, I'M UM, BEAVIS. UM, NO, UM, I'M LIKE BUTT-HEAD OR SOMETHING.

MEN ARE FROM MARS, WOMEN ARE FROM URANUS

 LIKE, IF YOU HAVEN'T NOTICED, CHICKS ARE DIFFERENT FROM DUDES.

 HEH HEH, YEAH, YEAH. THEY'VE GOT THINGEES AND BOOBS AND BUTTS AND...

 SHUT UP, DILLWEED. I'M TALKING ABOUT HOW CHICKS THINK DIFFERENTLY. YOU KNOW, LIKE, HOW THEY LIKE HORSES AND BON JOVI AND CRAP LIKE THAT. HERE'S SOME OTHER THINGS ABOUT CHICKS THAT DUDES JUST DON'T UNDERSTAND.

1) CHICKS ARE ALWAYS WEARING SHIRTS. DON'T THEY KNOW THEY HAVE BOOBS?

2) I HEAR CHICKS DON'T KNOW HOW TO PEE STANDING UP. BEAVIS LEARNED HOW TO DO THAT WHEN HE WAS 12.

3) CHICKS' PERFUME SMELLS LIKE FLOWERS AND CRAP. IF THEY WANT TO SMELL GOOD FOR US DUDES, THEY SHOULD RUB SOMETHING THAT SMELLS GOOD UNDER THEIR ARMS. LIKE PIZZA.

4) CHICKS ARE WUSSES. THEY'RE LIKE, SCARED OF BEAVIS.

5) CHICKS THINK DUDES THEY'VE NEVER MET ARE SEXY. THERE'S A LOT OF CHICKS AT SCHOOL ME AND BEAVIS HAVE NEVER MET. THEY MUST THINK WE'RE LIKE, REAL HOT.

6) CHICKS CAN READ YOUR THOUGHTS. LIKE THE TIME I WAS IN THE MALL AND I WAS JUST LOOKING AT THIS CHICK AND THINKING, "MMMM, YEAH, I'D DO HER." AND SHE CAME UP TO ME AND SAID, "DON'T EVEN THINK IT."

PEOPLE IN SERIOUS NEED OF SELF HELP

(1) FLABBY-O
HE'S GOT THE BODY OF A DUDE AND THE HAIR OF A CHICK. I THINK HE'S LIKE ONE OF THOSE TRANSYLVANIANS OR SOMETHING. ANY NORMAL DUDE WOULD DEFINITELY CHOOSE TO HAVE THE BODY OF A CHICK. YOU CAN ALWAYS SHAVE OFF THE HAIR.

(2) DIONNE WARWICK
SHE'S LIKE, ALWAYS ON TV TELLING PEOPLE TO CALL THE PSYCHOTIC NETWORK. SHE SAYS SHE CAN LIKE TELL YOUR FUTURE AND STUFF. SO, BEAVIS AND I CALLED HER ONCE AND SHE TOLD US WE HAD TO PAY HER $3.95 A MINUTE. HUH HUH. BUT THAT DIDN'T COME TRUE.

(3) YAWNI
HE TRIES TO HAVE HEAVY METAL HAIR, BUT HE LOOKS LIKE A WUSS. I THINK HIS NAME IS ITALIAN FOR "BORING."

(4) O.J.
HE GOT FAMOUS FOR DRIVING THAT WHITE TRUCK AND MAKING THAT JUICE. BUT EVEN THOUGH HE'S A FAMOUS DUDE, HE'S STILL NOT GOOD WITH CHICKS.

(5) MR. ROGERS

HE ALWAYS WEARS A SWEATER. IF HE WERE COOL HE'D WEAR A WINDBREAKER, LIKE ON COPS. THAT'D BE COOL. HE COULD GET ON THE RADIO AND SAY TO THE OTHER COPS, "UH, 10-4. ROGER, MR. ROGERS."

(6) CONAN

HE'S SUPPOSED TO BE THIS TOUGH BARBARIAN DUDE, BUT ALL HE DOES ON HIS SHOW IS SIT AROUND IN A SUIT AND TIE AND TALK LIKE A WUSS. HE NEEDS TO BE MORE LIKE XENA AND WEAR ANIMAL SKINS, AND LIKE, PICK A FIGHT WITH ALL THE PEOPLE WHO COME ON HIS SHOW.

(7) BUS DRIVERS

THEY'RE ALWAYS TAKING YOU PLACES YOU DON'T WANNA GO — LIKE SCHOOL— EVEN IF YOU ASK THEM TO TAKE YOU PLACES YOU WANNA GO, LIKE SWEDEN. THEY JUST DON'T LISTEN.

(8) PEOPLE WHO BUY SELF-HELP BOOKS

LOOK IN THE MIRROR, DUMBASS. HUH HUH HUH.

ROLE MODELS

Van Driessen says it's like important to find people you look up to. Beavis and I once looked up this chick's skirt. Huh huh huh. That was cool.

Beavis' Role Models:

Connie Chung
She like, called Newt Gingrich's mom a bitch. That was pretty funny, cuz she like, said the word "bitch" on TV.

Grover Cleveland
He's this blue puppet on public TV that tells little kids how to count and to quit taking drugs. And, he does a good job cuz you like never see little babies buying drugs.

Drummer for Def Leppard
After he lost his arm, he had to learn how to do everything with just one hand. Like, having to use one hand can make things hard, heh heh, if you know what I mean. He's brave. Heh heh heh.

That Guy with The Blurry Face and No Shirt
He was in the COPS episode filmed live with the men and women of Big Butte, Montana. Heh heh, Butte. This guy got real drunk and the cops had to use the taser. But this dude wouldn't take any lip from the cops, even when they beat the crap outta him and threw him in jail.

Madonna's daughter, Lord
I don't know what's so cool about Madonna's kid, but people are always praising Lord.

BUTT-HEAD'S LIST OF ROLL MODELS.
 THESE ARE MODELS I'D LIKE TO ROLL AROUND WITH,
IF YOU KNOW WHAT I MEAN:

TYRA BANKS
CINDY CRAWFORD
XENA
THAT FOOT MODEL FROM NEWSPAPER ADS
ALL THREE FRIENDS CHICKS
ALL THE BRADY BUNCH CHICKS – EXCEPT ALICE
ANY CHICK WHO'S EVER BEEN NAKED IN A MAGAZINE
ANY CHICK WHO'S EVER BEEN IN A MAGAZINE

ENVISION YOUR FUTURE

BEFORE YOU CAN GO FORWARD WITH YOUR LIFE IT'S IMPORTANT
TO SIT BACK AND IMAGINE WHAT YOUR FUTURE WILL BE.

BUTT-HEAD'S FUTURE

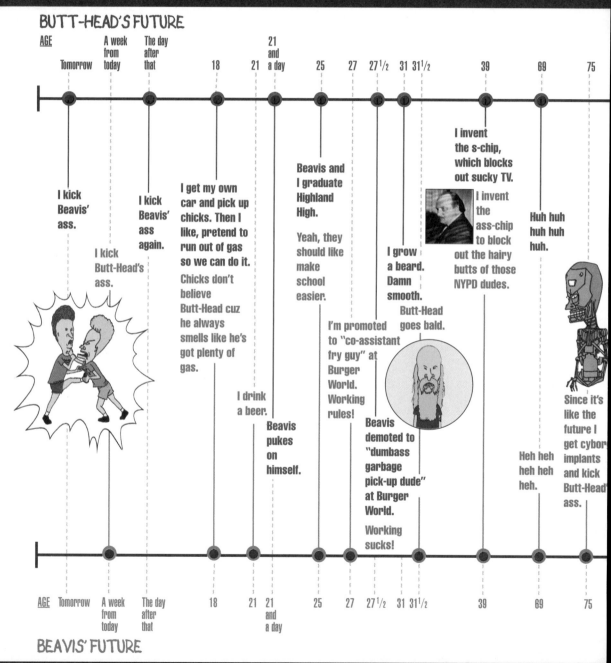

AGE

Tomorrow | A week from today | The day after that | 18 | 21 | 21 and a day | 25 | 27 | 27 1/2 | 31 | 31 1/2 | 39 | 69 | 75

I kick Beavis' ass.

I kick Beavis' ass again.

I get my own car and pick up chicks. Then I like, pretend to run out of gas so we can do it.

Chicks don't believe Butt-Head cuz he always smells like he's got plenty of gas.

Beavis and I graduate Highland High.

Yeah, they should like make school easier.

I grow a beard. Damn smooth.

Butt-Head goes bald.

I invent the s-chip, which blocks out sucky TV.

I invent the ass-chip to block out the hairy butts of those NYPD dudes.

Huh huh huh huh huh.

Since it's like the future I get cyborg implants and kick Butt-Head' ass.

I kick Butt-Head's ass.

I drink a beer.

Beavis pukes on himself.

I'm promoted to "co-assistant fry guy" at Burger World. Working rules!

Beavis demoted to "dumbass garbage pick-up dude" at Burger World.

Working sucks!

Heh heh heh heh heh.

AGE Tomorrow | A week from today | The day after that | 18 | 21 | 21 and a day | 25 | 27 | 27 1/2 | 31 | 31 1/2 | 39 | 69 | 75

BEAVIS' FUTURE

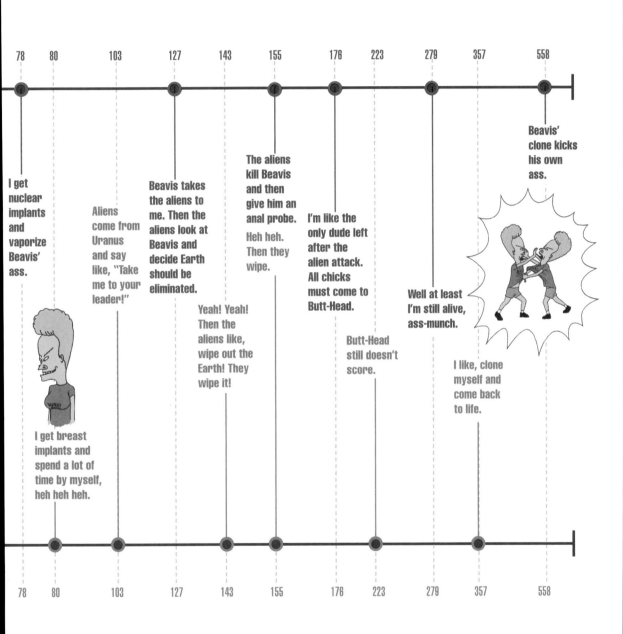

LIFE LESSONS FROM THE ROAD

Dumbasses who drive like to put stupid stickers on their cars.
These stickers tell you stuff that sucks, so we fixed a few of them.

WORLD'S GREATEST SELF HELP DUDES

ANDY ROONEY

D'YA EVER NOTICE THIS OLD GUY ON THIS 60 MINUTES SHOW ON TV WHO'S LIKE, ALWAYS TALKING ABOUT STUFF HE DOESN'T UNDERSTAND? HE ASKS QUESTIONS LIKE, "WHY DO THEY CALL IT 'ASPIRIN?' AFTER ALL, YOU DON'T PUT IT IN YOUR ASS." OR HE'LL TALK ABOUT FEDERAL TAXIS OR HOW HARD IT IS TO PICK UP TEENAGE GIRLS. YOU KNOW, CRAP LIKE THAT.

MAYBE HE'S CONFUSED CUZ HE'S SO OLD. I GUESS THAT'S WHY HE LIKE, FORGETS TO TRIM HIS EYEBROWS.

SEVEN HABITS OF HIGHLY DEFECTIVE PEOPLE

ME AND BEAVIS ARE LIKE, PRETTY SUCK-SESSFUL DUDES. YOU'RE PROBABLY ASKING YOURSELF, HOW DID WE GET TO WHERE WE ARE? WELL, IT WASN'T LUCK. THE SECRET OF OUR SUCK-SESS IS THAT WE DO THESE 7 THINGS EVERY DAY:

1. WAKE UP IN THE MORNING

IF YOU DON'T DO THIS THEN YOU CAN'T DO ANYTHING ELSE FOR THE REST OF THE DAY. UNLESS YOU WANT TO SLEEP.

2. LISTEN

SOMETIMES, OTHER PEOPLE HAVE REALLY COOL THINGS TO SAY. LIKE WHEN THAT DUDE ANDERSON'S FOOT GOT RUN OVER BY A LAWN MOWER. HE WAS SCREAMING, "CALL 911! 911!" WE LIKE, STOOD THERE AND LISTENED.

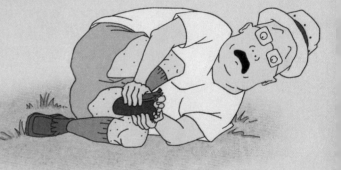

3. QUIT SMOKING

QUITTERS ARE WINNERS. BUT LIKE, IT TAKES A LOT OF SELF-CONTROL TO BE A QUITTER. BEAVIS HAD A HARD TIME QUITTING, BECAUSE HE DOESN'T KNOW HOW TO LIGHT A CIGARETTE IN THE FIRST PLACE.

4. TEACH A CHILD SOMETHING

VAN DRIESSEN SAID IT'S IMPORTAN TO SHARE WHAT YOU KNOW WITH CHILD OR SOMETHING.

I KNOW I COULD KICK YOUR ASS.

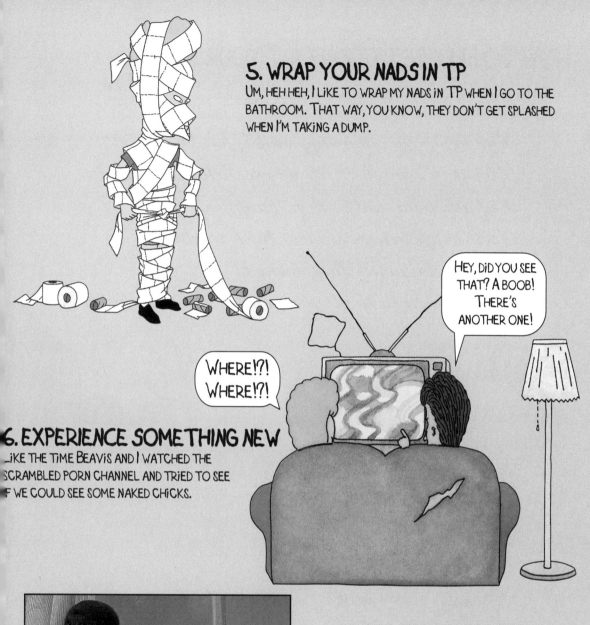

5. WRAP YOUR NADS IN TP

UM, HEH HEH, I LIKE TO WRAP MY NADS IN TP WHEN I GO TO THE BATHROOM. THAT WAY, YOU KNOW, THEY DON'T GET SPLASHED WHEN I'M TAKING A DUMP.

> HEY, DID YOU SEE THAT? A BOOB! THERE'S ANOTHER ONE!

> WHERE!?! WHERE!?!

6. EXPERIENCE SOMETHING NEW

LIKE THE TIME BEAVIS AND I WATCHED THE SCRAMBLED PORN CHANNEL AND TRIED TO SEE IF WE COULD SEE SOME NAKED CHICKS.

7. SPANK THE MONKEY

BUT, UH, WHY DO ALL THIS OTHER STUFF WHEN YOU CAN LIKE, GO INTO THE BATHROOM AND PROCRASTINATE. HUH HUH HUH.

HOW TO FEEL BETTER ABOUT YOURSELF

I woke up this morning and I felt bad.
I went to school. I felt worse. Then I went to
the bathroom and took a dump, heh heh.
I felt much better. I went back to class.
I felt bad again. That sucked!
I went back to the bathroom — I wasn't finished.

BeaVis

BUTT-HEAD'S LAW

ANYTHING THAT CAN SUCK, DOES

YOU GOTTA BE 21 TO DRINK, BUT YOU ONLY HAVE TO BE 14 TO GO TO HIGH SCHOOL. THAT SUCKS.

YOU DON'T HAVE ANY MONEY AND YOU WANT TO GET THIS BOOK THAT TELLS YOU HOW TO MAKE MONEY. BUT IT COSTS MONEY. THAT SUCKS.

IN A VIDEO STORE THEY ALWAYS HIDE ALL THE GOOD TAPES LIKE SPERMINATOR 2: FUDGEMENT DAY, MY OWN PRIVATE RIDE-A-HO, AND EDWARD PENIS-HANDS. BUT LIKE, THEY PUT TAPES OF CRAPPY KIDS' CARTOONS EVERYWHERE. THAT SUCKS.

CHICKS DON'T WANT TO DO IT WITH YOU UNLESS YOU'VE ALREADY SCORED. BUT HOW CAN YOU SCORE WHEN CHICKS WON'T DO IT WITH YOU CUZ YOU HAVEN'T SCORED. THAT SUCKS.

IN ENGLISH CLASS THEY LIKE, MAKE YOU LEARN ENGLISH, BUT LIKE, THE TEACHER IS SOME FOREIGN DUDE FROM BRITAIN WHERE THEY DON'T EVEN SPEAK ENGLISH. THAT SUCKS.

FARTKNOCKERS LIKE BEAVIS ARE ALWAYS HANGING AROUND COOL DUDES LIKE ME. THAT SUCKS.

SOMETIMES MY BUTT ITCHES ON THE INSIDE. THAT SUCKS.

ORANGE FREEZIES TASTE SO GOOD YOU GOTTA DRINK 'EM REAL FAST, BUT THEN IT FREEZES YOUR HEAD. THAT SUCKS.

PROFESSIONAL WRESTLERS GET PAID A LOT OF MONEY TO FIGHT, BUT IF YOU DO IT FOR FREE IN CLASS YOU GET KICKED OUTTA SCHOOL. THAT SUCKS. OH WAIT, UM, THAT DOESN'T SUCK.

A BAND LIKE METALLICA CAN BREAK UP, BUT THERE'S ONLY ONE BON JOVI, SO HE CAN'T BREAK UP. THAT SUCKS.

CHICKS DON'T CARE ABOUT OTHER CHICKS' THINGEES, BUT THEY'RE THE ONLY ONES WHO GET TO GO IN THE GIRLS' LOCKER ROOM. THAT SUCKS.

UNDERWEAR MODELS ARE ALWAYS WEARING UNDERWEAR. THEY SHOULD BE NAKED. THAT SUCKS.

HASSELHOFF. THAT SUCKS.

UNCOVERING CHILDHOOD MAMORIES

IF YOU HAVE PROBLEMS TODAY, IT'S PROBABLY BECAUSE OF STUFF THAT HAPPENED WHEN YOU WERE A KID. LIKE, IF YOU FORGOT TO GO TO SCHOOL AS A KID, THAT EXPLAINS WHY YOU HAVE TROUBLE COUNTING AND STUFF. SO IT'S IMPORTANT TO REMEMBER STUFF FROM WHEN YOU WERE A KID TO UNDERSTAND LIKE, WHO YOU ARE NOW.

BODY IMAGE

You'll feel better about yourself if you get in shape, cuz it makes it easier to get up off the couch and get some food from the fridge. Do the Beavis workout! Yeah, heh heh. Just do me!

Before

After

This is called the groin stretch. Stretching makes it bigger. Heh heh heh.

Real Man's Push-Up. Ugh, uhhh, one...

Chick push-ups are like, good for anyone too lazy to do a real push-up.

THE BUTT CRUNCHER IS MY FAVORITE EXERCISE. JUST SQUAT LIKE YOU'RE TAKING A DUMP. THIS IS GOOD FOR THE BUTT MUSCLE. SQUAT. POOP. SQUAT. POOP.

PELVIC THRUSTS ARE GOOD PRACTICE IN CASE YOU EVER GET TO DO IT WITH A CHICK.

I CALL THIS THE THINGEE BUILDER. IF YOU CAN'T TOUCH SOMEONE ELSE'S THINGEES, MAKE YOUR OWN. REPEAT AFTER ME — "I MUST, I MUST, I MUST INCREASE MY BUST." HEH HEH HEH.

DO THESE EVERY DAY AND YOU COULD HAVE A BUFF BODY LIKE MINE.

YOU COULD ALSO TRY SOME OTHER EXERCISES, LIKE THE BREAST STROKE, JERK AND PULL, OR JUMPING JACK-OFFS.

PAST LIVES

Some TV psychotics like Shirley MacLaine believe they were other people before they were born. Like, I'm not sure what the hell that means, but it might be cool to think about who you were if you lived in another time.

THE TURTLE AND THE HAIR

There once was this turtle who did everything real slow. Like, he was in the special class at school. One day, he was supposed to race this fast bunny. But before he got to the race, he saw this hair growing out of his butt. He was surprised because he didn't even know he had a butt. A lot of dumbasses don't know that turtles have butts.

So like, the turtle looked at the beard on his butt and figured it was time for him to become a man. He went down to the mall and scored with a bunch of turtle chicks. That took like 15 minutes or something. That's how he lost the race.

Moral: Dudes with beards score.

Butt Head

ASS-TROLOGY

Ass-trology like, rules the universe. It can tell your future. More important, if you want to do a chick, you need to like, know her ass-trological sign. Nobody knows where ass-trology comes from. Sometimes it seems like the ass-trologers pull it out of their butts.

ARIES

This is the sign of people who are uptight. Aries often lose their temper over any little thing. Coach Buzzcut is an Aries. He even gets mad when we don't come to class.

AQUARIUS

Aquarius like to tell people to do stuff like "Go to school!" or "Don't light that on fire!" Principal McVicker is an Aquarius. Everyone who is an Aquarius is a sonofabitch.

CANCER

The sign of people who smoke, like the Marlboro Man and that Smokey Bear guy.

CAPRICORN

Anderson is a Capricorn. It's the sign for people who are old. You can usually smell Capricorns cuz they wear those old people diapers.

GEMINI

Gemini is the sign of bands like Metallica and AC/DC. Geminis drink beer and throw TVs out windows.

LEO

This is like, the sign of chicks that are in love with Leonardo DiCaprio.

LIBRA
This is the sign of wusses. Stewart is a wuss. He's probably a Libra.

PISCES
Pisces think they're cool, because they are in touch with their feelings. Other people think they are fartknockers. Van Driessen is a Pisces.

SAGITTARIUS
Todd is a Sagittarius. This is the sign of people who kick ass and then kick some more ass, like Todd. Most Sagittarius are in prison.

SCORPIO
Daria is a Scorpio. Scorpios are the kinda people who are good at school and know lots of crap. They're pretty stupid.

TAURUS
No one knows much about Taurus cuz no Taurus ever got famous for doing anything good. That guy who sits on the corner outside Maxi-Mart all day is a Taurus. So is Tori Spelling.

VIRGIN
The sign of people who have never done it. This is Beavis' sign.

HOW TO BE A BETTER PERSON

CHECK IT OUT. AN ORGASMIC STORE, HUH HUH HUH.

IF YOU GO TO A NEW AGE HEALTH FOOD STORE, THE HIPPIES THERE ARE ALWAYS TALKING ABOUT HOW YOU CAN BE A BETTER PERSON. LIKE, I'M ALREADY A BETTER PERSON. I'M BETTER THAN BEAVIS. BUT IF YOU'RE A BUTTCRACKER LIKE BEAVIS MAYBE YOU SHOULD TRY SOME OF THIS NEW AGE CRAP.

AROMA THERAPY
DIFFERENT SMELLS CAN MAKE YOU FEEL DIFFERENT THINGS. LIKE THE SMELL OF FRESH NACHOS MAKES ME FEEL HUNGRY AND THE SMELL OF BEAVIS' FARTS MAKES ME FEEL LIKE KICKING HIS ASS.

AURA
THIS IS AN INVISIBLE BUBBLE AROUND YOUR BODY THAT HAS LIKE, DIFFERENT COLORS. WHEN BEAVIS GOES SWIMMING HE HAS A YELLOW AURA.

CRYSTALS
THESE THINGS LOOK LIKE DIAMONDS. THEY'RE SUP-POSED TO BRING YOU "GOOD FORTUNE," BUT THEY AREN'T WORTH ANYTHING AND COST A LOT OF MONEY.

INCENSE
INCENSE IS REALLY COOL, BUT YOU LIKE, HAFTA HAVE A SISTER TO DO IT. A NAKED SISTER. UH HUH HUH HUH.

MANTRA
A MANTRA IS LIKE WORDS YOU SAY OVER AND OVER AGAIN TO HELP YOU GET THROUGH THE DAY. BEAVIS' MANTRA IS "THANK YOU, DRIVE THROUGH."

NUMEROLOGY
NUMBERS HAVE HIDDEN MEANINGS, LIKE NUMBER TWO, HEH HEH HEH.

TAROT CARDS
HIPPIES ARE ALWAYS ASKING YOU TO PLAY TAROT CARDS WITH THEM. BUT IT'S A LOT HARDER THAN GO FISH OR THOSE OTHER CARD GAMES. LIKE, AS SOON AS THEY DEAL THE CARDS THEY TELL ME I'M GONNA LOSE EVERYTHING AND DIE.

BODY LANGUAGE

BODY LANGUAGE IS HOW PEOPLE COMMUNICATE WITHOUT TALKING. A CHICK MIGHT TELL YOU TO "GET THE HELL AWAY FROM ME." BUT IF SHE'S, LIKE, TAKING OFF HER CLOTHES AT THE SAME TIME, WHAT SHE'S TRYING TO SAY IS: "DO ME!" BODY LANGUAGE IS COOL CUZ SOMETIMES IT'S HARD TO THINK OF, YOU KNOW, LIKE, WORDS.

CHECK OUT HOW BEAVIS AND I CAN LIKE, EXPRESS OURSELVES WITHOUT TALKING:

MY BUTT ITCHES.

I'M BORED. THIS SUCKS.

MY BUTT STILL ITCHES.

I'VE GOT A STIFFY! BOOOOIIING!

HEY BABY. DO YOU LIKE WHAT YOU SEE? UH HUH HUH HUH.

I HOPE THAT TONY DANZA DUDE IS ON TV RIGHT NOW. HE'S FUNNY.

RELEASING STRESS

Life can be pretty stressful. Like when you're watching a video and they blur something out so you don't know what the hell is going on. Or like, when you get deported. You know, stuff like that. So here's some ways to help you relax when your life's a beach.

No, dumbass, it's like, "When your wife's a bitch."

Oh, yeah, yeah. That makes a lot more sense. Yeah.

TAKING A DUMP
PROS: A GOOD WAY TO DEAL WITH CRAP.
CONS: YOU NEED A BATHROOM.

UM, HEH HEH, NO YOU DON'T.

SCREAM THERAPY
PROS: YOU CAN SCREAM AS LOUD AS YOU WANT.
CONS: IF YOU DO IT TOO MUCH, YOU LOSE YOUR VOICE AND YOUR HEAD STARTS TO HURT.

COUNTING TO TEN
PROS: ZERO
CONS: IT JUST MAKES YOU MORE FRUSTRATED CUZ IT'S A PRETTY HIGH NUMBER. NUMBERS SUCK AN[D] MATH PISSES ME OF[F]

TAKE A FEW DEEP BREATHS
PROS: BREATHING IS LIKE, GOOD FOR YOUR HEALTH OR SOMETHING. AND IT'S PRETTY EASY, TOO.
CONS: BEAVIS JUST FARTED.

GET A PET
PROS: DOBERMANS,
PIT-BILLS,
HORNY TOADS
CONS: SEE "TAKING
A DUMP"

LISTEN TO MUSIC
PROS: AC/DC, METALLICA
CONS: CELINE DION, YANNI

BANGING A DRUM
PROS: YOU GET TO HIT STUFF.
CONS: YOU HAVE TO HANG OUT WITH
A DUMBASS WHO OWNS A DRUM.

BLOW THINGS UP THERAPY
PROS: YOU GET TO BLOW UP OTHER
PEOPLE'S STUFF.
CONS: PRISON

BUTT-READING

HOMELESS GYPSY CHICKS SOMETIMES TRY TO RIP YOU OFF BY TELLING YOU THEY CAN TELL YOUR FUTURE BY READING YOUR PALM. THAT'S CRAP. YOU CAN'T TELL ANYTHING ABOUT A DUDE JUST BY LOOKING AT HIS HAND. UNLESS HE JUST GOT DONE, YOU KNOW, UH HUH HUH HUH.

    TO REALLY FIND OUT STUFF ABOUT PEOPLE, YOU GOTTA READ OTHER PARTS OF THEIR BODY.

BUTT-CRACK READING

THIS WILL TELL YOU IF A PERSON HAS A JOB WHERE THEY BEND OVER A LOT, LIKE PLUMBERS OR THOSE CHICKS WHO WORK FOR THE PRESIDENT.

LIP READING

A QUICK LIP READING CAN TELL YOU IF A PERSON HAS KISSED A LOT OF PEOPLE— ESPECIALLY IF THEY HAVE LOTS OF SORES AND STUFF.

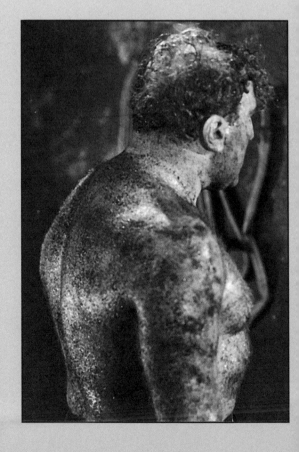

BACK HAIR READING

LOTS OF BACK HAIR TELLS YOU ONE THING — THIS DUMBASS ISN'T GOING TO SCORE.

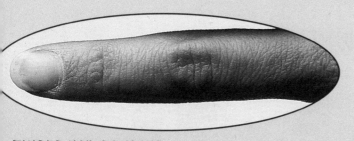

FINGERNAIL READING

TELLS YOU IF THEY LIKE TO PICK THEIR
NOSE — UNLESS THEY LIKE TO EAT IT, TOO.

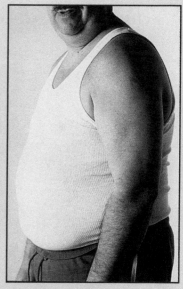

BELLY READING

THIS IS AN EASY WAY TO TELL IF SOMEONE
IS FAT. BUT SOMETIMES IT'S HARD TO TELL
IF THEY'RE FAT CUZ THEY EAT A LOT OR IF
THEY'RE LIKE, ABOUT TO BECOME A FATHER.

BEARD READING

THIS DUDE LOVES
COLLEGE MUSIC.

THIS DUDE WISHES HE
WAS ON COPS.

DAMN SMOOTH.

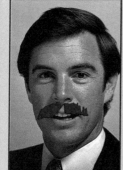

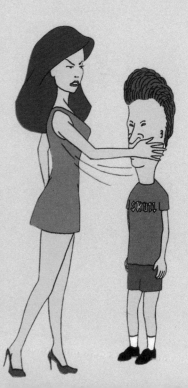

BOOB READING

NOTHING TELLS YOU MORE ABOUT A CHICK THAN A GOOD BOOB
READING. BUT THEY'RE REALLY HARD TO DO. YOU GOTTA BE SOME
KINDA EXPERT OR SOMETHING. SO, LIKE, KEEP PRACTICING.

WHAT IF I WERE BORN IN MEXICO?

What if I were born in Mexico?

My life would be like, really different. I'd wake up every morning and eat a breakfast burrito. I wouldn't hafta go to school, cuz like, the Highland High school bus doesn't pick anyone up who lives more than 10 miles away from school.

*I'd be foreign, which would suck,
cuz foreign dudes speak French.*

*And my name wouldn't be Beavis.
I'd probably have some kinda French name like
Señor Beavis.*

*And I never would have met Butt-Head,
um, unless Butt-Head was also
born in Mexico.*

So I guess it wouldn't be that different.

Beavis

WORLD'S GREATEST SELF-HELP DUDES

SALLY STRUTHERS

SHE'S THIS CHICK WHO'S ALWAYS ON TV TALKING ABOUT HUNGRY PEOPLE. SHE KNOWS A
LOT ABOUT HUNGRY PEOPLE BECAUSE SHE'S ALWAYS HUNGRY. ON HER COMMERCIAL SHE'S
ALWAYS TALKING ABOUT HOW IF YOU HELP PEOPLE YOU FEEL BETTER ABOUT YOURSELF. SHE
SAYS YOU CAN FEED A FAMILY OF HUNGRY PEOPLE FOR ONLY A PENNY.

THAT, LIKE, GAVE ME AN IDEA. ME AND BEAVIS WENT TO THIS STORE AND TOLD THE
CLERK DUDE THAT WE HAD A HUNGRY FAMILY AT HOME WITH TWO DADS, AN UNCLE, A GOAT
AND LIKE, THREE GERMAN DUDES. HE SAID HE COULDN'T GIVE US ANY FOOD, BUT HE WOULD
SEND SOMEONE OVER OR SOMETHING.

THE NEXT DAY THIS OLD CHICK CAME TO BEAVIS' HOUSE. SHE TOLD US SHE WAS LIKE A
SOCIALIST WORKER AND TOOK US TO SEE THIS FAMILY NAMED FOSTER. THEY GAVE US
FOOD AND LET US SLEEP ON THEIR COUCH AND WATCH TV. THAT WAS COOL. AND THEY
DIDN'T EVEN TAKE OUR PENNY.

DREAMS—WHAT THEY MEAN

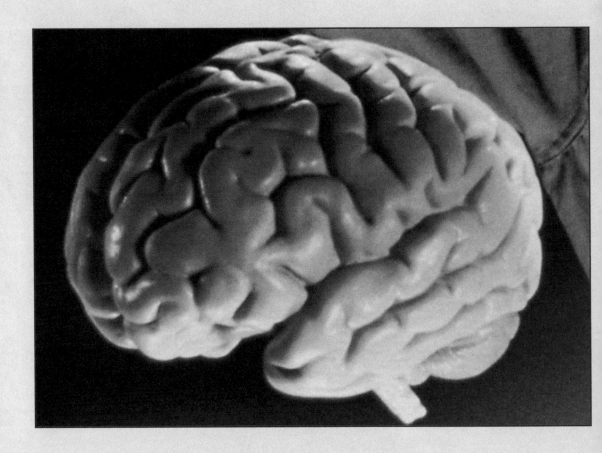

A LOT OF PEOPLE WONDER WHAT THEIR DREAMS MEAN.

YEAH, YEAH, LIKE EVER SINCE I WAS A KID I'VE DREAMT OF BECOMING A NINJA WITH THOSE CHINESE THROWING STARS AND TASERS, HEH HEH. LIKE, WHAT DOES THAT MEAN?

I'M NOT TALKIN' ABOUT THAT KINDA DREAM, DUMBASS. I MEAN THE KINDA DREAMS YOU HAVE WHEN YOU'RE ASLEEP. SCIENCE GUYS SAY DREAMS ARE YOUR BRAIN TRYING TO TALK TO YOU, BUT YOU'RE ASLEEP SO YOU DON'T KNOW WHAT IT'S SAYING. IT'S LIKE WATCHING ONE OF THOSE TV SHOWS FROM ENGLAND.

THIS CHART CAN HELP YOU UNDERSTAND WHAT YOU SEE IN YOUR DREAMS.

IF DREAM IS ABOUT...

IT MEANS....

BEING NAKED IN SCHOOL	YOU'RE A WUSS FOR THINKING ABOUT SCHOOL.
FALLING OFF A CLIFF	YOU, LIKE, CAN'T GET IT UP.

A BUNCHA NAKED CHICKS IN BIKINIS	YOU, LIKE, CAN GET IT UP. BOOOIIIING!
YOU'RE DOING IT WITH BEAVIS' MOM.	BEAVIS' MOM IS A SLUT.
YOU'RE GETTING BEATEN UP BY TODD.	TODD IS COOL.

SPIDERS CRAWLING OUT OF YOUR BUTT	YOU FORGOT TO WIPE, BUNGHOLE.
MEXICAN WRESTLERS	YOU PROBABLY ATE LIKE, SPAGHETTI OR SOME OTHER MEXICAN FOOD FOR LUNCH.
TWO MONKEYS DOING IT DOGGY STYLE.	HUH HUH HUH. HEH HEH HEH. THAT'S PRETTY COOL.
SWIMMING IN A POOL	THAT'S, LIKE, A WET DREAM.
BEAVIS SWIMMING IN A POOL	IT'S LIKE, TIME TO CLEAN THE POOL.
YOU'RE LIVING IN A WORLD WHERE TV SUCKS AND CHICKS DON'T WANNA DO YOU	YOU'RE NOT DREAMING.

CONFLICT RESOLUTION

IF YOU'RE LIKE US YOU PROBABLY MEET PEOPLE EVERY DAY WHO HATE YOU AND WANT TO BEAT YOU UP. BEAVIS AND I AREN'T FIGHTERS. WE'RE LIKE, LOVEMAKERS. HUH HUH. BUT, YOU KNOW, NOT WITH EACH OTHER. SO LIKE WHEN SOMEONE PICKS A FIGHT WITH US, WE LIKE, TURN THE OTHER BUTT CHEEK. HERE'S SOME WAYS YOU CAN AVOID CONFLICT, TOO.

FIRST, TRY TO TALK IT OUT.

THEN, JUST WALK AWAY.

IF THAT FAILS, ACT TOUGH.

WHEN ALL ELSE FAILS, LET THEM BEAT YOU UP — THAT WILL END THE CONFLICT.

ALTERNATIVE MEDICINE

IT USED TO BE THAT WHEN YOU WERE FEELING SICK YOU WENT TO THE DOCTOR AND GOT A SHOT IN THE BUTT. BUT NOWADAYS YOU DON'T HAFTA PULL DOWN YOUR PANTS FOR SOME FARTKNOCKER, CUZ THEY GOT THIS STUFF CALLED "ALTERNATIVE MEDICINE." IT WAS INVENTED BY THE SPIN DOCTORS AND THE CURE AND OTHER ALTERNATIVE BANDS. IT'S A WAY TO SELF-HELP YOURSELF WITHOUT GOING TO THE DOCTOR.

SYMPTOM

STOMACH ACHE

CONSTIPATION

HUNGRY

CAN'T SLEEP

HORNY

STEWART

HOMEWORK

NOT OLD ENOUGH TO BUY PORN

CAN'T SCORE

DEAD

CURE

1 GLASS OF SODA, 2 PIECES OF CHICKEN, SALT, KETCHUP, HOT SAUCE, 3 TACOS, AND 1 REMOTE CONTROL. USE THE REMOTE CONTROL TO TURN OFF THAT CRAP ON TV AND RELAX WITH A GOOD MEAL.

TELL BEAVIS TO HURRY UP AND GET THE HELL OUT OF THE BATHROOM.

TAKE 2 BAGS OF NACHOS OVER TO MY PLACE AND CALL ME A PIZZA IN THE MORNING.

WAKE UP, DUMBASS.

DO IT.

ROPE, ELECTRICAL TAPE

DROP OUT OF SCHOOL AND GET A JOB SO YOU WON'T HAFTA DO SO MUCH WORK.

BUY ONE OF THOSE NON-PORN CHICK MAGAZINES AND CUT THE CLOTHES OFF THE WOMEN.

LOWER YOUR STANDARDS.

UHH...MAYBE YOU SHOULD GO SEE A DOCTOR OR SOMETHING.

TWELVE STEP PROGRAM FOR DUMBASSES WHO NEVER SCORE.

1. ADMIT YOU NEVER SCORE AND THAT YOUR LIFE SUCKS CUZ YOU CAN'T GET SOME.

2. UNDERSTAND THAT THERE IS A POWER GREATER THAN YOU WHO CAN HELP YOU SCORE — CHICKS, DUMBASS!

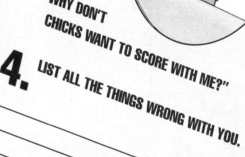

3. LOOK AT YOURSELF AND ASK: "WHY DON'T CHICKS WANT TO SCORE WITH ME?"

4. LIST ALL THE THINGS WRONG WITH YOU.

Note: If you're related to Beavis, feel free to use more space on the back.

BEAVIS AND I PUT TOGETHER THIS PAMPHLET FOR ALL YOU BUTT-MUNCHES OUT THERE WHO NEVER SCORE...
YOU KNOW, WITH THE LADIES. IF YOU DO EVERY STEP, YOU WILL SCORE. GUARANTEED.
   BUT WE NEVER SCORE.
      SHUT UP, DUMBASS.

5. FIX ALL THE THINGS WRONG WITH YOU.

6. MAKE A LIST OF ALL THE CHICKS YOU KNOW WHO YOU COULD SCORE WITH. Don't limit yourself. Include chicks you've seen on TV or chicks you see in the window across the street when you're hanging out in the bushes.

MAKE SURE THE CHICKS KNOW YOU WANT TO SCORE. Sometimes you can't just tell them. You hafta show them.

8. GET THEM TO SCORE WITH YOU.

9. IF YOU'RE STILL READING THIS, YOU OBVIOUSLY HAVEN'T SCORED.

10. ADMIT THERE'S SOMETHING REALLY WRONG WITH YOU AND YOU'LL PROBABLY NEVER FIX IT.

11. INHERIT A LOT OF MONEY. Rich dorks who aren't good looking always score, like that Bill Gates dude.

12. GIVE THIS PAMPHLET TO OTHER PEOPLE YOU WANT TO HELP SCORE. ESPECIALLY CHICKS.

ROMANCE, BUTT-HEAD STYLE

If you want to do a chick, it's like important to tell the truth. Honesty is supposed to be the best foreign policy for getting into a chick's pants.

Last night I was talking to this chick. And then I did her. WHOA, REALLY? HEH HEH HEH. THAT'S COOL. *Yeah, I was hanging out by the Maxi-Mart eating some nachos* REALLY? I WAS THERE, TOO. COOL. *and this chick drove up in like a really big foreign American car. She had these real big thingees, too.* UM, WAIT, I DON'T REMEMBER THAT. THERE WAS A FAT DUDE WHO DROVE UP IN A TRUCK. AND HE HAD REALLY BIG THINGEES. *Dammit, Beavis, this is my story. Shut the hell up.* OH, YEAH, HEH HEH. SORRY ABOUT THAT.

So like, she asked me if I knew how to do chicks. I told her, "I sure do." UM, HEH HEH, UM, NO YOU DON'T. *I told her how I did that chick in gym class.* UM, YOU MEAN THE CHICK THAT KICKED YOUR ASS FOR GOING INTO THE CHICK'S LOCKER ROOM? HEH HEH, THAT WAS COOL.

Uh, anyway, this chick got tired of talking and like, begged me to do her on the curb. So, you know, I did her. UM, HEH HEH, NO. *And then I got up and bought myself more nachos.* FARTKNOCKER! YOU SAID YOU WERE GOING TO GET ME SOME TOO! YOU LIED. *No I didn't, dumbass.*

Butt-Head
(AND BEAVIS)

EVERYTHING I NEED TO KNOW I LEARNED FROM COPS

Ignorance is no excuse.

Winners don't do drugs.

You have the right
to remain silent.

"Spread 'em" is not a request.
It's an order!

Prison loves little boys.

If you run
you will be shot.

Get your hands out of
your pants and keep
them where I can
see them!

There's nothing
funny about
the penal code.

This six-pack didn't
just walk here.
Now did it?

ACUPUNCTURE

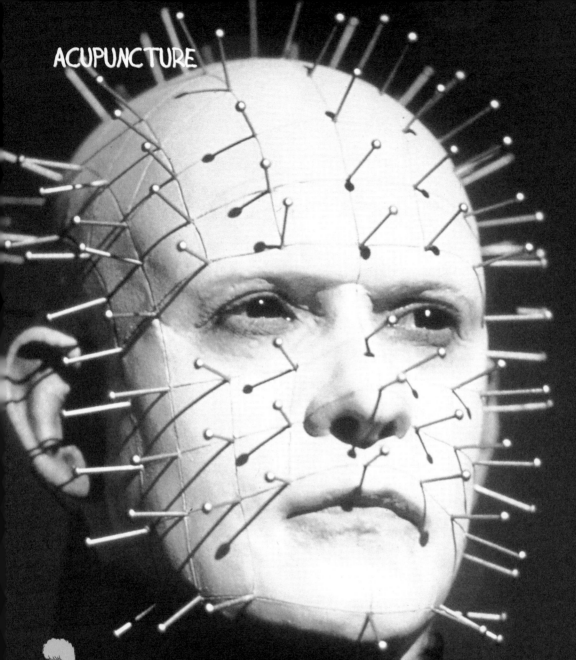

STICKING PINS IN YOURSELF IS SUPPOSED TO LIKE RELAX YOU AND MAKE YOU HAPPY AND STUFF. IT'S AN ANCIENT CHINESE SECRET, LIKE DOING LAUNDRY. BUT LIKE, IT DIDN'T MAKE ME HAPPY WHEN BUTT-HEAD STUCK A PIN IN ME. EXCEPT THE BLOOD. THAT WAS PRETTY COOL, HEH HEH HEH.

DUMBASS. THIS ACUPUNCTURE STUFF WORKS. THERE WAS THIS TIME I HAD A HEADACHE IN GYM CLASS AND I WENT TO SIT DOWN. BUT LIKE I ACCIDENTALLY SAT ON THE THIS NAIL STICKING OUT OF THE BLEACHER. MY BUTT REALLY HURT, BUT LIKE IT TOTALLY WORKED, CUZ I FORGOT ALL ABOUT MY HEADACHE.

WORLD'S GREATEST SELF-HELP DUDES

PAMELA ANDERSON

SHE HAD ONE SIMPLE IDEA: BIGGER THINGEES ARE BETTER.

DUMBASS, THAT'S TWO IDEAS.

OH YEAH, HEH HEH HEH, SO SHE'S LIKE TWICE AS SMART.

YEAH, YOU CAN NEVER HAVE TOO MUCH OF A GOOD THING. I'D LIKE TO SEE HER GET A THIRD ONE.

Self-help is all about helping yourself. Here's how Beavis and I help ourselves to stuff at the Maxi-Mart.

1. Go up to the counter and ask a question like: "If I were gonna steal some candy bars what aisle would they be in?"

2. Stuff some burritos into Beavis' pants. There's a lot of unused room in there.

3. At the drink machine, fill up your cup with a freezie, then pour it out and help yourself to another. That way, you get two.

4. Look at the pictures in the magazines and put them back without paying for them. Be sure to like, tear out the cool pages for yourself. Huh huh, you know, for future reference.

5. Take some donuts. If that clerk dude sees you, tell him you're pregnant and you need them for your kid.

6. Hide some ice cream in Beavis' shirt. There's a lot of room in there too.

7. An easy way to get stuff out of the store without paying is to go into the bathroom and flush it down the toilet. The hard part is figuring out where the stuff is going to come out.

8. Don't worry about the security camera. It's in black and white. Nobody watches black and white TV.

9. Stick a roll of toilet paper in your pants behind your butt. If you get caught, say you forgot to wipe.

10. Grab a handful of plastic sporks. They're free so you have to steal more than one to make it worth your while.

11. If the cops show up, tell them you're from Arkansas or something, and you didn't know you had to pay for this stuff. Or just, like, tell 'em Beavis did it.

LIFE LESSONS FROM MOVIES

MOVIES ARE A LOT LIKE REAL LIFE. EXCEPT YOU CAN LEARN STUFF
FROM WATCHING THEM.

VAN DAMN MOVIES
MORAL: KICK ASS OR BE KICKED

FREE WILLY
MORAL: IF YOUR WILLY IS THAT BIG, YOU GOTTA
LET IT ROAM FREE.

SPECIES
MORAL: LOVE ALL FORMS OF LIFE — ESPECIALLY IF
THEY COME IN THE FORM OF NAKED ALIEN CHICKS.

PORN MOVIES
MORAL: DON'T SIT NEXT TO PEE-WEE HERMAN
IN A THEATRE.

GANDHI
MORAL: BEING HUNGRY SUCKS.

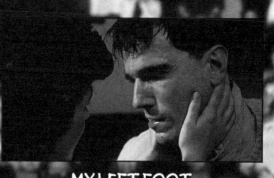

MY LEFT FOOT
MORAL: EVEN IF HE DOESN'T HAVE ANY HANDS, A REAL MAN FINDS A WAY TO SPANK HIS MONKEY.

FOREIGN MOVIES
MORAL: EVEN IF YOU CAN'T UNDERSTAND WHAT THEY SAY, YOU CAN TELL THESE MOVIES SUCK CUZ YOU CAN'T UNDERSTAND WHAT THEY'RE SAYING.

BABE
MORAL: EVEN IF YOU'RE LIKE, A FAT PIG, THERE'S SOME DUDE OUT THERE WHO THINKS YOU'RE A BABE.

SILENCE OF THE LAMBS
MORAL: PEOPLE WHO KILL PEOPLE ARE, LIKE, PRETTY COOL PEOPLE.

THE DAY I GOT FREE NACHOS

It was, you know, like any other day. I took some nachos up to the counter at Maxi-Mart. But then the clerk guy said, "Just take 'em. Go!" I was like, "No way. This is the greatest day ever." And the clerk guy was like, "Just get the hell out of here." He was hanging around behind the counter with this dude in a black ski mask, who kept saying, "Hurry it up, man." I guess they wanted to close the store early and go skiing or something.

So, I got the hell out of there just like he said. I went home and showed the nachos to Beavis. "Check it out, I'm like truly blessed or something." Beavis wanted some of the nachos, but I was like, "No way! Pay for your own, buttmunch."

I'll never forget that day, cuz like, sometime later that day the Maxi-Mart got robbed and the clerk guy was shot. He never worked there again. That sucked, cuz the new clerk made me pay for my nachos.

Butt-Head

TRANSCRIPT FROM THE SCHOOL PSUCKOLOGIST

SOMETIMES EVEN SELF-HELP GURUS LIKE BEAVIS AND ME CAN LEARN STUFF FROM OTHER SELF-HELP PROFESSIONALS. LIKE THE DAY WE WENT TO THE SCHOOL COUNSELOR.

HIGHLAND HIGH

Subjects: Beavis and Butt-Head
Sent by: Principal McVicker
Interviewer: Dr. Longstaff

School Psychologist's transcript
Strictly Confidential

Dr. Longstaff: Hello, Beavis and Butt-Head. Please take a seat. No, not on my desk. Yes, over there. Very good. Let's begin. Since the last time we talked, a few things have happened. Butt-Head, Principal McVicker tells me you interrupted class by daring Beavis to remove his shorts. Beavis, you went along with this.
Butt-Head: Yeah, it was pretty cool.
Beavis: It wasn't me, it was some Chinese dude!

Dr. Longstaff: Beavis, we can't learn from our mistakes unless we can admit them. There was no Chinese man, now was there?
Butt-Head: Yeah, there's no way some Chinese dude would have a wiener as tiny as Beavis'.
Beavis: Shut up, fartknocker! I'll kick your nads through your butt-hole.
Butt-Head: Settle down, Beavis! It's your fault we're here.

Dr. Longstaff: Actually Butt-Head, don't you think you had something to do with this?
Butt-Head: Uh, no. I'm not messed up, Beavis is messed up.
Beavis: I'm not messed up! That Chinese dude is messed up!

Dr. Longstaff: No one here is "messed up." But you both seem to have a problem controlling your behavior. I'd like to talk about your parents.
Butt-Head: Beavis' mother gets around. Huh huh huh.
Beavis: Yeah, she's a slut.

Dr. Longstaff: Hmm. I see. Not many boys say that about their mothers. I think this is an avenue we should explore further. Beavis, can you tell me more about your mother?
Butt-Head: Hey, Beavis, check it out, this guy wants to get to know your mother. Huh huh huh.
Beavis: Yeah, heh heh. I bet he wants to DO her.

Dr. Longstaff: No, no, that's not what I meant.
Beavis: This sucks. You know, you come to school, and some old dude just wants to do your mom.
Butt-Head: Yeah, this is like, sensual harassment.

Dr. Longstaff: What the hell are you talking about! Get out of my office! This interview is over.
Butt-Head: Whoa! This dude is really in a hurry. Huh huh huh, he must be horny.
Beavis: Yeah, it's just like when I order pizza or something, and like the delivery dude is too busy making out with my mom to give me my pizza. These guys should learn how to do their jobs.

Psychologist put on disciplinary suspension pending employment review. Seek replacement.

BEAUTY IS ONLY SKIN DEEP

EVERYONE WANTS TO CHANGE THE WAY THEY LOOK. THERE'S LOTS OF SELF-HELP BUTTMUNCHES WHO HELP FAT PEOPLE GET SKINNY. BUT THERE'S NO ONE TO HELP SKINNY GUYS LIKE ME AND BEAVIS TO GET FAT. THAT SUCKS, BECAUSE BEING FAT WOULD BE COOL.

YOU DON'T HAVE TO BUY A COUCH CUZ YOU CAN JUST SIT ANYWHERE ON YOUR BIG FAT BUTT.

YOU CAN HIDE FOOD AND STUFF, LIKE A TURKEY SANDWICH, IN THE FOLDS OF YOUR STOMACH.

WHEN YOU'RE HUNGRY, YOU DON'T HAFTA CHOOSE BETWEEN NACHOS AND PIZZA. YOU CAN HAVE BOTH.

CHICKS DIG YOU CUZ THERE'S LIKE MORE OF YOU TO LOVE. A LOT MORE.

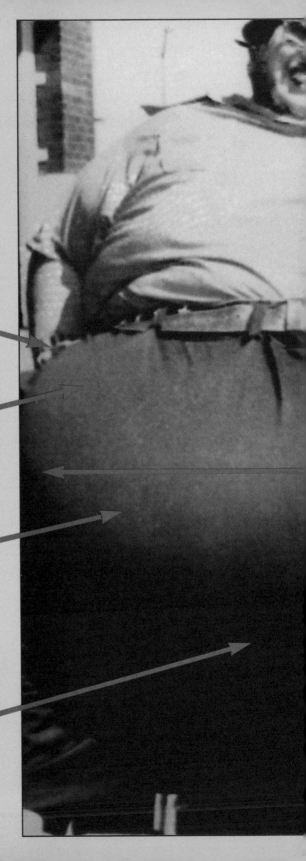

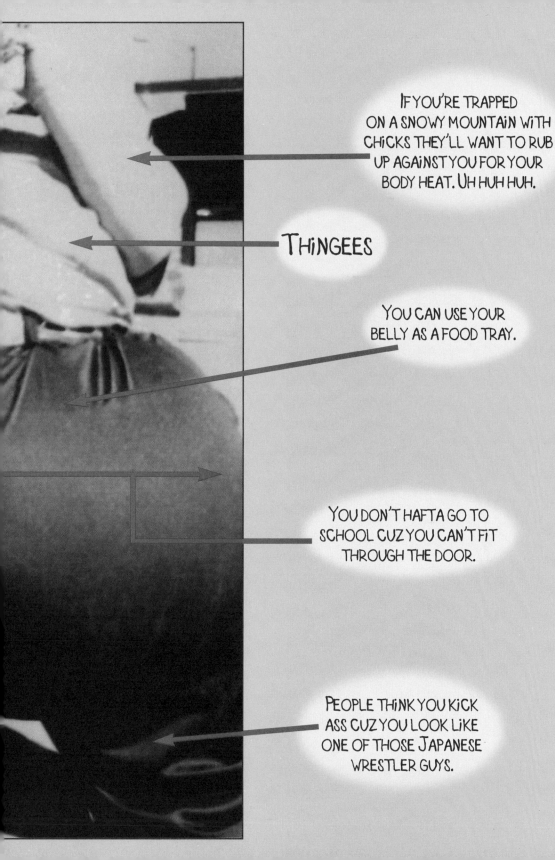

WORLD'S GREATEST SELF-HELP DUDES

URKEL

URKEL IS PART OF A LONG TRADITION THAT GOES ALL THE WAY BACK TO GARY COLEMAN AND WEBSTER. HE BELIEVES THAT EVEN IF YOU GET REALLY OLD, YOU CAN STILL ACT LIKE YOU'RE REALLY YOUNG ON TV. URKEL IS LIKE 40 OR 70 YEARS OLD OR SOMETHING, BUT ON TV, HE'S LIKE STILL IN HIGH SCHOOL.

LOTS OF FAMOUS PEOPLE ON TV BELIEVE IN URKEL'S FILOSOPHY, LIKE PEE-WEE HERMAN, AEROSMITH, AND THOSE DUDES ON BEVERLY HILLS 90269.

I'M GLAD I'M NOT ON TV, CUZ THEN I'D NEVER GET ANY OLDER AND I'D ALWAYS HAFTA BE IN HIGH SCHOOL. THAT WOULD SUCK.

THE WINNER IN MY JOCK STRAP

One day in gym class Beavis and me were playing dodgeball. And these two chicks were like, hitting us with their balls. Uh huh huh. That was pretty cool. But then Coach Buzzcut made us stop playing with the girls. That sucked. Buzzcut told us we needed some, like, motivation. This is what he said:

Are you boys gonna spend your whole lives getting beaten by a buncha girls? Yeah, I thought so! Let me share something I learned when I was stationed in Guam: any man who gets beat by a woman better get used to beating off! That's what we call natural selection. Until you learn to throw a ball like a man, your pathetic genes are never gonna reproduce!

Like, I'm not sure what the hell he was talkin' about, but if I can spend my whole life havin' some chick beat me, that'd be pretty cool. Especially if she, like, wears leather.

Butt Head

ART THERAPY

MOST PEOPLE THINK ART IS JUST FOR DUMBASSES. BUT WHEN YOU'RE LIKE, PISSED OFF OR SOMETHING, ART CAN SOMETIMES MAKE YOU FEEL GOOD. HERE'S SOME ART ME AND BEAVIS LIKE.

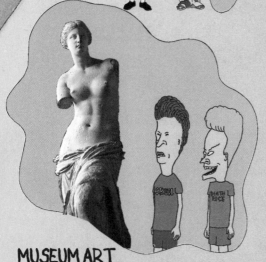

MUSEUM ART
THERE ARE TWO DIFFERENT KINDS OF ART IN MUSEUMS: CRAP AND STUFF WITH NAKED CHICKS.

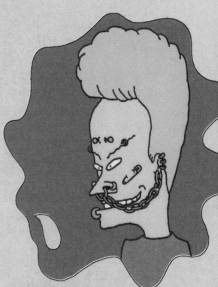

PORN ART
WHEN YOU CAN'T MAKE IT TO THE MUSEUM, GO TO THE MAXI-MART FOR SOME ART, IF YOU KNOW WHAT I MEAN. HUH HUH HUH.

TATTOO ART
THE PROBLEM WITH TATTOOS IS LIKE, USUALLY YOU'VE GOT TO LOOK AT SOME DUMBASSES'S BUTT TO SEE ONE, BUT YOU NEVER KNOW IF THE DUDE HAS A TATTOO THERE OR NOT UNTIL HE TAKES HIS BUTT OUT.

PIERCING
THEY CALL THIS KINDA ART "SUBMERSIVE" BECAUSE IT CAN BE KINDA DANGEROUS. LIKE, WHEN BEAVIS TRIED IT, HE GOT HIS BUTT PIERCED TOGETHER. NOW HE CAN'T MAKE ANY "ART" IN THE BATHROOM.

COMIC BOOK ART

ALL THE CHICKS HAVE BIG THINGEES AND THE DUDES BLOW STUFF UP. THE ONLY PROBLEM WITH THIS KIND OF ART IS THE WORDS.

TAKE THAT, YOU CRAVEN RAPSCALLION

POW!!

GRAFFITI ART

IF YOU'RE GONNA MAKE THIS KINDA ART, YOU GOTTA MAKE SURE NOBODY KNOWS YOU DID IT. OTHERWISE, PEOPLE MIGHT THINK YOU'RE SOME KINDA DUMBASS ARTY DUDE.

TV

SOME DUMBASS SAID TV WAS ART, BUT THAT'S A BUNCH OF CRAP.

MY ART

SINCE MOST ART SUCKS, SOMETIMES YOU JUST GOTTA MAKE YOUR OWN. BESIDES, CHICKS LOVE COOL ARTISTS LIKE ME THAT CAN CAPTURE THE TRUE ESSENCE THAT IS WOMAN. HUH HUH HUH. BUT OTHER CHICKS LIKE ARTISTS LIKE BEAVIS WHO ARE ALL POOR AND MESSED UP.

HOW TO GET AHEAD AND MAKE LOTS OF MONEY

IF YOU WANNA GET SOMEWHERE IN LIFE YOU GOTTA HAVE SOME CASH TO LIKE, PAY FOR THE BUS. BUT BEFORE YOU CAN MAKE MONEY, YOU GOTTA KNOW WHAT YOU'RE DOING. YOU KNOW, LIKE, BUY LOW AND UH, SELL WHEN YOU'RE HIGH. CHECK OUT THESE OTHER MONEY-MAKING TIPS:

DRESS FOR SUCCESS

PEOPLE WON'T GIVE YOU MONEY UNLESS YOU LOOK LIKE YOU ALREADY HAVE A LOT OR YOU HAVE, LIKE, NONE.

GET A RAISE

SO YOU CAN LIKE, GET AHEAD AND GET OFF AT THE SAME TIME. HUH HUH.

MONEY LAUNDERING

A LOT OF PEOPLE LAUNDER MONEY, SO IF YOU GOT TO THE LAUNDROMAT YOU CAN USUALLY FIND SOME CHANGE AT THE BOTTOM OF THE WASHING MACHINE.

HIRE ILLEGAL IMMIGRANTS

THEY'RE CHEAP. AND LIKE, WHATEVER YOU HAVE TO DO, YOU CAN TELL THEM TO DO IT FOR YOU.

GET WORKER'S CONSTIPATION

IF YOU GET HURT ON THE JOB YOU CAN GET WORKER'S CONSTIPATION. YOU GET TO STAY HOME FROM WORK AND STILL GET PAID. BUT TO GET THE CONSTIPATION, YOU GOTTA PROVE IT REALLY HURTS.

GO TO COLLEGE

IF YOU WANT TO GET DOWN TO BUSINESS, IF YOU KNOW WHAT I MEAN, YOU NEED TO LIKE, GO TO COLLEGE. CUZ ALL THE CHICKS THERE WANT TO DO IT.

LEARN TO USE A COMPUTER

THEN YOU CAN GET A JOB WHERE YOU SPEND THE WHOLE DAY DOWNLOADING NAKED PICTURES OF ALYSSA MILANO FROM THE NET.

BARGAIN

WHEN SOMEONE ORDERS SOMETHING THAT'S LIKE 5 DOLLARS, TELL THEM IT'S LIKE 3 DOLLARS. YOU KEEP THE CHANGE.

MONEY MAKES LIFE BETTER

NOW THAT YOU'VE GOT LOTS OF CASH, WHAT ARE YOU GONNA DO?
SPEND IT, DUMBASS! HERE'S HOW TO DIVIDE IT UP:

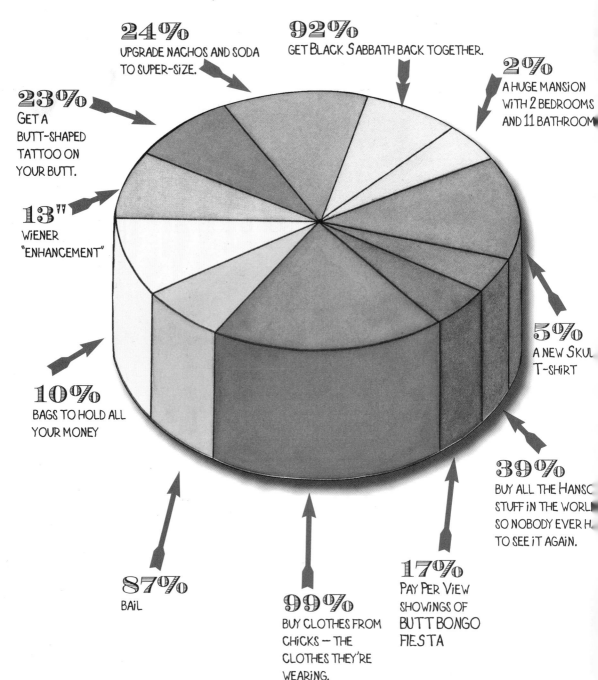

24% UPGRADE NACHOS AND SODA TO SUPER-SIZE.

92% GET BLACK SABBATH BACK TOGETHER.

2% A HUGE MANSION WITH 2 BEDROOMS AND 11 BATHROOM

23% GET A BUTT-SHAPED TATTOO ON YOUR BUTT.

13" WIENER "ENHANCEMENT"

10% BAGS TO HOLD ALL YOUR MONEY

5% A NEW SKUL T-SHIRT

39% BUY ALL THE HANSC STUFF IN THE WORLI SO NOBODY EVER H. TO SEE IT AGAIN.

87% BAIL

99% BUY CLOTHES FROM CHICKS — THE CLOTHES THEY'RE WEARING.

17% PAY PER VIEW SHOWINGS OF BUTT BONGO FIESTA

GROPE THERAPY

There was this time the school counselor sent me and Beavis to this thing called grope therapy. It sounded pretty cool. You know, a buncha cool people makin' each other feel better, by you know, feelin' each other up.

But when we got there, it sucked. It was just a buncha fartknockers sittin' around talkin' about their problems. It was kinda like Jerry Springer except nobody hit each other.

LIFE SUCKS, CHANGE IT!

When you're watching something on TV that sucks, you change it. So when your life sucks you should be able to change it, too.

Michael Jackson. His face sucked, so he changed it. And Van Halen. They don't like their lead singers so they change them every couple of years. And that Superman guy. His girlfriend fell in a ditch, so he like, flew around the Earth and went back in time to get her out.

But if you're not a famous dude like Van Halen or Superman, there's not a lot you can do.

So get used to it, dumbass.

Butt Head

THOUGHT QUESTIONS

If you've read the whole book, then you should be like, a better person or something by now. Here's some questions to see if you know what you've learned from this book.

1. How can I live in a world full of dumbasses without becoming a fartknocker?

2. How can I get in touch with myself if people keep telling me to put my pants back on?

3. What are my priorities? And like, what the hell are priorities?

4. Can I find happiness if everything sucks?

5. How can I feel better about myself if I'm not old enough to drink?

6. When I get older, will I get some?

7. How can I get out of an abusive situation if Butt-Head has me in a headlock?

8. Is it better to make a lot of money, drive a fast car and do a lot of chicks, or be some kinda dumbass who does stuff for other people?

9. How can I make a change in my life if the batteries in the remote control are dead?

10. If I'm okay and you're okay, then who the hell is buying all these self-help books?

Now that you've read this book,
you officially masturbate from the
Beavis and Butt-Head school of self-help.
Rip out this diploma and like, staple it to your wall.

I am Not a Fartknocker
Self-help Diploma

Let it be known that on this day _____ that
(date)

your Name
_____
(your name)

has suck-sessfully completed reading

Chicken Soup For The Butt

I am no longer the fartknocker I once was.
I promise to go out into the world and live life like
Beavis and Butt-Head taught me,

heh heh. huh huh. E Plurbus Butt-munch.

your name
_____
(your name)

Beavis and Butt-Head
(Beavis and Butt-Head)